THORNED THISTLE

OMMANDED
A THORNED THISTLE DARK ROMANCE

MERRIGAN CALDER

COMMANDED—A Thorned Thistle Dark Romance

© 2025 Merrigan Calder

This book is a work of fiction. The names, characters, places and incidents are products of the writer's imagination or have been used fictitiously and are not to be construed as real. Any resemblance to persons, living or dead, actual events, locale or organizations is entirely coincidental.

979-8-88649-231-6

Author's Note:

COMMANDED is a dark romance containing content some readers may find disturbing, including explicit BDSM content (bondage, impact play, discipline, power exchange), polyamorous relationship, explicit sexual content including MMF scenes, and on-page non-explicit death.

While this story ultimately features consensual relationships and an HEA, the journey there involves scenarios that may be triggering for some readers. Read responsibly.

Table of Contents

1

Kiernan

The rope slid through my fingers as I wrapped the sub's wrists behind her. Cross, loop, check tension. Her breathing had already shifted—slower, deeper, sinking into the headspace I'd guided her to dozens of times before.

"Too tight?" I asked.

"No, sir."

I secured the binding while Colin set everything we'd need within reach. Imelda's red hair fell forward as she knelt, patient and trusting.

I took three steps away.

"Apply the harness using a diamond pattern."

He picked up the longer rope, got behind his wife, and began wrapping her torso. The crimson contrasted sharply with her pale skin as he worked, creating the frame that would distribute pressure evenly. But my mind conjured olive skin instead. Dark wavy hair, not red.

"Tighter on the third wrap," I said, willing myself to remain in the scene.

Colin locked the harness into place with flawless execution.

"Now, the spreader bar."

He knelt to lock the cuffs around Imelda's ankles, forcing her thighs apart. The position put her on display—vulnerable, exposed, and trembling as her arousal became visible.

Everything was as it should be. So why did I feel so disconnected?

"Look at her," I ordered Colin. "Tell me what you see."

"She's beautiful, sir." His tone roughened with arousal. "The rope frames her perfectly. Her nipples are hard, and I can see how turned on she is—"

"Details," I snarled, cutting him off. "Don't make me ask twice."

I gave the command, but my mind was somewhere else. Instead of green, I was thinking about light-brown irises turning dark.

"Her thighs are shaking, sir," Colin continued. "She's so wet I can see it. Her breathing's changed—she's trying to remain still, like you taught her, but she wants to. She wants to be touched."

"Who should you be looking at?" I snapped at Imelda.

Her eyes found mine at once, glazed and unfocused. Exactly where she should be.

Except I wasn't.

"You don't acknowledge him unless I tell you to. You don't speak unless I ask you a question. Understood?"

"Yes, sir."

I turned to Colin. "Start at her knee and lick your way up. Slowly."

He obeyed my command, working his way higher with deliberate kisses while Imelda fought to remain motionless.

This should have been perfect. Every movement was orchestrated, every touch directed. But my thoughts continued to wander as Colin's mouth pleasured his wife and her breathing grew ragged.

Instead of clean-shaven skin scraping sensitive flesh, I envisioned a trimmed beard. Sandy-brown hair falling forward instead of dark. Another man's head, whose pupils were blown wide with arousal and submission, raised for permission.

"Hands on her breasts. Show me how she likes it."

He straightened, and his fingers found her nipples. He rolled them, then tugged, making her gasp and arch into his touch as much as the restraints allowed.

The sounds she made were genuine—a high, breathy whimper that should have sent heat straight through me.

All I heard was a different pitch. A different timbre. Someone who would sound rough and desperate when they begged, not soft. Someone who would fight their submission even as they surrendered to it, making every moan I extracted feel like a victory.

"Tell me what you need." I winced when my words sounded mechanical.

"Please, sir," Imelda begged. "I need his mouth. Please let him—"

The plea was too polished, the desperation too rehearsed.

"*Stop,*" I said, pausing the scene.

None of this was right. Colin froze with his hands on his wife's breasts.

"Sir?" Imelda cut through my thoughts.

I blinked. They studied me with worry. How long had I been standing there, silent?

The shift in energy was swift. Imelda's demeanor changed at the same time Colin switched from sub to protective husband.

"Neither of you has done anything wrong," I said before either could ask. "This is on me."

I knelt to release Imelda's ankle cuffs, using the rote motions to ground myself. The spreader bar came loose, and I set it aside.

"Are you okay?" Colin asked, already untying his wife's wrists.

"I'm not in the right headspace tonight. It's not fair to either of you to continue."

While Colin found the release points in the rope, they exchanged one of those married glances where an entire conversation took place wordlessly. I read understanding and concern in their faces, a shared decision to give me space.

I worked through the aftercare on autopilot, getting them water and the blankets kept in the suite's warmer. I asked the required questions, making sure they were stable before I let them leave.

"Do you want to talk about it?" Colin offered as they walked toward the door.

I shook my head and muttered my thanks.

"We're here if you need us," Imelda added. "As friends."

After they left, I stared at the crimson rope in my hands.

I didn't want Colin and Imelda.

My desire was for two *different* people, and it had grown to the point of obsession.

"Fuck," I muttered into the empty room as I straightened my clothes and walked out.

The club pulsed around me, but I passed through it without seeing, barely registering the fantasies displayed on the main floor.

The Thorned Thistle was busy tonight. The massive converted distillery space, with its exposed brick walls, industrial metal beams crossing the ceiling, and strategic lighting that created pockets of shadow and revelation, thrummed with music and energy. Around the perimeter, various scenes played out—a submissive kneeling beside his mistress, a flogging in one corner, where leather cracked on skin.

At the bar, I ordered a whiskey. The bartender set it in front of me.

"Everything all right, Master Kiernan?"

"Fine." The lie was automatic. For the first time in many years, the pleasure I'd always found here wasn't enough. The authority I'd always craved seemed hollow without the specific people I ached to command.

I finished the drink in one swallow and was halfway to the exit when I saw Callen Cavendish, the Marquess of Dunravin, heir to the Duke of Strathallan, code name Renegade, member of Unit 23, and the closest thing I had to a best friend. The two of us had founded the Thorned Thistle five years ago, along with three other partners. I'd needed something to build after everything fell apart. A place where I could be in control when the rest of my life had spiraled beyond my grasp.

He stood near the observation area, studying a wax-play scene with the critical eye of someone who knew the technique better than the person demonstrating it. He caught my approach in his peripheral vision and pivoted to greet me.

"I wondered if I'd see you here tonight," he said. "Or if you'd sleep for a week after wrapping the Labyrinth investigation."

"I could say the same about you."

"My body isn't ready to shut down," he said. "That briefing this afternoon didn't help."

"Same here."

We stood in silence, observing the club's activity. This was our ritual—the first night after returning from a mission, we'd end up here, decompressing in the only place where we could fully be ourselves.

"Planning to scene tonight?" he asked.

"I already did."

"That was quick. Even for you." He paused, and his eyes scrunched. "You ended it early. You never end scenes early."

I didn't answer. Callen knew me well enough to read my silence.

"Should I be worried?" he asked. "Or just impressed that something has finally rattled the great Archon?"

The dry humor was quintessential Callen—deflecting concern with wit. He didn't ask if this was about the past. He never did. That was the grace of old friendship— knowing which wounds to step around.

"Neither. I'm fine," I said, not ready to think about what had happened with the couple I'd been scening with for close to two years, let alone talk about it.

He made a sound that suggested he believed that about as much as I did. But he let it go, because that's what we did for each other.

I said good night and returned home through the tunnels that led from the club's undercroft to mine. The silence was deafening when I emerged from my wine cellar into the main castle, then made my way to the library that was my sanctuary. It was dark except for the embers glowing in the massive stone fireplace. I added wood, poured three fingers of my favorite whiskey, and stood at the window overlooking my land—nine thousand acres of wilderness stretched into the darkness. And slowly, I allowed myself to *breathe*.

During the Labyrinth investigation, I'd maintained the persona of my code name, Archon—the respectful "yes, boss" and "no, sir" deference, the quiet competence, the understated presence that made me practically invisible. The perfect operative. The man His Majesty's Secret Intelligence Service could trust to get the job done without drama.

Little did they know who I was when I dropped the facade.

Each kilometer of my earlier five-hour drive from Tarbert here put distance between that version of me and Kiernan Lockhart, Viscount of Greymarch—the man I truly was.

The duality had become second nature over the years. It had to. When you were trained to kill with your bare hands, to eliminate targets in twelve countries across four continents, or to be a ghost who ended lives without leaving traces, you learned to compartmentalize.

Unit 23 recruited only the best, whether it was for intelligence gathering, covert ops, or when necessary, permanent solutions to threats against the Crown. Other operatives I served with wore their danger openly. I'd cultivated the opposite approach, playing the supportive and dependable team player who blended into the background. But inside, I was an entirely different animal.

As I stared into the fire, my mind drifted where it had been circling for days—to them. Their code names—the field designations we all used on operations—were Prima and Vanguard. But I couldn't make myself think of them that way. Code names kept distance, reduced people to assets and objectives. In my head, where the wanting lived, they were Ophelia and Oliver.

Ophelia Okonkwo was the diplomat's daughter who spoke eight languages and had a mind sharp enough to cut. She'd exhibited the epitome of polish during our recent mission—the Labyrinth investigation Callen had mentioned. But I'd studied her. Observed her with an intensity that would have alarmed her. And I'd recognized what she couldn't see about herself.

She typically pulled her hair into a severe bun for briefings, but I'd caught her once in the corridor with it down, its waves spilling past her shoulders. The transformation was remarkable.

Other tells revealed themselves too. How her expression softened when someone took charge, a subtle shift she probably didn't realize she made. That her olive skin flushed easily was another tell. Color crept up her elegant neck whenever her boss spoke in a commanding tone, and she inhaled sharply when given a direct order, not from fear but from need. Her shoulders eased when someone else assumed control. She unconsciously deferred and yielded when authority was exerted.

She was a natural submissive who had no fucking clue.

Then there was Oliver Morse, the golden boy with the easy charm that came with knowing you were attractive.

I'd clocked him within fifteen minutes of meeting him. He tracked Ophelia during briefings with longing—no performance there—but his attention also lingered a fraction too long on certain male colleagues.

There were other telling details that suggested more than bisexuality.

When the Unit 23 commander entered a room, Oliver gave him space and deference that went beyond courtesy. This behavior showed not only with the commander, but with several of the more dominant personalities. He'd position himself slightly behind and to the left of them, subtly yielding to their authority.

Oliver was a skilled, intelligent, and capable operative. But he didn't want to be in charge. He craved someone else taking control, giving him orders, and letting him surrender the burden of command.

He was submissive. I was certain of it.

The memory of what had landed him in hospital rose unbidden—finding him in Brodick Castle's north wing corridor, the sound of impact echoing through the stone walls, his hair matted with blood where they'd struck him down. His body had been limp when I lifted him, a dead-weight in my arms that terrified me because I didn't know yet if he was breathing. Ophelia had dropped beside us, and she searched for his pulse. I recalled how calm she'd remained in the face of chaos. "He's alive. Weak pulse. We need help now."

We carried him out, working in perfect sync without having to speak. Her hands checked his vitals while mine bore his weight. I'd feared we were too late, then felt relief when he came to.

That was two weeks ago. Oliver had been in hospital in Glasgow ever since, and I'd driven there twice during the worst of it—once during the meningitis scare, once when an infection flared. I sat with Ophelia for hours while Oliver's body fought to recover. With every passing day, their connection deepened. Each time, I left without warning, furious at myself for wanting to be part of what was forming between them.

After the briefing earlier today—before I'd driven here from Glenshadow—ended with the usual wrap-up, Prima lingered. The same exhaustion on her face that I'd seen during my visits to the hospital was evident now as she briefed me on what came next for Oliver.

The infection had cleared, which meant he could be released tomorrow. However, the concussion meant he required twenty-four-hour monitoring for two weeks.

Fourteen days. The number lodged in my mind. That meant two weeks before he could return to Glasgow for medical clearance, until they returned to London and their jobs with MI6. The time I had to claim what I wanted was finite, and if I didn't, I'd be forced to let it go. Let them go.

When I asked about his family, she told me they lived in Australia, too far away to help.

The obvious solution was her. She'd been at his bedside for two weeks already and could provide the monitoring he required. But they were both based in London, eight hours away. He couldn't fly with the head injury, and that distance by car was too much in his condition.

She hadn't asked for solutions. She'd simply laid out the facts.

The answer came to me before she stopped talking. Greymarch sat four hours from Glasgow with staff, space, and a guest wing that no one ever used.

Rather than offer it as an option, I kept my mouth shut. She eventually nodded and left, and I spent the rest of the afternoon telling myself silence was the right call. Bringing them here meant having them under my roof, sleeping close enough to touch while I fought every instinct screaming at me to claim them both.

Mine. The word surfaced unbidden, fierce, and non-negotiable. I shut down the thought before it could take root. They weren't mine. They might never be. And wanting them this badly was a weakness I couldn't afford.

As I held the glass, the whiskey warming my palm, I knew I was going to do it anyway.

I took another sip, letting the burn of alcohol slide down my throat, but my mind wouldn't quiet. Finally, exhaustion won. I retreated to my bedroom in the castle's west tower, stripped down, and fell into bed, hoping for oblivion.

Sleep offered no escape.

The dreams came in fragments—Ophelia's hair spilling across my sheets. Oliver beside her, his eyes glazed with need. Their responses tangled together, "Yes, sir," and "Please," and my name on their lips.

Twice, I woke hard and aching. The third time, dawn was creeping across the horizon and I gave up on rest altogether. Every time I closed my eyes, they were there. Every silence was filled with the echo of their voices. Isolation only sharpened the wanting.

Resistance was pointless. I threw off the covers, got out of bed, and prepared to leave for the hospital.

In the great hall, Millie was arranging white roses and heather in the ancient stone vases. Their scent filled the space with a fragrance almost painfully beautiful. She raised her head when I passed through.

"Going somewhere, my lord?"

"Glasgow. I'll return late afternoon or early evening."

"Is something troubling you, Kiernan?"

I stopped and turned. Millicent Ogilvie had been Greymarch's housekeeper since my father's time. She'd been with me through every phase of my life, through growth and grief. She'd also witnessed my life implode several years ago. Not that she'd asked a single question then. She'd respected my privacy while I tried to keep my life compartmentalized, never passing judgment as far as I could tell. For her to ask if I was troubled, it was so far out of character that it jarred me.

"I'm fine," I snapped.

The tightening of her weathered hands on the rose stems said she knew I was lying, but she'd never press.

The drive to Glasgow took four hours. I pushed the speed limit where I could as the Highlands gave way to farmland, then to the gray sprawl of the city. Every mile brought me closer to them, and yet, I had no plan beyond needing to be there when Oliver was released.

The hospital smelled the same as on my last two visits—antiseptic and bleach. Fluorescent lights hummed overhead as I walked the now-memorized route to room 347, my heart rate climbing with every step.

I heard Ophelia speaking before I reached the door.

"The doctor said another hour at most. Then we'll sort out where you're staying."

I stopped with my hand raised to knock. Through the half-open door, a sliver of the room was visible—the edge of the hospital bed, the medical equipment with its steady beeping, and her shadow passing across the wall, graceful even in silhouette.

I knocked, then pushed the door open.

The clinical smell was stronger here, undercut by Ophelia's light fragrance that I'd caught during surveillance ops when we'd been confined in tight spaces together.

She stood by the window, sunlight catching her wavy hair. She turned when I entered, and her brows flared.

"Sir."

The word slipped out by habit, ingrained from the Labyrinth investigation. After my silence yesterday, she had no reason to expect me.

I scanned the room—the monitors showing Oliver's steady vitals, the IV stand with its saline drip, the gauze on the bedside table. I'd seen it all before on my previous visits.

Oliver was propped up with pillows, a white bandage wrapped around his head where they'd struck him. His color was better than on my last visit, but he was still pale. Exhaustion was evident in every line of his body when he sat up.

"Sir." He winced in pain. "I didn't expect—"

"Don't move." I crossed to him in three strides and reached out before I could stop myself, checking the bandage at his temple. The gauze was clean, without fresh bleeding, but the wound's edge was visible beneath it. "How are you feeling?"

"My head aches, and the light hurts. But I can handle it."

"What did the doctor say?" I asked Ophelia.

"He'll be in shortly to go over his discharge."

"Thank you for being here," Oliver said. "Both of you."

A knock interrupted whatever I might have said in response, and a doctor entered with a tablet tucked under his arm. He pulled a penlight from his pocket and shone it in Oliver's eyes, making notes between checks.

"Your color is better than yesterday." He clicked the penlight off. "Is someone able to assist you when you leave?"

Neither of us spoke, then Ophelia stirred beside me. "Perhaps Tag or Con could—"

"No." The word came out harsher than I intended. I forced my shoulders to relax and my jaw to unclench.

"Someone needs to commit to his care. Otherwise, he stays here, under hospital observation," the doctor said as he checked his mobile.

"I have a place north of Inverness. Greymarch." The words left my mouth before I'd made the conscious choice to say them. "It's isolated and quiet. Ideal for continued recovery."

Oliver's brow furrowed. "Sir, I couldn't impose—"

"It's not an imposition." I turned to Ophelia, and what I said next sealed my own fate. "You know his baseline. You'll monitor him."

She blinked, processing. "If you're certain…"

"I'm certain."

I turned to the doctor. "I'll take full responsibility for his discharge."

"Very well," he said, making another note on his tablet. "If you're both committed to his care, I'll process the paperwork." He walked toward the door. "If he complains of worsening headaches or vision problems, bring him in."

"Understood."

While we waited for the discharge paperwork to be completed, I stayed with Oliver while Ophelia left to get their bags from the hospital's guesthouse that had been her base for the last two weeks.

Oliver sat on the edge of the bed, pale and exhausted. Neither of us spoke.

When Ophelia returned, he took his bag into the bathroom to change. Through the doorway, I could see her unpacking his things and laying out clothes. They worked together easily, naturally.

He emerged in jeans and a shirt that hung loose on his frame, moving slowly, one hand on the wall.

"Ready?" I asked.

Oliver dipped his chin, wincing at the motion. "Thank you for this. I know it's…"

"You need somewhere to recover. I have the space."

We walked through the corridors together: Oliver under his own power but slower than normal, Ophelia close enough to help if necessary, and me leading the way.

Oliver paused at the hospital exit, squinting against the daylight.

"Light sensitivity," Ophelia murmured as he leaned on her.

I stepped to his other side on instinct, and together, we guided him to the car. His weight was heavy on my shoulder, sending protective, possessive desire flooding through my system.

I helped him into the rear passenger seat, and Ophelia climbed in beside him.

It took four hours to get to Greymarch. Oliver dozed within minutes, his body still weak from the battle it had waged to ward off infection. Ophelia sat beside him with her hand resting near his on the leather upholstery.

Every mile I traveled brought them closer to the world I had kept separate from everything else, and the walls of my constructed life cracked.

Did they sense, as I did, that everything was about to change? Or worse, that I was about to destroy them both?

2

Ophelia

Oliver's head rested on my shoulder as the Range Rover wound through the Scottish Highlands. His breathing had steadied out twenty minutes ago in a way it had not been during the first week after the attack. My hand stayed on his wrist, monitoring his pulse out of habit. Two weeks of sitting by his bedside had made me hypervigilant. I registered every change in his respiration and every shift in his color.

The head injury he'd sustained in the attack had nearly killed him. The worst was behind us now, but the memory of those terrifying first days lingered.

He'd survived. He was here. That should have been enough.

The doctors had insisted he have around-the-clock care, then return to Glasgow for clearance to resume normal activities. While the timeline should have relieved me, that I was headed to a place where I'd be responsible for making sure Oliver's recovery progressed as it should filled me with trepidation.

I'd spent six months fighting my attraction to him, pretending I didn't want him. How could I continue to do so with renewed forced proximity? Then again, wouldn't it be harder when he was cleared for work and we returned to Vauxhall Cross? Who knew how often I'd see him then.

I glanced at Archon as he drove. His dark hair was shorter than during the Labyrinth investigation, close-cropped in a way that emphasized the strong column of his neck. His posture had changed too. His shoulders were set and his jaw firm. Nothing about him was relaxed now, not like the understated operative who delivered intelligence and managed logistics without drawing notice.

He'd been a steady presence during Oliver's hospitalization. Twice during the worst of it, he'd driven four hours from where he lived to sit beside me in Oliver's room. We'd spent hours, waiting for test results, for any sign of improvement. Archon had brought me coffee without asking, sat close enough that our shoulders touched, and while he'd said little, he stayed.

I was grateful enough that I hadn't questioned why he'd make that drive. Grateful enough that I'd let my guard down in ways I shouldn't have with a colleague.

He navigated the roads without checking the GPS once, taking turns before the signs appeared and slowing for curves before they came into view. What else had I missed about him during the surveillance op?

The landscape shifted as we traveled north. Rolling farmland gave way to rougher terrain, and green fields were replaced by brown moorland that stretched to the horizon.

He slowed when we arrived at a set of iron gates mounted on ancient stone pillars. As he drove the Range Rover through, the name carved into the weathered surface became visible—*Greymarch*.

The castle rose from the ground like it had grown from the land itself. The pale stone tones and leaden-sky backdrop were so similar to it, the building seemed to merge with the clouds. The battlements on the twin towers spoke of a time when this place had needed to repel invaders. This wasn't an estate meant to impress visitors with its grandeur. This was a fortress.

Another structure rose beyond it, across a stretch of wild land, and my heart stuttered. *Dunravin*—the estate where I'd spent thirty-six hours on surveillance with Archon. Every window, approach, and blind spot in its security was mapped in my memory. The guest cottage, a small stone building tucked near the tree line where we'd set up our monitoring equipment, was visible from here.

"Where are we?" I asked as the vehicle slowed on the gravel drive.

"Greymarch. My family's estate."

"You never indicated…" I began, unsure what to say that wouldn't come across as an accusation.

His hands tightened on the wheel. "I did not."

He offered nothing more, no explanation for why he'd failed to mention this during our surveillance operation, when we had been stationed less than two miles from where he apparently slept every night he was not on mission.

I filed the question away. There would be time to pursue it later, when Oliver was stronger and I could focus on anything other than his recovery.

He stirred.

"We're here?" he asked.

"We're here," I confirmed.

He straightened, winced, then stared out the window at the castle looming above us. "Bloody hell. Archon lives *here*?"

"So it appears."

His laugh was weak. "I thought my family's estate was impressive."

Archon came around to help Oliver out of the car. When he wrapped his arm around his waist, steadying him, a muscle flexed beneath his shirt as he bore the burden without any effort. Oliver was not a small man, but Archon handled him as though he weighed nothing.

He led us inside to a great hall with three-story ceilings. It smelled of centuries of habitation, of lives lived and ended within the walls where tapestries hung. Their colors had faded, but their images remained visible—hunting scenes, battles, a family crest repeated in threads of gold. Flames leaped and crackled from the fire that blazed in a hearth large enough to stand in, but the warmth barely reached us across the vast stone floor.

A silver-haired woman waited near it. Her hands were weathered by decades of work, and she wore a gray dress that seemed designed to blend with the stone around her.

She assessed Oliver's unsteady gait, my hovering proximity, and Archon's bearing as he led us forward. The rapid evaluation was familiar—the same swift categorization of threat levels and power dynamics that I'd been trained to perform. This was no average housekeeper.

"Lord Greymarch," she said. "Welcome home."

She'd called him *Lord Greymarch*.

I steeled my expression as my mind raced. He was titled if the form of address was correct. Which meant this estate had been held for generations.

Who was this man, and why had he hidden his identity?

"Millie." Archon's voice carried differently here, deeper and more resonant, as if the castle itself amplified his presence. "These are colleagues who will be staying for a few weeks while one of them recovers from an injury."

Millie's gaze settled on me with open curiosity before looking at Oliver, who leaned against Archon's side.

"I'll ready the guest wing," she said. "The blue rooms?"

"Yes." Archon paused. "And please prepare a substantial dinner. They've had a long journey."

Millie nodded and slipped through a doorway without waiting for further instruction.

When Archon turned toward me, the firelight caught the planes of his face, throwing shadows across his jaw and his cheekbones. In the flickering light, his irises seemed almost black.

I thought about his hospital visits and how his attentiveness had seemed like more than casual concern—focused in a way I'd attributed to shared worry over Oliver. Now, I wasn't sure.

"Archon, I was wondering—"

"While we're here," he said, "use first names. No more 'Archon.' Here, I'm Kiernan. You're Ophelia and Oliver."

"Kiernan," I said under my breath. Had I known his first name before now? Most likely, I'd read it in a brief at some point but hadn't bothered to file it away in my memory.

As Kiernan led us through the castle, Oliver would rest a hand on the wall when his balance wavered, but I remained close enough for him to lean on me if necessary.

We passed by portraits lining the corridors, of generations of Lockharts who bore a strong resemblance to Kiernan. Men posed in military uniforms from wars I'd studied in school while women wore silks that had gone in and out of fashion half a dozen times.

"Your family has served in the military for generations," I observed.

"Every Lockhart man since the estate was granted has served the Crown." He paused before a portrait of a soldier in Napoleonic-era uniform; the resemblance to Kiernan was striking enough that it could have been a mirror. "Some more honorably than others."

He moved on without explaining.

Some doors, he opened, showing us sitting rooms and parlors with windows offering a view of the grounds, a music room, and several bedrooms that appeared untouched for years. Others, he passed without comment, what lay behind them remaining a mystery.

Kiernan didn't slow when we passed a heavy oak door with a brass handle that gleamed more than the others. He muttered something about a library as we continued. The deflection was subtle but deliberate—the kind of information control I'd seen diplomats use when steering conversations away from sensitive topics. Whatever lay behind that door, he didn't want us seeing it.

We reached a staircase that curved upward at the end of the next corridor.

"The west tower," he said, leading us away without breaking his stride. "My private quarters."

The guest wing was warmer than the rest of the castle, heated by radiators that hummed beneath tall windows. A sitting room with deep sofas in blue velvet faced a hearth already crackling with flames. Two bedrooms opened through separate doorways, each with a four-poster bed draped in fabrics that appeared old and expensive. The view from the windows stretched to the horizon beneath the heavy Scottish sky.

"You'll have privacy here," Kiernan said. "Millie can provide anything you need. Dinner will be served at nineteen hundred."

He left before either of us could respond, disappearing into the maze of corridors without a backward glance.

Oliver collapsed onto the nearest sofa with an exhausted groan. I sat beside him and reached for his wrist, checking his heart rate as I'd done countless times since the attack. The gesture was automatic now, as natural as breathing.

His pulse was steady and strong, better than it had been.

"He's not the same man we worked with," he mumbled before giving in to his exhaustion.

"No." I released his wrist but didn't step away from the warmth of him beside me. "It's like he's been playing a part. Or was."

"Exactly. Which version do you think is most authentic?"

I thought about his movements through the castle. The underlying command when he spoke to Millie. The wave of his arm as he showed us the portraits of his ancestors, the pride evident when he spoke of generations of service. The Scots had a word—*dùthchas*—for the deep, inherited connection between a person and their ancestral land. It was untranslatable to English, but watching Kiernan walk through Greymarch, I finally understood what it meant.

"I think this is who he really is."

When Oliver's hand found mine on the cushion between us and his thumb traced against my knuckles, warmth spread through me.

In the time we'd worked together prior to being assigned to the Labyrinth investigation, we'd shared glances that lingered too long, touches that meant more than they should, and tension that I'd pretended not to notice. MI6 regulations were clear about discouraging relationships between officers, and we'd followed them to the letter.

But the days I'd spent with him had stripped away my ability to pretend my concern didn't go beyond that of a colleague.

"You should rest before dinner," I said, pulling my hand away.

"Phee," he whispered. "You don't have to run."

"Rest," I repeated, and fled to my bedroom before he could respond.

I unpacked the single bag I'd brought from Glasgow, but nothing seemed suitable for dinner with a titled lord in his ancestral home.

Kiernan Lockhart baffled me. He owned a castle, lived next door to an estate we'd been surveilling, yet he'd never mentioned it. He was a man accustomed to guarding his secrets.

However, none of those things changed how my body responded when he did as much as say my name.

The dining room was colder than the guest wing, despite the fire roaring at the far end. A table, set with silver that gleamed in the candlelight, that could easily seat twenty, held three place settings clustered at one end. Kiernan sat at the head in a white shirt open at the collar and the sleeves rolled to his forearms, revealing tanned skin and a watch that probably cost more than my annual salary.

He was every bit the part of a lord holding court, and my simple black frock—the only one I'd packed—seemed woefully inadequate by comparison.

The wine breathed in a crystal decanter. Kiernan poured without asking, filling our glasses with a red that smelled of dark fruit and old wood.

"From the estate," he said when he caught me reading the label. "We don't produce much, but what we do is worth drinking."

The food was exceptional. Millie delivered course after course with the ease of someone who'd done this for decades. We'd started with a soup rich with root vegetables and herbs I couldn't identify, then had fish that melted on my tongue, and meat so tender I barely needed a knife.

Conversation was stilted at first, as it would be between three people who knew each other only through briefings and ops, and were trying to find common ground. Oliver, though, had a knack for drawing people out. He used his charm to coax stories from Kiernan about the estate, the land, and the history of the Lockhart family.

"We've held the Greymarch viscountcy since 1372," he said, swirling his glass. "We've survived wars, plagues, and changes of dynasty. The castle has been burned twice and rebuilt each time."

Oliver grinned. "The Morses have had our estate since 1156. You're practically new money."

Kiernan half smiled. "I'll try not to be offended."

"You should see Thornwood sometime. It's smaller than this, but the gardens are exceptional."

The two men traded barbs while I tried to focus on anything other than that persistent heat. My thoughts kept drifting to Kiernan—his hands as he lifted his wine-glass, long fingers wrapped around the stem, the flex of his jaw when he considered a response, his lower register when he talked about the land he loved.

He caught me staring more than once. We'd exchange looks across the table, and the air between us would thicken. His face remained unreadable. But there was no question recognition, an awareness and acknowledgment that I couldn't describe with words, passed between us.

"I have work to attend to," he said, rising abruptly before dessert. "Millie will see to anything you need."

He disappeared through a doorway I suspected led toward the library we were not allowed to enter.

Oliver and I finished our wine in near silence. The ease of our time together had evaporated with Kiernan's departure, leaving only emptiness.

"That was odd," Oliver finally said.

"Yes." I stared at the doorway where Kiernan had gone. "It was."

I knocked on Oliver's door an hour after we returned to the suite. The doctor's orders required regular monitoring, especially before sleep. That was the only reason I was here, or so I told myself.

He opened it wearing loose trousers and nothing else. I focused on why I was here rather than the expanse of his chest, the definition of his shoulders, and the trail of hair that disappeared below his waistband.

"Vitals check," I said, holding up the penlight I carried with me out of habit.

He stepped to the side to let me in, and I conducted the medical assessment, focusing on whether his pupils were equal and reactive and if his heartbeat was steady and strong. "Any headaches or nausea?"

"Negative, ma'am," he said with a wink.

I nudged him and smiled. "It's my pleasure."

"Thank you," he said, dropping his flirty tone.

"For what?"

"Staying with me at hospital. I know you could have returned to London, handed me off to a medical team. You didn't."

"I wouldn't do that, Oliver. You're my partner—of sorts, anyway."

"Is that the only reason?"

The air between us changed, and I stood to leave. "Get some sleep," I said. "I'll check on you in the morning."

My retreat was cowardly, and we both knew it.

Once in my own bed, I lay awake for hours while the wind howled outside and the old castle creaked around me. I thought about Oliver. About Kiernan saying my name and the command that lived beneath his words despite being polite. And how my body had responded to it.

Sleep came slowly, and when it did, I dreamed of two men surrounding me with their warmth.

I woke disoriented, then remembered I was at *Greymarch*, Kiernan's castle, and that Oliver was on the opposite side of the suite, recovering.

"Come in," he said when I knocked softly on his bedroom door.

He'd already showered and was dressed for the day. Once again, he seemed significantly better than yesterday. Color had returned to his cheeks, and his steps were less tentative.

"Nurse Ratched here for your morning vitals check."

He cocked his head.

"Sorry, obscure reference to a character from a decades-old movie."

"I can say with the utmost confidence that, based on the name alone, you're nothing like her."

"You may change your mind on day fourteen of our time here when you tire of me waking you up every morning."

"I'd never tire of waking up to you, Ophelia."

How easy would it be to allow myself to fall into his arms and tell him how much I wanted that? But I couldn't. Especially after my dreams last night.

After completing the morning vitals check, I hastily retreated to my own room, telling him I'd meet him later for breakfast.

I showered, spent too much time deciding what to wear, then went downstairs to the dining room where we'd had dinner.

A few minutes later, Oliver joined me. However, Kiernan was noticeably absent.

"His lordship left early for estate business," Millie informed us when she came in to see if we needed anything. "He sends his apologies."

Oliver and I exchanged a glance but said nothing. Whatever game Kiernan was playing, we were not going to question his staff about it.

We finished our morning meal, then decided to explore. Oliver needed to move to rebuild his strength, and the castle offered endless corridors to wander. We found more rooms that appeared unoccupied for years, perhaps decades. The castle was enormous, and it seemed Kiernan lived in only a small fraction of it.

We discovered a gallery of portraits extending the family history we'd seen in the great hall the day before, revealing more Lockharts. These women also wore elaborate gowns, and the men were in uniforms from wars long ended. One portrait in particular caught my attention. It was of a woman who resembled Kiernan. There was a fierce intelligence in her expression. I leaned forward to read the brass plate beneath it. "Helena Lockhart, 1890–1962."

"His grandmother, perhaps," Oliver mused. "I'd wager she could command armies."

"Like her grandson."

Oliver's expression sharpened. "Noticed that about our host, eh?"

"How could I not? Observation is part of the job."

"Right." His tone was knowing. "The job."

I continued, cutting him off before he could press further, but stopped when we got close to the library door. On impulse, I reached for the brass handle, and when it refused to turn, I pressed my ear to the old wood.

"Hear anything?" Oliver asked from where he'd walked farther down the corridor.

"Negative."

When I joined him, we were only steps from the west tower staircase.

Millie appeared as if summoned, materializing from a doorway I hadn't noticed. "Can I help you? The kitchens are this way if you'd like tea."

The redirection was polite but unmistakable. The west tower was not for guests.

We accepted the tea and spent the afternoon in the guest wing. Oliver rested while I read a book I'd found in the sitting room. Neither of us spoke about our enigmatic host.

That evening, Kiernan joined us for dinner. He asked about our day, but his concentration drifted as he spoke. He excused himself before the meal ended, retreating to wherever he went when he was not with us.

He'd done so twice now—joined us for dinner, then excused himself early, and vanished.

Clearly, Kiernan intended to be present but not accessible, available but not engaged. He'd invited us into his home but kept himself at a distance.

Later that night, I stood at my window, staring into the darkness. I'd spent two days in this castle and knew less about Kiernan Lockhart than when I arrived.

The intelligence operative in me wondered what secrets he kept.

My purpose, though, was to be here for Oliver while he recovered. That was the reason I'd agreed to stay at Greymarch rather than return to London. The days ahead felt like time that was on one part an eternity, and none at all on another.

My curiosity deepened, and I told myself I'd find out what he was hiding in that library and what secrets lived in the west tower—but was I truly brave enough?

I startled when, somewhere in the castle below, a door closed. The sound echoed through the stone walls, and my hand went to my hip before I remembered I had left my weapon in London.

3

Oliver

On day three, I woke feeling more like myself than I had since before the attack. The headaches had faded from a constant assault to a dull presence lurking at the edges of my skull, but my body ached with the restlessness of a man who'd spent far too long lying down.

I had too many days of forced rest ahead of me, in a castle that felt increasingly like a pressure cooker—Ophelia and I sharing a suite, our host being a mystery I couldn't stop picking at, and my own body betraying me.

Now, I needed air, needed to breathe something that didn't smell of old stone and the lingering medicinal tang that clung to everything I touched.

Except Ophelia had other ideas about my morning.

"Not until I check your vitals," she said when I mentioned wanting to take a walk. She was already reaching for the medical kit she'd appropriated with the blessing of the hospital staff.

I sat on the edge of my bed and let her take my wrist in her hands to register my pulse rate. I watched her as she counted the beats silently. Her dark hair was pulled away from her features that managed to be both delicate and fierce. A small furrow appeared between her brows as she concentrated.

I'd wanted her for as long as I could remember. The desirous ache had become as familiar as breathing. I'd told myself my reluctance to act was because MI6 frowned upon officers complicating matters with personal entanglements, but the truth was simpler and more pathetic—I was terrified she'd reject me.

We were both on leave now. The regulations that had kept us apart seemed distant here, irrelevant in this castle at the edge of the world. But I wasn't whole yet, wasn't the man I wanted to be when I finally confessed my feelings.

She shone a penlight into my eyes when I raised my head. Her face was close enough to mine that I was tempted to lean forward and kiss her.

"You'll live," she pronounced, clicking the light off. "I think we can manage a walk on the grounds, nothing strenuous. If you start feeling unsteady or if your head hurts, we return. No arguments."

"Yes, doctor."

"I'm not a doctor."

"You certainly play one convincingly." I got up, testing my balance. The room stayed steady around me—a marked improvement from two days ago, when standing had made the world tilt like a carnival ride. "Shall we?"

A cold wind cut across the landscape, carrying the scent of peat, distant rain, and the wild emptiness that seemed to define this place. After days trapped inside, first in hospital, then within the castle's ancient walls, the vastness of it made me dizzy—though I was not about to admit that to Ophelia.

We walked slowly, following a path that wound away from the main entrance toward the ruins of an old chapel. She kept pace beside me, adjusting her stride to match my appalling stamina. Each step required more effort than it should, and my legs trembled with the strain of what I once would've considered modest exertion.

"Beautiful, isn't it?" she said, gesturing at the landscape rolling toward the horizon. "Bleak, but beautiful."

"The Morses have their estate in Kent," I said. "Rolling green hills, ancient oaks, a river perfect for punting." I paused to catch my breath, leaning on a lichen-covered stone that might have been part of a wall centuries ago.

"But this—I understand why a man would love this land. It's breathtaking in its honesty."

"Its honesty?"

"It doesn't pretend to be anything other than what it is. The land is beautiful and brutal and utterly indifferent to human concerns. There are no manicured gardens here, no artificial lakes designed to impress visitors. There is only rock and heather and sky."

Ophelia studied me with an unreadable look. "That's surprisingly philosophical for a man who claims to think primarily about cricket and whiskey."

"Near-death experiences have a way of inspiring reflection." I pushed off from the stone and resumed walking, though at a slower pace. "Also, the cricket season doesn't start for months, and I'm not allowed hard spirits yet, so I'm forced to find alternative topics for contemplation."

Her laugh was quiet, and the sound of it warmed me more than the weak sunlight struggling through the clouds.

"What do you make of our host?" I asked as we turned toward the gray bulk of Greymarch that rose against the darkening sky. From this distance, the place commanded the same attention it did up close.

Ophelia's gaze remained fixed on the fortress ahead of us, and she didn't speak right away. "He's not who I thought he was."

"Nor I." At the Labyrinth briefing, I'd barely noticed him. Now, Kiernan Lockhart silently commanded attention whenever he entered a room. I'd noticed it during dinner the previous nights—how my thoughts drifted toward him even when I was trying to focus on Ophelia.

I noticed powerful men all the time. It was part of the job—assessing potential threats, determining who might be dangerous and who was merely posturing. That was all this was. Our host deserved the same assessment as any other player on the field. The fact that my gaze lingered on the breadth of his shoulders and the strong line of his jaw meant nothing. Even as I thought it, I knew the lie for what it was.

We reached the castle's main entrance and paused to scrape the mud from our boots on the iron grate set into the stone. I was winded, though I hated to admit it, and my legs shook with the effort of the walk, but my mind remained clear. The headache hadn't worsened, and I counted that as a victory.

On our way to our suite, we walked past a music room we'd seen on our tour with Kiernan and, this time, went inside. The space was dominated by an old but obviously valuable grand piano. Sheet music sat on the stand— Chopin, I noted, one of the nocturnes—as if someone had set it aside mid-practice and never returned.

"Do you think he plays?" Ophelia asked, resting her fingers on ivory keys that had gone pale yellow with age.

"I've no idea." I tried to picture Kiernan's hands on the keys with the same controlled power he brought to everything else, and pushed the image away. "Perhaps it belonged to a previous generation."

He joined us for dinner that evening, appearing in the doorway as Millie was setting out the first course—some sort of cream soup that smelled of leeks—and I straightened in my chair when he crossed the threshold.

"I hope you don't mind the company," he said, taking his seat at the head of the table. He wore a charcoal-gray jumper tonight that stretched across the expanse of the shoulders I was increasingly obsessed with. "The estate accounts can only hold my attention for so long before I require human conversation."

"We're hardly scintillating dinner companions," I muttered. When I reached for the wine Millie had poured, Ophelia raised a brow. "I'm allowed," I said, sounding more like a child than a grown man. The red was excellent—rich and full-bodied, with a depth that spoke of patient aging. "Phee has been regaling me with the latest developments in field medicine, and I've been complaining about my head. Not exactly riveting discourse."

A ghost of a smile crossed Kiernan's features, softening the stern lines of his face. "You underestimate yourselves." He turned toward Ophelia, and his posture eased—still commanding, but more open than I'd seen him be during mission briefings. "How are you finding Greymarch? I know the castle can be somewhat overwhelming for newcomers."

"It's beautiful," she said. "The architecture alone is fascinating. Some of those corbelled ceilings must be centuries old."

"From the fourteenth, in fact." Kiernan's tone warmed as he spoke about his home, losing some of its cool reserve. "The Lockharts have been adding to the castle piece by piece for six hundred years. It's more of an archaeological dig than a home at this point—every renovation reveals foundations from an earlier era, walls that were built over older one, secrets layered on mistruths."

The man was a puzzle I wanted to draw out further. I'd never been able to resist piecing together a mystery—especially one that kept revealing unexpected layers. "How long have you been with Unit 23?"

"Seven years." He took a spoonful of soup. "I was recruited to MI6 from special forces. Then Typhon stepped in, saying he needed someone who understood both tactics and logistics—who could plan missions but also execute them when necessary."

"I've heard the skill set required for the unit goes far beyond what you've mentioned." I tried to picture the man across from me younger, leaner, running ops in hostile territory with weapons and violence instead of spreadsheets and supply chains. It wasn't difficult. "Which branch of special forces?"

"The one they don't officially acknowledge exists." His tone made it clear the subject was closed.

That was fair enough—I shifted tactics, turning to topics where he'd seemed more willing to engage. "It must be difficult, managing an estate this size while serving the Crown."

"The land manages itself, for the most part." Kiernan set down his spoon, and when he spoke again, his voice dropped into a lower register that made the hair on my arms stand up. "These moors have been here for millennia. They don't require my intervention. What they require is respect—an understanding that we are visitors here, not masters. The land endures. We're merely its temporary stewards."

I looked away, focusing on Ophelia. I concentrated on how her hair turned to burnished copper where it caught the light, on the graceful line of her neck, the intelligence in her brown eyes, and the subtle curve of her lips—all safe and familiar territory.

"Oliver mentioned his family has had their estate since the twelfth century," she said, picking up the conversation. "I suppose old families understand that kind of stewardship."

"That's right," I confirmed. "Though I suspect my ancestors were rather more interested in mastering the land than respecting it. We were Norman invaders, after all. Not known for our humility or our deference to existing traditions."

"The Lockharts were raiders before we were lords," Kiernan said. "Border reivers, cattle thieves, men who took what they wanted and dared anyone to stop them. We came to respectability late and unwillingly."

"Who manages your family's property now?" Ophelia asked, turning to me.

"Distant cousins I met a handful of times on visits to the estate. The last time I was there was before I left for university and my parents and sister moved to Australia."

The conversation flowed from there, loosened by wine and the intimacy of candlelight.

"Do you play the piano?" Ophelia asked, gesturing toward the music room we'd passed earlier. "We saw the Chopin piece on the stand."

Embarrassment crossed his features before he steeled them. "Badly, I'm afraid. My mother was the musician, and she used to play for hours while my father read in the library. I'd fall asleep, listening." He paused, swirling his wine. "I kept up with lessons, but I never had her gift."

"That's a lovely image, the three of you," Ophelia said.

"It was a good life," he said softly. "This place holds many fond memories."

"Running an estate like this must be demanding," I commented.

"Millie keeps it from falling apart, while I try not to make a mess of the accounts." The corner of his mouth lifted. "Yet I do manage to do so frequently."

I laughed. The image of Kiernan wrestling with ledgers while Millie tutted disapprovingly was endearing.

"What about you?" he asked, turning to Ophelia. "Where did you grow up?"

"Everywhere and nowhere. As you know, I was a diplomatic brat, and we moved every two or three years—Cairo, Vienna, Singapore, Washington. I learned to pack a suitcase before I knew how to ride a bicycle."

"Sounds lonely," I commented.

"It was, but it also taught me to read people quickly and figure out who was safe, who was genuine, and who was putting on a show." Her eyes landed on Kiernan for no longer than a second before she turned away. "Some people are harder to read than others, though."

"So I've been told," he responded with a wink.

The conversation wandered to the challenges of maintaining ancient properties, the sheep that grazed the eastern pastures, and the gamekeeper who had served three generations of Lockharts. Kiernan spoke more expansively than he had on previously, offering glimpses of a life I'd not considered.

He loved this place. That much was obvious in every word, every gesture, every lingering glance out the darkened windows toward the moors beyond.

When the evening stretched long, Millie brought out a cheese course, then whiskey—which I was forbidden from consuming. The aroma alone was torture.

I allowed myself to relax into the conversation, continuing to trade stories and observations, almost forgetting the weirdness of our situation. We were three strangers who'd worked together at a distance, now thrown into an intimacy none of us had anticipated.

When Millie cleared the last of the dishes, I expected Kiernan to make his usual excuses and disappear into the depths of the castle. Instead, he pushed his chair from the table and gestured toward the doorway. "Join me for a walk?"

Ophelia caught my eye, and her raised brow mirrored my own surprise.

He led us to the great hall, a place that held more warmth than I remembered from our first day here. Kiernan crossed to a sideboard where crystal decanters caught the firelight. He poured whiskey for himself and Ophelia, then glanced at me.

"Not allowed," I grumbled.

"Water, then. Millie would have my head if I sabotaged your recovery."

"She wouldn't be alone in that," Phee teased.

We sat in chairs arranged near the fire.

"Is that your ancestors' military collection?" Ophelia asked, motioning to a display case.

"It represents every Lockhart who ever served," he responded. "Six centuries of questionable decisions and occasional heroism."

He rose, and we followed him to the case. Inside lay the accumulated artifacts of a family at war, arranged with the care of a devoted curator. A sword from Culloden bore a notch in its blade. Campaign medals from the Napoleonic Wars, the Crimea, and both World Wars gleamed on the dark velvet under them. A set of letters tied with a faded ribbon showed handwriting that was cramped and urgent.

"My great-great-grandfather wrote those from Sebastopol." Kiernan nodded toward the envelopes. "His wife kept every one, though half of them are complaints about the food and the other half are too inappropriate to display."

The image of this stern, controlled man descending from someone who wrote filthy letters from the front lines struck me as humanizing.

Ophelia had drifted to a smaller case where a single medal lay on velvet. A Victoria Cross.

"My grandfather was in Burma in 1944. He carried three wounded men to safety under enemy fire, then returned for a fourth. They found him unconscious with a bullet in his shoulder. The man he'd dragged half a mile through the jungle lay beside him."

"He survived?" Ophelia asked.

"Lived another forty years. He never spoke about it except once, when I was sixteen and stupid enough to ask." He shook his head and grinned. "He told me that courage wasn't the absence of fear. It was deciding that something else mattered more."

In the flickering light, Kiernan looked different than he had an hour ago—or maybe I was finally letting myself see what had been there all along. He was more than a Unit 23 operative, more than the enigmatic lord of this castle—he was a man shaped by generations of duty and sacrifice, carrying a weight I was only beginning to understand.

"What about the dishonorable ones?" I asked. "You said some served more honorably than others."

He laughed. "Ah. The fourth viscount was a spectacular coward, who bought his way out of every battle he was meant to fight. And my great-uncle fled to Argentina in 1922 under circumstances the family has always refused to discuss." He took a sip of whiskey. "We don't display their contributions."

"Every family has its scoundrels," Ophelia said.

"The Lockharts have more than our share," he mused. "We're not good at moderation. When we commit, we do it completely. For better or worse."

When Kiernan finally excused himself with an apology about early morning obligations, I was surprised by how much I wanted him to stay.

Ophelia and I lingered a while longer. In the quiet left by Kiernan's absence, I became acutely aware of how close she sat, of how the firelight caught the curve of her cheek, of the subtle rise and fall of her breathing.

My pulse quickened when she reached for my hand and our fingers intertwined. Neither of us spoke or pulled away.

Eventually, we made our way to the east wing and our quarters, saying a quick good night before retiring to our respective rooms. Part of me wanted to follow her, to finally know the taste of her lips in what would be our first kiss. But I wasn't all the way myself yet. When the day came that Phee and I acted on our attraction, I wanted to be as whole a man as I'd ever been, able to give her pleasure I knew I could, not be compromised by the onset of another debilitating headache.

I had time to heal, to find my footing, to figure out what I wanted from this strange interlude before real life reclaimed us.

On the fifth day, I woke eager to venture beyond the confines of my bedroom and the sitting room that had become my prison unless I was accompanied by Ophelia. Rain streaked the windows in sheets, blurring the world beyond into gray-green smears. Had the weather been better, I would've suggested another walk.

"I want to explore," I told her over breakfast, where Millie had laid out eggs, toast, and thick rashers of bacon that smelled like heaven. And which I ate with an appetite I'd not had in weeks. "There's an entire castle here, and I've seen approximately three rooms."

"You've seen far more than that, *and* you're meant to be resting."

"I've rested so much I'm going mad." I reached for my tea, noting with satisfaction that my hand barely trembled. "Besides, you can't tell me you're not curious. A medieval castle in the Scottish Highlands, owned by a man who locks entire wings and disappears for hours at a time—"

"He's entitled to his privacy."

"Of course he is." I gave her my most innocent look—the one that had gotten me out of trouble at Eton and into trouble everywhere else since. "I merely want to walk the halls and perhaps find a billiards room where I can embarrass myself with my lack of coordination."

Phee shook her head, clearly not fooled in the slightest. But curiosity warred with caution in her eyes, and I knew which would win. She was as intrigued by our mysterious host as I was, even if she was better at hiding it.

"I'm in," she said at last. "But if you start looking pale or unsteady, we're going straight to your room. No arguments, no feigned charm, and definitely no pouting."

"I wouldn't dream of doing any of those things."

This time, she rolled her eyes.

Greymarch revealed itself in layers, like an old book whose pages had been shuffled and rebound a dozen times. The central section, where our rooms were located, connected to older wings through corridors designed to confuse invaders—narrow passages that turned sharply, stairs that led to landings with no obvious purpose, doors that opened into rooms within rooms within rooms. I understood how one might live here for decades and not discover all of it.

We stumbled upon an armory that would have made my ancestors weep with envy. Swords and pikes and ancient rifles lined the walls—some of which bore the Lockhart crest, while others appeared to be trophies from wars fought across continents. I lingered before a glass case containing a set of matching dueling pistols.

"Beautiful," I murmured, studying the craftsmanship. "And deadly."

"Rather like their owner," Ophelia added dryly.

I shot her a look, but she was already heading toward the door, a smile playing at the corners of her mouth. I followed, suppressing my own amusement.

We found a conservatory in a wing that faced south, chasing a sun that rarely appeared. Now it held only dead plants. The iron framework of its ceiling sagged in places, and rain hammered on panes of glass that hadn't been cleaned in years. The air smelled of rot and mildew, making me anxious to leave.

"It must have been magnificent once," Ophelia said, picking her way around a fallen palm frond gone brown and brittle. "Imagine it filled with tropical plants, warm and alive, while the moors froze outside."

I filed the image away for a time when she and I might create such a space together, romantic fool that I was turning into.

We explored until exhaustion caught up with me, then returned to our suite. I spent the remainder of the afternoon reading a Victorian mystery I'd found in our shared sitting room. There were too many characters and not enough plot, but it served to pass the time.

That evening, Millie brought a message from Kiernan offering his apologies, saying estate matters requiring his attention would keep him from joining us for dinner, and that he hoped we'd understand.

I was sure Ophelia shared my opinion that the dining room seemed emptier without him, but neither of us mentioned it aloud.

We retired early, and I lay in the darkness of my bedroom, listening to the wind howl around the castle's towers, rattling shutters and finding every gap in the ancient stone. My head ached—not badly, but enough to keep me from drifting off—and my body was restless despite the day's exertions.

I tried to read, but eventually gave up on the pretense of either it or rest and rose, crossing to the window. The clouds raced across what little moonlight managed to penetrate them, and the world beyond was a shifting darkness broken only by the occasional flash of distant lightning over hills I couldn't see.

I was about to return to my bed when I spotted a figure crossing the courtyard below. Whoever it was, walked with purpose despite the rain that must have been soaking him to the bone. When he turned into the moonlight, I recognized Kiernan's stride, along with his broad frame.

Pressing closer to the glass, I saw him head toward a stone structure set apart from the main castle that I hadn't noticed before. He disappeared inside, and a moment later, the Range Rover he'd driven us here in pulled out and turned down the long drive. Red taillights glowed until it rounded a bend and vanished into the darkness.

I glanced at the clock on my nightstand, which read close to midnight.

Where did a man go at this hour, in weather that made the roads treacherous in daylight, let alone at night? The nearest village was miles away and barely more than a collection of stone cottages and a pub that would have closed hours ago.

I considered looking for another vehicle, which was absurd—I was recovering from a concussion, didn't know the roads, and Kiernan's comings and goings were none of my business. He was entitled to leave his own home as he pleased, at whatever hour suited him.

I stood at the window for too long, wondering. Eventually, I returned to bed, but sleep remained elusive. I lay in the darkness, trying to construct logical explanations for his departure.

An emergency, perhaps—a tenant in trouble on some distant corner of the estate, livestock in distress, estate business that couldn't wait until morning. Or perhaps duty had called him away. Had Typhon summoned him for a mission on behalf of Unit 23? We were all on leave, but it could be canceled. Missions didn't respect schedules.

I tossed and turned as my innate curiosity kept my mind reeling.

Hours later, I heard the crunch of gravel through the rain's dying patter. Headlights swept across my ceiling, cutting bright arcs through the darkness. I waited, listening to a car door open and close.

It was zero four hundred now, which meant Kiernan would've had time for a round trip to Inverness, long enough for a meeting or a rendezvous or a task that required the cover of darkness, long enough for a hundred possibilities, each more intriguing than the last.

"He left around midnight," I said in a hushed tone to Ophelia over breakfast the next morning. Millie had cleared away our plates, and we sat alone in the dining room with cooling cups of tea. "He drove off into the storm and didn't return until nearly dawn."

"I wonder where he went," she murmured as she tapped her lower lip with her index finger.

"I assure you that the possibilities one conjures in the middle of the night are virtually endless," I said with a wink that made her smile.

Her mood shifted quickly, though. "He's hiding something," she said at last.

I nodded. We'd be here nine more days, and the question was no longer whether Kiernan Lockhart had secrets. Certainly, the locked rooms and midnight drives pointed to a life I doubted had much to do with his duty to the Crown. The question was what those secrets were, and whether they posed any danger to the two people staying under his roof.

4

Kiernan

I woke shortly after I'd drifted off, with the taste of a dream lingering on my tongue.

The images scattered as I reached for them—dark hair spread across white sheets, a man's groan, two bodies intertwined while I lurked in the shadows. I pressed the heels of my hands to my sockets until the fragments dissolved.

They were here. In my home. Sleeping in the guest wing I'd offered like a fool who believed he could handle the proximity.

During the Labyrinth mission, I'd studied them, planning how I might eventually have them. Now, they were here, and the only plan I had was avoidance. The irony wasn't lost on me.

I got up and crossed to the window, staring out at the land that had always given me peace. Today, it didn't.

After dressing, I made my way downstairs.

"You're up early, my lord," said Millie, who was already in the great hall.

"Estate business." The lie came easily. "I'll be in my library most of the day. Please let our guests know I send my apologies."

She dipped her chin and returned to her work without pressing, but her eyes lingered for a moment too long. She'd obviously noticed the shadows under my eyes and the tension I carried. Millie had witnessed me at my worst. She wouldn't ask, but she'd watch.

In the room that was my refuge, I sat behind the desk my father had used and his father before him, surrounded by ledgers and correspondence that demanded attention. I stared at the pages without reading a word, but it didn't matter. This was manageable.

They were not. But Oliver would recover, they would leave, and I'd return to the solitude that kept everyone safe. A few weeks of distance, and I'd stop imagining her laugh at my dinner table. Stop picturing him in my bed. Stop craving them with a ferocity that bordered on obsession.

I almost believed it.

As hard as I tried to focus on the columns of numbers, my mind continued circling to them.

Ophelia's beauty wasn't what had drawn me to her initially. It was her mind—the way she'd analyzed intelligence with an acuity that impressed even Typhon and her quiet competence that never demanded recognition. During our mission, I'd observed her adapting to every shifting variable without complaint, solving problems before others noticed they existed.

Oliver was no less compelling. His wit was a weapon he wielded with skill, but underneath the charm was kindness. I'd seen it in how he treated Millie, asking about her grandchildren as if he actually cared, and in how he deferred to Ophelia without ever diminishing himself. He'd thanked me for the room, the meals, and the hospitality, with an earnestness that couldn't be anything but authentic.

They were remarkable people, and that was the problem. They deserved a man who could meet them as equals, not one who would consume them for his own pleasure.

By afternoon, the ledgers had blurred into meaningless columns. I pushed away from the desk and crossed to the window, drawn by activity on the grounds beyond.

Ophelia and Oliver walked the formal gardens. He moved with more strength than days before. She stayed close, drawn to him as if she couldn't help it. They orbited each other like binary stars, caught in a gravity neither could escape.

They stopped near an old oak tree, and Oliver said something that made her laugh. I tamped down my jealousy, but it repeatedly clawed its way to the surface.

I should have continued my work and let them have this moment. Instead, I reached for my coat.

I told myself it was a host's duty. They were guests on my land. I should ensure they didn't wander into the boggy ground near the north pasture or stumble across the gamekeeper's traps. Responsibility—not desire—carried me down the stairs and out through the kitchen entrance.

The lie lasted until their faces came into view. Oliver's surprise gave way to genuine pleasure. Ophelia's guarded smile did nothing to hide her curiosity.

"We were admiring this tree," Oliver said. "Ophelia thinks it's older than the castle."

"She's right." I stopped a few paces from them. "It was here when the first Lockhart laid the foundation stones. Family legend says he refused to cut it down. He built around it instead."

"Stubborn," Ophelia observed.

"A family trait."

She smiled again. "I'm beginning to notice."

"Shall we walk?" I asked.

"That would be lovely," she responded right after I caught a look pass between them.

I hadn't intended to lead them anywhere in particular, but my feet knew this land better than my conscious mind. Soon, we were climbing the gentle slope toward the standing stones on the ridge.

"Neolithic," I said when Oliver asked about them. "No one knows who placed them here or why. My grandfather used to tell me stories about druids and blood sacrifices. I think his intent was to frighten me away from playing here."

"Did it work?" Ophelia asked.

"The opposite. I spent half my childhood convinced I'd find ancient treasure if I dug deep enough." I paused at the largest stone and ran my hand across its weathered surface. "I never found anything but earthworms and my mother's fury at the state of my clothes."

"I can picture you as a boy, covered in mud and hunting for treasure." Oliver's laugh was so warm and unexpected that my guard slipped.

"That was before my father died and I became lord of everything you see."

"How old were you?" he asked.

"Twenty-three."

"It's beautiful, Kiernan," Ophelia said quietly. "I understand why you love it."

When I looked at her, an openness she rarely showed was visible. The wind had caught her hair, and she looked dreamy as she took in the view. I wanted this moment to last longer than I had any right to.

"My father used to bring me here when I was young. Before he got sick. We'd sit on that stone there, and he'd point out the boundaries of the estate. He told me that, one day, it would all be mine to protect."

"Twenty-three was so young. How did you manage?" Oliver asked.

"I learned to pretend." I faced the path. "We should return. The weather's getting nasty."

"Thank you for showing us this," Oliver said a few minutes later when the castle came into view. "I know you're busy."

"Estate business will keep." The admission surprised me. "It's been some time since I've walked these grounds with anyone."

I glanced at Ophelia, wondering if she was curious enough to ask who with before. I was disappointed when she didn't. Not that my answer was all that interesting.

The last person I could recall being out here with was a groundskeeper.

I left them at the entrance to the guest wing and retreated to my library while I still had the sense to do so. But even in the space I considered sacred, I couldn't escape the feeling of them beside me on that ridge. The way I'd begun to relax in their presence.

I was walking a tightrope, but for the first time in years, I didn't care.

The storm broke shortly before midnight when I made the decision to visit my club. The tunnels sometimes flooded in weather like this, so I drove. However, the rain was coming down so hard I could barely see the road.

The Thorned Thistle was busy tonight despite the weather. I parked in the private lot, made my way inside, and found Callen in the observation gallery overlooking one of the main performance spaces, a glass of whiskey in hand.

"You look like hell." He didn't glance away from the scene below as I joined him at the railing. "How's Vanguard recovering?"

"Well enough."

He raised a brow. "At Greymarch."

"As you're well aware."

"Why, Kier?"

"He needed somewhere quiet. I had the space."

"Of course." His tone said he didn't believe a word of it. Not that I expected him to. Sometimes, it seemed he knew me better than I knew myself.

"Come." He gestured toward the front of the viewing area. "Gus is doing rope work tonight."

We claimed chairs with an optimal view. Below us, two dozen members had gathered in the space that had been configured for the evening—a wooden-frame structure in the center, soft lighting, and seating for observers.

Gus was one of the founding partners of our club, and rope work was his specialty. His submissive for the evening was a woman I recognized—a regular who enjoyed being displayed. She knelt before him, wearing nothing but a silk robe that wouldn't stay on her body for long.

"We begin with conversation," Gus announced. "Before a single strand touches her skin, I know her limits, her desires, and her fears. This isn't about binding a body. This is about earning the gift of surrender."

He spoke to his submissive, words meant only for her. She nodded, and the robe fell away.

What followed was artistry. Gus worked with hemp dyed deep burgundy, creating intricate designs across her body—functional and beautiful. He narrated his process as he checked her circulation, placed knots to avoid pressure points, and adjusted the tension to create different sensations.

His technique faded into the background. My attention was on the sub's face when the binding tightened around her. Most compelling was the moment when she stopped fighting and yielded to his control.

In my mind, her face became Ophelia's.

I imagined her in that space, kneeling before me, with her hair unbound and her eyes full of trust. I'd start with her wrists, wrapping the rope in deliberate loops as the color rose in her olive skin. She'd tremble—not from fear, but from the anticipation she didn't know she possessed.

I'd bind her with aching slowness, savoring every gasp, every shiver. The rope would frame her breasts, create diamonds of exposed flesh across her stomach, and force her shoulders back and her chin up. She'd be beautiful in her surrender—more beautiful than she'd ever allowed herself to be. And Oliver would watch.

The image seized me. Oliver on his knees beside her, aroused and waiting for my commands. He wouldn't be bound—not yet. He'd be free to touch her, to taste her, but only with my permission. Only when I told him where to put his hands, his mouth, his cock.

"Kiss her neck," I'd say, and he'd quiver as he obeyed. "Lower. I want to hear her moan."

Ophelia would arch into his touch, restrained and helpless to do anything but receive the pleasure I orchestrated. Oliver would look up at me for approval, for direction, for the next command that told him how to worship her body.

"Use your tongue," I'd order, and he'd lower himself between her spread thighs. I'd witness her pleasure building under his mouth, his submission displayed in every movement. I'd tell him to speed up or slow down, when to add his fingers and make her scream.

Then, as soon as she was close, trembling and on the edge, I'd make him stop.

"Please," she'd beg. "Please, sir, I need—"

"You need what I give you." I'd circle them, running my hand along the rope that held her, gripping Oliver's hair to tilt his face up toward mine. "You come when I allow it. Not before."

I'd position him behind her, still on his knees. "Inside her," I'd command. "Slowly."

He'd obey. He'd always obey. And they'd look at me as their bodies joined—seeking my approval, my permission, my control over their pleasure.

"Kiernan."

Callen saying my name shattered the fantasy.

I blinked, disoriented. My knuckles had gone white on the arm of my chair. Below us, Gus had finished. The submissive hung suspended in an intricate web, while observers applauded.

I'd missed all of it.

"You were somewhere far away." There was no judgment in Callen's tone, only observation. "Somewhere that put that look on your face."

"It's nothing."

"We've known each other too long for you to get away with deflection." He rose and gestured toward the bar. "Come. You need a drink, and I need to understand why my oldest friend looks like a man being torn apart."

We claimed a corner where we wouldn't be overheard, and Callen ordered two whiskeys.

"They're getting to me."

"I suspected as much." He swirled his glass. "Tell me."

I did, but not everything. Not about the fantasies that had consumed me since I'd met them, not the bone-deep certainty that they were inexplicably mine. But about the impulsive offer for them to stay at Greymarch that I was already regretting.

He listened without interrupting. When I finished, he was quiet long enough for me to wonder if he'd comment.

"You want them."

"In ways that terrify me."

Callen understood the darkness in me because he shared it—we'd recognized it in each other before we had words to name it. He knew my history better than anyone alive.

"What happened was a long time ago," he said. "You're not the same man."

"Am I not?" I set my glass down. "The wanting feels the same—the intensity, the consuming need. What makes you think it would end differently?"

"Because you're asking the question." He set his glass down. "The man you were then wouldn't have. He'd have taken what he wanted and dealt with the consequences later. That you're here, torturing yourself with doubt, tells me you've learned from the wreckage."

I longed to believe him. To believe the years of solitude had changed me, that I'd become someone capable of wanting without destroying.

I could still see the look on my sub's face when I'd ended it. How our third had crumbled. And in my nightmares, I heard every word said when the news came a year later via a call in the middle of the night. It still woke me with guilt searing through my chest.

"I can't risk it," I said. "Not with them."

"Then, they must leave." It wasn't an accusation; it was the truth. "If you can't trust yourself, remove the temptation. Find another place for him to recover. Let them go before this becomes a fire you can't put out."

Sending them away would hurt worse than the memories. Oliver recovering somewhere else, Ophelia caring for him without me nearby—it was unbearable.

That, more than anything, told me how far gone I already was.

"When is the next partners' meeting?" I asked, changing the subject.

Callen allowed the deflection. "Next month. Why?"

"Just making sure I could be there."

He shook his head, rose, and clasped my shoulder. "If and when you're ready to bring the subject back around to your guests, I'll be willing to listen."

Before I could object, not that I would have, he left.

I stayed at the club for another two hours, observing scenes I didn't see, drinking whiskey I didn't taste. By the time I returned to my car, the storm had eased and the roads were slick but passable.

The drive to Greymarch took longer than it should have. I took it slow, delaying the moment when I'd be close to them again. Breathing the same air. Fighting the same impossible battle.

It was nearly four in the morning when I pulled into the courtyard. The castle loomed in the darkness, windows black except for the faint glow of banked fires.

They'd be asleep. Safe in their beds in the guest wing, unaware of where I'd been or what I'd imagined doing to them.

I didn't go to my bedroom. Instead, I walked to the end of the hall and unlocked the door to the playroom—a space I hadn't entered since they'd arrived.

The door swung open on silent hinges, and I stood on the threshold.

I'd built this space before the Thorned Thistle existed, when I was still learning what I was and what I needed. It gave my darkness somewhere to live that wouldn't bleed into the rest of my life. Here, I could be the man

I truly was—commanding, controlling, the architect of surrender.

Now, I imagined them here.

Ophelia on the St. Andrew's cross, wrists secured above her head, body stretched and displayed for my pleasure. Her breath would come fast and shallow as I circled her. I would trail my fingers across her heated skin. She'd try to predict what came next, but the beauty of the cross was that she wouldn't be able to turn. She could only wait, feel, and trust.

Unlike in my fantasy at the club, Oliver would be on his knees beside a bench farther away, rather than close to her, with his hands clasped behind him. He'd be hard—he'd always be hard when she submitted—but he wouldn't be allowed to touch himself. He'd do nothing without my permission, because that was the gift he craved even if he didn't know it yet.

I'd make them wait. Make them desperate. I'd draw out their pleasure until they begged, then I'd give them what they needed. What only I could give them.

The fantasy was so vivid I could almost hear them. Ophelia's soft moans as I marked her skin with my flogger—measured strokes, building sensation, never more than she could take. Oliver's rough groans as I granted him permission to touch, to taste, to worship her under my direction.

I was achingly hard, my body responding to the images that existed only in my mind.

I shut it down before it could consume me, exited the playroom, and locked the door.

Later, alone, I'd take care of it. Yes, I still scened. I gave subs what they needed, witnessed them come undone under my command—but I never took my own release with them. That was the line I'd drawn after what happened.

Three more days passed in the same pattern.

I emerged for meals when I couldn't avoid them, making polite conversation, then escaping to my library as soon as I could.

I spent hours staring at paperwork, reading the same paragraphs over and over without absorbing a word while my mind drifted to them again and again.

The distance was killing me, but the alternative was worse.

On the fifth day, my restraint cracked.

I emerged from the library in the late afternoon, my mind so full of numbers and estate reports that I didn't see her until we nearly collided.

"Kiernan." Ophelia stumbled, and her hand flew to her chest. "I didn't realize you were—I was, um, exploring. I didn't mean to disturb you."

She was close. Too close. I could smell her fragrance—the same light scent I remembered from the hours spent in the surveillance cottage and during hospital visits when she'd leaned into me unconsciously.

"You could never disturb me," I murmured.

Color rose in her cheeks, but she didn't step away.

The space around us constricted as I became aware of her quickening breath, dilated pupils, and the flush of her skin.

Her body knew what her mind was only beginning to understand.

"We've hardly seen you." She spoke barely above a whisper. "I thought perhaps we'd offended you."

"No." I wanted to reach for her, to cup her cheek, and kiss her until she forgot the questions I couldn't answer. "You've done nothing wrong. The fault is mine."

"Then, why—"

"Because I can't be near you," I blurted. "Because it makes me desire things I have no right to want."

The color in her cheeks deepened from pink to rose.

"Kiernan, why do you think you have no right?" My name from her lips nearly undid me.

I should have walked away. I didn't.

"I don't do relationships. I don't let people in. It's not what I'm built for."

"Has it occurred to you that we might be capable of deciding that for ourselves?"

The question stopped me cold. No one had ever challenged me like that, not in those words.

For a moment, neither of us stirred. Then she lowered her gaze and let her arms fall to her sides.

Submission. The unconscious gesture of a woman yielding to authority she didn't consciously recognize.

It was yet another nail in the coffin of my tenuous restraint.

"Forgive me," I said as I walked away.

I sat in my bedroom and accepted the truth I'd been avoiding.

Distance wasn't working. The club wasn't working. My walls were crumbling more with every day they stayed, every meal we shared, every glimpse I caught of them walking the grounds or laughing together in the garden.

I'd told her the truth, though not all of it. I ached to command them together, to own their pleasure and their surrender in ways that would consume all three of us.

I had two choices. I could send them away and save them from what I was. Find another place for Oliver to recover and return to the solitude that had kept everyone safe.

Or I could let them stay while I destroyed everything I touched. The same way I had before.

I knew which choice I should make.

I also knew, with sick certainty, that I didn't have the strength to make it.

The wanting had already won.

5

Ophelia

Kiernan's words echoed long after he'd disappeared.

Being near you makes me want things I have no right to want.

He desired me. He'd admitted it aloud in a way that made my skin prickle with heat, then he'd walked away as if the confession cost him nothing—as if he could deposit those words between us and retreat to his tower without consequence.

I should have been relieved. The distance he maintained, the hours when he disappeared, the meals where he barely looked at me—all of it had been driving me mad. At least now I understood why.

Except understanding made it worse.

Rather than act on that desire, rather than let me respond, he'd fled. The man who set my heart racing had run from a single moment of honesty. But Kiernan wasn't an average man. I'd known that from the moment we met at Glenshadow, realized it more deeply during our hours together at Dunravin, and acknowledged it with sharp clarity during the nights at Oliver's bedside when he appeared and disappeared like a storm I couldn't predict.

I replayed it—how close he'd stood, the rough edge to his words, how I'd lowered my gaze, not knowing why I was compelled to do so. I could not overcome the overwhelming need to yield to him.

I had to put this in a box. That's what I did with feelings—labeled them, filed them, and dealt with them later or never. Except this wasn't something I could manage. Kiernan had looked at me like he could see straight through every wall I'd built, and instead of feeling exposed, relief washed over me. That terrified me more than anything.

When I returned to my room, the fire had burned down to embers, leaving the room dark, but I didn't turn on the light. I stood frozen, recalling Kiernan's words.

He'd spoken as if the wanting itself was dangerous, as if desire was a force to be contained rather than acted upon. What could a man like Kiernan Lockhart want that he believed was forbidden?

I crossed to the window. The west tower was visible from here—a dark spire disappearing into a cloud-scattered sky. A single light burned in the uppermost window. Was he standing there now? Was he thinking about me the way I was thinking about him? I pressed my forehead on the cold glass and tried to steady my breathing before turning away and shedding my robe as I crossed to the bed.

The sheets were cool on my overheated skin, but they offered no relief. I lay in the darkness, hyperaware of the weight of my breasts and the throbbing between my legs.

My mind drifted to the hospital where I'd spent two weeks with Oliver, acknowledging that I'd been falling for him then. What kind of person did that make me?

Now, I wanted both of them—the man who'd been in the hospital bed and the one who'd sat vigil beside me. I craved them with an intensity that made my blood rage, and I didn't understand how that was attainable.

Sleep was impossible. Every time I closed my eyes, I saw Kiernan's face, then Oliver's. The sheets tangled around my legs as I rolled from side to side, and the pillow grew warm beneath my cheek.

Sometime after midnight, I heard footsteps in the corridor—footsteps that were heavy, measured, and deliberate. They paused near my door, and I went still. For one wild moment, I thought it was Kiernan, that he'd changed his mind, that he was going to knock, that I'd open the door and he'd be standing there, desperate with desire like I was.

After several seconds, the footsteps continued. A door opened and closed down the hall—a servant, probably, or Oliver unable to sleep.

I told myself I was relieved, that it was better this way, that whatever existed between us would only complicate an already complex situation. We were guests in his home. Oliver was recovering. There were a dozen reasons why acting on this attraction would be foolish.

None of them made the ache go away.

I fell into restless sleep sometime before dawn. I dreamed of Kiernan's hands on my flesh, his body pressing me into the mattress while I arched up to meet him. I woke gasping, my nightgown clinging to me, damp with sweat, and the space between my thighs slick with need.

While I managed another hour of sleep, I still woke with his name on my lips and an ache that bordered on pain. I was acting like a teenager with her first crush instead of a grown woman with a career and a life.

I took a shower, hoping it would help. I stood beneath the spray and let the water sluice over my shoulders and down my spine. It was hot enough to redden my skin and strong enough to pound the tension from my muscles. I reached for the soap and began washing—arms first, then stomach. When my palms skimmed my breasts, I shuddered.

The sensation was electric. My nipples were sensitive from a night of restless need, my body primed and desperate for contact. I told myself to move on, to finish and get out, but my mind had other ideas. I lingered. My thumbs brushed across the hardened peaks of my breasts, and I bit back a moan.

Kiernan's hands. The thought came unbidden—what would they feel like? Larger than mine. Rougher. He would know exactly when to be gentle and when to squeeze hard enough to make me gasp. He would—

I forced myself to stop this nonsense, then finished washing quickly, keeping my touch impersonal, refusing to let my mind wander. But when I stepped out and caught my disheveled reflection in the mirror, I knew I was losing this fight.

Breakfast was an exercise in torture. Millie had laid out a spread in the small dining room—eggs and bacon, toast and preserves, and a pot of coffee that filled the room with its rich aroma. Oliver was already seated when I arrived, looking more rested than he had in days.

"Sleep well?" he asked.

"Well enough." The lie came easily. "You?"

"Better than I have in a while. I think I'm finally on the mend." He raised his coffee cup in a mock toast. "Another week, and I'll be ready to take on the world. Or at least a flight of stairs without getting winded."

I smiled despite myself. This was us—the easy rhythm we'd fallen into over six months of working together. Somewhere along the way, colleagues had become friends.

"Will Kiernan be joining us?" I glanced at the empty chair at the head of the table when Millie appeared.

"Lord Greymarch sends his apologies." Her face gave nothing away. "Estate matters require his attention this morning. He hopes to join you for dinner."

Estate matters—of course. He was avoiding me.

"Phee? What's going on?"

I raised my head. "Sorry. I'm distracted."

"Clearly. Anything you want to talk about?"

Yes. No. I don't know.

"Just restless," I said instead. "I'm not used to having nothing to do." Extended leave was always like this—a few days were idyllic, but when it stretched beyond two weeks, my mind craved work. A mission. An op. Hell, I'd welcome a pile of paperwork.

"Tell me about it." He stood and refilled his plate. "Another few days of this, and I'll be climbing the walls. Literally."

I laughed despite myself. "Please don't. Kiernan would never forgive us if you re-cracked your skull on his property."

"Speaking of our host—have you noticed anything odd about him?"

"Odd how?"

"His behavior runs hot and cold at what feels like a whim. Not to mention the constant disappearing act."

You have no idea, I thought, remembering the heat in Kiernan's eyes.

"He's a private man," I said. "Some people are."

"Privacy is one thing. This feels more like reclusivity." Oliver returned to the table. "Maybe I'm paranoid. Occupational hazard."

I forced a smile. "I empathize."

We finished breakfast in silence, then separated. I told Oliver I had work to catch up on—a fib, but he didn't question it.

I'd brought a book from London, but the words blurred on the page. My mind kept returning to the same questions, the ones I couldn't answer no matter how many times I turned them over. I'd read articles about polyamory, seen it discussed as if it were perfectly normal, but those people seemed confident in their choices. Enlightened while I was confused, believing there was a flaw in my wiring that made me incapable of wanting what I was supposed to want—one person, one love, one neat and tidy relationship.

That wasn't all that troubled me. I kept thinking about the way my body had softened when Kiernan looked at me, the way I'd longed to bare my throat and wait for his instruction. I'd never known that with anyone. I'd always been the one in control—in bed, in relationships, in every part of my life. I didn't yield. I didn't submit. Except apparently I did, for him, and wanting it made me feel like a stranger in my own skin.

I set down the book and stood, too restless to sit any longer. The room became suffocating, as though its elegant furnishings were closing in around me. I needed air. Movement.

I stood in the corridor, not knowing which way to turn. The main staircase was to my right, and it led to the grand hall. To the left, the passage wound deeper into Greymarch's maze of rooms and hallways, where the library was and the west tower stood.

I turned left.

My footsteps echoed off the stone walls as I walked. Greymarch was quiet at this hour.

The library wasn't hard to find. I'd memorized the castle's layout during our first day here, an old habit from training. Know your exits, your routes, and the geography of any space you might need to navigate in a crisis. I hadn't expected to use that knowledge like this.

The door was similar to others I'd seen, except a more modern lock had been added. Was Kiernan somewhere on the other side of it right now? Maybe working at a desk, reviewing ledgers or correspondence? Or was he doing exactly as I was—thinking about what had passed between us?

I almost knocked, but didn't.

What would I say? *You told me you wanted me, then you ran, and I haven't been able to think about anything else since?* That was hardly the basis for a productive conversation. I could demand explanations, but he'd made it clear he wasn't ready to give them. I could confess my own desires, but the thought of that vulnerability made my stomach clench.

I lowered my arm and stepped away. Some battles weren't meant to be fought head-on. Some required patience, strategy, and the willingness to wait for the right moment. I'd learned that in my career. I could apply it here.

I returned to my room the way I'd come, leaving the library and its occupant undisturbed. Once there, I sat on the window seat Oliver and I had shared. The perch had a clear view of the grounds, the hills, and the ever-changing Highland sky. I curled up on the cushions and watched the clouds roll across the gray expanse overhead, letting myself feel what I'd been fighting since we arrived here.

I wanted him. The admission landed with the weight of truth too long denied. I yearned for Kiernan Lockhart with an intensity that frightened me, and I had no idea what to do about it.

The suite door opened, and Oliver stepped through. I was struck again by how much better he looked. The shadows beneath his eyes had faded, and color had returned to his cheeks. He walked with more certainty now, less of the halting steps of a man guarding against vertigo.

"There you are." He crossed to where I sat and settled beside me, near enough to feel the warmth radiating from his body. "I was starting to think you'd vanished too."

"Too?"

"As Millie told us at breakfast, our host has made himself scarce." He stretched his legs out until his feet nearly touched mine. "Not that I'm complaining, since it means more time with you."

I studied him. Six months of working together had turned a colleague into someone I trusted, someone who made me laugh, someone whose absence would leave a hole I couldn't fill. I couldn't lose this. Whatever was happening with Kiernan, whatever these feelings meant, I couldn't let them cost me Oliver.

I craved them equally, but what if keeping one meant losing the other? I couldn't bear making the choice.

The hint Oliver dropped was clear. I should have said a quip in return, acknowledged the flirtation while keeping it safely contained—that was what I would have done a week ago, what the version of me who existed before Kiernan's confession would have done without thinking.

Instead, my eyes traveled over his face, along the cut of his jaw and the curve of his mouth. He was beautiful. I'd always thought so in an abstract way, the same way one acknowledges that a sunset is breathtaking or a piece of music is stirring. But sitting here with him so close, with the memory of Kiernan's confession burning through me, that detachment was gone.

"Phee?" His voice was soft. "What are you thinking about?"

"Sorry." I pulled my foot away, breaking the almost-contact between us. "My mind's been elsewhere today."

"Mine too. This castle does strange things to a person."

"What kind of strange?" I asked.

Oliver's eyes dropped to my mouth long enough for me to notice. "The kind that makes you question things you thought you knew about yourself."

My heart hammered. This conversation had veered into dangerous territory, and I wasn't sure how to steer it to safety. I wasn't sure I wanted to.

Something crossed Oliver's face. His shoulders tensed, and when he spoke again, it was at a near-whisper. "I've been thinking about what happens after."

"After?"

"Soon, I'll be cleared to return to London. To MI6 and pretending we're nothing more than colleagues."

I'd been avoiding this thought—the ticking clock over everything we were feeling in this strange, suspended moment. Our time at Greymarch was always temporary, a parenthesis in our real lives, a chance to recover and regroup. Then what? Return to Vauxhall Cross and act as though none of this had happened? Return to cool distance and rigid restraint while my body burned with awareness every time he walked into a room?

"Is that what you want?" I asked. "To go back to pretending?"

Oliver turned to face me. "No. It's not." His tone lost its usual lightness. "I've spent months acting as though I'm not attracted to you, Phee. All those reasons to keep my distance? They made sense in London." He shook his head. "Not anymore."

His confession mirrored what stirred inside me—the same exhaustion with lying to myself, the same hunger for honesty.

"We'll have to face it eventually," I said. "The real world doesn't disappear just because we're hiding in a castle."

"I know." His hand slid across the cushion between us, and this time, it didn't stop short. He weaved our fingers together. The connection felt tentative and certain all at once. "But we have a week. Maybe we figure out what this is before we have to decide what to do about it."

His thumb traced a slow circle on my palm. The touch was gentle, almost innocent, and yet it sent fire unfurling through me. But as I looked at Oliver—even as my body responded to his nearness, his want—I saw another face superimposed over his. Dark hair instead of sandy brown. A man who would never suggest figuring things out. A man who would take.

I was thinking about Kiernan while Oliver held my hand. And the worst part was, I didn't want to stop.

"I think I'll rest before dinner," I said, pulling away too quickly. I stood from the window seat. "Will you be all right?"

Disappointment flickered across his face—or maybe understanding. "Always am." He sighed. "See you at dinner."

I fled before I could do anything foolish. Before I could tell him the truth—that my fantasies had started tangling together in ways I couldn't untangle. Two men who couldn't be more different, and yet who'd both taken up residence in my thoughts.

I remained in my room until an hour later, when there was a knock at the suite door. Millie stood in the corridor, with her coat already buttoned.

"Lord Greymarch asked me to let you know he's cooking dinner tonight. He's given me the evening off and wondered if you might like to help him in the kitchen."

"The kitchen?"

"He's already started the preparations." There was a twinkle in her eye. "I tried to argue, but he insisted. He said it had been too long since he cooked for anyone."

After she left, I stood frozen on the threshold. Kiernan had avoided me all day. He'd avoided Oliver too. Now, he wanted us to help him cook dinner?

Oliver came out of his room. Clearly, he'd overheard the invitation.

"This should be interesting," he said, stepping closer to me. "I can't cook to save my life, but I'm excellent at eating."

When we arrived, Kiernan stood at the counter, with his sleeves rolled to his elbows, chopping vegetables.

"I hope you don't mind the change of venue," he said without raising his head. "Millie deserved a night off, and I realized I've been a poor host."

"I thought you were busy with estate matters," I snapped, unable to hide my irritation.

His knife stilled. "Yes. I was. Apologies."

Oliver broke the tension. "What are we making? And please tell me whatever my job is can't ultimately ruin dinner. For example, I'm more than comfortable opening wine."

That earned a smile from Kiernan. "There's a Burgundy breathing on the counter. Glasses in the cabinet to your left." He gestured toward a cutting board at the other end of the island. "Ophelia, if you're willing, the onions need dicing."

We fell into an awkward rhythm. Oliver poured wine and stayed out of the way, apart from stealing bits of cheese from a board Kiernan had set out.

I worked on the onions, blinking away the sting and wondering if this was punishment for snapping at him.

"You're holding the knife wrong."

I looked up. "Excuse me?"

"You're going to lose a digit." Kiernan set down his own knife and stepped behind me. "May I?"

I nodded.

He repositioned my hand. "Curl your fingers like this." He adjusted my grip. "You control the cut as the blade follows your knuckles."

His breath stirred my hair, and I almost leaned into him.

"Now." His mouth was near my ear. "Slow, even strokes."

I forced myself to focus on the onion, cutting through it cleanly but with a rhythm steadier than my heartbeat.

"Better." He stepped away, and I missed his warmth.

I glanced over at Oliver, and he grinned. He didn't appear jealous, more curious.

We cooked. Or Kiernan did while Oliver and I followed instructions. *Crush the garlic. Stir the sauce. Taste for seasoning.* He navigated his kitchen with an ease that revealed how often he must do this alone. He reached for tools and ingredients without looking, adjusting the heat and timing by instinct.

"My mother taught me," he said when Oliver commented on his skill. "She believed every Lockhart should be self-sufficient. My father could barely boil water, and she was determined I wouldn't be the same."

"She sounds formidable," I said.

"She was." His voice softened. "She died when I was nineteen. Cancer. It was quick, at least."

I thought of my vibrant and very-much-alive mother. Guilt pricked at me for every phone call I'd rushed through and every visit I'd postponed.

"I'm sorry," said Oliver.

"It was a long time ago." Kiernan returned to the stove. "I prepare her recipes when I need to feel close to her. This was her favorite. Beef stew with vegetables. Astonishingly simple."

"Not if you're the one responsible for the onions," I muttered, making them both laugh.

We ate at the kitchen table rather than in the formal dining room. The wine flowed, and the food was extraordinary. The stew was rich and savory, and each bite tasted better than the last. Kiernan seemed more relaxed than I'd ever seen him. Perhaps good food and easy company had loosened the tension he usually carried. Our conversation wandered from childhood memories to favorite books to the absurdities of intelligence work.

When he laughed at something Oliver said—a real laugh, deep and unguarded—I wished I could bottle the sound.

This was what I'd wanted to see. The man beneath the title and beneath the command. Someone who missed his mother and cooked her recipes to feel close to her. Someone who could laugh without calculation. Someone capable of warmth despite all his walls.

After dinner, Oliver insisted on washing up while Kiernan and I dried. The domesticity of it was at once strange and familiar, especially when our shoulders occasionally brushed.

"Thank you," I said when Oliver finished washing the last of the pots. "For tonight."

"It was selfish, really. I've been hiding, and that's not fair to either of you. I'm not good at this," said Kiernan.

"This?"

"Letting people in," he said, almost too quietly to hear. "I've been alone a long time. I'd forgotten what it was like to want to be with people."

The admission cost him. It showed in the clench of his jaw. Before I could respond, Oliver put his hand on my shoulder.

"Time to check my vitals?"

"Yes, of course." I folded the dish towel and set it on the counter, hating that our evening was coming to such an abrupt end.

Kiernan's arm grazed mine as he brushed past me. I couldn't tell if it was an accident or intentional.

"I'll not forget you called me a scoundrel," he whispered before disappearing in the opposite direction. "Sleep well," he called out behind him.

I didn't. Sleep, that is.

After making sure Oliver was stable and settled, I retreated to my room, but being alone only made things worse.

My desire had become unbearable. My body ached with it, and the hunger only sharpened with every passing minute. Nothing I tried made it go away. Every time I tried to sleep, I could feel Kiernan's warm breath on my neck and hear him whisper in my ear. *I'll not forget you called me a scoundrel.*

God, what was wrong with me? Why did him simply teasing me make me want to beg him to fuck me?

I changed into sleep clothes and got in bed. Tossing and turning didn't help. I couldn't focus on my book, so I finally gave in.

My hand slid beneath the covers, beneath the silk of my nightgown, and I exhaled slowly as I reached between my legs. I knew how to chase pleasure, how to bring myself to the edge and over it. No man had ever managed it—I'd had lovers, competent and attractive men who'd tried their best, but my body had never surrendered to anyone but myself. I'd learned to fake what was expected, to act satiated. I'd had lovers who complained I was distant, friends who said I was hard to read. I'd taken both as a compliment.

I'd assumed I simply wasn't wired for passion. That the consuming desire other women described was an exaggeration or a fantasy.

Being here told me how wrong I was. What would it feel like to surrender? To let someone else hold the reins, make the decisions? The thought should have repulsed me. It didn't. It made my thighs press together and my breath come faster.

Tonight, I needed the release.

Oliver's face surfaced first, and the image felt safe and expected. I let it form—his gaze darkening with desire, his mouth hovering above mine as he whispered my name. This was a fantasy I could control.

My fingers traced slow circles as I imagined his weight pressing into me, his lips tracing a path down my throat, and his breath hot against my ear as he told me how beautiful I was, how long he'd ached for this. The pleasure built steadily. I arched into my own touch and let the images sharpen—his hands on my breasts, his mouth on my flesh, his body covering mine as we rocked together in the darkness.

Then the fantasy changed. The hands on my skin changed. They were rougher, more demanding. The image was Kiernan now.

I hadn't called him forward. He'd simply appeared, displacing Oliver as if he belonged there. His hand fisted in my hair, tilting my head to expose my throat. His mouth descended not in a kiss but in a claiming. His teeth scraped my pulse point as he growled, *"Mine."*

The pleasure sharpened. I tried to return to the safety of fantasy-Oliver, but my mind refused. It craved Kiernan.

The image dissolved and reformed. I was somewhere else entirely. Kneeling. Stone beneath my knees. My head bowed, my hands in a position of surrender.

I thought of a book I'd found in an airport years ago, the cover garish enough that I'd hidden it inside a magazine. The story was about a woman on her knees. A man commanding her surrender. I'd told myself I was reading it out of boredom, that it was absurd—who would actually want that? But I'd read every page before tossing it in a bin after the flight ended.

I allowed the fantasy to continue. A hand gripped my chin and tilted my face upward. Then the voice blended with Oliver's, both of them issuing a single command that brought me to the edge of release.

The fantasy fractured, and I stared at the ceiling. My chest heaved, and my body trembled. I'd been imagining two men at the same time, commanding me together, and my body had responded with a surge of desire so intense it terrified me.

I pulled my hand away and rolled onto my side, curling into myself. The overwhelming desire remained, but I couldn't bring myself to finish what I'd started.

A sound from outside my room cut through my restless haze, and I sat up when I recognized the creak of Oliver's door hinges. Footsteps passed my room, quiet and measured, the tread of someone trying not to be heard. The clock on my nightstand showed half past midnight.

Where was Oliver going at this hour?

I considered following. My hand reached for the covers, ready to throw them off and pursue him, but I didn't. Whatever he was seeking, he needed to find it alone. Or perhaps I was simply a coward—afraid that following him would lead me somewhere I wasn't prepared to go.

I rested on the pillows, listening for any sound of his return. The castle was quiet around me. I told myself I would wait ten minutes. If there was no sign of him, I'd go after him.

The seconds ticked by slowly, and moments before I was about to get up, I heard footsteps, then a knock at the door. I crossed the room and pulled it open.

Oliver stood in the sitting area of the suite. His face was pale and slick with sweat, and his hands shook at his sides. He looked like he'd seen a ghost—or become one.

"Phee," he whispered, then fell into my arms without speaking another word.

6

Oliver

The walls were closing in.

My feet landed on the cold floor when I swung my legs over the side of the bed. The shock of it helped, grounding me in something other than the restless energy thrumming beneath my skin. My body had been demanding movement for hours, and I'd denied it long enough.

The headache that had plagued me for days had finally faded to almost nothing. My strength was returning. My legs were steadier when I stood, and my muscles no longer trembled from simple exertion. I was healing, and my body knew it, and now, it wanted to do something other than lie in the dark.

Ophelia. Her name surfaced the moment I let my thoughts drift. The way she'd laughed at three nights ago, her whole face transforming with it. The warmth of her hand when she checked my pulse each morning, her fingers lingering at my wrist longer than required. The silk of her dress at that first dinner, skimming curves I wanted to trace with my tongue.

I'd buried my attraction to her for months, telling myself it was a bad idea. Now, whatever reasons I'd come up with seemed irrelevant. She'd stayed with me. By my side. Whatever had existed between us before had deepened into a bond that stretched far beyond a working relationship.

Now, all I wanted was to cross the sitting room to her door. I wanted to kiss her until neither of us could breathe, bury myself inside her, and forget everything except how she would feel wrapped around me, her nails digging into my flesh as I drove us toward release.

I knew how to want Ophelia. I had been doing it for six months, fighting it every day. Except, going to her room at this hour felt presumptuous. She needed rest as much as I did, maybe more.

I stood and crossed to the window, but it wasn't enough. I had to burn off my restlessness before it drove me mad.

I pulled trousers on, slipped out of my room, and walked, not knowing where I was heading, letting my feet choose the path while my mind churned through thoughts of Ophelia. The taste of her lips when I finally kissed her. The sounds she would make when I touched her. How her body would arch beneath mine when I finally gave in to what we'd wanted.

The castle was silent at this hour, the staff long since retired, the fires burned down to embers that cast no light into the hallways.

The corridor narrowed as I continued on, wandering into a wing I hadn't explored before. The ceilings lowered, and the air grew colder. The sconces here were unlit, leaving only the pale light from the moon filtering through the windows. Dust coated the floor in a fine layer, disturbed by a single set of footprints leading toward a door at the far end.

I stopped. Every instinct I'd honed through years of operative work told me to stop. This was a private space, clearly unused except by one person.

But the footprints were fresh, which meant someone had been here recently, perhaps tonight.

I should return to my room, respect the privacy of my host, forget I'd ever found this part of the castle, and push away the questions burning in my chest.

My feet carried me forward anyway.

The door was fitted with hardware that looked as old as the castle itself. Everything in this corridor was coated with dust and neglect, everything except the brass handle, which gleamed bright, polished by years of hands touching it.

When I reached for it, it turned without resistance, and the door swung open.

As I stepped inside, my brain tried to make sense of what I was seeing.

There was a cross on the far wall and a padded bench in the center of the room. Cabinets filled with things I'd only ever seen in porn—floggers, paddles, restraints, rope—were on the far wall. Everything appeared to be arranged with care, maintained, and ready for use.

Fire rushed through me, settling in my hardening cock. I'd never been in a room like this, never sought out anything like this, never imagined myself anywhere near restraints and implements designed for pain and pleasure intertwined.

I stepped farther into the room.

This was not casual experimentation I was witnessing. This was not a passing curiosity indulged on lonely nights. This was a lifestyle maintained over years.

Someone used this room. Someone strapped people to that cross and bent them over that bench and put collars around their throats. Someone wielded those floggers and canes and made people beg for more.

My fingers traced the leather restraint on the cross. Its softness was the kind that came from years of use. How many people had been secured here? How many had felt these bonds tighten around their flesh while someone decided what came next?

The image seized me without warning. Not some anonymous body strapped to the cross, but mine. My wrists in those restraints. My muscles tensing in anticipation as a voice commanded me to hold still, to take whatever was given, to surrender every ounce of control I'd spent my life hoarding.

I jerked my hand away as my mind rejected what my body clearly craved. I was the one who took charge, who guided, who decided. So why did the idea of being bound make my heart race? Why was my cock achingly, undeniably rock-hard, straining beneath the thin fabric of my trousers with an urgency that bordered on pain?

The bench drew me next. Its leather was cool and smooth beneath my touch. I imagined being positioned here, face-down, straps securing my wrists and ankles while a hand traced across my bare skin—testing, teasing, deciding where to strike first while I waited, helpless, aching for whatever came next.

I made my way over to the cabinets, stopping when one holding collars caught my attention. They rested on black velvet—some plain leather bands, others more elaborate, studded with metal or lined with fur. One collar sat apart from the rest. It was heavier than the others, with a single word tooled into the surface in elegant script—SLAVE.

I stared at it, imagining the weight of it around my neck. The pressure at my pulse point.

None of this made sense—why I was still standing here, why my body was reacting like this, why I couldn't make myself turn around and walk out the door.

This wasn't who I was. So why couldn't I leave?

A sound of footsteps cut through the silence, and I spun toward the door. My heart seized, and dread settled low in my gut when I saw Kiernan standing in the doorway.

His face was a mask of fury. His jaw clenched so tight the muscle jumped beneath his skin. Every line of his body radiated anger.

This was his room. His cross. His bench. His collars. Kiernan was the one who used these implements, who strapped people down and made them beg.

"What the fuck are you doing in here?"

His words were quiet, controlled, and more terrifying for it. When I opened my mouth to respond, nothing came out.

I was standing in his dungeon with an obvious erection. There was no explanation that would make this acceptable.

Kiernan stepped into the room, and the door swung shut behind him. He stalked over to us like a predator closing on prey, every step measured and deliberate. He walked like a man who knew exactly what he was capable of and had spent years learning how to wield it.

I backed up until my shoulders hit the cabinet, rattling the glass.

Kiernan kept coming. He stopped inches away, near enough that his heat bled into my space and his breath ghosted across my face. If either of us swayed forward, we would be touching.

His pupils had blown wide despite the fury on his face. Whatever he was feeling, it wasn't only anger.

"I asked you a question."

"I couldn't sleep." The words came out unsteady. "I was walking. I didn't know this was here."

He raised a brow. "You didn't know."

"No."

His focus swept down my body with deliberate slowness, lingering on my chest, my stomach, then drifting lower. It landed on my erection and stayed there long enough that fire spread up my face and down my neck. I should have been humiliated, should have wanted to disappear. Instead, part of me wanted to drop to my knees.

When our gazes locked again, I couldn't read what I saw there.

No one moved, but my pulse pounded in my ears.

He took a step back. "You don't belong in here."

I pushed off the cabinet, but my legs were shaky. When I reached out to steady myself, Kiernan grabbed my arm.

"Return to your room. Forget what you saw."

A sound escaped me that might have been a laugh if it had not been so strangled. "Forget?"

"That's what I said."

"Yes, sir." The words slipped out. I had no idea where they'd come from or why my voice sounded quiet and calm, nothing like the chaos ricocheting through my skull.

Kiernan's expression flickered, and for a split second, I saw hunger. It was gone as quickly as it had come.

I didn't wait. I jerked my arm loose, then skirted around him and left.

I made it halfway down the corridor before my legs gave out again, forcing me to catch myself against the wall. I pressed my forehead to the cold stone, my lungs seizing while my heart raced and my hands shook.

What the hell had just happened?

I'd discovered that my host kept a sex dungeon in his castle. That was strange enough, but the rest of it—my body's response, the images that had rushed through me when I saw the cross, and how I'd looked at Kiernan when he stood inches away from me, close enough to touch—was worse.

I couldn't explain it or even reconcile it in my own mind. My words echoed. "Yes, sir," I'd said. Why? And why had it felt so right?

I shoved away from the wall, needing to get as far from this wing as I could.

I needed Ophelia. The thought crystallized with sudden clarity. Her warmth. Her steadiness. The familiar comfort of wanting someone I understood how to want. To touch her and be touched.

I reached our suite and walked over to her door. Raising my fist to knock before I lost my nerve.

Every second stretched into an eternity as I waited for it to open. When it did, Ophelia stood before me in a silk nightgown that skimmed her thighs. Her eyes widened with surprise.

"Oliver? What's wrong?"

I stepped forward and fell into her arms when she opened them to me. I buried my face in her neck and breathed in her scent. When her arms came around me, some of the chaos quieted.

Then, desire flared again. I found her mouth with mine and kissed her. It was gentle, then desperate and devouring. I poured all the confusion and terror and want of the past hour into it. She gasped against my lips, and I swallowed the sound, pressing forward, walking us farther into her room.

"Oliver—"

"I need you. Please, Phee."

She searched my face in the darkness. I didn't know what she saw there, but whatever it was made her pull me down for another kiss. This time, her urgency matched mine. Her fingers fisted in my hair, and she pressed her body to mine with an abandon that set my blood on fire.

I pushed her against the wall and slid my hands beneath the silk of her nightgown.

We tore at each other. Her fingers yanked at my shirt, and her nails scraped across my chest. My mouth found her throat, her collarbone, her breast, biting, then soothing. She gasped and writhed, and her leg hooked around my hip to pull me closer.

The kiss turned almost angry. Months of denial, and now this—this raw collision of want and confusion and need. I hiked her nightgown higher. Her thighs were bare beneath my palms when my hand slid between her legs.

She was wet. Slick and hot and ready, and the moan that escaped her throat was raw with need. I groaned into her mouth and slid my fingers through her folds, feeling her body welcome me.

"Yes." She gasped. "Oliver, yes—"

We were lost in the taste of each other. Her hands were everywhere, and I couldn't get close enough, couldn't touch enough of her, couldn't—

The door opened behind us.

We froze, then turned. Kiernan stood in the doorway, his eyes dark and his voice low and absolute.

"Did I tell you to stop?"

7

Kiernan

Sleep was impossible.

I stood at my bedroom window, staring out at the darkness beyond. The grounds of Greymarch stretched below me, invisible in the moonless night. Somewhere out there, the loch lapped against the shore, the wind rustled through the pines, and the world went on as if nothing had changed.

Except everything had.

Oliver's face kept surfacing in my mind. The shock when he'd turned to find me in the doorway. The flush on his cheeks. The unmistakable bulge in his trousers as he stood before my cabinet of collars, his palm flattened on the glass like he wanted to reach through and touch them.

He'd stood in my playroom, surrounded by implements of control and surrender, visibly aroused.

Then he'd said it. Two words that had almost destroyed me. *Yes, sir.*

I pressed my forehead against the window. The chill did nothing to cool the heat still coursing through me.

I'd sent him away. Told him to forget what he'd seen. As if forgetting were possible. As if either of us could unsee what had been revealed in that room.

He wanted this. Maybe he didn't understand it yet, maybe he was fighting it the way I'd fought when I was first introduced to the lifestyle, but his body knew, and God help me, I wanted to show him everything.

My unyielding desire had been manageable before tonight. Painful, yes. Relentless, yes. But contained. I could look at them across the dinner table and remind myself why I couldn't have them. I could retreat to my tower and let the ache subside into a dull, familiar throb.

Now, the container had cracked. Oliver had seen what I was. He'd stood in the heart of my hidden self and responded with arousal instead of revulsion. Had looked at me with those green eyes and said *Yes, sir* like the words were pulled from deep within him.

I couldn't unknow that. I couldn't unfeel the surge of possessive desire that had flooded through me when I'd heard him speak.

The clock on my nightstand showed half past midnight. I should try to sleep. Tomorrow would require composure, distance, and the reconstruction of the walls that had taken years to build.

Instead, my feet carried me to the door.

The corridor was dark, but my body navigated the familiar path with the same rhythm my mind churned. I wasn't going to them. I was burning off restless energy the way I'd done a thousand nights before.

The lie lasted until I reached the guest wing.

I stopped at the entrance to the corridor where their rooms waited. My pulse hammered, and my fists clenched at my sides.

Return to your tower. They're not yours to take.

A sound reached me through the darkness. Muffled. Distant. But unmistakable.

A moan.

I froze.

Then I heard another sound. Ophelia's voice. Her words were unclear, but the tone was unmistakable. It was breathless, urgent, and wanting.

They were together. Right now, in one of those rooms, they were touching each other. Doing what I'd imagined them doing in my weakest moments. What I'd forbidden myself from picturing because the images were too vivid, too tempting, too likely to destroy the last of my restraint.

I should leave. Every rational part of my mind screamed at me to turn around and walk away. Whatever was happening in that room was none of my concern. They were adults. They were free to do as they pleased with each other.

Still, I walked forward. Every step felt inevitable. Each one came harder than the last. The sounds grew louder as I approached—soft cries, rustling fabric, the wet sounds of mouths meeting skin.

I stopped outside Ophelia's partially open door. A sliver of darkness showed where it had been left ajar, as if the universe were testing me. Tempting me. Daring me to look.

Don't.

I did.

Through the gap, I could see them. Oliver had her pinned to the wall, her nightgown hiked up around her thighs, his hand working between her legs. Her fingers gripped his shoulders, and she was panting, writhing, and chasing the pleasure he was giving her.

They were beautiful together. Tangled and lost in each other.

My cock was hard. Painfully so. Straining beneath my trousers with an urgency I hadn't felt in years.

The wise thing would be to close this door, return to my room, and pretend I never saw this.

Instead, I pushed it open.

They froze and turned, staring at me with identical expressions of shock, chests heaving, skin flushed with the arousal that the interruption had not diminished.

"Did I tell you to stop?"

The silence stretched between us. Oliver's chest rose and fell with rapid breaths, but neither of them pulled away from the other. Neither of them tried to cover themselves or stammer excuses.

I stepped into the room and closed the door behind me.

The click of the latch echoed through the darkness, and I crossed the room toward them.

Oliver tracked my approach, his fingers still pressed to her heat. She was trembling, and her gaze darted between him and me as if she could not decide who posed the greater danger.

I stopped within arm's reach. Near enough to smell her arousal and his sweat. Close enough to see how they both leaned toward me, drawn by a gravity they didn't understand.

"Continue." The command came out low and absolute, a voice that expected obedience and received it.

Oliver's breathing hitched. He searched my face, but I gave him nothing but the weight of my expectation.

His hand began stroking.

Ophelia gasped, and her eyes fluttered closed as Oliver's fingers resumed their work, stroking through her folds with a deliberateness that had not been there before. He was performing for me now. They both were.

"Slower." I kept my voice even. "I want to hear her."

Oliver's rhythm changed, drawing out each stroke until Ophelia whimpered. The sound went straight to my cock.

I knew how to do this. I had commanded dozens of scenes like this, orchestrating pleasure without participating, directing bodies without touching them. The distance kept everyone safe.

"Kiss her neck," I told him. "Just below her ear."

He complied. Ophelia's fingers gripped his shoulders, and her hips rocked against his hand. Arousal built in my own body as they rocked together, her chasing her release under my direction.

This was enough. I could give them this—give them each other, give them the commands that heightened every sensation—and walk away untouched. I'd done it before. I could do it again.

"Faster now. Make her come."

Oliver's fingers quickened. Ophelia gasped, and her whole body tensed. I watched as she climbed, teetered on the edge, then came apart.

She sagged against Oliver, trembling in the aftermath. He held her steady, his own breath ragged and his cock hard against her hip. God, I wanted them.

I should let the scene end here. I'd given them what they needed. There was no reason to stay.

Then Ophelia opened her eyes.

She looked at me through a haze of bliss, her mouth soft and her skin flushed. Her gaze dropped to my chest, to my hands clenched at my sides, to the erection I couldn't hide, and her face changed. Not with desire alone. Recognition. She saw what this was costing me.

"Kiernan." My name from her lips was a question and an invitation. She reached for me.

I stepped away, and she dropped her hand.

Confusion flickered across her face, then worse. *Understanding.*

"You're not going to touch us." It wasn't a question.

"No."

I'd said the word countless times to people who'd wanted more than I could give. Then, it had been final. Now, it might not be.

Oliver's expression was unreadable, but the question was forming in his mind. Why? Why command them through that, why stand close enough to feel the heat of their bodies, why look at them with hunger I couldn't hide—then refuse to take what they were offering?

I couldn't explain. I couldn't tell them about those who'd crumbled under the weight of my wanting. I couldn't make them understand that the wall was not punishment but protection. That I stayed outside because those I'd permitted entry ended up broken.

"Get some sleep," I said. "Both of you."

I turned toward the door.

"No."

Ophelia's voice stopped me. I turned around as she crossed the room toward me, naked and unashamed, her eyes blazing.

She stopped inches away from me. "You don't get to walk into this room and take control and make me come, then pretend you don't want this."

"What I want is irrelevant."

"Bullshit."

The word might as well have been a slap. I stared at her, this woman who should've been afraid of me, who should have been grateful for whatever scraps I offered. She didn't flinch.

"I see you," she said. "I've seen you since the day we arrived. You stare at us like you're starving. Then you lock yourself away and pretend you're made of stone." She stepped closer. "You're not, Kiernan. I can see you're not."

I looked down at my hands. She was right. They were trembling.

"You don't know what you're asking for."

"Then, tell me."

I couldn't. The words lodged in my throat. Years had passed since I'd given anyone what she was asking for. Not the subs who wondered why I never took my own pleasure. Not even Callen, who saw more of what I kept hidden than anyone.

Ophelia reached for me again. This time, I remained where I was.

Her palm pressed flat against my chest, right over my heart. The heat of it burned through my shirt, searing into skin that had not been touched in years. My whole body went rigid, and I couldn't draw in air.

"How long?" The question was quiet. Gentle. It undid me more than any demand could have because she saw it. I didn't understand how, but she did.

"A long time." The words scraped out of me.

"How long?" she repeated.

I looked over her shoulder, and my eyes met Oliver's.

"Seven years," I confessed.

Her eyes widened. "Why?"

I forced myself to hold her gaze. "Because I break people."

"Maybe we're not as fragile as you think."

"Maybe you are."

She should have pulled away. She should have heard the warning in my voice and retreated to safety. Instead, she curled her fingers into my shirt and pulled me closer.

"Touch me," she said. "Or tell me to stop. But don't stand here, pretending you don't want me."

My restraint snapped. I felt it happen. She was too close, her skin too warm, her eyes too knowing. I could smell her arousal mixed with Oliver's sweat. I could hear his breathing behind her, ragged and waiting. I could feel my own heartbeat pounding against her palm.

Every instinct screamed at me to push her away. To say no and mean it.

Instead, I gripped her neck, dug my fingers into her flesh, and kissed her.

Seven years without real intimacy, and now this. Her mouth was soft and open and welcoming. Her body pressed against mine, and her hands slid up my chest to wrap around my neck. I groaned against her lips, a sound so foreign I wondered if it came from me.

My hands found her waist, her hips, pulling her closer until there was no space between us. She was naked, and I was still clothed, and her warmth radiated through the fabric.

Yet it wasn't enough.

Ophelia stared at me when I broke the kiss. Her lips were swollen, and her eyes wild.

"Oliver. On the bed. Now." The words came out like the command they were.

He obeyed without question, crossing to the bed and sitting on the edge. His cock was hard against his stomach, his whole body taut with tension. He was waiting. They were both waiting.

I looked at Ophelia. "Remove my shirt."

Her hands trembled as she reached for the buttons. She fumbled with the first one, then the second, her fingers clumsy with anticipation. I stood motionless and let her peel away the armor I'd expected to wear forever.

My shirt fell open, and she pushed it from my shoulders. It dropped to the floor.

The first touch of air against my bare skin made me shudder. Then her hands were on me, palms resting on my skin, and I had to close my eyes against the intensity of it.

It had been so long since anyone had touched me like this that I'd forgotten how it felt. The intimacy of skin against skin. My nerve endings were overwhelmed by the sensation they'd been denied for so long.

"Kiernan." Her voice was soft. "Open your eyes."

I did.

"You're shaking."

"I know."

"Does it hurt?"

"No." The word came out rough. "It's too much. It's not enough. I don't—" I stopped, unable to explain the war raging inside me. The part that wanted to devour her whole. The part that wanted to run before I destroyed her.

She rose on her toes and kissed me again, soft and slow. "Take what you need," she whispered.

The last of my resistance collapsed.

I lifted her off her feet and carried her to the bed, laying her down next to Oliver. They looked up at me—naked and wanting and waiting—and I felt the coiled tension inside me release.

I unfastened my belt. Let my trousers fall, and stood naked before them.

Ophelia's eyes roamed down my body, lingering on my cock, hard and aching and desperate for touch. Oliver's gaze darted away, then returned, his jaw tight.

"Lie beside her and touch her," I told him. "Her breasts. Slow."

His thumbs brushed across her nipples. Ophelia arched and moaned, making my cock throb.

I climbed onto the bed and positioned myself over her. My mouth found her throat, her collarbone, then traveled lower. Every kiss was a reclamation of what I'd denied myself for too long.

"Suck her nipple. Hard," I told Oliver. He did, and she cried out.

I kissed down her stomach, across her hip, and settled between her thighs. The first taste of her made me groan.

She was wet and wanting, and I'd forgotten—God, I'd forgotten what this was like. The intimacy of it. The power. The ecstasy of giving pleasure.

"Kiss her," I told Oliver. "I want to hear her moaning into your mouth."

Their lips met as I worked her with my tongue. The sounds she made were muffled by his kiss. I pushed two fingers inside her and felt her clench around me, her whole body quivering.

I could have stayed here for hours and never ask for anything in return. It was what I always did—giving without taking. But this was different. So different. I drank in her essence, felt her tightness squeezing my fingers.

She'd told me to take what I needed, and fuck me if I didn't need.

I lifted my head and shifted my body. "Oliver. Between her legs. Your mouth where mine was."

He shifted without hesitation, positioning himself where I'd been. He lowered his mouth, and she cried out when his tongue found her clit. His technique was rougher than mine, but her body didn't seem to care.

I crawled up the bed until I was kneeling beside her head. She turned to look at me, her eyes heavy-lidded with want.

"Please." The word slipped out without permission. "Please, sir."

The title sent fire through my veins. I traced my thumb across her lower lip. "What do you want?"

"You. I want to taste you. Please."

I guided myself to her mouth, and when her lips closed around me, I nearly came.

The sensation was overwhelming. I gripped the headboard to keep from collapsing. My whole body shook with my struggle not to lose control.

"Fuck." The word tore out of me. "Ophelia—"

She hummed around my cock, and it reverberated in my spine, in my skull, in every cell of my body. Oliver was still working her with his mouth, she was moaning around me, and I was drowning in passion I'd denied myself for so long.

"Stop." The command was ragged. Oliver lifted his head. Ophelia released me, looking up with concern.

"Did I—"

"No." I was panting, trying to regain control. "I need—I want—"

I couldn't find the words. I was a master at commanding others, and now, I couldn't command my own voice.

"Tell us," Ophelia said. "Whatever you need."

I looked at her. At Oliver. At these two people who'd chiseled away every defense I'd built.

The words stuck in my throat. *I want to feel again. I want to remember what it's like to be human. I want to stop being so goddamn alone.*

She pulled me down and kissed me. "Take me, Kiernan."

I couldn't. It was more than I could bear. "On your hands and knees," I told her. Then turned to Oliver. "On your knees behind her." A condom packet sat on the nightstand. I didn't know where it came from, but I thanked God it was there. I reached for it, so tempted to open it with my teeth and roll it on his length, but it was too soon for that. Far too soon. I handed it to him instead.

"Inside her. Slow," I said once he was sheathed.

He pushed forward, and she moaned as he filled her. Oliver's jaw clenched with restraint, and Ophelia's face went slack with ecstasy as every inch of him disappeared inside her.

"Deeper."

He buried himself to the hilt, and they both went still as if they waited for my next directive.

I shifted and knelt in front of her, my cock inches from her lips. Her eyes met mine, and I cupped her face in my hands.

"This is what I am." My voice was barely a whisper. "This is what I need. If it's—"

She turned her head to press a kiss against my palm and nodded.

I guided my cock to her mouth for the second time. She took me in, and this time, I didn't try to stave off my release. I let the pleasure wash over me, let it drown me.

"Move," I told Oliver. "Match my rhythm."

We found it together. He thrust into her as I withdrew from her mouth, then I pushed forward as he pulled away. She was suspended between us, filled at both ends.

The pleasure built, higher than anything I'd let myself feel. I was going to come, and I couldn't stop it.

Oliver's pace increased, driving into her with more force. I matched him, my hips rocking in counterpoint. Ophelia was shaking between us, her entire body quivering on the edge.

"Come," I commanded her. *"Now."*

She came with a scream muffled by my cock. Her whole body convulsed, and her inner muscles clamped down on Oliver hard enough to drag a groan from his throat.

"Again."

Oliver's thumb found her clit. Within moments, she was coming again, harder than before.

"Oliver. Now."

He buried himself deep and let the orgasm tear through him.

Then it was my turn.

Years of denial crested and broke. I came with a groan, pleasure flooding through me, whiting out my vision and my thoughts and everything except the feeling of her mouth around me and the knowledge that I had finally, finally let myself have this.

Afterward, I couldn't move.

I collapsed on the bed. My chest heaved. Ophelia curled against my side with her head on my chest. Oliver lay on her other side, one hand resting on her hip.

No one spoke.

The silence should have given me time to think about how I'd broken every rule I'd made for myself. I'd let them in. I'd taken what I wanted. And now, I was lying in the wreckage of everything I'd built. It should've shattered me, but it didn't. Ophelia's hand was warm against my skin. Oliver's breathing was steady and calm. And for the first time in longer than I could remember, the wanting didn't feel like a weapon.

I lay still until their breathing deepened into sleep, then extracted myself from the tangle of their limbs.

I stood at the edge of the bed. They'd shifted in my absence, drawn together by some unconscious gravity. Ophelia's head rested on Oliver's shoulder. His arm curved around her waist. They looked peaceful. Content.

The solitude of my tower waited—safe and protected. But I didn't go.

I stood in the darkness, observing them in sleep.

I should leave.

Instead, I stayed.

8

Ophelia

My mind was several seconds behind my senses when I woke pinned between two male bodies.

A heavy arm lay draped over my waist, and heat radiated from behind me. The scent of cedar and whiskey and sex surrounded me. Where was I? How had I gotten here?

As the memories surfaced, I recalled Kiernan's hands on my skin and his voice in my ear, commanding and demanding. Oliver thrusting inside me while Kiernan's dark, hungry focus riveted on every motion. The three of us had tangled together in ways I'd never imagined, never knew I wanted, never understood I needed.

Except that wasn't entirely true. I'd known. That night, alone in my room, when my fantasies had shifted from Oliver to Kiernan to them commanding me together—I'd known then, but I'd been too afraid to acknowledge it.

I stopped breathing when the arm around my waist flexed, pulling me closer—Kiernan was awake. When I turned my head, his eyes met mine. They were unreadable.

"Don't move." His voice was rough, stripped of his usual polished control. In this light, with his hair disheveled and his jaw shadowed with stubble, he looked younger and more human, less like the untouchable superior I'd worked alongside.

I held still as his attention traveled over my face, then past me to Oliver's still sleeping form.

"How do you feel?" he asked.

The question was simple. The answer wasn't.

My body ached in unfamiliar places—my thighs, my hips, the tender spots where his fingers had gripped hard enough to bruise. But beneath the physical awareness lurked a strange, unsettling sense of exposure, as if he'd peeled away layers I hadn't known existed and seen the raw truth underneath.

"I don't know," I said.

He nodded once, accepting the honesty. Then he extracted himself with a grace that shouldn't have been possible, given how we'd worn each other out hours before.

His muscles flexed as he crossed the bedroom and pulled on his trousers. Even that simple motion made my mouth go dry.

He paused at the door. "Twenty minutes. Breakfast. Both of you."

Then he was gone.

Oliver stirred beside me, and his arm curled around my waist in an unconscious echo of what Kiernan had done moments before. "What time is it?"

"Early." I turned to face him. He looked sleep-soft and vulnerable, with his sandy hair falling across his forehead—God, he was beautiful. And now, he was mine. They both were.

I had no idea what came next.

"He wants us downstairs in twenty minutes," I said.

"Of course he does." Oliver sat up with a wince, likely as sore as me from our escapades. "Did he seem…?"

"I don't know what he seemed." I pushed myself upright, hyperaware of my nakedness in a way I hadn't been while we were still under the sheet. "He's impossible to read."

"He's not." Oliver didn't look away. "He's intentionally difficult."

We dressed in silence, pulling on clothes—mine from my closet, his from the pile on the floor.

Kiernan was already seated when we arrived, dressed in charcoal trousers and a white shirt with the sleeves rolled to his elbows. Tea sat on the sideboard next to dishes of bacon and eggs. He didn't look up from the tablet in his grip when we entered.

"Sit."

I obeyed instinctively. So did Oliver.

The command had been simple, but my body had responded before my mind could intervene. I'd done the same thing last night—followed his orders as if obedience was an instinct rather than a choice. The memory of kneeling in my fantasy rose unbidden, and heat crept up my neck.

Millie appeared with fresh toast and disappeared again without a word.

The silence stretched. Oliver poured himself a cup of tea, and I reached for a piece of toast, not that I had an appetite.

Kiernan set his tablet down.

"That's not how I do things."

His tone was flat and controlled, and the warmth from earlier this morning had vanished. Oliver tensed beside me.

"What do you mean?" he asked.

"Last night," Kiernan continued, "was not how this works."

I braced myself. This was it, then. He was going to tell us it had been a mistake, that whatever had sparked between the three of us during those desperate, hungry hours was an aberration, never to be repeated.

The words didn't come.

Instead, Kiernan studied us both with a weight that made me fidget. "What happened between us wasn't planned. It wasn't negotiated. It wasn't safe."

"Safe? But we used protection." Oliver's tone was low.

Kiernan's attention shifted to him. "That's not what I was referring to. Neither of you knows what you're dealing with."

"Then, explain it," I snapped as much as said. Was my irritation because I'd gotten so little sleep or because I sensed Kiernan withdrawing.

He held my stare without blinking. Then his mouth curved—not a smile, but close.

"If we're going to continue," he said, "there are things you need to learn."

The words stunned me. I'd been so certain he was ending this before it could begin. Instead, he was opening a door where I'd expected a wall.

"Continue?" I repeated.

"Did you think last night was it?" His tone carried an edge of dark amusement. "It was the beginning. A chaotic, uncontrolled beginning that I should never have allowed."

"You didn't allow anything," Oliver said. "We were all there. We all chose it."

"You chose what you didn't understand." Kiernan rose and looked out the window. The light behind him caught the tension in his shoulders and the rigid line of his spine. "What I want from both of you—what I need—requires more than instinct. It requires knowledge. Consent that's truly informed, not given in the heat of the moment."

I exchanged a glance with Oliver. His face mirrored my own confusion, my own curiosity, my own desperate hope that this wasn't a rejection dressed up in pretty words.

"What exactly do you want?" I asked.

Kiernan faced us. He was in silhouette from the light behind him, so I had no idea what to expect he'd say next.

"I'm a dominant." I'd heard the word before but had no real understanding of what it meant. "Not only in bed, though that's part of it. It's how I'm wired. How I've always been. I need control, and I need partners who want to surrender it."

His words resonated with a part of me I'd spent years pretending didn't exist—the part that had always responded to authority with more than respect, that had melted under his commands last night, that had found peace in obedience. The part that had conjured fantasies of kneeling without understanding why.

"A dominant," Oliver repeated. His knuckles had gone white around his cup.

"In the BDSM sense, yes." Kiernan studied us, assessing. "Do you know what that means?"

"I know the term." Oliver sat forward. "Whips and chains, people in leather."

"That's the surface. The aesthetic some people prefer." Kiernan returned to the table, but he didn't sit. He stood over us, and the position—him looking down, us looking up—was deliberate. Significant. "The reality is more complex. It's about power exchange. One person yielding control to another, within negotiated boundaries and complete consent."

"And you want that from us," I said. "Both of us."

"I want to explore it with you. If you're willing."

The qualifier mattered. It was in his tone, in how he held himself—giving us the option to walk away, to pretend last night hadn't happened, and to return to the distance we'd maintained before.

Except I couldn't pretend, not now that I knew the feeling of his hands on my body, what his voice did to me when it dropped into that commanding register, and what it meant to have the two of them at once, filling spaces I hadn't known were empty.

"I'm willing," I said.

Oliver tensed. "I need to understand more before I can answer that."

"That's exactly what I was hoping you'd say." Kiernan pulled out the chair across from us and finally sat. The tension in the room eased—still present, but less fragile. "What I'm proposing is education. Before anything else happens between us, you both need to understand the world you're stepping into."

He was negotiating. I recognized the tactics—establish authority, define terms, create structure where chaos had reigned. I'd seen ambassadors do the same thing after border skirmishes. What surprised me wasn't his approach. It was how badly I wanted to agree.

"The world?" I asked.

"The BDSM community has its own vocabulary, its own codes of conduct, and its own structures for ensuring everyone involved is safe and satisfied." He reached for his tea, and the mundane gesture contrasted sharply with the weight of his words. "Last night, I violated most of those structures. I let desire override judgment, and I'm not proud of that."

"It didn't feel like a violation." I barely managed a whisper.

"Because you trust me." His focus met mine, and the force of it stole my breath. "You trusted me without knowing what that trust meant and without understanding what you were giving up or what you were agreeing to. That's not fair to either of you."

Oliver leaned forward. "What happens now?"

"Now, I teach you." Kiernan set down his cup. "I'll teach you the terminology, the dynamics, and the difference between a healthy power exchange and abuse. You'll learn what it means to be submissive—what that word entails, not the stereotypes you've absorbed from popular culture."

"Submissive," Oliver said with no inflection.

"Does that word bother you?"

"I don't know," Oliver said through clenched teeth.

"Then, we'll explore that." Kiernan's tone softened. "Submission isn't weakness, Oliver. It's trust. It's choosing to let go, to let someone else carry the weight of decisions, because you believe they have your best interests at heart."

Oliver's resistance warred with curiosity on his face. He'd been raised in a world that equated masculinity with control, strength with dominance, and the idea that surrender could be its own form of power clearly didn't fit his mental framework.

It fit mine better than I wanted to admit.

"What kind of things will you teach us?" I asked, giving Oliver time to think while satisfying my own curiosity.

Kiernan turned his attention to me. "Everything you need to understand what you're consenting to. Safewords and how to use them. The difference between limits—hard ones you'll never cross, soft ones you might negotiate. Aftercare, and why it's essential. The psychological components of dominance and submission, not limited to the physical."

"What happens after the education?" My words came out steadier than expected.

"Once you've learned what this world looks like, you'll decide if you want to be part of it—with me and with each other." He looked between us. "This isn't a world you can enter halfway. If we do this, all three of us need to be committed to the dynamic and to each other."

The weight of what he was proposing settled over me. This wasn't a casual arrangement or a convenient outlet for the attraction that had built over weeks. He was talking about structure. Rules. A future that terrified and thrilled me in equal measure.

"I have questions," I said.

"I'd be concerned if you didn't."

"You mentioned safewords. What are those, exactly?"

Kiernan rested his forearms on the table's edge. "A safeword is an agreed-upon term that either partner can use to stop a scene immediately. No questions asked, no judgment given. In most dynamics, people use a traffic light system. Green means everything is fine, continue. Yellow means slow down, check in, you're approaching a limit. Red means stop everything immediately."

"And you respect that?" Oliver asked. "If someone says red, you stop?"

"If someone says red, I stop." There was no hesitation in Kiernan's answer. "That's nonnegotiable. A dominant who ignores safewords isn't a dominant—they're an abuser. Without it, nothing else matters." His voice roughened. "These aren't arbitrary rules. I've seen what happens when they're ignored."

I absorbed his reaction. It aligned with the man I'd observed over the past weeks—the one who'd asked permission before entering Oliver's hospital room, who'd given us the choice to refuse his offer of Greymarch, who'd checked in multiple times last night despite the frenzy of desire that had consumed us all.

"What about limits?" I asked. "You mentioned hard and soft."

"A hard limit is an act you will not do. Ever. Under any circumstances. For some people, that might be certain acts. For others, it might be specific scenarios or dynamics. Hard limits are respected completely and never pushed."

"And soft limits?"

"Soft limits are things you're uncertain about or have reservations around. They might be areas you want to explore eventually but aren't ready for yet. They might be activities that require more trust before you're willing to try them." He let that sink in. "Soft limits can be negotiated, but only with explicit discussion and enthusiastic consent from everyone involved."

Oliver sat forward. "How do you even figure out what your limits are?"

"Through honest conversation. Through being willing to examine what excites you and what frightens you." Kiernan's attention shifted between us. "There are tools that help with that process. But before we get there, I need to know this is something you both truly want to explore."

The question hung in the air. I knew my answer. I'd known it since last night, maybe longer.

At last, Oliver spoke. "I need to understand one thing first."

"Ask."

"This dynamic you're describing. The dominance and submission. Is it about more than sex?"

Kiernan considered the question. "For some people, D/s—that's shorthand for dominance and submission— exists only in the bedroom. For others, it extends into other aspects of the relationship. How much it permeates your life depends on what the people involved want and agree to."

"What do you want?"

The direct question appeared to catch Kiernan off guard. Longing flashed across his face before he suppressed it.

Silence. He wasn't going to make this easy.

"So what happens next?" I asked.

"That depends on you." He looked between us, then rose and crossed to a cabinet near the window. When he returned, he held two slim booklets with plain covers.

He placed one in front of me, one in front of Oliver.

"What is this?" Oliver asked.

"A questionnaire. Activities, scenarios, dynamics— you mark what interests you, what doesn't, and what you're curious about." Kiernan returned to his chair. "It's how I learn where your boundaries are. And how you learn them too."

I opened mine to a random page. The questions were blunt, specific, leaving no room for ambiguity.

Have you ever been restrained during sexual activity? Yes / No / Maybe / Curious

"And if we have questions while we're working through these?" I asked.

"I'll be in the library."

Then he was gone, leaving us alone.

Oliver stared at the open page in front of him for a long time without speaking.

"Are you all right?" I asked.

"I don't know." He stared at the booklet in front of him. "Are you?"

"We don't have to do this," I said. "Either of us. He gave us the choice."

He looked at it again, then at me. "Is this something you want to do?"

I remembered the peace that had washed over me last night when I'd stopped thinking and surrendered, the rightness of following Kiernan's commands, and the freedom of giving up control.

"It is," I responded. "What about you?"

Oliver turned the page, skimmed what was on it, and his eyes widened. "This is..."

"Intense?" I asked as I read one of the questions. *Have you ever fantasized about being told what to do by a sexual partner?* I marked "Yes" without hesitation. Maybe I would've answered differently before last night, but now, it was almost all I could think about.

"There's some kinky shit in here," he muttered.

I shrugged a shoulder. "If this doesn't interest you, no one is forcing you to participate."

His eyes bored into mine. "So it's this or nothing?"

"I can't say for sure. All I know is before last night, every orgasm I'd had was self-induced."

His brow furrowed. "Seriously?"

I huffed as much as sighed. "Oliver…"

"Sorry, none of my business."

"Actually, if you're interested in pursuing this—whatever it is—it is your business. If you're not, then don't fill this out." I picked up the questionnaire and waved it at him.

We stared at each other for several seconds, then he flipped to the first page and began marking things.

The next question stared up at me when I did the same.

Have you ever fantasized about surrendering control completely during a sexual encounter?

Another "Yes."

Have you ever fantasized about being observed during sexual activity?

My face heated as I remembered Kiernan's focus on us last night, the way he'd tracked every reaction, every gasp. I marked "Yes" again.

The questions continued, each one probing deeper. Some were easy—clear "nos" that required zero thought.

Others made me pause, examining desires I'd never acknowledged.

Have you ever fantasized about being praised for obedience?

The memory of Kiernan's words rose unbidden. *Good girl.* I couldn't remember if he'd actually said that or if I'd imagined it, but either way, the thought made me melt, made me want to earn more of them.

I marked "Yes."

Across the table, Oliver's pen scratched in stops and starts.

Every so often, his breath caught. Or mine did.

Have you ever fantasized about submission to multiple partners?

Have you ever fantasized about witnessing your partner being with someone else?

Have you ever fantasized about seeing your partner with someone of the same sex?

I paused on that one. Before last night, it had never occurred to me. Many of the things in this questionnaire hadn't. But the idea of seeing Kiernan and Oliver together sent desire coiling tight inside me.

I marked "Curious," then changed my answer to "Yes."

The questions went on and on—pages of them. By the time I reached the end of the first section, my mind was spinning. But beneath the overwhelm, clarity emerged.

When I looked up, Oliver was studying me.

"I'm on page six."

"I'm on page six too," I responded.

"It's a lot."

"It is."

Oliver closed his journal and stared into space.

"Done?" I asked.

"Done."

"How do you feel?"

He laughed—a short, sharp sound that held no humor. "Like I took an exam I didn't study for. And also, like I might have passed it anyway."

I understood. The same strange sense of accomplishment lived in my own chest, alongside the lingering uncertainty.

"What now?" Oliver asked.

"We find out what we do with what we've learned."

9

Oliver

The questionnaires lay open on Kiernan's desk, side by side—mine and Ophelia's, spread out for examination.

"You've both marked bondage as a yes." Kiernan's finger traced down my page. "Restraints. Being restrained. Restraining a partner." He looked between us. "Interesting symmetry."

I adjusted my position in the leather chair with Ophelia beside me. We'd been at this for nearly an hour—Kiernan dissecting our answers with the detachment of a surgeon reviewing scans.

"Pain." He flipped a page. "You've both marked curious. Not yes, not no. Curious." He let that settle. "That's honest. Pain is complicated. It exists on a spectrum, and most people don't know where their limits fall until they're tested."

"How do you test it?" Ophelia asked.

"Gradually. With trust." He closed her questionnaire and set it aside. "Which brings us to the foundation of everything we do. Safewords."

He stood and rested on the edge of his desk with his arms crossed.

"Red means stop. Everything stops. No questions, no negotiations, no pushing through. If either of you says red, the scene ends immediately and we move to aftercare. Understood?"

We nodded simultaneously.

"Yellow means slow down. Use it if you're approaching a limit, or you need time to process. When I hear yellow, I pause, I check in, and we decide together whether to continue or redirect." He uncrossed his arms. "Green means continue. I'll check in periodically during scenes. When I ask for a color, you answer honestly. Not what you think I want to hear. Not what you think you should feel. What you actually feel in that moment."

"What if we can't speak?" I asked.

The corner of his mouth twitched. "Good question. Hand signals. Three taps means red—on my arm, on the furniture, on each other. Two taps for yellow. One tap or a thumbs-up means green." He demonstrated on the desk. "If you're restrained in a way that prevents tapping, we negotiate alternative signals beforehand. Nothing happens without a clear method of communication."

He picked up my questionnaire again and flipped to a page near the middle. "Let's discuss some specifics." His finger trailed down the page. "Exhibitionism. You marked yes. Voyeurism. Also yes." His eyes lifted to mine. "But public scenes, you marked as curious. Explain the distinction."

Heat crept up my neck. Discussing this with Ophelia present—with Kiernan's eyes pinning me in place—felt like standing naked in a spotlight.

"Being seen by someone I trust is different than by strangers," I managed. "The first feels intimate. The second feels…exposed."

"Good. That's a useful distinction." He made a note in the margin. "We'll start with intimate exhibition. Strangers can wait until you've built more confidence."

He turned to another page. "Sensation play. You've marked yes to ice, feathers, wax. But you marked curious on electricity." He looked up. "What's the hesitation?"

"I don't know what it feels like. Hard to say yes to something I can't imagine."

"Reasonable. We'll demonstrate with a violet wand when you're ready. Low settings only until you understand the sensation." Another note in the margin. "What about this one?" His finger tapped a line lower on the page. "Being commanded to pleasure yourself. You marked that as yes, but I noticed you hesitated when you wrote it. The pen pressure changed."

I stared at him. "You can tell that from looking at the page?"

"I can tell many things." He gave nothing away. "Why did you hesitate?"

Because admitting I wanted to stroke myself while Kiernan watched felt like confessing to something I didn't fully understand. Because when I'd stood in his play-room two nights ago, staring at that collar, my body had responded before my mind could catch up. Because the fantasy had featured his eyes specifically—not Ophelia's, not some abstract observer's. Because I'd tried to change my answer twice before leaving it.

"It felt self-indulgent," I said instead. "Asking for that."

"Submission isn't self-indulgent. Knowing your desires and communicating them clearly is the foundation of everything we build here." He set my questionnaire aside and picked up Ophelia's. "Your turn."

She straightened in her chair, and her composure slipped for the first time.

"Praise," Kiernan said. "You've marked it as essential. Not yes—essential. With three underlines." His voice softened almost imperceptibly. "Tell me about that."

"I need to know I'm doing well. If I don't know whether I'm pleasing my partner, I spiral. I start second-guessing everything," Ophelia confessed.

"Previous partners didn't provide adequate feedback?"

"Previous partners took what they wanted and assumed I was fine."

Kiernan's brow furrowed. "That won't happen here. I'll tell you when you're pleasing me. I'll tell you when you're exceeding expectations. And if something isn't working, I'll redirect you clearly rather than letting you flounder." He held her gaze. "You'll never have to guess with me."

The tension in Ophelia's shoulders eased. I reached over and took her hand.

Kiernan continued through her questionnaire, discussing her interest in sensory deprivation, her curiosity about role-play, her firm no on anything involving her face being covered. When he reached the section on multiple partners, he stopped.

"You've marked yes to being shared. Yes to seeing your partners together. Yes to being the focus of multiple people's attention." He looked between us. "These align well. Oliver's answers mirror yours in this section."

I hadn't known that. Knowing Ophelia wanted the same things made my cock strain, especially when I allowed myself to envision what that might mean.

"Hard limits," Kiernan said, flipping the page of my questionnaire. "These are nonnegotiable. Things that are off the table entirely, regardless of context or mood. Oliver, you've listed…" He scanned the page. "Blood play. Breath play. Anything involving bodily waste." He raised his head. "Standard limits. Sensible."

"And Ophelia's?"

"Similar, with a few additions." He glanced at her page. "No humiliation. No degradation. No name-calling during scenes."

Ophelia winced, and I filed it away.

"My limits align with yours," Kiernan said. "I don't engage in edge play that risks permanent harm. No blood, no breath restriction, no psychological degradation.

"There's something else we need to discuss. Something that goes beyond activities and limits." He leaned on his desk again. "Structure. Accountability. Consequences."

Ophelia straightened beside me.

"Your questionnaires show interest in rules, in having clear expectations. But rules without consequences are merely suggestions. I need to understand how you each process correction. When you've done something wrong—not a mistake but a choice—what helps you move past it?"

The question landed differently than the others. This wasn't about what turned us on.

Ophelia chuckled, but it held no humor. "I process it badly."

Kiernan waited.

"I'm not good at forgiving myself," she admitted. "I can let something go when the other person has clearly let it go. Not before."

"And if they say they've let it go but you don't believe them?"

She didn't answer, which was an answer in itself.

"I'd rather someone be angry with me than...nothing," she added. "Silence. Pretending everything's okay when it isn't."

"What about you, Oliver?" he asked.

I considered the question. "I don't know. I've never..." I shook my head. "I've never been in a dynamic where that was part of it."

"That's an honest answer." He didn't push. "Discipline in a D/s context isn't about cruelty or control for its own sake. It's about maintaining the structure that makes the dynamic feel safe. When a rule is broken, the correction clears the slate. Guilt is processed, forgiveness is given, and we move forward without it festering."

"What kind of correction?" Ophelia asked.

"That depends on the infraction and the people involved. For something like breaking a boundary we've established—" He held her gaze. "Spanking. Impact that stings but doesn't damage. Enough to make an impression, followed by aftercare and real forgiveness."

My heart stuttered at the matter-of-fact way he said it.

"Correction may bring up feelings of shame—that's natural when you've broken someone's trust. But I won't use that shame against you. I won't mock you or call you names. The goal is accountability followed by forgiveness, not making you feel small.

"This would only apply to rules we've explicitly agreed to," Kiernan continued. "Not arbitrary expectations I haven't communicated. And it would never happen in anger. If I'm truly upset, we talk first. Correction happens when we're both calm and clear about why it's needed."

"And if we don't want that?" I asked. "If punishment isn't something one of us is comfortable with?"

"Then, it's not part of your dynamic with me," he said it the same way he'd said everything else—without pressure, without judgment. "This isn't a requirement. It's a tool that works for some people and not others. I'm explaining how I approach it so you can make an informed choice."

"I would prefer structure and accountability," Ophelia said.

Kiernan's face softened. "Noted."

He looked at me, waiting.

"I'm not saying no," I said slowly. "I'm saying I need to understand it better before I agree to it for myself."

"Also noted. And completely reasonable."

He set the questionnaires aside. "Everything else is open for negotiation, exploration, and discovery."

Kiernan allowed the statement to settle. Then his voice shifted—still calm, but with an edge of command that hadn't been there before.

"One more thing. A rule that begins now, not later." He looked between us. "From this moment forward, your pleasure belongs to me. Neither of you comes without my presence and my explicit permission. Not alone. Not together. Not until I say."

Ophelia's gasp was barely audible.

"Understood?" Kiernan asked.

"Yes," Ophelia said.

I nodded. "Understood."

"Good."

Ophelia stirred beside me. "And if we break this rule?"

The question hung in the air. I realized I'd been wondering the same thing.

"Then, there are consequences." Kiernan's tone carried no threat—only certainty. "Specifically, what we discussed earlier. Spanking. Prompt, proportional, and followed by forgiveness."

"How prompt?" she asked.

"As soon as practically possible. Discipline loses its effectiveness when it's delayed." He waited. "And the other partner will likely be present. Transparency matters in a dynamic like ours. We don't hide things from each other, including correction."

I tried to imagine it—Ophelia bent over Kiernan's knee—and shuddered.

"You're both clear on this?" Kiernan asked. "This rule begins now, and breaking it has real consequences that we've just defined. I need verbal confirmation that you're agreeing to that."

"Yes," Ophelia said. "I understand, and I agree."

He looked at me.

"Yes," I said. "Agreed."

Ophelia leaned forward. "What about you? Do you have a safeword?"

"Dominants can safeword too. It's rare, but it happens. If I say red, the same rules apply. Everything stops."

"Has that ever happened?" I asked.

He held my gaze for a beat too long. "Once."

He didn't elaborate. I didn't push.

"When we scene together," Kiernan said, "we're entering a structured dynamic. A scene has a beginning, a middle, and an end. It has negotiated boundaries, clear communication, and defined roles. It's not casual sex—it's intentional. Deliberate. You'll know when we're in a scene because I will tell you."

I wanted to ask him how soon we could get started since my cock had never been as hard as it was right now.

"One more thing. When we're scening, you call me sir. Not Kiernan. Not Archon. *Sir.*" His attention shifted between us. "Outside of scenes, you may use my name. But when I'm commanding you, when I'm controlling your pleasure or your pain, I'm sir. Clear?"

"Yes, sir," Ophelia said.

The title should have felt strange on my tongue. But when I echoed her—"Yes, sir"—it came out the same way it had in the playroom. Natural. Right. As if some part of me had been waiting years to say it.

Kiernan gave a single nod.

"The playroom," I said. "When do we—"

He went rigid. "Not yet."

"Why not?"

"Because you're not ready." He pushed off from the desk and crossed to the window. "You've read about this. You've answered questions about it. But you haven't seen it. Not properly. Not in a context where you can observe without pressure to participate."

Ophelia and I exchanged glances.

"Tonight," Kiernan continued, facing the window, "I want to take you to Thorned Thistle. My club." He turned to face us. "You'll see healthy dynamics in practice. See how scenes unfold, how partners communicate, how trust functions in real time."

He returned to the desk but didn't sit. Instead, he stood before us, arms crossed.

"But I need to be clear about something before you agree to go. Tonight won't be purely observation."

Ophelia's body went still.

"I intend to direct scenes between us while we're there," he continued. "Touching. Oral. Possibly more, depending on how the evening unfolds and what you're both comfortable with. You'll be participants, not spectators."

The words settled over me. I thought about the questionnaires, about everything we'd marked yes to. This was the reality of those abstract questions.

"If you'd rather tonight be observation only, we can do that," he added. "I'll show you the space, explain what you're seeing, and bring you home without any engagement. It's your choice, and there will not be negative consequences if that's what you prefer."

He looked between us.

"But I need to know what you're consenting to before we go. Not when we're already there. Not when you're caught up in the environment. Now, when you can think clearly."

Ophelia's questioning eyes met mine. What did I want?

I thought about the two men in the questionnaire discussion. The scene Kiernan had described where submission and dominance played out in real time. The idea of seeing Ophelia fall apart under his direction, or being observed myself.

"Full participation," I said.

Ophelia nodded. "Me too."

"You're certain?" Kiernan pressed. "Once we're there, you can still safeword out of anything. Red stops everything; yellow slows us down. Those apply throughout the evening, for any reason. But I want you going in with clear expectations."

"I'm certain," Ophelia said.

"Yes," I confirmed.

Again, he nodded once. "We'll leave at nine. I'll have appropriate clothing sent to your rooms." Something almost like anticipation crossed his features before he suppressed it. "Perhaps, after tonight, you'll understand what you're really asking for."

I stood to leave, and the room tilted.

The headache came on like a blade behind my left eye—vicious, terrifyingly familiar. I gripped the arm of the chair, and the room swam.

"Oliver?" Ophelia's voice came from far away.

Kiernan was in front of me, his hands on my face, tilting my head toward the light. The dominant had vanished. In his place was a sharper man—clinical, focused, afraid.

"Look at me." He held my chin steady. "Follow my finger. Don't move your head."

I tracked his finger left, right, up, down. The motion made the pain worse, but I didn't complain.

"Pupils equal and reactive," he muttered. "Nausea?"

"Some."

"Vision changes? Ringing in your ears?"

"No. Just the headache."

"Scale of one to ten."

"Seven. Maybe eight."

His mouth pressed into a line. "Ophelia, get him to the settee in the sitting room. I need to make a call."

She helped me to my feet, her arm steady around my waist. The walk to the next room felt endless. Every step sent a fresh spike through my skull.

"Is it bad?" Ophelia whispered as she lowered me onto the settee. "Like before?"

I didn't answer. I didn't know.

Through the partially open door, I heard Kiernan's voice—low, clipped, urgent.

"I need you to walk me through concussion warning signs." A pause. "Yes, it's Oliver." Another pause, longer this time. "No, I don't want to discuss why he's still at Greymarch."

Whoever was on the other end spoke at length. Kiernan listened, occasionally interjecting with clinical questions—my symptoms, the timeline, when I'd last slept properly.

"And if the pain doesn't subside in an hour?" A long silence. "Understood. I'll drive him to Glasgow myself if it comes to that."

When he returned, he carried a glass of water and two pills. His face was composed, but his eyes betrayed him—a tightness that hadn't been there before.

"Take these. Rest. If the pain worsens or you develop new symptoms, we leave for the hospital. Now."

"Tonight—"

"Is off the table unless you're fully recovered." His tone brooked no argument. "Your health comes first. Always."

I swallowed the pills. Kiernan sat in the chair across from me, watching. Not commanding, not seducing—just watching. Making sure I was all right.

An hour passed. The pain receded—slowly at first, then more steadily. By the time the clock struck six, it had faded to a dull throb.

"Overexertion," Kiernan said when I reported the improvement. "Your body is still recovering. You've been pushing yourself too hard."

I thought about the nights I hadn't slept, the restless hours pacing the corridors, the physical activities that had left me breathless. He wasn't wrong.

"Tonight," I said. "I still want to go."

He studied me. "If there's any return of symptoms—"

"I'll tell you immediately. Red means stop, remember?"

His face shifted—surprise, maybe, or approval. "Yes. It does."

The tunnels beneath Greymarch stretched farther than I'd realized. We walked for nearly twenty minutes. Dim sconces lined the stone corridor, casting long shadows on the walls. Kiernan led us, his footsteps steady and unhurried. None of us spoke.

"You should know," Kiernan said without breaking stride. "Callen Cavendish is one of the founding partners. So is Angus Drummond."

I nearly tripped on the uneven stone. We spent three weeks with both of them during the Labyrinth investigation.

"They'll see us," I managed.

"Yes." Kiernan glanced at me. "And you'll see them. That fear you're feeling right now? They felt it once too."

He didn't elaborate, and I didn't ask.

Ophelia walked beside me, her heels clicking on the flagstones. She wore what Kiernan had chosen for her—a deep-green dress that barely covered her thighs, the neckline plunging to reveal the curve of her breasts. No bra. No underwear. She'd blushed when she emerged from her room, but the look Kiernan gave as he took her in made her cheeks pinken for an entirely different reason. My guess was, if he put his hand between her legs, she'd be drenched with desire.

"Beautiful," he'd said and left it at that.

My own outfit felt almost pedestrian by comparison. Dark jeans, black button-down shirt with the sleeves rolled to my forearms, leather boots. When I'd asked why, Kiernan had simply said, "You'll blend in better this way."

I hadn't asked what I'd blend in with.

When we came to a door at the end of the tunnel, Kiernan produced a key, and the lock turned with a click.

He pushed it open, revealing a narrow stone staircase that curved upward into darkness. Music pulsed faintly from above.

"Rules," Kiernan said as we climbed. "Stay with me at all times. Don't speak to anyone unless I introduce you. If someone approaches you directly, defer to me." His voice echoed off the stone. "What you see tonight stays here. These people trust this space with their secrets.

That trust is sacred. And remember—red and yellow are always available to you. For any reason. At any moment. No explanation required."

At the top, Kiernan pushed another door open, and we stepped into a world I hadn't known existed.

The main floor of Thorned Thistle resembled a high-end lounge with leather sofas, dim lighting, and a bar staffed by attractive men and women dressed in crisp black. Music played at a volume that encouraged conversation without drowning it out. Well-dressed people mingled with drinks in hand, their laughter and chatter indistinguishable from any upscale club in Edinburgh or London.

Details emerged as my eyes adjusted. A woman in the corner wore a collar of braided leather. A man knelt beside an armchair, his head resting against his companion's thigh. Subtle power dynamics played out in every interaction—who stood, who sat, who spoke first, who waited for permission.

"This is the social floor," Kiernan said, guiding us through a crowd of nearly fifty people with a hand on each of our lower backs. "Members gather here to connect, negotiate, and decompress. The scenes happen below."

We descended another staircase, this one curving downward into warmer air and lower light. The architecture changed—exposed stone walls, wrought-iron fixtures, alcoves shrouded in shadow. Doorways lined the corridor, some open, some closed. From behind the closed ones, I heard sounds that made my heart race.

"Observation rooms," Kiernan said. "Pay attention and learn."

He led us to an alcove with a large window—one-way glass, I realized. Inside, a woman was bound to a wooden frame, her arms stretched above her head, her body naked except for a blindfold. A man circled her slowly, trailing something across her skin. Leather strands that left pink marks in their wake.

Ophelia tensed beside me.

As the scene unfolded, the woman's body relaxed into each stroke rather than tensing against it. Her lips parted on sounds we couldn't hear through the glass. The man spoke to her constantly, and she nodded or shook her head in response.

I glanced at Kiernan. He wasn't paying attention to the scene. He was studying us.

His eyes followed Ophelia's face, her breathing, the flush creeping down her throat. Then he turned to me, and I felt the weight of his assessment—cataloging my responses, filing them away.

"Oliver." His words took on that edge I was beginning to anticipate. "Behind her."

I acted on instinct, positioning myself behind Ophelia. Kiernan's hand found mine and guided it beneath the hem of her dress.

"She's aroused," he said. "Feel it."

My fingers slid between her thighs and found her slick and swollen. She shuddered against me.

"Keep your hand there," Kiernan ordered. "Feel how her body responds to what she's seeing."

On the other side of the glass, the man brought the flogger down across the woman's thighs. Her spine arched, and her mouth fell open in a silent cry. Between my fingers, Ophelia clenched.

"She likes that," Kiernan observed. "The impact. Notice how wet she gets when the leather strikes skin."

He was right. Each time the flogger connected, Ophelia grew slicker against my hand. Her hips twitched, seeking the friction I wasn't giving her.

"Not yet," Kiernan told her.

The man in the room set the flogger aside and stepped behind the bound woman. He pressed himself against her and reached around to cup her breasts. Even through the glass, I could see how her body melted into his.

"Surrender," Kiernan said. "She's giving him everything. Her pleasure, her pain, her trust." He glanced at Ophelia. "You understand that, don't you?"

"I do," she said, barely above a whisper.

"Show me. Bear down on Oliver's hand. Let him feel how much you want this."

She did. Her inner muscles clenched, her thighs pressed together to trap my fingers on her clit, and I felt the desperate pulse of her arousal and the heat of her need.

"Good girl." Kiernan's voice was velvet and steel. "Oliver, one finger inside her. Slowly."

I obeyed. She was so wet I slid in without resistance. Her whole body shuddered.

"Hold it there. Don't move."

The scene continued. The man freed the woman from her bonds, bent her over a padded bench, and entered her from behind. Ophelia whimpered against my shoulder.

"Another finger," Kiernan said.

I added a second, and she clenched around me, her breathing ragged.

"Now, curl them forward. Find the spot that makes her shake."

I pressed upward, and Ophelia's knees nearly buckled. Only my arm around her waist kept her standing.

"There," Kiernan said with satisfaction. "Keep pressure there. Thumb on her clit. Slow circles."

I worked her as he directed, feeling her climb toward release. Her hips rocked against my hand, her moans muffled.

"She's close," Kiernan observed. "I can see it in the flush of her skin and the tension in her thighs." He stepped closer, his mouth near her ear. "You want to come, don't you?"

"Yes," she gasped. "Please."

"When the woman comes, you come. Not before."

Ophelia whimpered but obeyed, her eyes fixed on the glass. On the other side, the man gripped the woman's hips, and his pace increased. The woman's mouth opened in what had to be a scream.

"Now," Kiernan said.

I pressed hard against that spot inside her, ground my thumb on her clit, and Ophelia fell apart, coming with a strangled moan that she buried in my shoulder.

I held her through the aftershocks, feeling her pulse around my fingers.

"Beautiful," Kiernan said. He lifted her chin with two fingers, studying her face. "Aftercare is important. The man in the scene is holding her now, wrapping her in a blanket. That tenderness matters as much as the pain that came before."

Ophelia nodded, still trembling.

"Can you walk?"

"I think so."

"Good. We have more to see."

We drifted to another window. This room held two men—a dominant with his hand fisted in the submissive's hair, controlling the rhythm as he fed the man his cock, pressing deeper until tears streamed down the man's cheeks.

My mouth went dry.

I looked away, steeling my reaction but powerless to control the hardening of my cock.

Kiernan guided us onward.

We observed three more scenes. A woman dominating another woman—Ophelia's hand found mine and squeezed tight. A rope suspension that turned the human body into art. A sensory deprivation scene where the submissive floated in darkness, responding to touches she couldn't anticipate.

Through all of it, Kiernan paid more attention to us than the scenes. And through all of it, I tracked Ophelia's responses—how her breathing changed, the flush that spread across her skin, how she pressed her thighs together.

Finally, we stopped in a shadowed alcove. Ophelia was trembling again, her arousal rebuilt from everything she'd witnessed.

Kiernan noticed. "She needs release again." His eyes met mine. "And you've been patient."

He looked at Ophelia. "On your knees."

She sank down without hesitation. Her hands found my belt, my zipper, then her mouth found me.

I braced one hand on the wall.

Kiernan stood beside us, close enough for me to smell his subtle cologne. His eyes never left my face as Ophelia worked me with her tongue.

She took me deeper, and my hips jerked forward. Kiernan's hand landed on my shoulder, holding me steady.

"Easy," he said. "Let her set the pace."

His grip tightened, and heat surged through me that had nothing to do with Ophelia's mouth. His hand on me. His voice in my ear. His eyes holding mine.

"What about you?" I managed. "Don't you want—"

"Yes."

The word hung there.

"Then, why—"

"You're not ready for what I want."

Before I could respond, Ophelia did something devastating with her throat. I came hard, my vision whiting out, and when I opened my eyes, I looked at Kiernan first.

He watched me with hunger. Or maybe possession.

Ophelia rose, wiping her mouth after Kiernan offered her a handkerchief.

"Come," he said. "One more thing."

There was a bed draped in dark silk, soft amber lighting, and a chair positioned in the corner of the private room where he took us to.

"On the bed," Kiernan told Ophelia. "Oliver, get her naked."

I peeled the dress over her head, leaving her bare on the sheets.

"Now, sit in the chair."

I retreated to the corner. From here, I had a clear view of everything.

Kiernan undressed—shirt first, then trousers. He stood naked, and I noticed things I shouldn't. The scars on his ribs and shoulder blade, the dark hair trailing down his stomach to his thick and hard cock.

I tried to look away, but couldn't.

He positioned himself between Ophelia's thighs. She wrapped her legs around him, pulling him closer.

"Oliver." Strain roughened his words. "Come over here. Kneel at the side of the bed."

Once again, I did as he commanded without hesitation.

After rolling on a condom, he entered her slowly. The sound she made echoed through the room. Then he began to thrust.

I was learning Ophelia's sounds, her responses, but Kiernan drawing them from her was different. He fucked her with control, each thrust deliberate, playing her body like an instrument.

"There," she panted. "God, right there—"

His hand fisted in her hair, exposing her throat for his teeth. She moaned when he bit down.

I couldn't stop myself from grasping my own cock.

His pace increased, and a bead of sweat trailed down his spine.

Why couldn't I look away? What was wrong with me? This was about Ophelia.

"Come," Kiernan commanded her. "Now."

She broke. He fucked her through it until she was whimpering, then his own rhythm faltered. His hips snapped once, twice, and he came with a groan that reverberated through me.

He stayed buried in her, chest heaving. Then he lifted his head and looked directly at me.

Our eyes met. His were dark, pupils blown. I felt pinned by that stare—exposed.

What had my face revealed?

He studied me for four heartbeats, then looked away.

I returned to the chair, hard and confused, trying to sort out what had affected me most.

The return walk to Greymarch was silent.

Ophelia leaned against me, exhausted, as Kiernan led us through the tunnel.

When we emerged into the castle, he spoke.

"Get her to bed. I have work to do."

His words were clipped. The warmth from the club had vanished.

I adjusted my grip on Ophelia. At the last moment, I turned around.

"Kiernan."

He stopped.

"What you said. What is it you want that I'm not ready for?"

The silence stretched.

"Go to bed, Oliver."

"That's not an answer."

"No." He turned away. "It's not."

He disappeared around a corner, and I was left with Ophelia's weight beside me and a question I wasn't sure I wanted answered.

What did Kiernan want, and why did part of me hope the answer involved me?

10

Ophelia

I didn't remember much of the walk from the Thorned Thistle to the castle. Exhaustion had made my legs unsteady, and I'd leaned against Oliver most of the way. Kiernan had been ahead of us, silent the entire time.

Oliver had brought me to my room. "Get some rest," he'd said, echoing Kiernan's clipped instructions. I'd heard his footsteps fade down the corridor, heard a door open and close, then nothing.

Now, I lay in the darkness and stared at the canopy above my bed. My body thrummed with an energy I couldn't release.

Kiernan's rule echoed in my mind. *Your pleasure belongs to me. Neither of you comes without my presence and my explicit permission.*

I pressed my thighs together and tried to think about something else.

It didn't work.

Every time I closed my eyes, I was at the club, in that shadowed alcove with Oliver's fingers sliding between my thighs.

She's aroused. Feel it.

Kiernan's voice had been so calm. So controlled. Like he was conducting an experiment, and we were his willing subjects. He'd guided Oliver's hand beneath my dress and ordered him to touch me, and I'd nearly collapsed from the intensity of being handled like that. Directed. Used.

I'd loved every second of it.

The woman in the first scene had surrendered so beautifully, and the whole time, Oliver's fingers had been inside me. He'd held still because Kiernan told him to, and my own arousal built without relief.

Not yet. Patience. Watch the scene.

I'd wanted to scream. I'd wanted to grind against Oliver's hand until I came apart. But Kiernan's command had held me in place more effectively than any restraint.

That was the part I couldn't stop thinking about. Not the physical sensation—though, God, that had been intense—but how his voice had wrapped around my will and squeezed. How I'd obeyed without question, without hesitation, because pleasing him had become more important than my own release.

I rolled onto my side and hugged a pillow to my chest.

The second scene we watched had been between two men. Oliver went rigid behind me the moment we'd stopped at that window. His chest rose faster, and when I glanced in his direction, his arousal was evident.

I sensed before he did that it wasn't only the power exchange that had his hardness straining against his trousers, but the men themselves.

No doubt Kiernan had picked up on it before I did, since he seemed to pick up on our every response as though he was filing it away for future use.

My thoughts drifted, then and now, to how much I *knew* Oliver's responses to Kiernan ran deeper than he'd acknowledged. Kiernan had made his desire known too when he told him that what he wanted, Oliver wasn't ready for. God, that thought alone had my pussy weeping.

Seeing them together, being part of that dynamic, Oliver finally surrendering to what he so obviously needed—I pressed my hand between my legs.

This was what I'd fantasized about that night, alone in my room. Before the club, before Kiernan had touched me. I'd imagined them both commanding me together, and my body had responded with a need that terrified me. Now, I understood why.

The memory unfurled as I touched myself.

After the second scene, Kiernan had guided us onward. More windows. More dynamics. A woman with a strap-on fucking another woman who begged for more. A rope suspension that made the bound man look like he was flying. A sensory-deprivation scene where the blindfolded submissive responded to every touch with a full-body shiver.

Through all of it, Kiernan had tracked our responses with predatory focus. Every gasp, every flush, every shift of weight—he'd noted it all.

At one point, I'd felt eyes on us that weren't Kiernan's. When I'd turned, I'd caught a figure near the bar watching our group with an intensity that felt targeted rather than curious. Not the idle interest of club members observing newcomers. Something sharper. When I'd looked again, they'd disappeared into the crowd.

I'd mentioned it to Kiernan. He'd scanned the room, seeing nothing suspicious. "Probably a member curious about new faces," he'd said. But his jaw had tightened almost imperceptibly, and he'd kept us closer after that.

Oliver had barely spoken. When I'd reached for his hand, he'd squeezed mine with urgent pressure, like I was the only thing keeping him grounded.

I'd wanted to tell him it was okay. That wanting Kiernan didn't change anything between us. That desire didn't have to fit into neat categories. But it wasn't my place. He had to figure it out himself.

When Kiernan had finally stopped in a shadowed alcove and told me I deserved a reward, I'd nearly wept with relief. The arousal had been building for over an hour. Every scene, every command, every moment of Oliver's fingers holding still inside me had wound me tighter.

Make her come. Quietly.

Oliver had obeyed. He knew my body now—knew the rhythm I needed, the pressure, the pace. He'd worked me with focused intensity, and I'd fallen over the edge. However, it was what came after that I couldn't stop replaying.

Ophelia. On your knees.

I'd sunk down without hesitation. The stone floor had been hard beneath my knees, but I hadn't cared. Oliver's belt, his zipper, his cock in my mouth—I'd taken him eagerly. I was grateful for the chance to give pleasure after receiving so much.

Kiernan had stood beside us, and the tension between them was almost palpable. Oliver's hand had landed on my head, guiding my rhythm, but he hadn't looked away from Kiernan. When his hand had gripped Oliver's shoulder, Oliver had made a sound that had nothing to do with what I was doing to him.

I thought about how Oliver's body had gone still when Kiernan touched him. His hips had jerked forward—not from my mouth, but from that single point of contact on his shoulder. His pupils had blown wide when Kiernan leaned closer.

He'd wanted Kiernan to kiss him. I'd seen it in how his lips had parted, how his head had tilted almost imperceptibly toward the other man. He probably hadn't even realized he'd done it. But I had.

I'd felt the moment everything shifted. The moment Oliver stopped fighting and started wanting. His hips had stuttered, and he'd gasped before coming down my throat with Kiernan's name on his lips.

Not sir. Not Archon. *Kiernan.*

I didn't think either of them had noticed. But I had, with a surge of satisfaction that surprised me.

My fingers worked faster now, chasing the memory.

The private room. Kiernan ordering Oliver to undress me. How Oliver's hands had trembled as he'd peeled the dress over my head.

Sit in the chair.

Oliver had retreated to the corner while Kiernan undressed, but his attention had lingered on Kiernan's shoulders and chest, then on his cock.

I'd wondered then what Oliver was thinking. Whether he was horrified by his own responses or starting to accept them. Whether he understood what it meant that he couldn't stop looking at another man's body.

I'd wondered, too, what it would feel like to watch them together. To see Oliver finally give in to what he wanted. To see Kiernan's control applied to Oliver's resistance until it crumbled. Then he'd ordered him to kneel at the side of the bed. To watch.

The thought had made me clench around nothing.

Then Kiernan had been inside me, and I'd stopped thinking about anything except the feel of him.

He'd fucked me like he did everything else—with complete control, absolute focus, and relentless intent. Every thrust had been deliberate. Every angle calculated. He drew sounds from me I hadn't known I could make.

Even lost in sensation, I'd been aware of Oliver's presence. Imagined his hand pressed against his jeans. His focus on us—on Kiernan—with an intensity that bordered on desperation.

The knowledge hadn't made me jealous. It had made me want it for him.

When Kiernan had commanded me to come, I had. Instantly. Completely. The orgasm crashed through me, and I'd screamed without caring who heard.

Then Kiernan had found his own release, and I'd felt him pulse inside me. In the heat of the moment, we'd both looked at Oliver, and it was as though the three of us were connected by a current that ran between all of us.

Oliver's face had been raw. Exposed. Hungry. He wanted this. Wanted us. Wanted *him*.

I'd thought about it during our walk through the tunnels. What it would mean to share Kiernan with Oliver. What it would mean to watch them together, to be part of something that included all three of us equally.

I'd thought I might feel threatened. Another person wanting what I wanted. Competition for Kiernan's attention.

Except that wasn't what I felt at all.

What I felt was excitement. Possibility. The sense that we were building toward something none of us had experienced before—something bigger than any pairing could be on its own.

I was close now. So close. My fingers worked my clit in tight circles while my other hand pinched my nipple the way Kiernan had shown me he liked.

The rule didn't matter. I needed to take the edge off so I could sleep. I'd be good tomorrow. I'd be obedient. I'd—

"Ophelia."

I froze.

Kiernan stood in the doorway. The light from the corridor silhouetted him. I couldn't see his face, but I could hear the ice in his voice.

"What are you doing?"

My hand was still between my legs. There was no point in lying.

"I couldn't sleep," I whispered. "I—"

"Was breaking my rule." He stepped into the room and closed the door behind him. "I was very clear. Your pleasure belongs to me. Did you forget?"

"No."

"Did you think I wouldn't know?"

I had thought that. I'd been wrong.

He crossed to the bed and looked down at me. His face was unreadable in the darkness, but ice threaded his words.

"Get up. Go to Oliver's room. Tell him to come here. Now."

"Kiernan, I'm sorry—"

"You will be." He turned away. "Go."

Oliver followed me to my room. He wore only loose sleep pants, his chest bare. "What's going on?" he asked.

"Ophelia broke a rule," Kiernan said without turning around. "She touched herself without permission. Now, she needs to be punished, and you need to watch."

"Punished how?" Oliver asked.

Kiernan turned. "Twenty strikes. She'll count each one. If she loses count, we start over." He motioned to me. "Come here, Ophelia."

I crossed to him on shaking legs. He guided me to stand at the end of the bed, then sat on the edge of the mattress.

"Over my lap."

My bare breasts pressed into the bedding as I draped myself across his thighs. My ass was raised and vulnerable. The position was humiliating and exposing and arousing all at once.

Kiernan's hand rested on my spine. It was warm and steady.

"Oliver. Sit in that chair. Don't look away."

I heard Oliver cross the room. Heard the creak of the chair as he sat.

"Ophelia." Kiernan's voice softened slightly. "Do you understand why you're being punished?"

"Yes, sir. I broke your rule."

"What rule?"

"My pleasure belongs to you. I'm not allowed to come without your presence and permission."

"And did you come?"

"No, sir. You stopped me before—"

"But you would have. If I hadn't walked in."

Shame burned through me. "Yes, sir."

"This is about trust," Kiernan said. "I gave you a boundary. You tested it. Now, you learn there are consequences." His hand stroked down over my ass, gentle and warm. "Twenty strikes. You'll count each one and thank me. Do you understand?"

"Yes, sir."

"What's your safeword?"

"Red."

"Use it if you need to. There's no shame in it." His hand lifted from my skin. "We begin."

The first strike landed with a sharp crack. Hot, stinging pain bloomed across my right cheek.

"One," I gasped. "Thank you, sir."

"Good girl."

The second strike hit the left side. Harder than the first.

"Two. Thank you, sir."

The third and fourth came in quick succession, and I jerked with each impact. The pain was bright and immediate, impossible to ignore.

"Three. Thank you, sir. Four. Thank you, sir."

By the fifth strike, my skin was on fire as much from shame as from the punishment. I'd disappointed him. I'd broken his trust. I deserved this.

"Five. Thank you, sir."

Kiernan's hand rubbed over my heated flesh, and I hissed at the contact.

"Five down," he said. "Fifteen to go. How do you feel?"

"I'm sorry," I whispered. "I'm so sorry."

"I know. But sorry doesn't erase the transgression. Only consequences do." His hand lifted again. "Continue."

Six through ten came harder than the first five. Each strike drove a cry from my throat. The pain layered on itself, building into something that consumed my entire awareness. I couldn't think about anything else. Couldn't think about the club, about Oliver, about my own arousal. There was only the pain and Kiernan's voice.

"Seven. Thank you, sir. Eight—" My voice broke on a sob. "Thank you, sir."

"You're doing well," Kiernan murmured. "So well. Keep going."

"Nine. Thank you, sir. Ten. Thank you, sir."

He stopped. His hand stroked over my punished skin, and I whimpered at the gentleness after so much pain.

"Halfway," he said. "The shame is fading, isn't it? The guilt is burning away."

He was right. Somewhere between five and ten, the shame had transformed. It was still there, but it had become something else. Something cleaner. Each strike felt like penance. Each burst of pain absolved me a little more.

"Yes, sir," I whispered.

"That's the purpose of punishment. Not to hurt you. To free you." His fingers dipped between my thighs, and I heard his sharp intake of breath. "And your body understands that, even if your mind is still catching up. You're wet, Ophelia. Dripping."

I could feel the slick evidence of my arousal. The pain had unlocked something in me. Every nerve ending was alive, every sensation amplified.

"Ten more," Kiernan said. "Then you're forgiven."

Eleven through fifteen broke me open.

I'd spent my life maintaining my composure. Embassy dinners where I smiled through insults. Negotiations where I swallowed my rage to close deals. I'd believed control was my greatest strength. But draped across Kiernan's lap, waiting for his hand to fall, I discovered something terrifying. I didn't want to be in control anymore. I wanted to shatter.

The pain was intense now, each strike landing on already-tender flesh. I sobbed into the mattress, tears streaming down my face, but I didn't ask him to stop. I didn't want him to stop. Each impact drove me deeper into a space where nothing existed except his hand and my skin and the exquisite agony of surrender.

I lost myself somewhere around fourteen. The sting had morphed into warmth and pressure and release, all tangled together. My body was shaking, my mind was floating, and every strike felt like a gift. I counted and thanked him with each one.

Kiernan rubbed my inflamed skin, spreading the heat, and I moaned at the sensation.

"Five more," he said. "You're almost there. You're doing beautifully."

"Please," I whispered. I didn't know what I was asking for. More pain. More praise. More of him.

"Please what?"

"Please finish it, sir."

Sixteen through nineteen came fast and hard. I screamed into the mattress with each one, but I counted, I thanked him, and I held on.

The twentieth strike was the hardest of all. It landed across both cheeks, a final burst of fire that consumed everything in its path. I screamed, then collapsed, boneless and sobbing.

"Twenty. Thank you, sir."

"Perfect." His hand rested on my burning skin. Possessive. Warm. "Such a good girl. You took your punishment beautifully."

I was crying freely now. The pain had broken through my defenses, and everything was pouring out—the tension of the evening, the loneliness, the hungry need to please, the fear that I wasn't enough, the relief of being held accountable. Kiernan's hand stroked up and down my spine.

"Shh. You did well. The punishment is over." He helped me sit up, then pulled me onto his lap and cradled me against his chest. "You're forgiven. The slate is clean."

I buried my face in his neck and sobbed. He held me through it, his hands gentle as he murmured words I couldn't decipher.

"You're mine, Ophelia," he said. "And I take care of what's mine. That includes discipline when you need it. Do you understand?"

"Yes, sir," I whispered against his throat.

"Good girl. Oliver?"

I'd forgotten he was there. I turned to look at him and saw him gripping the arms of the chair. His knuckles were white, and his sleep pants tented with obvious arousal.

It was his face that caught my attention, though. He looked wrecked. Devastated. Like witnessing my punishment had shattered something inside him. But he wasn't looking at me. He was looking at Kiernan.

"Come here," Kiernan said.

Oliver rose from the chair, his legs unsteady as he crossed the room like a man in a trance.

"On your knees."

His obedience was automatic, instinctive. He sank down, and his eyes dropped to the floor, then rose again to meet Kiernan's.

His surrender had been instinctive. Natural.

Did he know that yet? Did he understand what his body was telling him?

"Ophelia took her punishment," Kiernan said, adjusting my position so I was on his lap, his hardness pressed against my arse. He draped my legs over his thighs, then spread them wide open. "Now, she gets her reward. Make her come with your mouth."

Oliver's eyes were riveted to my exposed center, and he swallowed hard.

"Yes, sir."

He leaned forward, and his tongue found me.

I moaned and arched into the contact. Kiernan's arms wrapped around me, holding me in place, keeping my legs open.

"That's it," Kiernan murmured in my ear. "Let him taste how wet you are. Let him feel what the punishment did to you."

Oliver licked through my folds, circled my clit, and thrust inside me. The pleasure was sharp after the pain, almost too much to bear. Even as the sensation built, all my attention was on Oliver. He was aroused. Desperately so. And not only from tasting me.

Then Kiernan's hands found my breasts.

He cupped them, kneaded them, and rolled my nipples between his fingers until I whimpered. His mouth was against my ear, his voice a low rumble.

"I'm going to clamp these soon. Pretty little clamps with a chain between them. Would you like that?"

"Yes, sir," I gasped.

He pinched harder, and I cried out. Oliver's tongue never stopped, but I saw his eyes fix on Kiernan's hands on my breasts.

"Watch him," Kiernan murmured in my ear, and I did.

Oliver gripped my thighs with bruising force.

Every command Kiernan gave, every word of praise or instruction, wound Oliver tighter.

"And this—" Kiernan's hand slid down my stomach, past where Oliver was working, to my swollen clit. He pinched it between two fingers, and I nearly screamed. "What if I clamped this too? A pretty jewel right here, keeping you on edge?"

Oliver groaned, and the vibration shot through my core.

"Please—"

"Please what?"

"Please, sir, I want—I need—"

Oliver's tongue pressed flat against my clit at the same moment Kiernan pinched my nipple with his opposite hand, and I broke.

The orgasm crashed through me with devastating force. I screamed and convulsed in Kiernan's arms while Oliver kept licking and Kiernan kept pinching, and the ecstasy went on and on until I was sobbing from the intensity.

When it finally stopped, I shook and cried, more wrung out than I'd ever been in my life.

"Beautiful," Kiernan said softly as he held me. "That's what happens when you earn your pleasure instead of stealing it."

I couldn't speak.

"Oliver. Stand up."

His mouth glistened with my arousal, and he looked dazed, almost drugged, as he rose.

"Come here," Kiernan said. "On the bed. Hold her."

Oliver climbed on and lay beside us. Kiernan transferred me into his arms, and I curled against Oliver's chest, still crying softly.

"This is aftercare," Kiernan said. "After intense experiences—punishment, heavy scenes, overwhelming orgasms—the body needs care. Reassurance. Connection."

Oliver wrapped his arms around me. "What do I do?"

"Hold her. Stroke her hair. Tell her she's safe, she's good, she's cherished." Kiernan's hand settled on Oliver's head, his fingers threading through his hair. "Ground her with your touch and your voice."

"You're safe," Oliver murmured against my hair. "You're so good. I've got you."

His body shifted against mine, and he grew hard where we pressed together. His lids had drooped, his mouth fell open, and a flush crept up his neck.

Kiernan's fingers worked slowly, stroking through the strands, scratching lightly against his scalp. Oliver made a barely perceptible sound, but I heard it.

"Good," Kiernan said, and Oliver shivered at the praise. "You're taking care of her. That's what she needs right now."

Oliver nodded, but his attention had fractured. Half of him was focused on holding me, murmuring reassurances, being present. The other half was lost in the sensation of Kiernan touching him.

Oliver's hips pressed forward infinitesimally, seeking contact.

Through it all, Kiernan praised him. Kept drawing responses Oliver didn't know he was giving.

I looked up and caught Kiernan staring at Oliver with a look I recognized. Hunger. Patience. Certainty.

He knew.

Oliver pressed his lips to my forehead, but his body arched subtly into Kiernan's touch. Seeking more. Needing more.

He had no idea what he was revealing. But Kiernan did. And now, so did I.

11

Kiernan

I'd endured seven years of celibacy, discipline, and channeling every ounce of my desire into control. Years spent observing—commanding—others in scenes at Thorned Thistle while I stood apart, untouchable, unreachable.

It wasn't for lack of trying. In that first year, I'd willed myself to attempt normalcy. A woman at a conference— attractive, willing, uncomplicated. We'd gone to her hotel, and when she'd kissed me, nothing but ice spread through my chest. My body rejected the intimacy with a violence that left me shaking.

Six months later, I'd tried again. Someone from the lifestyle—no expectations, no romance; I only wanted physical release between consenting adults. She'd been skilled and patient. And I couldn't perform. My body simply refused. The harder I pushed, the more it retreated, until I'd had to stop the scene entirely.

After that, I stopped trying.

I'd built the club to give myself purpose when everything else had crumbled. But I'd never let myself fully participate—not the way I once had. Not since I'd proven to myself exactly what kind of man I was.

One night with Ophelia had shattered all of it.

My body thrummed with the memory of being inside her as I stood at my bedroom window. The tight heat of her. The sounds she'd made when I'd commanded her to come. How she'd clenched around me like she never wanted to let go.

I wanted her again. The need was a constant ache, a hunger that my lengthy abstinence had made ravenous. I wanted to bend her over my desk and fuck her until she screamed. I wanted to tie her to my bed and spend hours wringing orgasm after orgasm from her body. I wanted to claim every inch of her until she forgot anyone else had ever touched her.

I had three days to do it. Three days to claim her—or lose her forever.

Except she wasn't the only one I wanted.

I closed my eyes and let myself feel the desire I'd been holding at arm's length since the moment I'd met Oliver. How my pulse quickened when he challenged me. How my cock hardened when he submitted, even reluctantly. How I'd imagined, more times than I could count, what it would feel like to have him on his knees before me.

Last night had nearly broken my restraint.

Punishing Ophelia had been necessary, a lesson in consequences that she'd needed to learn. But watching Oliver watch me—the way his breathing had changed, the evidence of his arousal in his sleep pants, how his eyes had tracked my hand rising and falling on her arse—had tested every ounce of my control.

The fantasy of ordering him to fuck her had played out in vivid detail even as I'd delivered each strike. I'd tell him to stand, to strip, to position himself behind her while she was still draped across my lap. I'd watch his face as he sank into her wet heat—the shock of pleasure, the loss of control, the desperate sounds he'd make as he thrust. Then I'd stand behind him with my hands on his hips and my cock pressing against his virgin hole. He'd freeze, then tremble as I breached him for the first time. I'd slide into him inch by inch while he was still buried in her, and the three of us would be connected in the most intimate way possible.

I'd fuck him slow at first. Let him adjust to the stretch, the fullness, the overwhelming sensation of being taken while taking. His moans would vibrate through Ophelia's body. Her clenching would drive him deeper into madness. And I'd control it all—the pace, the depth, the timing of every orgasm.

When I finally let him come, he'd shatter. He'd scream my name and spill inside her while I spilled inside him, and we'd collapse together, spent and sated.

The vision had made me so hard I'd nearly lost count of the strikes.

I'd nearly said the words. Nearly commanded him to take her while I prepared myself to take him. The only thing that had stopped me was knowing he wasn't ready—not physically or mentally. Oliver had never been with a man. His body would need preparation. His mind would need time.

I turned from the window and crossed to my closet. Behind the row of suits, a panel slid aside to reveal my private collection. Toys I'd acquired over the years. The kind of implements of pleasure and pain that I'd used on countless partners before my self-imposed exile. These items had never made it to the playroom. At first, because it was too painful for me to even enter the space. Then I'd all but forgotten them. Until now.

My fingers brushed leather at the back of the compartment. A collar—simple, elegant, custom-made. I hadn't touched it in seven years. I withdrew my hand as if burned and focused on what I'd come for.

My fingers closed around a set of plugs—graduated sizes, smooth silicone, designed to stretch and prepare. I'd start them both on these, Ophelia first, then Oliver. Let them get used to the sensation of being filled. Let them learn to associate penetration with pleasure.

I'd have Ophelia wear hers during dinner. She'd squirm in her seat, hyperaware of the fullness inside her, and each time she did, it would send sparks of sensation through her body. By the time we retired to the bedroom, she'd be desperate.

Oliver's introduction would take longer. He'd resist at first—the vulnerability of it, the submission required to let me put anything inside him. But I'd make it good for him. I'd work him open with my fingers while Ophelia distracted him with her mouth. By the time I slid the plug home, he'd be begging for more.

I selected a prostate massager next, curved and weighted, designed to drive a man out of his mind. Oliver would clench to stop the intrusion, control his responses, and refuse to let himself feel how good it was. But once I found the right angle, he'd understand that submission wasn't weakness. That letting someone else control your pleasure was its own kind of power. That the surrender I was asking for would give him more than he'd ever imagined possible.

They'd learn that lesson. And I would be the one to teach them.

I replaced the panel and dressed for the day, my mind already planning. Tonight, we'd return to Thorned Thistle. I'd show them scenes they hadn't witnessed before—MMF dynamics, male submission, two men sharing a woman, sharing each other, building a bond that transcended traditional pairings.

Ready or not, I was done waiting. I didn't have a choice. In three days, they'd be gone, and I'd have missed my chance.

I found them at breakfast, seated across from each other at the long table in the morning room. Ophelia looked rested. Her skin glowed, and a grin played at her lips when she saw me. Oliver looked like he hadn't slept at all. Dark circles shadowed his eyes. His jaw was tight. His hand trembled as he lifted his cup. Worst of all, he couldn't look at me.

"Good morning," I said, taking my seat at the head of the table.

"Good morning, sir," Ophelia replied.

Oliver's cup clattered on the saucer. "Morning," he managed.

I studied him while I poured my tea. He was wound tight. His shoulders were rigid. His breathing was shallow. The aftereffects of last night were written all over him—the confusion, the arousal, the desperate attempt to understand what he'd felt while watching me punish Ophelia.

What he'd felt when I'd touched his hair.

"We're going to Thorned Thistle again tonight," I announced.

Oliver's head snapped up, his eyes meeting mine for the first time, panic warring with desire and fear in their depths.

"Again?" The word caught in his throat.

"There are dynamics you haven't observed. Things I want you to see." I held his gaze. "Unless you'd rather remain here."

The challenge hung between us. We both knew he wouldn't refuse. Couldn't refuse. The need to understand what was happening to him would drive him forward even as fear urged him to retreat.

"No," he said quietly. "I'll come."

I allowed myself a small nod of satisfaction.

Ophelia's focus shifted from Oliver to me as the conversation played out. Recognition had flickered across her face last night when he'd responded to my touch. She wasn't threatened by it. If anything, she seemed intrigued.

She understood that this could only work if all three of us wanted each other. That my desire for Oliver didn't diminish my desire for her—it enhanced it. Made us stronger. More complete.

"Wear what is waiting in your rooms," I told them both. "We'll leave after dinner."

As difficult as it was, my instincts told me it would be best if I left them on their own until then. I didn't doubt their yearning would rival mine in the hours between now and our departure. Ophelia's punishment last night would be fresh on their minds, so neither would be tempted to self-satisfy nor would they seek to find pleasure in each other.

The tunnels felt longer tonight. Ophelia's hand brushed mine occasionally as she walked between Oliver and me.

I'd chosen a deep-blue dress for her tonight that was elegant as well as revealing. Oliver wore dark jeans and a gray Henley that was tight across his torso and clung to his body in a way that made me want to push him up against the side of the tunnel and grind my cock into his.

When we emerged into the club, the crowd was already gathered on the social floor. I spotted Callen immediately, and he noticed us.

"Kiernan." He greeted us with a warm smile. "Twice in one week. People will talk."

"Let them."

His eyes flicked to Oliver and Ophelia. "Can I get you all a drink? Gus and Rafe are holding a table."

We followed him across the room. Gus rose when he saw us, his massive frame dwarfing the chair he'd been sitting in, and a grin spread across his face. "Ophelia and Oliver. Welcome. It's nice to see you both."

Oliver's spine went rigid, but he quickly recovered as he watched Gus pull Ophelia into a hug.

"Rafe, meet Oliver and Ophelia."

He rose when he saw us, taking the stance of a man who'd spent years in special forces. That constant coiled energy never left him. It was evident in everything he did.

"Kiernan. Good to see you." He shook Oliver's hand, then Ophelia's. His gaze had lingered on each of them until another man—a dom—approached our table and leaned close to Rafe's ear. Whatever he said made my friend nod once and follow him to a quiet corner.

Oliver tracked the two men, swallowing hard when Rafe's shoulders dropped and his chin dipped. Good. He was starting to see it.

"Drinks," Callen announced, setting glasses on the table. We stayed for one round, and all the while, my focus remained on Oliver. He tried to act normal, to make appropriate responses, laugh at the right moment, and engage in small talk. But his attention kept drifting to the corner where Rafe stood with the other man. He watched how Rafe's posture had changed, the quiet intimacy of their exchange.

His defenses were crumbling.

"Ready?" I asked when we were finished with our drinks.

Oliver's nod was jerky. "Yes."

I led them down to the observation level. Past the rooms they'd seen on their first visit, where standard scenes of domination and submission took place. Instead, we entered a different wing. One I'd been saving.

There were two men and a woman in the first room we stopped to view. She was on the bed while one man knelt between her thighs and the other at her head. She pleasured him with her mouth while the first man fucked her. But what made the scene remarkable was what happened next—the man at her head reached down and gripped the other man's face, pulling him up for a deep, claiming kiss while she writhed beneath them.

Oliver's sharp intake of breath was audible.

I stayed silent and watched as the flush crept up from his collar, then as his fists clenched at his sides.

On the other side of the glass, the scene evolved. The woman was on her hands and knees now. One man still fucked her while the other fed her his cock. But the men's eyes were locked on each other. Their hands reached across her to grip each other's arms.

Oliver's chest rose and fell faster. His lips had parted, and he no longer watched the woman at all. He was watching the men.

Then they changed positions. The one who'd been fucking her withdrew and stood by her head. The second man took his place behind her. But before he entered her, the first man reached across and wrapped his hand around his partner's cock. He stroked him twice, three times, then guided him into her body.

Oliver made a small, choked sound. His hand twitched toward his groin before he caught himself.

He didn't know I'd seen. He thought he was hiding it. He wasn't.

When Ophelia glanced at me and I shook my head, she looked away.

Neither of us spoke. Oliver lingered in whatever he was feeling, and I let the images burn into his mind without words to rationalize them away.

When the scene ended, I led them to the next room, where two men were scening. The dom had his sub pinned to the wall. Their mouths were fused together as the more powerful of the two ground his hips into his partner's. Then he dropped to his knees and took the sub's cock into his mouth.

While Oliver didn't make a sound, his reactions were reflected in the glass.

His breathing had gone ragged. His hands trembled, and his cock was visibly hard, straining in his jeans.

The man on his knees worked his partner, taking him deep, then easing off to tongue the head, before swallowing him again.

Oliver's hips turned as his body sought the friction his mind wouldn't allow him to pursue.

The scene progressed, and the dom rose and turned the other man to face the wall. He retrieved lubricant, slicked his fingers, and began to prepare his partner.

Oliver's whole body went rigid as he watched the fingers push deeper and the sub's arse clench involuntarily. One finger became two. When the dom added a third finger, the man's mouth fell open on a silent moan. He stretched and prepared and opened him up.

Oliver's hand drifted toward his cock, but he didn't touch himself.

Had he reached the point in his desire where he could admit to himself that he wanted another man's hands on him? To be on his knees? To be opened and taken?

When the dom finally positioned himself and pushed inside his partner, Oliver swayed toward the glass.

His face revealed everything as the dom fucked his partner with long, deep strokes. With every thrust, Oliver tensed and released, synching his own rhythm with theirs.

"Enough," I said when I couldn't bear not touching him. "We're leaving."

Oliver blinked rapidly, like a man waking from a dream.

He didn't ask questions or protest. He nodded once and followed Ophelia and me toward the exit.

He couldn't look at me, and that was exactly what I wanted.

We remained silent on the return trip to the castle, and when we emerged into Greymarch, I stopped in the corridor.

"Ophelia. Go to your room. Oliver and I need to talk."

She studied me, then him, before nodding once and disappearing down the hallway.

"Come." I motioned for him to follow me to the library.

The room was dark except for the fire I'd had laid earlier. The flames cast shadows across Oliver's face as he fought to steady his breathing.

I closed the door behind us.

"Sit before you fall down."

He rested on the arm of the sofa and dropped his head into his hands. "I don't understand what's happening to me."

"Yes, you do."

"I've never—" He looked up at me with wild eyes. "And now, all I can think about is—" He cut himself off.

I crossed the room slowly, giving him time to stop me if he needed to.

He didn't.

I stood within reach, close enough that he had to tilt his head to look at me.

"Tell me what you can't stop thinking about," I said.

"You," he whispered. "I can't stop thinking about you."

"And what do you think about?"

"Your hands in my hair. On my shoulder at the club. On me."

"What else?"

He swallowed convulsively. "I think about your mouth when you give commands, when you praise me. I want—" He shook his head. "I don't know what I want."

"I do."

His whole body went still when I cupped his jaw.

"Tell me to stop," I said.

Again, he didn't. Instead, his eyes held mine as I bent toward him. His lips parted, and his breath came in short, shallow gasps.

"Tell me to stop, Oliver. Say it now, and I will. I'll walk out of this room, and we'll never speak of it again."

"I can't." His voice broke on the words. "God help me, I can't."

I kissed him—not gently or tentatively. I claimed his mouth like I'd wanted to since the moment I met him. My tongue swept between his lips, and he opened for me with a moan that vibrated through my entire body.

His hands fisted in my shirt and drew me closer, and I let him. He sunk into the sofa, and I braced my knee beside his hip, letting him drag me down until I was half on top of him and my weight pressed him into the cushions.

The kiss deepened. His tongue met mine with awkward eagerness.

I broke away long enough to breathe. "Touch me."

His hands traveled up my chest, hesitant at first, then over my shoulders. His hips rolled into mine, and his hard cock pressed against my thigh.

"Kiernan, please—"

My hand slid down his chest, over his stomach, and to the bulge straining beneath his jeans as I thrust my tongue into his mouth. He cried out when I gripped him through the denim.

"Please what?" I asked.

"I don't know."

"Yes, you do."

When I squeezed him, he arched off the sofa, and a broken sound tore from his throat. His gaze was raw when he met mine, desperate and confused and burning with need.

"What does this make me?" he asked.

"It makes you human."

His jaw worked. He was processing and fighting and surrendering all at once.

"Show me, Kiernan," he whispered.

The sound of my name on his lips—not sir, not Archon, but Kiernan—broke my restraint.

I kissed him once more. It was deep, claiming, and full of promise. Then I pulled away.

"Find Ophelia," I said, my voice rough with want. "Bring her to my bedroom."

<h1 style="text-align:center">12</h1>

Oliver

My lips still burned from Kiernan's kiss as I walked to find Ophelia.

His taste lingered, and my heart slammed into my ribs as I walked to our suite. His hands had gripped my jaw like he owned me, and I'd let him. I'd done more than let him. I'd taken everything he gave.

This was what my body had known that night in the playroom, when I'd stood before that collar and hardened without understanding why. This was what "Yes, sir" had meant when it slipped out unbidden. My hand trembled when I raised it to knock on Ophelia's door.

She opened it wearing silk pajamas and her hair loose around her shoulders. Her eyes searched my face, and her expression shifted.

"Oliver." She brushed her fingers along my jaw. "What happened?"

"I kissed him. Or he kissed me."

Her brows flared, but rather than surprise or jealousy, she appeared relieved and even desirous.

"Finally," she murmured.

"He wants us to join him in his bedroom. Right now."

Her pupils dilated when she nodded, then her hand found mine as we walked to the west tower, where Kiernan's bedroom door stood open.

He waited near the fire that burned in the massive hearth. He'd removed his shirt, exposing the dark hair that dusted his chest and trailed past his navel. Firelight played across the planes of his stomach, the ridges of his muscles, the broad set of his shoulders.

"Close the door," he said as his gaze tracked our approach with dark hunger.

The latch clicked shut and sealed the three of us in warm amber light.

"Tonight, we begin." He spoke in a low tone. "The three of us together. But before we go further, there's something we need to discuss."

I tensed, wondering what rules he was about to set forth.

"How long has it been since you were tested?"

The question caught me off guard, but it shouldn't have. Of course he'd ask.

"Six weeks ago," Ophelia said. "SIS requires quarterly screenings. I'm clean."

"In hospital," I added. "Also, clean."

Kiernan nodded. "Unit 23 has the same requirements. My last test was five weeks ago." He looked from me to her. "I haven't been with anyone since. But I won't assume anything, and neither should you."

His gaze darted to mine, then hers. "Which means we have a choice. I want you bare, but that's a decision we make together."

I twitched at the thought of feeling her with nothing between us.

"No condoms," Ophelia whispered.

I swallowed. "Agreed."

Kiernan's eyes darkened as he got closer. "Then, tonight, nothing separates us." Heat radiated from his bare skin, and his scent surrounded me as he traced my jaw with his fingertips and tilted my face up toward his.

"Look at me," he commanded.

His dark gaze held mine.

"You're allowed to want this." His thumb brushed my lower lip and pressed until I opened to him. "You're allowed to want me."

He lifted my shirt over my head and tossed it aside, then his palm pressed flat on my chest, right over my pounding heart.

"Racing," he observed.

"Yes."

"Afraid?"

"No."

His hands slid up my arms and trailed over the muscles of my biceps. They crossed my shoulders and traveled down my spine. They were rougher than Ophelia's and broader and stronger. I shuddered as calluses scraped across my skin.

"Touch me too," he commanded.

When I rested my palms on his chest, his coarse hair scratched my skin. I spread my hands wide and felt his heartbeat. His pulse ran steady where mine raced.

His shoulders were broader than mine by inches, and his pectorals were dense and defined. The muscles jumped, and I dragged my thumbs across his nipples and watched them harden into stiff peaks. His breath caught, and I throbbed in response.

His muscles tensed and flexed when I touched the flat planes of his stomach. I counted six distinct ridges of abs that were hard as stone.

"Lower," he said.

My fingers shook at his belt.

"Go ahead."

The buckle clinked in the quiet room, then I unzipped his trousers, pushing the fabric down his thighs. He stepped out and kicked them aside.

His cock jutted, thick and hard. It was flushed deep red, heavy, and bigger than mine, with veins that roped along the length. The head was broad and swollen, and a bead of moisture gathered at the slit. I stared at it and at him.

"More, Oliver."

I wrapped my fingers around the velvet-soft skin over rigid flesh like silk stretched over steel. As I stroked up his length, his breath grew deeper and rougher.

His hips eased forward and pushed into my fist. I found a rhythm that went up with a twist at the top and down with a squeeze at the base. I learned what made his breath catch, what made his stomach muscles clench, and what made his hardness pulse.

A low sound tore from his chest, and his hips jerked. "Join us," he said over my shoulder.

Ophelia pressed into my back. Her nipples were hard points beneath the silk of her pajamas and poked into my shoulder blades. Her hands slid around my waist, and her nails dragged across my stomach. She worked at opening my jeans, and my aching erection sprang out and slapped on my belly. She pushed the fabric down my legs, and I stepped out too.

Now, Kiernan and I were naked. Her hand wrapped around me from behind and pumped me while I worked him.

"My God." Kiernan grabbed my neck, and his mouth crashed into mine. This kiss was hungrier than in the library and more demanding. His free hand wrapped around me, overlapping Ophelia's. My knees nearly buckled as they stroked me together, sliding up and down my shaft in tandem.

Kiernan leaned away enough to look down. Our erections were hard and leaking, so close to touching. When he wrapped one large hand around both of us and stroked, a rough sound escaped me.

Ophelia kissed her way up my neck from behind. Her teeth grazed my earlobe, and her tongue traced the shell of my ear. I was caught with her softness on one side and his hardness on the other. Her hands roamed my torso and pinched my nipples while his continued playing with our cocks.

"Get on the bed," he said, motioning to me and Ophelia.

She climbed onto the massive four-poster first and left her silk pajamas discarded on the floor. Her olive skin glowed bronze in the firelight as she stretched out on the dark sheets with her legs parted. Her sex glistened wet and pink and swollen.

"Oliver." Kiernan's speaking my name anchored me. "Get her ready for us."

When she opened her legs, I breathed in the musky scent of her arousal, then lowered myself to her center.

She gasped when I found her swollen pearl of flesh. She threaded her hands in my hair, and her nails scraped my scalp as she held me close to her. I circled slow and steady with teasing strokes around the sensitive bud.

Her taste flooded my mouth, and I traced her folds to gather more of her wetness.

The mattress dipped behind me as Kiernan's weight settled behind me, spreading me open. His hand slid down my spine, dragged over each vertebra, then the curve of my arse, landing between my cheeks.

"Color?" he asked.

"Green." The word came out strangled.

"Then, keep going. Focus on her."

His finger pressed my hole, but he didn't push farther. The pad only circled the sensitive ring of muscle. No one had ever touched me there, and the vulnerability of it sent electricity up my spine.

"Relax." His lips brushed my ear. "I'm not taking you tonight. But I want you to understand what's coming."

His finger circled my entrance and pressed enough to make the muscle flutter. I resumed working Ophelia with my tongue. The dual sensation overwhelming me—my mouth on her clit, his finger teasing my hole, and pleasure spiking from both ends of my body.

My cock ached and throbbed.

When I sucked Ophelia's clit and flicked it, her thighs trembled. Her moans grew louder and more desperate. Her hips ground into my face, and her fingers yanked my hair.

"She's close. Don't let her come yet."

When I eased away, Ophelia whimpered.

"Oliver," she pleaded, her voice ragged and thin. "Please."

"He doesn't have permission to give you what you want." Kiernan positioned himself beside Ophelia's head. "That's my decision."

He bent to kiss her and swallowed her frustrated whine. One hand cupped her breast, and he rolled her nipple to a stiff peak. He toyed with her for what seemed like a few minutes to me, but must have felt like an eternity to her.

"Now," he finally said. "Make her come, Oliver. Then I want your mouth on me."

I buried my face between her thighs. Two fingers slid into her wetness. Her inner walls were hot and slick and gripped me tight. I curled them forward and searched for the rough patch of tissue on her front wall. Her whole body jerked when I found it.

I rubbed that spot in small circles while relentlessly working her clit fast. Her moans climbed in pitch, her knees clamped around my head, and she fluttered around my fingers.

Then she came, arching off the bed and lifting her hips.

Kiernan kissed her, and she screamed while I worked her through her orgasm, drawing out every spasm, flutter, and aftershock until she collapsed, boneless, on the sheets.

My face was slick with her arousal as I sat back on my heels.

Kiernan's dark and hungry eyes met mine across her trembling body. His cock stood rigid and was flushed nearly purple. A steady drip of precome trailed down the underside.

"Come here."

I knelt before him, close enough to smell his musk. His erection was inches from my face—thick and impossibly hard.

"Use your safeword if you need to," Kiernan reminded me.

I leaned forward and wrapped my lips around the head. He groaned above me as I took him deeper. The sound rumbled in his chest and resonated within me. His hand found my hair, and he twisted the strands and held fast as he guided my head.

The stretch of my jaw to take in his girth bordered on painful, but I breathed through my nose and relaxed, letting him in. The head—heavy, hot, and leaking—rested on my tongue.

"Slower," he said. "Take your time. Feel it."

My tongue dragged along his length, and I traced the underside, following the thick vein that ran from base to tip. The ridge beneath the head was pronounced and formed a flared edge where I lingered. His hips jerked forward, forcing more of him deeper.

"That's it. Right there."

I circled the head and swirled around the swollen crown, dipping into the slit where moisture continued to gather. The salty and bitter taste intensified, but I lapped at it like it was honey, drawing more from him and swallowing it down.

His grip in my hair tightened until pain bloomed across my scalp. I moaned around him, and the vibration made him curse under his breath.

"Deeper."

I opened my jaw wider, and when he thrust, it triggered my gag reflex and made my eyes water. I pulled off with a wet gasp.

"Perfect." His thumb brushed the tears from my cheek. "You're doing so well."

I tried again, breathing deep, and swallowing around him as he pushed forward. I fought the urge to gag as his hips rolled, and I let him fuck my face.

My erection throbbed. It was untouched and leaking and harder than it had ever been in my life.

"Hollow your cheeks and suck."

My cheeks caved in around him, making obscene sounds.

The rumble in his chest went straight to my balls. "Enough." He pushed me away. "If you keep going, I'll come, and that's not how I want tonight to end."

Ophelia had recovered enough to watch us. She was propped on one elbow, and her free hand drifted to circle her clit.

"Did I give you permission to touch yourself?"

Her hand froze. "No, sir."

"Then, stop."

She jerked her hand away and rested her palms flat on the sheets.

"Oliver. On your back."

When I rolled over and stretched out on the mattress, my hardness jutted toward the ceiling. It was so rigid the skin stretched taut, aching more with every heartbeat. Kiernan positioned Ophelia above me until she straddled my hips. Her slick heat hovered above me, warmth radiating from her core.

"Take him inside you. Slowly. I want to watch."

She wrapped her hand around me, positioned me at her entrance, then sank down inch by torturous inch.

Slick heat enveloped me, and her inner walls gripped my cock, stretching around me as she took me in. The visual of me disappearing inside her was nearly my undoing.

She sank until she was so deep I could feel the entrance to her womb kissing the tip of my cock.

My hands found her hips, and I dug into her soft flesh hard enough to leave bruises while I fought the desperate urge to thrust up into her.

"Keep still." Kiernan pinned me to the mattress, his palm hot over my racing heart. "Let her set the pace."

She rode me slowly. She rose until only the tip remained inside her, then sank down until I bottomed out again. She repeated the motion over and over. It was deliberate, controlled, and maddening.

Kiernan's hand held me still. My instincts screamed to slam her down and take what I needed. But his palm kept me pinned to the mattress, forcing me to lie there and take whatever she gave.

Then he stood behind her and cupped her breasts, filling his palms with her soft flesh. He kneaded them, rolled her nipples, then pinched until she gasped.

She moaned and ground down harder onto me, clenching around me enough for me to see stars.

His eyes locked on mine over her shoulder as I came apart.

"Kiernan." His name, raw and desperate, tore from me. *"Please."*

"Please what?"

"Touch me."

His hand left her breast and reached between her thighs. He wrapped it around the base of my cock and squeezed.

The added pressure made us both cry out. She clenched harder around me, and I throbbed deeper. His calloused touch was a new point of contact and a new source of overwhelming pleasure.

"Like this?"

"Yes. God, yes."

He worked the exposed length of my erection while she rode me. His callused palm dragged over my sensitive flesh with each rise and fall of her hips. His other hand returned to her breast and tugged her nipple.

The three of us moved in tandem, setting my nerve endings on fire. Pressure built at the base of my spine, and my balls drew up.

"She's going to come." Kiernan's voice was rough and strained with his own arousal. "You're going to feel it. But you don't have permission yet. You hold it."

"Yes, sir."

Ophelia's head fell on Kiernan's shoulder, and she clenched around me in rhythmic waves. She squeezed and released over and over and massaged my length with every spasm of her orgasm.

My muscles locked and trembled with the effort of staving off the release that threatened to rip through me. I bit my cheek until I tasted blood.

"Such good control." Kiernan's praise washed over me. "You've earned your reward."

He lifted Ophelia off me, and she whimpered at the loss. He set her aside on the mattress, and she collapsed onto it, boneless and panting. Aftershocks still rippled through her.

Then Kiernan seized my legs and spread them wider until I was completely exposed. He looked down at me with hungry eyes as his head descended.

I cried out with the first touch of his tongue. When he took me in, it was a revelation. Hot, wet suction engulfed me as he worked me with a skill I'd never experienced. He swallowed half my length in one smooth motion, and when his throat constricted around me, I nearly came on the spot.

He cupped my balls, rolled them gently, then tugged, adding another layer of pleasure. His other hand pressed my hip down and held me in place.

My hands fisted in the sheets until my knuckles were white and my head thrashed on the pillow. Broken sounds—groans, whimpers, and curses—came out of me. My hips fought to thrust, but his grip held me still.

He pulled off long enough to speak. "Come for me, Oliver. Now." When he sucked in the head and his cheeks hollowed, pleasure overwhelmed me and I erupted.

I seized as the violent and all-consuming orgasm exploded, obliterating every thought. I pulsed and emptied everything I had. He swallowed around me, his throat drawing out wave after wave.

Guttural noises I didn't recognize tore out of me. He continued sucking, milking me until I had nothing left to give.

Finally, I collapsed on the mattress, spent and shattered.

Shattered. That was the right word. Whatever walls I'd built around myself—around this part of myself—lay in rubble. I'd knelt for him. Obeyed him. Let him use my mouth, hold me down, decide when I could find release. And instead of feeling diminished, I felt free. Like I'd been carrying something heavy for so long I'd forgotten it was there, and he'd simply taken it from me.

The fire had burned low, and the room was quiet except for three sets of uneven breathing that slowly settled.

Kiernan stretched out, pulling Ophelia to his side with her head pillowed on his shoulder. His free hand found mine, and our fingers interlaced.

"You haven't—" My voice was wrecked and barely a rasp, but he was still hard.

"Tonight was about you. Now, sleep," he commanded.

Ophelia's breathing had already deepened, but I couldn't rest yet.

Instead, I kept watch on Kiernan as his cock softened. Tomorrow, I'd wake him with my mouth, make him lose that iron control, and come down my throat. I'd have Ophelia on her knees, fucking her while Kiernan watched and making her scream my name.

If he gave me permission to.

13

Ophelia

I woke to Oliver's arm heavy across my waist and Kiernan's hand tangled in my hair. Sunlight cut through a gap in the curtains and fell across the three of us in a bright stripe.

Oliver stirred behind me, and his lips brushed my shoulder.

"Morning," he murmured.

Kiernan's eyes opened. Dark and alert, already awake beneath the surface. He looked at how we looked, tangled together in his sheets, and he smiled.

"Breakfast," he said. "Then we talk."

We met in a smaller dining room, where Millie had set out eggs, toast, bacon, and a pot of tea strong enough to strip paint. We ate in silence at first, our knees bumping beneath the table. Oliver kept stealing strips of bacon off Kiernan's plate until Kiernan gave him a look that made him grin and reach for another one anyway.

My mobile vibrated in my pocket, and Viper's name appeared on the screen.

"Sorry. I should take this," I said, pushing from the table to step into the hallway.

"Prima." Viper's tone was clipped as always. "Your leave ends Thursday. What are your plans?"

Thursday. Two days. While I'd acknowledged the amount of time we had left at Greymarch, hearing it out loud from my boss made it feel more real.

"I can report Friday morning, ma'am."

"Right. First, there's another matter to be addressed."

Pinpricks of dread flooded my system. "Yes, ma'am?"

"Typhon is making noise about you joining Unit 23."

"I'm honored."

"Yes, well, I can't say I'm thrilled about you transitioning out of your position with MI6; however, the likelihood we'll conduct more collaborative missions in the future is strong."

"Yes, ma'am," I repeated. "Regarding Morse—"

"Right. He's my next call. Before we can discuss his future within SIS, he'll require medical clearance to return to active duty. It may not happen right away."

Not right away. Did that mean Oliver would remain in Scotland—at Greymarch—while I'd have to return to London? Or would that even be required?

"May I ask what role I'd fill in the unit?" I didn't have training as an assassin, which I understood to be a requirement to be on the team.

"He mentioned you'd start off as a handler when I expressed my concern about how well your skill set fit the unit."

"That's good to hear."

"Before we ring off, is there anything else I should know, Prima?" she asked.

My eyes widened, and the pinpricks returned. "No, ma'am," I responded, hoping the lie wasn't apparent.

"Good. Typhon will contact you directly with the next steps. Until then, consider your leave extended."

I stood in the hallway and stared at my mobile after the line went dead.

When I returned to the breakfast table, both men raised their heads.

"That was Viper," I said, taking my seat.

Kiernan raised his head. "And?"

"She mentioned that Typhon expressed interest in my joining Unit 23."

When Kiernan's brow furrowed and he looked away, it felt like a slap in the face.

"I could turn it down," I said too quickly.

"Why would you do that?" Oliver asked. "That's good, isn't it? You'd be brilliant."

I shrugged a shoulder, wishing Kiernan would look at me again. He didn't.

"She also mentioned you'd be her next call," I said to Oliver. "She indicated that your medical clearance to return to work might not happen right away."

Oliver's fork paused. "Not right away? What does that mean?"

"You almost died." Kiernan's tone held little inflection. "Your body must heal."

"I feel fine."

"You're not." His sharp voice caught me by surprise.

Oliver stabbed at his eggs but didn't speak.

Finally, Kiernan turned to me. "Did she say anything about when you'll be required to return to London?"

"Only that I'd remain on leave until I spoke with Typhon."

I hoped he'd respond positively to that news, but when he merely nodded once, I felt deflated.

"So, what are your plans?" Oliver asked.

"I haven't had a chance—"

"What do you want to happen?" Kiernan's eyes bored into mine.

"I don't know," I answered honestly.

"I want to not think about it until I'm forced to." Oliver's tone was joking, but his eyes weren't.

"That's avoidance," I said.

"That's survival." He settled into his chair. "Look, two weeks ago, I was still in hospital, feeling worse than I had at any other time of my life." He turned to me. "Before that, I spent six months fantasizing about you. And now, I've discovered I'm attracted to men, which is news to me. Can we live in the moments we're given, then figure the rest out later?"

"I'd like that," I finally said when neither Kiernan nor I spoke for several seconds.

"Good." Kiernan pushed away from the table and left the room.

"I hate it when he does that," Oliver said under his breath.

"Maybe he was hoping I'd respond differently."

He shook his head. "Then he wouldn't have said 'good.'"

When he reached for my hand, I took it, wishing I was as optimistic as he was.

"Maybe he's off to the playroom to find things he can torture us into multiple orgasms with."

I smiled. Yes, Oliver was a far better positive thinker than I was.

"How's a walk sound?" I asked after we finished eating.

"Not as good as what I had in mind." He wriggled his eyebrows.

"We can't," I whispered.

Oliver took two steps toward me, leaning in close enough that his warm breath brushed my neck. "But wouldn't it be worth it?" He reached up and ran his hand over my hardened nipple. "Oh, the things I'd make you do, Phee…"

I squeezed my thighs together and leaned into him, about to submit, when Kiernan's footsteps sounded behind us.

"I've got estate business to see to. You—" He stopped dead still when he came around the corner. "My library. *Now.*"

"Sir—"

Before Oliver could say another word, Kiernan stalked toward us and gripped his neck. "What part of now did you not understand, *sub*?" He sounded cold and hard—conveying none of the warmth he'd shown at breakfast before his mood changed. This was the dom we'd witnessed at Thorned Thistle. The man who commanded us without shouting.

Oliver swallowed hard. "Sir, we weren't—"

"Weren't what?" Kiernan gripped harder. "Weren't about to break my rules the moment I left the room?"

Oliver's cheeks flushed crimson.

"I gave you one directive. Your pleasure belongs to me. Not to yourselves or one another. To me." He turned to look at me. "Have you forgotten?"

"No, sir." I sounded small but not frightened. If anything, I'd happily take another punishment, knowing that when it was over, the orgasm would be mind-blowing.

"Yet you chose to disobey."

It wasn't a question. There was no point in denying it. Oliver's hand had been on my breast. My nipple still tingled from his touch. We'd been seconds away from more.

Kiernan released Oliver and stepped away. His posture was rigid, but hunger burned in his gaze, barely masked as anger.

"What part of my order wasn't clear?"

My mind raced. Order? Which one? I had my answer when he turned and walked away, expecting us to follow.

Oliver and I exchanged a glance—his panicked, mine uncertain—before we trailed after him like chastened children.

The curtains in the library were drawn to block the morning light, making the room cool and dark. Kiernan crossed to his desk—a massive oak piece that dominated one corner of the space—and began arranging papers as though we weren't standing there. My heart pounded, wondering what came next.

"Lock the door," he said without looking up.

Its click echoed in the quiet room when I turned it.

He didn't acknowledge us. He sat in his leather chair, reached for another stack of documents, and uncapped a pen. The scratch of writing filled the silence.

Nervous energy radiated off Oliver when he fidgeted beside me.

Minutes passed. Kiernan continued working. We continued standing.

When the tension had wound tight enough to snap, he spoke a single word. "Strip."

Oliver made a choked sound. "Sir—"

"Did I stutter?" Kiernan continued to work, not even raising his head. "You wanted to touch each other so badly. Fine. I'll give you what you wanted. *Naked. Now.*"

Beside me, Oliver pulled his shirt over his head, and I reached for the hem of my jumper. The rustle of fabric was loud in the quiet room.

I removed my bra and let it fall. My jeans followed, then my knickers. The cool air raised goosebumps across my skin as I stood naked before Kiernan's desk while he continued reviewing documents as though we weren't there.

Oliver had stripped down as well. His cock stood hard and flushed, straining toward his stomach.

Kiernan's attention lifted at last. It traveled over me slowly, clinically, then drifted to Oliver, his expression revealing nothing.

"Ophelia. Come here."

I approached the desk on unsteady legs.

"Kneel." He pointed to the floor beside his chair. "Here. Face the room."

While the thick Persian rug cushioned my knees when I sank down, it didn't change the fact that the position left me exposed and vulnerable. Anyone who entered would see me at once—naked and kneeling at his feet like a pet.

Kiernan's hand settled on my head. He threaded my hair with absent affection, the way one might stroke a cat while reading.

"Oliver. There's a chair by the fireplace. Bring it here. Position it facing Ophelia."

Oliver retrieved the wingback chair and placed it where Kiernan had indicated—directly in front of me.

"Sit. Hands on the armrests. Keep them there."

Oliver's fingers gripped the leather hard enough for his knuckles to go white.

"Good boy." Kiernan raised a brow when Oliver visibly bristled, then returned to his work. His hand remained woven in my hair, alternating between pulling and stroking. "Now. Since you seem incapable of controlling yourselves, I'm going to help you learn."

The scratch of his pen resumed.

My heart raced, and my skin prickled with awareness. Oliver sat across from me, rigid and straining. Neither of us spoke. Neither of us moved.

Time stretched. Five minutes. Then ten. Kiernan worked through his stack of papers with maddening focus while I grew increasingly aware of the brush of air across my peaked nipples, the ache building at my core, and the slow pulse of need that intensified as the minutes passed.

A bead of moisture gathered at the tip of Oliver's hardness.

"Don't even think about it," Kiernan said without looking up. "If either of you comes without permission, the consequences will far exceed what you experienced last night."

I squeezed my thighs together. The small motion drew his attention.

"Spread your legs."

I obeyed. The position opened me completely—to the air, to Oliver, to Kiernan's peripheral vision. Wetness gathered, threatening to drip onto my thighs.

"Better." His hand tightened in my hair, tilting my head until I was looking up at him. "You're drenched, aren't you?"

"Yes, sir."

"From what? Are you thinking about what you and Oliver were about to do?"

"No, sir." I swallowed. "From waiting. From being here. From you."

Satisfaction flickered in his eyes, and he half smiled.

"Good girl." He released me and returned to his work. "Oliver. Describe what you see."

"Sir?" Oliver sounded hoarse.

"You heard me. Tell me what you see when you look at her."

Oliver's erection pulsed toward his stomach as he studied me.

"She's…she's beautiful. Her skin is flushed. Her nipples are hard." He swallowed. "She's drenched."

"Go on."

"She's breathing fast. Her fists are clenched. She's trying to remain still, but she can't stop herself." His register dropped lower. "She wants to be touched."

"And you?" Kiernan asked. "What do you want?"

"To touch her. To touch myself. I want—" His eyes flicked to Kiernan, then away. "I need you to tell me what to do."

"That's the first honest thing you've said all morning."

Kiernan set his pen down and rose from the chair. He circled around the desk, passing me without a glance, and stopped behind Oliver's chair.

"You touched her without permission. You were going to make her come without my knowledge." When he grazed Oliver's bare shoulders, he flinched at the contact, then melted into it. "That tells me two things. One, you don't respect my authority. Two, you can't control yourself around her."

"I'm sorry, sir."

"Sorry isn't enough." Kiernan's hands slid down Oliver's chest, over his pectorals, across his stomach. He stopped before reaching his straining cock.

Oliver groaned when Kiernan fisted him. The raw, desperate sound went straight to my core.

"You're so hard," he murmured near his ear. "How long have you been like this? Since breakfast? Since you saw her across the table and started planning what you'd do to her the moment I left?"

"Yes," Oliver gasped when Kiernan tightened his grip. "Yes, sir."

"Hmm." Kiernan stroked him once, twice, three times. Slow and deliberate. "And if I let you come right now? Would you learn anything?"

"No—I don't—please—"

Kiernan's hand stilled. "No. You wouldn't." He released him entirely and stepped away. "You'd come, and then you'd forget. You'd do it again the first chance you got."

Oliver's erection bobbed toward his stomach again, flushed and leaking.

"So instead, we're going to do this my way." Kiernan returned to his chair. "You're going to stay exactly where you are until I decide differently. It may take all day."

"But, sir," I began. "We can't—"

"Can't what?" His dark gaze pinned me in place. "Can't wait? Can't control yourselves? That's the problem, Ophelia. You think your pleasure belongs to you. It doesn't."

He returned to his papers.

The next hour was agony. I tried not to watch the clock on the mantle, but I couldn't stop myself. Periodically, Kiernan would pause his work and attend to us. He'd stroke my hair, then continue down to trace my collarbone, my breasts, the curve of my waist. But never lower, never where I wanted him most. Never where I needed him. Other times, he'd rise and circle Oliver's chair, trailing his hands across his shoulders, his chest, stroking him until Oliver shook and moaned, then releasing him before he could come.

The pattern was unpredictable. He'd touch me, then Oliver, or only one of us. He'd simply look at us. The weight of his attention alone was enough to make me clench around nothing.

My arousal pulsed through me, coiled tight in my belly, and slicked my thighs. My nerve endings were on fire, screaming for stimulation that never came.

"Ophelia." Kiernan's voice cut through the haze, and he pushed his chair away from the desk. "Stand and come here."

I rose on shaking legs and approached him.

"Bend over. Legs spread."

When I leaned forward and pressed my palms to the cool oak, Oliver's breath caught behind me and Kiernan's chair creaked.

"Look at her, Oliver. See how wet she is." His finger traced down my spine, over the curve of my arse, and between my cheeks. I trembled. "She's been dripping for the past hour. Desperate. Aching." His finger slid through my folds, and I cried out. "All that yearning, and she can't do anything about it. Can you, pet?"

"No, sir," I cried.

"That's right." He circled my entrance, teasing, then pushed one finger inside. My walls clenched greedily around him. "Your body knows who it belongs to. Even if your mind hasn't caught up."

He added a second finger and thrust—slow, steady strokes that built the pressure without providing relief.

I rocked into his hand, chasing more, but he'd anticipated me. As soon as I got close, he'd slow down or stop entirely, leaving me gasping and on the edge.

"Please," I whimpered. "Sir, please—"

"Not yet." When he withdrew, I nearly sobbed. "On your knees. Where you were before."

I sank down, shaking.

"Look at me." Kiernan lifted his glistening fingers to his mouth and sucked them clean before returning to his work.

The second hour was worse.

Kiernan made several calls—estate business, from what I could gather. He conducted them with perfect composure, remaining calm while Oliver and I suffered in silence.

He hadn't forgotten us, though.

When one call ended, he'd gesture one of us forward. He'd stroke Oliver's hardness with one hand while making notes with the other. He'd call me to him and stroke my pussy while speaking to his solicitor about property boundaries. It was clinical and controlled, and he always stopped before we could orgasm.

Small, broken noises escaped Oliver's lips despite his best efforts to remain silent. His cock was an angry red and so hard it looked painful. Whenever Kiernan touched him, he jerked like he'd been electrified.

I wasn't faring any better. The yearning had become unbearable. I'd lost track of how many times he'd brought me to the edge and left me there. I was a wound-up spring, ready to shatter at the slightest provocation.

Kiernan set his mobile on the desk. "Get on the sofa."

Oliver sat at one end, and I sat as far away from him as the small space allowed.

"No." Kiernan rose and stepped closer. "Together. Oliver, rest on the arm. Ophelia, sit with your back to his chest."

We rearranged ourselves. Oliver's breath was hot and ragged as he pressed into me.

Kiernan crouched in front of us.

"You want to touch each other so badly." His words were soft, almost gentle. "I can see it. Feel it. The way you're trembling." He reached out and brought Oliver's hand to my breast. "Go ahead."

Oliver's breath caught. "Sir?"

"Touch her. You have permission."

Oliver's thumb brushed my nipple, and I arched into the contact, moaning.

"That's it." Hunger was apparent in the words he spoke. "Show me what you wanted to do this morning."

Oliver's other hand traced my hip, my thigh, then dipped between my legs. When he found my clit, I cried out and jerked in his arms.

"Feel how wet she is?" Kiernan asked.

"God, yes." Oliver sounded wrecked as he circled, stroked, then slipped inside me. "She's soaked."

"Because of me. Because I made her wait." Kiernan leaned closer. "You could learn from that, Oliver. The anticipation is half the pleasure."

Oliver's rhythm grew more urgent. He thrust his digits into me while his thumb worked my clit. The pressure built, spiraling higher, faster—

"Stop."

Oliver's hand froze, and I sobbed with frustration.

"Not yet." Kiernan's fingers closed around Oliver's wrist and tugged his hand away from me. "Now." He rose and returned to his desk. "The two of you on your knees. Over here, where I can see you."

More time passed. I could no longer see the clock, so I couldn't tell how long we remained there. It should have gotten easier. I was so far gone that the edge had become my constant state. But Kiernan knew exactly how to keep us suffering.

Eventually, he abandoned the pretense of working and studied us while he asked questions.

"Oliver. How badly do you want to come?"

"More than anything, sir." his voice was barely recognizable. "Please. I can't—"

"Not yet." Kiernan glanced in my direction. "Ophelia. If I told you to make him come right now, would you?"

The question made my heart stutter. "Yes, sir."

"Even though you haven't come yourself?"

"Yes." I swallowed. "I want—" I looked at Oliver. "I want to give him that."

Kiernan was quiet. When he spoke again, his demeanor had changed.

"You're learning," he said softly, cupping my face and kissing me.

When he pulled away, his hand fisted in Oliver's hair and he kissed him with the same intensity. Oliver groaned as Kiernan lifted him to his feet.

"Ophelia, on your knees in front of him."

When I knelt, his cock bobbed in front of my face, flushed and leaking. I looked up, waiting.

"Use your mouth."

I took him in without hesitation.

Oliver's cry echoed through the library. His hands flew to my head, then jerked away—realizing he hadn't been given permission.

"Good boy," Kiernan murmured. "You can touch her."

Oliver's touch was gentle as I worked him with my lips and tongue, and I could feel him pulse.

"You do not have permission to come," Kiernan said, reaching down to tug on one of Oliver's nipples. "If you do, you won't again for days."

Within minutes, he was trembling, his breath coming in harsh gasps. "Sir, I'm going to—"

 Kiernan's hand gripped my neck. "Stop."

I eased away, but it was too late.

Oliver's whole body convulsed.

Kiernan's hand stroked through my hair. "Good girl. You did beautifully. Remain on your knees but watch."

I looked up at him with longing. I was wound tight—aching and empty.

"Please, sir." I barely recognized my own voice. "Please."

"Come here," he said to Oliver instead.

When he approached, he turned him to face the desk and bent him over the oak surface. Fabric rustled, then his belt clinked. "Ask for it."

Oliver groaned. "Please."

"Please what?"

"Punish me." The plea tore from him.

"For what?"

"Coming without permission."

Kiernan circled the desk and held the belt near Oliver's face. "You have a choice. I warned you that if you came, it would be the last time you did for days."

Oliver whimpered.

"Or you can accept the strike of my belt. Which will it be?"

"The belt, sir. *Please.*"

"How many?"

Oliver's words were raw. "Twenty, sir?"

Kiernan tapped his hand with the leather. "Twenty? Ophelia, does that seem fair? You received the same for touching yourself."

I shook my head as tears spilled over onto my cheeks. "I don't know," I cried.

"Thirty," Kiernan said without inflection, sparing me from further comment. "He touched you without permission. He made you an accomplice to his disobedience. Then he came when I explicitly told him not to."

Oliver's forehead dropped to the desk, and his shoulders shook.

"Count them," Kiernan told me. "Out loud. If you lose count, we start over."

The first crack of leather on skin made me flinch. Oliver jerked, but he didn't cry out.

"One," I whispered.

The second strike landed harder. Oliver gripped the far edge of the desk, knuckles bone-white.

"Two."

Kiernan found a rhythm—steady, measured, each blow landing with devastating accuracy. By ten, Oliver was breathing in harsh gasps. By fifteen, tears streamed down his face. By twenty, he was sobbing openly and trembling.

"Twenty," I counted.

Kiernan paused. His hand stroked down Oliver's spine with tenderness. "Ten more. You're doing well."

"Please—" Oliver's voice cracked. "Sir, I'm sorry. I'm so sorry."

"I know." Kiernan's tone gentled, but the belt cracked again.

"Twenty-one."

Each remaining strike landed harder than the last. Each one echoed through me as if he was striking me too. By the time I counted thirty, my throat was raw.

Kiernan set the belt aside, then helped Oliver stand. He turned him gently and drew him to his chest. Oliver collapsed into him, sobbing. Kiernan held him, one hand cradling his head, and the other rubbing slow circles on his shoulder, avoiding the punished skin below.

"It's over," Kiernan murmured. "You took it beautifully. I'm proud of you."

Oliver clutched Kiernan's shirt. He shook with the force of his emotion—not only from the pain, but from the release. The guilt he'd been carrying since he came without permission was purging itself through his tears.

"Ophelia." Kiernan looked at me over Oliver's shoulder. "Come here."

I stood and crossed to them on unsteady legs. Kiernan drew me into their embrace. I wrapped my arm around Oliver's waist and rested my cheek on his shoulder. The three of us stood tangled together while Oliver's sobs gradually quieted.

"Neither of you will come again until I give you permission," Kiernan said eventually.

My body throbbed at the words. I was still achingly aroused—hours of edging had left me raw—but I understood now.

"Yes, sir," I whispered.

Oliver nodded.

"Good." Kiernan released us. His expression changed again—still commanding, but warmer now. "Get dressed."

We gathered our scattered clothes in silence. Every motion reminded me how unsatisfied I was. My nipples brushed my bra, and I whimpered. Oliver winced as the fabric of his trousers scraped his welted skin.

When we were dressed, Kiernan stepped forward.

"We're going to Thorned Thistle tonight," he said. "But not yet. First, you're going to help Millie prepare dinner."

Oliver blinked. "Sir?"

"You heard me. Kitchen duty. You'll assist with whatever she wants—chopping, stirring, setting the table. You'll be useful and polite and focused on the task at hand." He half smiled. "And you'll do it while remembering exactly how aroused you are. How much you want release."

My legs pressed together involuntarily.

"When you reach for a knife, you'll feel the ache between your legs," Kiernan continued. "When you bend to retrieve a pot, you'll remember what it felt like to be spread open on my desk. And when dinner is finished and we walk through those tunnels to the club, you'll be trembling with need."

He crossed to the door and unlocked it.

"Go. I'll find you when it's time."

The kitchen was warm and fragrant with roasting vegetables when we arrived. Millie looked up from her chopping board, her face creasing with surprise.

"Lord Lockhart sent us to help," I said.

"Did he, now?" Millie studied us. Whatever she concluded, she kept it to herself. "Right, then. Oliver, you're on potato duty. Ophelia, start on the salad."

We worked in silence at first. The mundane tasks should have been grounding—washing lettuce, peeling potatoes, arranging vegetables on a platter. But Kiernan had been right. Every motion amplified my awareness of my want.

When I bent to retrieve a colander from the lower cabinet, the phantom press of Kiernan's fingers ghosted through me. When I reached up for the olive oil, my nipples brushing my shirt sent sparks racing down my spine. The kitchen was warm, and my skin was flushed, and every breath I drew carried the memory of Oliver's mouth on me—denied at the last moment, leaving me gasping and empty.

Beside me, Oliver was faring worse.

He repositioned himself relentlessly, unable to find a position that didn't aggravate his welted skin or remind him of his own unfulfilled arousal. When Millie asked him to check on the roast in the oven, he bent down and his breath caught audibly. His hand shook as he basted the meat.

"Are you all right?" Millie asked, not unkindly.

"Fine," Oliver managed. "Just—tired."

She nodded once, then returned to her work.

An hour passed. Then two. We set the table in the formal dining room—crystal glasses, silver flatware, cloth napkins folded into intricate shapes. The trips I made from the kitchen to the dining room were their own small torture. By the time Millie declared everything ready, I was vibrating with tension.

Oliver caught my hand as we left the kitchen. His grip was tight, bordering on frantic.

"I don't know how much more I can take," he admitted.

"We can take whatever he gives us. That's the point."

His laugh was uneven. "When did you become the expert?"

"Last night. When I learned what happens when you earn it instead of stealing it."

Kiernan spoke from the doorway. "Time to get ready."

I almost asked about dinner, then thought better of it. My hunger wasn't for food anyway.

14

Oliver

The clothes laid out on my bed made me hard despite everything—or perhaps because of it.

Black leather trousers and two wide cuffs with O-rings on the outside lay on the bedspread, and nothing else.

I stripped off my shirt and jeans, wincing as the fabric dragged across my still-tender arse, where Kiernan's belt had left welts I'd feel for days.

The leather trousers were tight, molding to my body like a second skin, and the weight of the cuffs was grounding as I fastened them around my wrists.

When I caught my reflection in the mirror, I barely recognized myself. This was who I was becoming. Who Kiernan was making me.

Ophelia was already in the corridor when I emerged, wearing a dress so thin her nipples were visible. The black material skimmed her curves, ending mid-thigh, hiding nothing.

My mouth went dry. "Kiernan's waiting," I managed.

We found him outside the playroom. His gaze traveled over us with dark approval that made me strain beneath the leather.

"Beautiful." He traced a finger down Ophelia's spine, and she shivered. "Both of you."

He opened the playroom door, then motioned for us to go in first.

A leather bench dominated the center of the room. On a side table sat a small case that made my stomach clench in anticipation.

"Tonight is about preparation." Kiernan closed the door behind us.

He crossed to the case and opened it. Nestled in velvet were three plugs—graduated sizes, all smooth black silicone. My arse clenched involuntarily.

"These stay in until I remove them." His voice dropped to that register that made my spine straighten and my cock throb. "You'll wear them during dinner. You'll eat and drink and make polite conversation, and by the time we leave for the Thorned Thistle, your bodies will be aching for what comes next."

I couldn't breathe. Having a toy inside me—there—for hours…

"Ophelia. Bend over the bench."

His finger was slick with lubricant and circled her entrance but stopped short of penetration.

"Relax." He rested his hand on her spine. "You've done this before?"

"Once. A long time ago."

"Then, you know the key is patience." As the tip of his finger pressed inward, she exhaled slowly. "Good. Yes, like that."

Her nails made indentations in the leather, and she gasped as he positioned the plug, then gradually worked it all the way in.

"Stand," he told her before turning to me. "Your turn, Oliver. Strip but leave the cuffs on."

When I did, my erection sprang free. I started toward the bench, but Kiernan stopped me.

"You've never had anything inside you." It wasn't a question.

"No."

"Then, we go slowly. If you need to stop, you say red. If you need me to slow down, you say yellow. Understood?"

"Yes, sir."

He motioned to Ophelia. "Move under the bench and suck him off while I work him open."

She positioned herself beneath me, and when I bent over, her tongue circled my length.

"Focus on her," Kiernan ordered from behind me. "Let her distract you."

Her lips wrapped around me at the same time Kiernan's slicked finger pressed into my hole.

I jerked at the dual sensation—wet heat engulfing my erection, cool pressure circling my entrance. My body didn't know which sensation to chase.

"Breathe." Kiernan's voice was steady. "Push back. That's it."

His finger breached me.

The intrusion was strange—not painful, but foreign. A pressure I'd never felt before. Ophelia took me deeper. Her tongue worked the underside of my cock, and I groaned as the sensations blurred together.

"Good." Kiernan added a second finger. "You're doing so well. Feel how you open for me."

As he stretched me, my muscles relaxed despite myself. Then he crooked his fingers forward and touched a spot that made my muscles seize.

"There. Right there," he said with dark satisfaction.

Pleasure exploded in me—sharp and bright and nothing like I'd ever experienced. I throbbed in Ophelia's mouth, and my hips jerked backward, trying to get more of that pressure, that impossible sensation.

"Fuck—" I gasped. "I can't—it's too—"

"You can. And you will." He withdrew his fingers, and I nearly sobbed at the loss.

He crossed the room, opened a cabinet, then returned with a different case.

"This is a prostate massager," he said. "It's going to stay where it is until I remove it. When you take a breath, you'll feel it pressing on the spot I just found."

I jerked, dripping.

"Ophelia. Keep him distracted."

She took me deep again as Kiernan inserted the toy. The tip was wider than his fingers, and my body resisted, then slowly yielded as he pressed forward.

"Relax. Let it in."

I seized the bench so hard the leather creaked. The stretch burned, but beneath it was a spark of pleasure, building as the toy pushed deeper. Ophelia sucked me hard. Her tongue swirled around the head, and I focused on that as Kiernan worked the massager into me.

"We're close." His voice was gentle now. "The widest part…and…there."

I closed around the base, and it settled into place, making me cry out. The pressure was constant, inescapable. As he'd warned, the thing moved when I inhaled. I was so close—so fucking close—

"Don't." Kiernan's command echoed in the haze. "Don't you dare come until I say."

I shook as I struggled to obey. Ophelia eased off, pressing soft kisses to my length while I fought for control. The device ground without mercy, and dawning horror crept over me—this sensation wasn't going to fade.

"Stand up. Both of you."

Ophelia rose first. I tried to follow, but my knees buckled, and I grabbed the edge of the bench, breathing hard.

I tried to scream, but nothing came out. As much as I wanted the agony to end, I wanted to come more. As soon as he'd allow it.

"Oliver?" Kiernan crossed to me and gripped my jaw, forcing eye contact.

"I can't—you have to take it out."

"Use your safeword."

"No."

"Then, you'll leave it in. You'll do so because I told you to. Because you want to please me. And because by the time I finally let you come tonight, it's going to be the most intense orgasm of your life."

I twitched.

"Dinner's waiting," he said, positioning himself on my opposite side from Ophelia.

I took one cautious step. Then another. Each one was agony—the toy nudging, pressing, sending waves of sensation impossible to escape. I dug my fingernails into Kiernan's arm hard enough to leave marks.

By the time we reached the dining room, I was shaking.

Dinner, more formal than they previously were, was torture.

Candles flickered in silver holders, and stemware caught the light. Millie had set the table with the good china, as if this were a celebration rather than an exercise in torment.

Millie had outdone herself. Roast lamb with rosemary and garlic. New potatoes glistening with butter. Spring vegetables that Ophelia and I had helped prepare.

I tasted none of it.

Kiernan cut into his meat with infuriating calm. "The lamb is excellent."

I made a sound that might have been an agreement. Or a whimper. I wasn't sure anymore.

Across from me, Ophelia's cheeks were heated. Her movements were measured, deliberate—the guarded motions of someone trying to remain still. When our eyes met, my own need stared back at me.

We were both drowning. And Kiernan was watching us sink with dark satisfaction.

"More wine?" He lifted the bottle, the picture of a gracious host.

"Please."

His hands were steady as he poured, while mine trembled. The wine was excellent—a rich Bordeaux that deserved to be savored. I drank it like water, hoping the alcohol might dull the relentless stimulation.

It didn't.

When I reached for my glass and the device ground inside me, my hand jerked, nearly knocking the crystal over.

"Problem?" Kiernan smirked.

"No, sir." The words came out strangled.

I was grateful when Ophelia's gaze met mine. It was a reminder that I wasn't alone in this exquisite hell. But it didn't help. Nothing helped. I was trapped in a body that had become a live wire, and the man whose gaze missed nothing controlled my pleasure.

Kiernan asked about the book Ophelia had been reading. She answered in fragments when she shifted in her seat. He inquired about my recovery, whether I'd been sleeping better. I managed monosyllables while fighting the urge to beg.

Twice, I clutched the edge of the table hard enough that my knuckles went white. Kiernan watched me with knowing eyes, eating calmly while I fell apart.

"Dessert?" he asked when the main course was cleared.

"No." The word came out too fast, too urgent. I forced myself to add, "Thank you, sir."

His smile widened. "Perhaps later, then."

By the time he declared dinner finished, I was wrecked. Flushed. Sweating. I'd been hard for so long it hurt. Standing when he told us to rise took all of the control I possessed.

"Time for the club," he said.

The walk to the wine cellar was endless. Each step drove it deeper and increased the pressure. Regardless of how cautious I was, the stimulation was relentless.

At the cellar door, Kiernan paused.

He unlocked the latch. "Remember, your bodies belong to me tonight. Your pleasure, your pain, your responses—all of it is mine. You will feel. You will want. You will ache. And you will not come until I decide you've earned the privilege."

The walk in the tunnel seemed endless.

I could barely think. Ophelia's hand found mine in the darkness, her grip as urgent as my own.

When we emerged into the club, the change in atmosphere was immediate. Music pulsed in the space—something low and rhythmic that seemed to sync with my heartbeat. The air was warmer here, heavy with anticipation and the faint musk of bodies in motion.

Kiernan walked us straight onto the main floor.

Heads turned. Eyes traveled over my bare chest, the cuffs on my wrists, and my obvious bulge. I felt exposed in a way that had nothing to do with the lack of clothing. They could see my hunger. My need. The way I trembled.

A woman in a corset caught my eye and smiled knowingly. A man at the bar raised his glass in what might have been appreciation or amusement. I kept my gaze forward, focused on the broad expanse of Kiernan's shoulders, as he guided us over to Callen, who waited by the bar.

There were two cushions on the floor beside the leather armchair where Kiernan sat—positions clearly intended for us.

He settled his hand on my shoulder. "Kneel, then rest on your heels."

I sank down, and the position drove the massager impossibly deeper.

The pressure was constant now, unrelenting. There was no readjusting, no way to escape it.

"Kiernan." Callen looked at us with obvious appreciation. "I see you've been busy."

"They're learning."

Ophelia knelt beside me, close enough that our shoulders almost touched. Her breathing was uneven. When I glanced at her, the flush spread down her chest, and her thighs pressed together as if she could create friction through sheer force of will.

People stopped to speak with him. Club members I didn't recognize, faces I couldn't focus on because my attention was consumed by the massager's relentless stimulation.

"Lovely pair," someone commented. "Yours?"

"Mine," Kiernan confirmed, his fingers tightening on my shoulder.

Mine. I was his.

"How long have you been training them?"

"Not long. They're naturals."

A woman crouched down to my eye level. Her perfume was heavy, floral. She studied my face with an appraiser's gaze.

"He's beautiful when he's desperate," she said to Kiernan. "Those eyes. Like he's about to break."

I was. I was going to shatter. I couldn't take much more of this—the pressure, the need, the humiliation of kneeling here while people discussed me like I was an object to be evaluated.

"He's stronger than he knows."

His touch was claiming and steadying, as he squeezed my shoulder, then stroked my hair. I leaned into it without meaning to, starving for any contact, any anchor.

More people came and went. Conversations happened above me that I couldn't follow. Time lost all meaning. There was only the burn in my knees, the throb of my cock, and Kiernan's hand in my hair—the only thing keeping me tethered to reality.

When he finally rose, I was close to tears.

"Come, I have one more thing planned before we leave." Kiernan led us down to the observation level, but instead of stopping at the windows, he opened a door and motioned us inside. The room beyond was small and intimate, with a bed draped in dark silk, soft lighting, and a large mirror on the same wall as the door.

"This is a performance suite," Kiernan explained. "The glass is two-way. They can see everything. We can't see them."

The mirror reflected the bed, the three of us, and my flushed and desperate face. Behind it, anyone could be watching—or no one at all.

"Color?" Kiernan looked between us.

"Green, sir," Ophelia said.

"Also green."

"Good." He looked at me. "On the bed. Oliver, on your back."

I obeyed, so hard I hurt.

"Ophelia. Remove your dress and straddle his face. You're going to come on his tongue while they watch."

She stripped and climbed over me, positioning herself above my face. Through the haze of my own need, I noticed she was so wet, so swollen. She needed this as badly as I did.

"Louder," Kiernan ordered. "I want to hear you."

I pulled her down and buried my tongue in her folds.

She cried out, and I worked her frantically—circling her clit, thrusting into her, doing everything I could to make her come.

I was so hard. So needy. So fucking close to breaking.

"That's it," Kiernan murmured, coming to stand beside us. "Show them who you belong to," he said, reaching out to pinch her nipple. "Come now, beautiful girl."

Ophelia's thighs clamped around my head as she came with a scream, flooding my mouth with her release. I licked and sucked until she collapsed sideways onto the mattress.

I lay there, panting, aching, praying I'd be allowed my own release soon. I'd done as he'd asked. Everything he'd asked. Surely now—

"Kiernan stroked her cheek. "You did well. Now, let's go."

"Please," I begged. "Sir, I need—"

"Not here. Not yet." He helped Ophelia up and handed her the dress.

I barely made it through Kiernan's bedroom door before my knees gave out.

He caught me, lowering me to the bed with surprising gentleness. He unfastened my trousers and stripped them away, leaving me naked except for the cuffs.

"Ophelia, take off your dress, then go into the bathroom, remove and clean the plug, then return and join us."

Her footsteps faded. Then Kiernan's weight settled behind me on the mattress.

"On your hands and knees."

When I did, the shaking increased.

"Tell me how this feels," he said from behind me, rocking the toy gently. I arched off the mattress as the sensation intensified, and I nearly came.

"Fuck—please, I need—"

"What do you need?"

"I need to come. Please. I've been—during dinner, the tunnels, I can't—"

"Not yet." He looked up as Ophelia returned. "Crawl under him and spread your legs. Oliver, make her come again. No hands."

She positioned herself beneath me, and I lowered my mouth to her cunt while Kiernan worked the thing into me in slow circles.

When I moaned, the vibration made her gasp. The toy hit my prostate again, and my hips jerked helplessly into empty air. I was trapped between them—giving pleasure, denying my own—and it was driving me out of my mind.

I kept working her, desperate to make her come, desperate for Kiernan to finally give me release. When her legs locked around my head and she screamed and came, relief flooded through me.

"Good girl," Kiernan said to her. "Now, watch."

Ophelia got out from under me, and fabric rustled, then Kiernan's clothes hit the floor, followed by the click of the lube bottle.

Then his hands gripped my hips from behind.

"I'm going to fuck you now." His tone was controlled despite the hunger in it. "And you're going to come with me inside you. If you don't want that, use your safeword now."

"I want it." The words tore from my throat. "Please. God—"

He withdrew the massager, and I sobbed at the emptiness, but only for a moment.

First, the cool lube drizzled on my entrance, then the head of his cock pressed against it—thick and hot. He pushed forward, and I stretched around him, opening, yielding. The burn was sharper than before, but beneath it was the spark of sensation, building as he pressed deeper.

"Breathe," he murmured. "Let me in."

I willed my body to relax, and he slid deeper. Inch by inch, filling me, stretching me as I'd never experienced. When he bottomed out, his hips flush with my arse, I felt impossibly full. Claimed. Complete.

"Mine," he groaned. "Both of you are mine."

Then he thrust.

The first punched a groan from my chest. He'd angled himself perfectly—every stroke dragged across my prostate, sending lightning through my veins. I couldn't think, couldn't breathe, could only feel him taking me, owning me.

"Touch yourself," he ordered. "Stroke yourself while I fuck you."

My hand wrapped around my erection—finally, finally—and I stroked in time with his thrusts. The dual sensation was overwhelming. Pleasure built, spiraling higher and higher until I couldn't tell where one ended and another began.

"*Now.*" He stuttered with his own approaching climax. "Come now."

An orgasm crashed through me like nothing I'd ever experienced. My body seized. The world went bright, and I jerked as I spilled over my fist and onto the bed. Kiernan's thrusts stuttered, he buried himself deep, and the pulse of his release vibrated inside me as he came.

For several heartbeats, we barely breathed.

Then he eased out gently, rolled me over, and collapsed between me and Ophelia. His hand found mine, then hers, linking the three of us together.

I was drifting toward sleep when Kiernan's mobile buzzed on the nightstand.

He reached for it lazily, still half-tangled with us. But the moment he read the screen, he went rigid.

"Kiernan?" My voice was thick with exhaustion. "What is it?"

He was already out of bed, pulling on his trousers. "Remain here. Do not leave this room."

He was gone in an instant, leaving us staring at each other in confusion.

15

Kiernan

A package arrived, my lord. Hand-delivered. Urgent.

I read it twice, then glanced at Oliver and Ophelia, who were still tangled together on my bed. Oliver's eyes were closed. His breathing was deep and even, and one arm lay across Ophelia's waist. Her dark hair spread across the pillow like silk, and she watched me with quiet curiosity.

Mere moments ago, I'd been inside Oliver for the first time. Had felt him come apart beneath me and heard him cry out my name like a prayer.

Ophelia's eyes were bright with tears and desire and joy as she watched us.

Then, I felt as though I had everything. Dread settled over me as my gut told me how naive I'd been to believe that was possible.

"Kiernan? What is it?" Oliver asked.

"Remain here," I snapped. "Do not leave this room."

Ophelia's brow creased. "Is everything all right?"

After pulling my trousers and shirt on—not bothering with buttons—I left without responding.

My bare feet were silent on the stone floors as I made my way to the great hall where Millie waited beneath the portrait of my grandfather. In the dim light, her face was drawn tight, and she held a wrapped package in both hands as if it might bite her.

"It was left at the gate, my lord. The groundskeeper found it twenty minutes ago." Her voice was low, hushed, as if she sensed danger seeping from it. "No one saw who delivered it."

I took it from her. The wrap was plain brown, the kind you could buy at any shop. No postmark. No return address. My name was printed in block letters—not handwritten.

"Thank you, Millie. That will be all."

She hesitated, then retreated without another word.

I carried the package to the library and locked the door behind me.

I set it on the desk and stood over it, studying the clean folds, the neat tape, the utter anonymity of it. The instincts I'd honed during my tenure with MI6, then Unit 23, screamed a warning.

I retrieved a letter opener from the drawer, sliced through the tape with one clean motion, and the paper fell away. I did the same to open the box, then dumped its contents.

A manila envelope landed with a heavy thud. It was thick with contents I already knew I didn't want to see.

I opened it too, then upended it over the desk.

Photos spilled across the polished wood.

The first image showed Oliver and Ophelia walking the grounds of Greymarch. They were laughing, her hand on his arm, their faces turned toward each other with the easy intimacy of lovers. Behind them rose the eastern tower of my castle, unmistakable with the backdrop of the gray Highland sky.

Someone had been on the grounds of Greymarch.

The second image showed me standing at the library window. This window. The silhouette was clear enough— my height, my build, the distinctive line of my shoulders. I was looking out at the grounds, unaware that I was being observed, captured, and documented.

The third showed all three of us in the conservatory. Oliver's brow was furrowed, and Ophelia leaned on me, with her hand on my chest. My arm was around her waist, pulling her close.

I spread the remaining images across the desk with numb fingers. A dozen, then two dozen, then more. Each one a violation. Each one proof that our privacy had been an illusion.

The progression told a story. Walks on the grounds, day after day. Dinner in the formal dining room, visible on the opposite side of the tall windows. The three of us in the library, tangled together on the sofa. Every tender moment and stolen glance—all of it recorded by someone with a telephoto lens and the patience of a predator.

Except those weren't the worst of them. My hands went still as I sifted through images from the Thorned Thistle. The semi-private room. Glass walls designed for exhibitionism, for the thrill of being seen by willing observers inside the club. Not for this. Never for this.

Most were from our scene earlier tonight, captured in crisp detail by someone who should never have been able to get close enough to take these shots.

I had to look away and breathe deeply until the roaring in my ears subsided.

My mind raced with the implications. Someone had gotten inside the club. Past the security measures that Rafe had spent years building. Past the vetted membership, the private entrances, the staff who would die before betraying a member's identity.

I turned over the final image and found a single sheet of paper beneath it.

The words were typed and centered on the page. No signature. No identifying marks.

Did you think no one was watching? They leave tonight. The photos go public if they're still there by morning.

I read it once. Then again.

Whoever sent this wanted Oliver and Ophelia gone.

I gripped the edge of the desk and willed myself to breathe. To think. To push past the ice in my veins.

Who?

The question spiraled outward, branching into a thousand possibilities. One of the founding partners' enemies? A rival establishment? Someone I'd crossed in my years with Unit 23—a target who'd escaped, a colleague I'd wronged, an enemy I'd made without knowing it?

The list of people who might want to destroy me was long. I'd spent nine years doing the kind of work that bred grudges. I'd killed in service to the Crown. I'd ruined lives, ended careers, toppled criminal empires. Any one of a hundred people might want revenge.

Except this felt different. Personal. The demand wasn't for money, information, or access. The demand was that I end this specific relationship. That I send them away.

Why?

The images could destroy their careers. MI6 didn't officially forbid relationships between operatives, but there were limits to institutional tolerance. Pictures of two agents in a BDSM club with a third party—another operative, no less—would end their advancement. Their security clearances would be revoked. Their employment terminated. Viper would have no choice but to cut them loose, no matter how valuable they were. And Typhon certainly wouldn't pick either of them up for the unit.

The evidence could also destroy the Thorned Thistle. Everything we'd built over five years—the trust, the discretion, the sanctuary we'd created for people like us—would be gone in an instant. Every member could be exposed. All secrets laid bare. Careers ruined. Marriages ended. Lives shattered.

They could also destroy me. A viscount caught on camera in acts that would make the tabloids salivate for months. My family name dragged through the mud. My position with SIS compromised, my usefulness as an operative ended. I didn't care about that. I'd survived worse. I'd survived loss and grief and years of self-imposed isolation. Exposure was nothing in comparison.

What I couldn't survive was to be the reason Oliver and Ophelia were burned.

In an age of deepfakes and AI-generated images, photographs alone proved nothing. If the worst happened, they could claim fabrication. The technology existed to create images indistinguishable from reality—and that same technology provided cover for denying reality when it was captured on film. It wasn't a perfect defense. The accusation alone would cause damage. But it was something. A thread to pull later, when the immediate threat was mitigated.

Nothing changed that I'd brought this on them. By wanting them. By letting them in. By convincing myself I could have this, that I deserved happiness, that my darkness wouldn't poison everything it touched.

I'd been a fool.

I had to get them out. Tonight. Now.

If I told them the truth, they'd want to stay. I knew them well enough to be certain of that. Oliver would dig in his heels, would insist on facing the threat together, would refuse to leave my side. Ophelia would analyze and strategize, would want to identify the sender, would argue that running solved nothing.

They'd be right.

Running solved nothing. But it did buy time.

The only way to protect them now was to make them leave. Tonight. Without explanations, without arguments, without giving them time to refuse.

I had to make them hate me enough to go.

I reached for my mobile and rang Callen's number.

He answered on the second ring. "Kiernan. It's late." His voice was rough with sleep, but alert. We'd both been trained to wake quickly.

"I need a helicopter. Now. To take Oliver and Ophelia to the Glasgow safe house."

Silence stretched across the line. I could picture him sitting up in bed, all traces of sleep vanishing as his mind transitioned into operational mode.

"What's going on?"

"I can't explain. Not yet. Trust that they need to leave tonight."

"Kiernan—"

"Please."

We'd been friends since we were kids, yet I could count on one hand the number of times I'd used that word with him. I gave orders, made requests, and issued commands. I didn't beg.

Callen heard it. Whatever he'd been about to say died in his throat.

"Twenty minutes," he said. "I'll transport them myself."

"Thank you."

I ended the call before he could ask anything else.

Twenty minutes. Twenty minutes to prepare myself to destroy everything I'd built with them.

I gathered the photos, stacked them neatly, with the edges aligned and faces down, then slid them into the manila envelope along with the note. I locked it in the bottom drawer of my desk and poured myself a whiskey that I drank in two swallows.

The burn gave me a focal point to distract me from an ache worse than any I'd ever known.

I set down the glass and walked out of the library, prepared to destroy my own heart.

The corridor stretched before me, dark and cold. My bare feet made no sound on the stone. The castle felt different—not a refuge but a trap. I'd let two people inside my walls, and someone was watching the whole time.

The only thing left was to fail them one more time, in a way they'd never forgive.

I stopped outside the door. Put my hand on the wood and couldn't make myself turn the handle. Three breaths. Four. My fingers were numb when I finally pushed it open.

They were sitting on the bed. Ophelia was wearing Oliver's white linen shirt. His bare shoulders were visibly tense with worry as he put on his trousers. They'd been talking—I could see it in the way they turned to me with matching expressions, the concern that creased both their brows.

"Kiernan?" Ophelia's voice was soft. "What's wrong? You've been gone almost half an hour."

I couldn't look at her. If I did, I'd break.

"You're leaving. Tonight."

The words came out flat and dead, the voice of a man already gone.

Oliver stood. "What are you talking about?"

"Pack your things. A helicopter is waiting."

"A helicopter?" Ophelia stood, and the shirt fell to her thighs. "I don't understand. What's happened?"

I turned toward the door.

"Kiernan." Oliver's hand caught my arm. His grip was strong, and his fingers, the ones that had clutched the sheets an hour ago, that had dug into my arms as I fucked him, were warm. "Talk to us. What the hell is going on?"

I looked at his hand, then up at his face. The confusion there, the fear beginning to dawn, the edge of anger that would soon consume everything else, nearly broke me. I came so close to telling them everything. The words were right there. Instead, I jerked away.

"Pack."

I walked out before either of them could argue.

Behind me, I heard Ophelia's voice break when she said my name, and Oliver's sharp and vicious curse. I heard the bed creak as they scrambled to make sense of what was happening.

I didn't stop walking until I reached my library.

I poured myself another whiskey and stood at the window, staring out at the dark grounds. The moon had set, leaving the gardens shrouded in shadows. Backlit, whoever was watching could see me. Let them. Give them a front-row view of me doing as they demanded.

From deep in the castle, I heard muffled voices and drawers opening and closing. When a door slammed shut, I flinched like I'd been struck.

The helicopter's approach announced itself as a distant thrum from the north. The sound grew louder, filling the night, drowning out the wind, the silence, and the sounds from the guest wing. Callen was coming in fast, the way he always did when something was wrong.

I drained my whiskey and went to meet him.

He walked into the main hall, still pulling on his jacket, his hair disheveled, his eyes sharp with questions. This man had stood beside me at my parents' funeral, and I'd been with him when he discovered his family's estate had been used to transport weapons of mass destruction, all orchestrated by a once-beloved caretaker. We'd bled together, killed together, and kept each other's secrets.

In all that time, he'd only seen me like this—broken—once before.

"They're in the guest wing," I said, cutting him off. "Get them out."

"Kiernan." He stopped in front of me, close enough for me to see the concern etched into his features. "What's happening? What am I walking them into?"

"Nothing. They'll be safe in Glasgow. They need to be away from here."

"And you?"

"I'll handle it."

His expression hardened, then he relented. "I'll take care of them," he said.

I nodded and turned away before I could say anything else. Before I could beg him to tell them I was sorry. Before I could ask him to explain what I couldn't explain myself.

Knowing it would be impossible to watch them leave, I stood in the library and listened to the sounds of the castle emptying. Footsteps on stone. Voices in the entrance hall—Callen's low murmur, Oliver's sharp questions, and Ophelia's silence that was somehow worse than her tears. The heavy front door opening, then closing in finality.

The helicopter's rotors spinning up. The pitch rising, the blades biting into the air. The sound growing louder, then lifting.

Then fading.

Then gone.

I pressed my forehead to the cold glass and stayed there until I could breathe again.

I waited until the night had swallowed the last echo of the helicopter's passage and I was certain they were truly gone. Then I poured another whiskey. This time, my hand shook so badly I spilled half of it across the desk.

I didn't bother cleaning it up.

The images waited in the locked drawer. The note with its anonymous threat. Evidence of a predator I couldn't identify, couldn't track, couldn't fight until I knew who the fuck they were.

I'd done what I had to do. Whatever came next—the exposure, the destruction, the ruin of everything I'd built—they would be safe. Far from Greymarch. Far from me. Far from whatever darkness had followed me here and was now demanding its due.

The fire crackled low, the last of the logs falling into embers. The library pressed in around me, heavy with shadows and the ghosts of what might have been. The sofa where I'd first kissed Oliver, where he'd pulled me down and opened for me. The rug where Ophelia had knelt at my feet while Oliver watched from the chair. The desk where I'd worked while they waited, desperate and denied.

Every corner of this room held a memory now. Every surface a reminder of what I'd had for far too brief a time.

I sank into the chair behind my desk and let my head fall into my hands. The whiskey burned in my throat. The silence rang in my ears. And the full weight of what my life now was settled over me like a burial shroud.

They would hate me for not confiding in them. That was the point.

Hatred was safer than love. Distance was safer than closeness. If they hated me, they wouldn't return. Wouldn't put themselves in danger. Wouldn't give whoever was watching another chance to destroy them.

I told myself this was the right choice. The only choice.

I told myself the hollow ache in my chest would fade with time.

I told myself a lot of things, sitting alone in that library while the fire died and the darkness crept closer.

None of them were true.

I unlocked the drawer and spread the damning evidence across the desk one more time. I studied each image with an operative's eye, looking for clues—lighting that might indicate time of day, reflections that might show the photographer's location.

Nothing. Whoever had taken these knew how to avoid leaving traces.

However, everyone made mistakes. And I had resources. Callen, Gus, Rafe, and our silent partner—a man more lethal than the four of us combined. The full weight of Unit 23, if I could find a way to bring them in without exposing what they contained.

Whoever you are, I will find you.

It wasn't a thought. It was a vow.

I would make them pay for every violation, stolen moment, and hour of happiness they'd poisoned with their surveillance.

I would destroy them. Tomorrow.

Tonight, there was only the silence. The empty castle. The knowledge that I'd had everything and cut it out of my own chest with my own two hands.

I picked up one picture—the three of us in the library, laughing together about a joke I could no longer remember.

We looked happy and whole, like people who believed they had a future.

I stared at it until my vision blurred. Until my throat ached from not making a sound.

Then I turned it face-down, locked it away with the others, and poured another drink.

16

Ophelia

The helicopter touched down a little after zero two hundred hours.

I knew the exact time because I'd been staring at my phone since we lifted off from Greymarch, watching the minutes crawl past like they meant something. Like tracking them might help me understand how my entire world had collapsed in the span of thirty minutes.

One moment, I'd been tangled in silk sheets between two men who brought me greater pleasure than I dreamed possible. The next, Kiernan's phone had buzzed on the nightstand. He'd left the room. And when he returned—

The rotors wound down with a whine that scraped along my nerves. Oliver's hand found mine in the darkness of the cabin, and I squeezed back just as hard. We hadn't spoken since Greymarch. There were no words for this. No framework I could apply, no logic that would make it make sense.

Kiernan had looked at us like we were strangers. Like the last twelve days hadn't happened. Like he hadn't held and commanded us.

You're leaving. Tonight.

When the helicopter door slid open, cold Scottish air rushed in, carrying the smell of rain and industrial exhaust. A figure waited on the tarmac—tall, broad-shouldered, face cast in shadow by the dim security lights.

I recognized him from Thorned Thistle. Rafe Harding—head of security for the club, and one of the founding partners. We'd barely exchanged ten words with him during our visits. He'd been a presence in the background, watchful and silent.

Callen said something to him as we climbed out—a quick exchange I couldn't hear over the fading noise of the rotors. Then Callen returned to the cockpit, and the helicopter lifted off, leaving us behind with a man who clearly had no intention of explaining anything.

The concrete was slick beneath my feet, and Rafe reached out to steady me when I stumbled. I'd thrown on clothes in a daze before we left Greymarch—jeans, a jumper, whatever my hands had found first.

"This way." Rafe's voice contained no warmth, no sympathy, no acknowledgment that he was shepherding two people whose lives had mysteriously imploded. He turned and walked toward a squat concrete building at the edge of the landing pad.

Oliver followed—a solid presence, the only thing grounding me to this moment. His hand brushed mine, and I reached for his.

The building turned out to be a safe house. I recognized the type at once—high security, minimal comfort, the kind of place Unit 23 used for witness protection or agents who'd been compromised. Reinforced doors. No windows on the ground floor. The faint hum of electronic countermeasures in the walls.

Rafe led us through a sterile corridor and into a common room that looked like it had been designed by someone who'd read about furniture but never actually sat on any. Gray sofa. Gray chairs. A kitchen area with a coffeemaker that probably dispensed something technically containing caffeine. The fluorescent lights buzzed overhead, casting everything in a sickly pallor.

"You'll be in an apartment on the second floor." Rafe gestured vaguely. "You'll be safe here."

"Safe from what?" Oliver's voice sounded rough and raw. Tension coiled in his shoulders as he stepped forward, every line of his body betraying the effort it took not to grab Rafe and shake answers out of him. "What the hell is going on? Why did Kiernan—"

"I don't have any answers for you."

"What the hell?"

Rafe's expression didn't change as he led us to the lift. Stone would have shown more emotion. "Kiernan's orders. You're safe here. That's what matters."

"That's not good enough." My voice came out steady, controlled—utterly at odds with the chaos churning inside me. "We deserve an explanation."

"I'm not in a position to give you one." Rafe met my eyes, and something flickered there. Regret, maybe. Or exhaustion. "Get some sleep. There's food in the kitchen. I'll check in tomorrow."

He turned toward the door.

"Rafe." Oliver's voice stopped him. "You know something. I can see it."

Rafe stood with his hand on the door handle, facing away from us. "Whether I do or not doesn't change anything. I'm following orders."

The door clicked shut behind him.

Oliver let out a breath that was almost a laugh—sharp, bitter, disbelieving. He ran both hands through his hair and gripped the strands like he wanted to tear them out.

"What the fuck?" he said quietly. "What the actual fuck?"

I sank onto a gray sofa like the one in the common area. The cushions were exactly as uncomfortable as they looked. My body ached with exhaustion, but my mind wouldn't stop spinning.

I'd been half asleep, warm and sated, with Oliver's arm draped across my waist when Kiernan's phone buzzed. He'd gone still, slipped out of bed, and the door had closed behind him. No explanation, just an order to remain where we were, not to leave the room.

When he returned, everything was different. *He* was different. His face had been carved from ice, his voice stripped of every note of warmth I'd learned to listen for since we'd arrived at Greymarch. He'd looked at us like we were problems to be solved, obstacles to be removed.

Pack your things. A helicopter is waiting.

He gave us no explanation and no apology. He delivered orders in that cold, commanding tone, and when

Oliver had grabbed his arm, demanding to know what was happening, he'd jerked it away.

Then he'd walked out, leaving us alone and baffled.

Oliver dropped onto the sofa, beside me. Not touching, but close enough that heat radiated off his body, the same helpless rage that was building behind my ribs.

"The text," Oliver said. "Something happened."

I nodded. I'd been thinking the same thing. Turning it over and over, trying to find an angle that made sense.

"He was gone for what, thirty minutes? Maybe less?"

"Less."

Oliver shook his head. "What happens in half an hour that makes someone—" His jaw clenched.

That makes someone throw away what we'd barely started to build, I finished silently. "Something he read changed everything."

Oliver held his head in his hands. "From who? About what?"

I didn't have an answer. The questions kept multiplying, but the data points were too few, the variables too unknown. I couldn't solve an equation when I didn't even know what I was supposed to be calculating.

He reached over and took my hand, his palm warming my cold fingers.

"We should try to sleep," he said, but neither of us got up.

Hours crawled past.

I couldn't say exactly what we did during that long stretch between Rafe's departure and dawn. We didn't sleep—that much I knew. We sat on the uncomfortable sofa, talking in fragments that went nowhere, sometimes in silence. Oliver made coffee, and I drank it without tasting it.

At some point, his head fell on my shoulder. I let him rest with his breath on my neck and stared at the wall while my mind refused to stop churning.

I kept asking the same questions, trying to make any sense of it. Nothing did. The thing that kept catching in my chest, the splinter I couldn't work free, was how fast he'd done it. How efficiently he'd dismissed us. One moment, we'd been three people experiencing something I never imagined. Closeness. Connection. The next, Oliver and I were being loaded into a helicopter like cargo.

He hadn't hesitated. Hadn't wavered. Hadn't given us even a moment to understand before he'd cut us out of his life like we were nothing.

The worst part was that some small, terrible voice in my head wasn't even surprised. Because hadn't I always known, on some level? That it was too good to be true? That men like Kiernan Lockhart didn't fall for women like me, didn't build lives with people they'd known for a few weeks, most of which were spent as operatives on a mission?

I'd let myself want anyway.

Now, I was sitting in a safe house in Glasgow at zero four hundred, and the man I'd given my submission to had thrown me away without a word of explanation.

Gray light began seeping under the door—dawn breaking over a city I couldn't see. Oliver stirred and lifted his head with a groan.

"Tell me that was a nightmare," he mumbled.

"I wish I could."

He sat up properly, dragging a hand over his face. Even in the dim light, he looked terrible—shadows under his eyes, lines of strain around his mouth, the golden warmth completely drained from his complexion.

I probably looked worse.

"I'm not staying here," Oliver said.

I turned to look at him. "What?"

"I'm not staying in this bloody safe house like a good little operative following orders." His jaw was set, that stubborn line I'd learned to recognize. "Kiernan doesn't get to decide where we go. He doesn't get to pack us up and ship us off and expect us to wait."

"Where would we go?"

"London." He said it like it was obvious. "To our lives. Our jobs. Our homes." A muscle jumped in his cheek. "I'm not giving the bastard the power to dictate anything else."

Something blossomed in my chest. Not hope—it was too early for hope—but something close to it. Purpose, maybe. Direction.

"You'll need to see your doctors first," I said. "Get cleared for travel."

Oliver blinked, then let out a short laugh. "Right. The head injury. I'd actually forgotten about that."

"We should, since we're already in Glasgow. I'm sure the doctor would be willing to see you a couple of days ahead of time."

"One day."

I nodded once. The last thirteen days were a blur. Time I wanted equally to remember for the rest of my life and wipe from my memory entirely. "Right."

"And if they clear me to fly?"

"Then, we go to London." I met his eyes, and for the first time since we'd landed, I felt something other than numb despair. "Together."

The decision steadied me. This was what I knew how to do—assess a situation, identify objectives, execute a plan. My heart might be breaking, but my training remained intact. Compartmentalize. That's what they'd drilled into us at MI6. Put the emotions in a box, deal with them later, focus on the task at hand. I'd never been particularly good at it before. Apparently, devastation was an excellent teacher.

We'd waited two hours between the DTI MRI they'd done and for the results to be read. A different doctor than the one who'd discharged him flipped through Oliver's records.

"Your scan looks good." He set down the chart. "The infection is fully resolved, no signs of complications. How are the headaches?"

"Manageable," Oliver said. "Mostly gone."

"Dizziness? Nausea?"

"No."

"Vision problems?"

"None."

The man nodded, making a note. "I'd like to schedule a follow-up in two weeks, but I don't see any reason you can't resume normal activities. However, given your line of work, I'm not clearing you to return yet."

"What about air travel?" Oliver asked.

He glanced between us. "How long of a trip?"

"Just to London," I responded. "Home, actually." Hearing the word, even said to myself, felt like a knife to my chest.

"Should be fine. Stay hydrated, and if you experience any sudden severe headaches or vision changes, get to an A&E immediately." He handed Oliver a printed summary. "Take care of yourself, Mr. Morse."

We walked out into a gray Glasgow morning. The city stretched around us—concrete and glass and the distant gleam of the Clyde—utterly indifferent to my entire world having collapsed twelve hours ago.

"So," Oliver said. "Airport?"

When I nodded, he got out his phone to search for flights. I watched him—the focused furrow of his brow, how his fingers attacked the keyboard—and felt a swell of gratitude that I wasn't doing this alone. That whatever we'd lost last night, I still had him.

Even as I thought it, a colder voice whispered in the back of my mind. *Do you? Do you have him without Kiernan? Or was what you had only possible because of the three of you together?*

I pushed the thought away. There would be time to face it later. Right now, we needed to get home.

The flight was ninety minutes of staring out the window, trying to stop the thoughts racing through my head. Oliver sat beside me, his hand resting on mine. We'd barely spoken since leaving the hospital.

What was there to say?

I thought about all the flights I'd taken in my life. Diplomatic missions with my parents. Training exercises for MI6. The helicopter ride to Glenshadow, where I met the man who'd changed my life in a few short days.

I'd flown into Scotland for the Labyrinth investigation, thinking I knew what was waiting for me. A surveillance op. Targets to observe. I hadn't known about the castle in the Highlands. The viscount with shadows in his eyes who taught me about things I hadn't known I wanted until he showed them to me.

Now I was flying out again, and everything I'd discovered about myself felt like a cruel joke. A door that had opened enough to show me what was on the other side before slamming shut in my face.

Oliver squeezed my fingers as the plane began its descent. "We're going to be okay, Phee."

My eyes bored into his. "Are we?"

He brought my hand to his lips and kissed my palm. "One way or another. I promise."

My flat felt wrong.

I stood in the doorway, keys still in my hand, and tried to remember the last time I'd been here. Close to two months ago?

The space looked like it always did—tidy, minimal, everything in its proper place. My books arranged by subject and height in the cases. My grandmother's tea set displayed in the glass cabinet. The view of London through windows that felt too large now, letting in too much dismally gray light.

Oliver came in behind me, carrying our bags. He set them down by the door and looked around.

"Nice place," he said.

"Thanks."

The word felt hollow in my mouth. I crossed to the kitchen and opened the refrigerator, then closed it again when I saw the empty shelves.

"I should order food," I said. "Are you hungry?"

"No."

Neither was I. But asking about food was normal. Ordering takeaway was normal. If I could keep doing normal things, maybe eventually something would start to feel that way again.

I ordered Thai from the place down the street. Oliver sat on my sofa—a real sofa, soft and cream-colored, nothing like the gray monstrosity at the safe house—and stared at the wall. I sat beside him and stared too.

The food arrived. We picked at it without enthusiasm. The pad thai tasted like cardboard, or maybe my taste buds had simply stopped working along with everything else.

"He didn't even give us a reason."

I looked up. Oliver was still staring at the wall, but his jaw was tight, his hands clenched on his thighs.

"Nothing," he continued, his voice rough. "He told us to leave like we were nothing."

"Oliver—"

"I trusted him." The words came out jagged, broken at the edges. "I trusted him with things I've never—" He stopped, shaking his head. "And he threw me away."

My throat tightened, and I turned to face him fully.

"I know."

"Do you?" He finally looked at me—and there it was. The raw hurt beneath the anger, the devastation he'd been holding together through sheer force of will. "Because I keep thinking I must have missed something. Must have done something wrong. And I can't figure out what, Phee. I've been going over every moment of our time with him—"

"You did nothing wrong."

Oliver's breath hitched, his composure fracturing. Not completely—he was too strong for that, too skilled at holding himself together.

"I thought he saw me," he said quietly. "For the first time in my life, I thought—" He stopped, pressing the heels of his hands against his eyes. "God. I'm pathetic."

"You're not." I leaned in until our shoulders touched. "You're hurting. We're both hurting. That's not pathetic, Oliver. That's human."

He dropped his hands and looked at me. In the dim light of my flat, with the remains of untouched Thai food between us, he looked younger than I'd ever seen him. Vulnerable in a way that made my heart ache.

"I don't know how to do this," he admitted. "I don't know how to pretend my life didn't change in a profound way."

"Neither do I."

"So what do we do?"

I didn't have an answer. The silence stretched between us, heavy with grief and confusion.

Oliver didn't respond at first. Then he said, "He's done this before."

"What do you mean?"

"The way he shut down. Like he flipped a switch." Oliver's brow furrowed. "It didn't feel spontaneous. It felt practiced. Like he knew exactly how to destroy us quickly and completely. Like he knew the most efficient method."

My breath caught. He was right. It had felt rehearsed.

A knock at the door shattered the silence.

We both went still. It was after midnight. No one knew we were here.

The knock came again—three sharp raps that echoed through my flat like gunshots.

17

Kiernan

I didn't sleep.

When the first gray light crept across the grounds, I was still in the library, still standing at the window where I'd watched the helicopter disappear hours ago. The whiskey decanter was dry, and my body ached with an exhaustion I refused to acknowledge.

The castle felt hollow in a way it hadn't before. These halls had held laughter and warmth that came from having them here. Ophelia's voice echoing in the corridors. Oliver's footsteps on the stairs. The three of us tangled together in spaces that had known only solitude for years.

Now, all that remained was a lingering, painful stillness. Too quiet. Too empty.

I forced myself to put one foot in front of the other, because standing still meant drowning in the absence.

My steps echoed in the cavernous corridors as I made my way to the west tower. I paused at the entrance to my playroom and rested my hand on the doorframe. The equipment waited in the shadows—the St. Andrew's cross, the bench, the restraints. We'd used this space once together, but that single night had mattered more than I could have anticipated. I remembered Ophelia's trust and Oliver's surrender when his composure finally cracked. The room smelled like them—perhaps a phantom scent—but I couldn't bring myself to enter.

I'd made a vow to never use this room with anyone again and had broken it within a week of Oliver and Ophelia arriving.

I shut the door and locked it.

My own bedroom was far worse.

I stood in the doorway of the master suite—the room that had been mine alone for three years, the room I'd opened to them. This was where I'd woken with Ophelia's head on my chest and Oliver's arm thrown across my waist. Where we'd talked in the dark about nothing and everything. Where I'd let myself believe, for the first time in years, that I might have this.

The sheets were still tangled from our final hours together, and pillows were scattered where we'd thrown them. This was where I was when Millie's text arrived. Right before everything fell to pieces.

Oliver's book sat on the nightstand, its spine cracked at page one hundred forty-six. I remembered him reading it, propped against the headboard while Ophelia dozed on his shoulder, his free hand absently stroking her hair. My hand on his thigh. The three of us breathing together in the space that had become ours for far too short a time. He hadn't thought to grab it when Callen arrived— none of us had been thinking clearly.

Through the open bathroom door, Ophelia's hair tie lay coiled on the counter, dark strands still caught in the elastic. And her robe hung on the back of the door. Small things, forgotten in the rush to leave.

I couldn't sleep here tonight. Couldn't lie on sheets we'd shared and reach across the mattress to find only cold space where warm bodies should be.

They'd left pieces of themselves scattered around. Small things that would haunt me for months. But that I'd keep. Every time I entered this room, I would remember what it had held. What had been destroyed because of me. What I'd known would be, yet I risked it anyway.

Another vow broken. Never bring anyone to Greymarch. I'd held that line for years, only scening at the club, never allowing anyone in my private spaces.

Then two people arrived, and I shattered every boundary I'd built. If I'd kept my vow—if I'd never brought them here—those photos wouldn't exist.

I walked out and closed the door behind me. Not sure when I might enter again. If ever. Millie could transfer my things to another room. To another part of the castle. She wouldn't mind. In fact, she'd prefer it.

I'd spent the hours since the helicopter departed turning the question over and over. Who would want Oliver and Ophelia gone—specifically them, specifically from my life? Who would want to wound me in the most precise way possible?

That I couldn't figure it out meant I was overlooking a crucial detail.

Callen arrived at zero nine hundred.

I heard him before I saw him—the soft scrape of the hidden door behind the library bookcase, the creak of one of the tunnel passages that connected Greymarch to the network of Jacobite escape routes running beneath the Highlands. The hidden entryways had been built three centuries ago, when my ancestors needed ways to travel undetected. If only I could escape the nightmare of what sat before me now.

Callen emerged from behind the shelving unit. There were shadows under his eyes and tension in his shoulders that spoke of too little sleep.

"You look like hell," he said in greeting.

"Thank you for the observation."

He crossed to the sideboard and poured himself a whiskey without asking. That was his right. Callen was my best friend in the world, closer than a brother. The last few hours had proven that more than any other time in my life. Except once. I shoved those memories down before they could surface.

"Rafe rang from Glasgow." He turned to face me, glass in hand. "Said they were wrecked when he left."

"They're alive and safe. That's what matters."

"Is it?" He took a long swallow of whiskey. "Because from where I'm standing, you nuked a relationship that was actually making you human again."

"I didn't have a choice."

"There's always a choice, Kier. What in the bloody hell happened?"

I crossed to the desk and unlocked the bottom drawer. The manila envelope sat where I'd left it, thick with its poisonous contents. I reached for it, then dropped it in front of him.

"This."

Callen set down his glass and reached for it. His face shifted as he sorted through the contents—going still when he came to the exterior shots, his jaw tightening as he recognized the angles. Then his expression went flat at the club photos.

"These were taken over the last couple of days." His voice was controlled. That of an operative assessing a threat. "But whoever sent these has been watching you far longer."

"Yes."

"The shots from outside were taken from the tree line." He held up one of the photos, studying it with narrowed eyes. "Long lens. Six hundred millimeters, maybe better. High-end surveillance gear."

"Can you trace it?"

"Maybe. If they bought or rented locally." He set that photo aside and picked up another. "This one's from outside the dining room. Clear line of sight through the windows. They knew your routines. Knew when you'd be in that room, where you'd sit."

Someone had seen us sharing meals, falling into a connection that felt like hope. They'd captured those moments and turned them into weapons.

Callen picked up the note and read it more than once, his expression hardening with each pass.

"Christ." He set it down like it had burned him. "No demand for money, only for them to be gone. Who would want that?"

"I've been asking myself that question all night." I walked over to the window, unable to look at those photos any longer. "Whoever did this knows me, Cal. Knows what I value. Knows that threatening them was the fastest way to bring me to my knees."

"That's a short list."

"Too short. None of the people who know me that well would do this."

He gathered the photos and slid them into the envelope. "Which means someone's been watching long enough to figure it out. Or someone talked."

The second possibility sat between us, ugly and unspoken.

"I need Rafe here," I said. "Gus too. We have to work this together. And we need to read Snow in."

"Emergency channel." Callen was already pulling out his mobile. "I'll send the alert."

The five of us had established a secure line years ago—encrypted, untraceable, known only to the founding partners of the Thorned Thistle. We'd never had to use it for anything like this.

Within seconds of Callen sending the message, responses came in.

"Rafe's already headed this way from Glasgow. He should be here within the hour." He glanced at the screen again. "Gus is leaving Edinburgh now."

I'd read the message he'd sent. While he'd told them enough for them to understand the urgency, they had no idea how bad the situation truly was.

Callen's mobile buzzed. He glanced at the screen. "Snow."

He typed rapidly, then held the device over the desk and photographed the contents spread across the blotter—the surveillance shots, the club photos, the note—and sent them through the encrypted channel.

We waited.

Snow never used voice calls. Never video. In all the years I'd known him, I'd never seen his face outside of in person, and even then, he had a way of being present without being memorable. No photographs existed. No recordings. He was a ghost who happened to be one of the most dangerous men alive.

Three dots appeared on Callen's screen. Then a message:

I'm on it.

Nothing else. No questions about who, or how, or what we planned to do. Three words, then silence— already hunting, already working angles none of us would see until he chose to reveal them.

Callen pocketed his phone. "Well. That's Snow."

It was, and whoever had sent these photographs had just made themselves his target.

Rafe arrived at ten thirty, his face thunderous. "Fucking show me."

I handed him the envelope. "Jesus Christ," he muttered as he sifted through the images. "Someone got inside my club." He dropped into a chair and accepted the whiskey Callen poured him. "Inside the private rooms. Past every obstacle I've spent five years building."

When he reached the club shots, a muscle jumped in his jaw. "This is impossible."

He stood and spread the photos across the desk, studying the angles and lighting with fierce concentration. "The semi-private rooms are surveyed only by our own cameras. Access is restricted to members who've been vetted for years. No one brings phones or recording devices into those spaces—we have detection equipment at every entrance."

"Someone bypassed it," Callen said.

"Someone made a bloody fool of me." Rafe's voice was quiet, which made it more dangerous. I'd seen him kill men with less anger in his eyes.

"The angles on these shots," I said. "What can you tell from them?"

Rafe held up one of the photos, turning it to catch the light. "This was taken from above. There's a maintenance catwalk near the ceiling—we use it for lighting adjustments before events. Members don't have access."

"Staff do," I said. "The regular crew, along with the technicians we bring in for special events."

"All vetted. All watched." He shook his head. "But someone either slipped through the vetting, or…"

"Or someone we trusted betrayed us."

The words hung in the air, heavy with meaning none of us wanted to accept.

"I'll tear the fucking place apart." Rafe's expression hardened. "Review every access log, every camera feed, every member and staff member who's been through those doors in the last two months. Someone got in, which means someone left a trail. No one's that good."

"Do it."

"And when I find them—" He met my eyes, and the promise was unmistakable. Rafe knew how to make people disappear as well as the rest of us. Other than Snow, no one was as good as him. "When I find them, we'll have a conversation about boundaries."

Gus arrived twenty minutes later, looking harried from the drive. He read the situation the moment he walked in—three grim faces, photos on the desk beside the envelope, and the kind of tension that meant we were at war.

"Tell me," he said simply.

Between the three of us, we explained the surveillance, the threat, and the demand that Oliver and Ophelia leave. He listened without interrupting, his expression growing grimmer with each detail.

"Surveillance like this costs money," he said, setting down a photo of the Greymarch grounds. "High-end equipment, long-term positioning, access to a secure facility—none of that comes cheap. Someone funded this."

"Can you track it?"

"Possibly. Purchase records of the equipment, certainly. If they rented a property near Greymarch for the stakeout, there's a paper trail." He glanced at Rafe. "And getting inside the club would require either bribery or an existing relationship with someone who has access. Either way, money changed hands."

"Run it," I said. "Whatever you need."

He nodded, already pulling out his laptop. "I'll start with suppliers in Scotland. Cross-reference them with any unusual transactions in our member database—large withdrawals, payments to unfamiliar accounts. If someone on the inside was bought, I'll find the receipt."

For the next hour, we worked the problem.

Rafe set up in the corner with his own computer, pulling feeds and access logs from the club's servers. The familiar rhythm of his typing filled the library—rapid bursts, followed by long pauses, then muttered curses as lead after lead went cold.

"Another dead end," he said after the fourth such pause. "The catwalk access logs show nothing unusual. Standard maintenance visits, all during closed hours, all by vetted personnel."

"Which means either the logs were altered, or whoever did this had legitimate access," Callen suggested.

"Or they found another way up." Rafe loaded a schematic on his screen. "There's an external fire escape on the east side. It's alarmed, but if someone knew the system…"

"Check it," I said. "Every possible entry point. I want to know every way someone could have gotten up there without triggering your sensors."

Gus worked from the sofa, multiple windows open on his screen as he reviewed financial records no one should have the ability to access. He typed deliberate sequences on the keyboard.

"The equipment used for those exterior shots," he said without looking up. "There are only a handful of suppliers in the UK who stock that level of kit. I'm cross-referencing purchases in the last six months with known associates, anyone who might have a connection to us."

"How long?"

"Days, maybe longer. Money's good at hiding, especially when the person spending it knows what they're doing." He glanced up. "But I've also got feelers out to some contacts in the banking sector. If any large or unusual transactions moved through Scottish accounts in the last two months, they'll flag it."

I sat at my desk, staring at the photos I'd spread across the blotter.

"The positions," I said, thinking aloud. "They're not random. This one was taken from the ridge beyond the garden wall—that's a difficult climb in daylight, let alone at night. And this angle here, through the conservatory glass—you'd need to know exactly where to stand to get this shot."

Callen looked over my shoulder. "Someone who's been here before. Or someone who did extensive reconnaissance."

"The guest list," I said. "Everyone who's visited Greymarch in the last year. Deliveries, maintenance workers, anyone who's set foot on the property."

"I'll have Millie pull the records." Callen made a note on his phone. "What about the staff? How many people work the grounds?"

"Six. All of them have been with the family for over a decade. I'd trust any of them with my life."

"We still check," Rafe said flatly. "You trusted your club too, and someone got in."

The words stung—him more than me. And he was right. Trust was a vulnerability. I knew that. In my personal life as much as within Unit 23. "Typhon," I muttered under my breath. The unit's commander would need to know of this compromise. Maybe not of the club, but of me personally.

"Not yet," Callen said. "Not until we know more."

Rafe's mobile buzzed. He glanced at the screen, and his expression changed.

"Message from the safe house. Oliver and Ophelia are leaving."

I cringed. "Where are they going?"

"Doesn't say. One of my people is following at a distance." He was already typing a response.

The next twenty minutes were agony. Callen paced by the window, and I stood at my desk, unable to sit, unable to focus on anything but the silence from Glasgow.

When Rafe's mobile buzzed again, all four of us went still.

"Hospital," Rafe read aloud.

Some of the tension in my chest eased. That made sense. Oliver had been due for a follow-up. They were being responsible, not reckless.

"Keep someone on them," I said. "I want to know the moment they leave."

Rafe nodded, already sending the message.

We returned to work, but my concentration was fractured. Every few minutes, my eyes drifted to Rafe's mobile, waiting for the next update. The photos on my desk mocked me—evidence of how badly I'd failed to protect them, how thoroughly someone had invaded our privacy.

Another hour passed. Gus found a potential lead—a shell company in Edinburgh that had purchased surveillance equipment matching the specifications of the exterior shots. He started pulling the thread, following the money through layers of misdirection.

Then Rafe's mobile buzzed.

"They're leaving the hospital." He read the message, and his brow furrowed. "Headed to the airport."

"Did you say *airport*?" The word came out sharper than I intended. "They need to stay in Glasgow. At the safe house."

"Apparently, they have other plans," Rafe muttered.

I crossed to the window, hands clenched at my sides. They were leaving. Running to somewhere I couldn't protect them.

"Kiernan, you can't have it both ways. You can't hide this threat from them by forcing them to leave in the middle of the night without an explanation." Callen's voice was steady. "Did you expect them to remain in a safe house indefinitely?"

"They don't know what they're facing."

"Precisely. Because you didn't confide in them. However, they're intelligence officers. They know how to take care of themselves."

Gus looked up from his laptop. "I can check airline manifests. If they're flying commercial, I can find the booking."

"Do it."

His fingers flew across the keys. Thirty seconds later, he had an answer.

"Heathrow." He glanced at me. "They'll be in London in under three hours."

Three hours. Then they'd be exposed—out in the open, with no idea that someone might be waiting for them.

"We should alert Snow," Callen said.

He sent a message through the secure channel. No response. Typical Snow—he'd surface when he had information to share, and not a moment before.

"We need someone else waiting. Put a detail team together," I said.

"On it," Callen responded.

Time dragged on as we waited.

Rafe eventually headed for the tunnels, laptop tucked under his arm, expression murderous.

"I'll tear apart every inch of the place," he said at the passage entrance. "Every access point, every camera angle, every staff member who's ever worked for us. If there's a breach, I'll find it."

Gus followed shortly after.

"Someone funded this," he said, clasping my shoulder as he passed. "Money always leaves a trail, no matter how well they try to hide it. I'll find it."

Callen and I remained in the library, waiting for word from London.

The fire had burned low. The whiskey decanter sat empty on the sideboard. Outside, the afternoon light was already fading toward dusk—winter days in the Highlands were brutally short.

"You should eat," Callen said. "Sleep."

"I'll sleep when this is over."

He didn't push. He knew me well enough to understand that some arguments weren't worth having.

My mobile buzzed. A message on the encrypted channel. *Snow.*

I opened it at once, Callen reading over my shoulder.

On them. Followed from Heathrow. At her flat now.

We have a team tracking them, I responded.

His response came in seconds. *I know.*

Some of the tension in my chest eased. I sent another message. *Any sign of surveillance?*

The typing indicator appeared. Disappeared. Appeared again. In all the years I'd known Snow, I'd never seen him hesitate—not even in text.

Then his response appeared. *Van across the street from her building. Blacked-out windows. Engine running. No one in or out.*

The world tilted beneath my feet.

Another message arrived. *Going in. Will handle.*

I typed rapidly. *Keep them safe. Find out who's behind this.*

His final message was characteristically brief. *That's why I'm here.*

The line went dead.

18

The text came through at twenty-one hundred hours.

Unknown number. One word: *Ostrich.*

My spine straightened, and I showed the screen to Phee. Her eyes widened.

Fourteen, I responded.

Three seconds. Then: *Carmine.*

It was the correct response to a code that changed every six hours. Only MI6 personnel with high-level clearance had access to it. Whoever was texting me was legitimate.

Another text followed almost immediately. *Now open the fucking door.*

Once opened, the man on the other side didn't wait to be invited. He pushed past me into the flat—average height, athletic build, features that seemed to slide out of focus even as I looked at them. The kind of face designed to be forgotten.

"You're being relocated," the stranger said. "Come with me."

No explanations. But whoever he was, he had the code that meant exactly what he'd said—that we were being relocated. Within SIS, whether MI6 or Unit 23, that sequence meant you followed orders immediately. Without question. Anything else would be considered a refusal of a direct order.

"Transport is waiting. Two minutes."

Phee already had her go bag when I swept past her to get mine.

As we followed him to the lift, I spotted three more agents in the corridor. One entered it with us. When the doors opened in the underground car park, a black SUV sat waiting.

We'd barely gotten in when it sped off.

"Moved where?" I asked. "Why?"

Neither the mystery man nor the driver responded.

The building was in Southwark, overlooking the Thames—a glass-and-steel tower with a private entrance and a concierge who nodded without asking questions. The stranger led us into a lift that required a key card and a six-digit code.

The doors opened directly into the penthouse. Floor-to-ceiling windows wrapped the space, offering a panoramic view of the London skyline—the Shard glittering to the east, St. Paul's dome lit against the darkness, the Thames a shadowed ribbon far below. The floors were pale marble, the furniture sleek leather and polished chrome. A Steinway grand piano sat in a corner near the glass, its black lacquer gleaming.

"Stay here," the stranger said. "Someone will be in touch."

"Wait." I turned, but he was already stepping into the lift. "Who's going to—"

The doors slid shut.

Ophelia's footsteps were silent on the marble as she walked through the space. "This isn't a safe house."

"No." I walked through the flat, taking in the details. Expensive but impersonal. The kind of place that looked staged rather than lived in. "It isn't."

A photograph on a side table caught my eye. A woman holding a little boy; she was blonde, elegant, and smiling at the camera. The boy couldn't have been more than four or five, dark-haired and serious-eyed.

Something nagged at me. The woman's face. I knew her from somewhere.

I picked up the frame and studied the image. Where had I seen her before?

"What is it?" Phee asked.

I turned the photo toward her. "She looks familiar, but I can't place her."

Phee took the frame, examined it, then shook her head. "I don't recognize her."

I continued staring at it, knowing it was going to drive me mad until I figured it out. I knew her. I was certain of it. But from where?

We explored the rest of the flat—bedrooms, a study lined with books, a bathroom with a soaking tub that overlooked the river. Everything was pristine and expensive. Yet nothing told us who owned it or why we'd been brought here.

"This is going to bother me all night," I muttered, picking the photo up again.

Then it clicked.

"Wait." My voice came out sharp. "I know where I've seen her."

Phee raised her head.

"There's a painting hanging in the family wing at Greymarch. It was above a fireplace."

Our eyes met.

"You're right," Phee said, barely above a whisper. "I remember it."

"That's his mother." My stomach dropped, and I clenched my fists. "This fucking penthouse belongs to him. Jesus. He's still controlling us." I set the framed photo down harder than I meant to. "He threw us out without a word, then has us collected and delivered here? What are we, packages? Property he's transferring between storage units?"

My hands shook with fury I couldn't contain.

"Maybe there's a reason—"

"Then, he should have told us what it was." I stopped in front of the window and rolled my shoulders. Phee came up behind me, wrapped her arms around my waist, and rested her cheek on my shoulder.

Her warmth grounded me, and for a moment, neither of us spoke.

"We need to find out who he is," she said quietly. "We're missing something, and whatever it is, it's the reason he sent us away."

She was right. The Kiernan we got to know during our brief stay at Greymarch didn't throw people away without an explanation.

"Let's get to work." I grabbed my laptop from the go bag.

Our computer screens cast a blue light across the marble floor when we set up at the dining table. The flat's wifi was secure—of course it was—and our credentials got us into the standard personnel databases without issue. What it contained was minimal, but maybe we'd still find some detail that would give us our first clue.

Kiernan Lockhart. Archon. Unit 23.

His service record was exemplary. Multiple commendations. A career trajectory that marked him as exceptional.

"Look at this." Phee turned her screen toward me. "Seven years ago. Extended personal leave."

"How long?"

"Six weeks."

"Reason?" I asked.

"Classified. Above our access level." She scrolled further. "But look at the timeline."

She loaded two documents up side by side. Before the leave, he'd been on the standard MI6 command track—driven, committed, excellent interpersonal skills, strong leadership potential. After, he'd transferred to Unit 23.

"That's not a demotion," I said slowly, working through it. "Unit 23 is elite. But it's also…"

"Independent," Phee finished. "No team command. No direct reports. Operatives who work alone or in small cells, brought in for specific missions."

The kind of role where a man could excel without ever having to be responsible for anyone else's well-being.

"So he was on track to lead teams, then something happened, and he chose a path where he'd never have to."

Phee's voice was soft. "What happened to him?"

I stared at the screen. Somewhere in those classified files was the answer. But we couldn't reach it. Not from here. Not with our clearance.

"We're stuck," I said. "Unless we can find another way in."

Phee closed her laptop. "We'll figure it out tomorrow."

Once in bed, we reached for each other in a way that was both desperate and primal.

My mouth found her throat, and her hands traced the planes of my chest. The heat that had always sparked between us was there. When she wrapped her legs around my hips and pulled me closer, I ground into her with a groan. This was what we'd been circling before Greymarch—stolen glances across briefing rooms, accidental touches that lingered too long, tension that had simmered between us until it finally boiled over.

Except it didn't feel right. The mechanics worked. Every touch landed where it should. Her body responded, arching beneath me. I kissed down her neck, tasting her skin, trying to find the spark that would ignite us the way it had before. Her fingers threaded through my hair. Except the fire that had consumed us at Greymarch burned at half strength. A pilot light where there should have been an explosion.

I leaned away. "It's not—I still want you. I do."

Her eyes searched my face. "I feel it too. It's like…"

"Like we're playing a duet that was written for three."

I rolled off her and sat on the edge of the bed with my elbows on my knees and my head in my hands. She sat up behind me and rested her palm between my shoulder blades.

He'd seen something in us—something we hadn't seen in ourselves. The way I responded to his commands. How Phee had bloomed under his attention. We'd both needed him.

"It doesn't mean we don't work," she said softly. "It means we work differently than we thought."

"We need to get him back," I added.

When sleep finally took me under, I dreamed of Greymarch.

The playroom materialized around me. Silk ropes bound Ophelia's wrists to the headboard of the bed where she lay, waiting. Naked with her legs spread. Her eyes were soft with trust, with need.

Kiernan stood behind me. His hands slid around my waist, and his arousal pressed into me through the thin fabric of my trousers.

"She's beautiful, isn't she?" His voice was low. "Look at how she waits for you. How wet she is already, just from watching us."

Phee's thighs glistened. Her chest rose and fell with rapid breaths.

"Take her," Kiernan commanded. "Show me how you worship her."

His hands worked my belt. The leather slithered free, and he pushed my trousers down, freeing my cock and wrapping his fingers around my length with a grip that drew a low sound from my throat.

"Not yet." He stroked me once, twice—enough to make me desperate. "You come when I tell you. Not before."

I positioned myself between Ophelia's thighs, then entered her and thrust hard.

She cried out, and her body opened for me with heat and pressure and the exquisite grip of her inner walls.

Kiernan's eyes burned as he watched us.

"Slowly," he said, stretching out beside us. "Let me see everything."

I set a rhythm—slow, deep strokes that made her arch and writhe beneath me. Her bound wrists tested the give of the silk, and her heels dug into my back. Through it all, Kiernan's presence was a physical force.

His hands gripped my hips when he knelt behind me, and I heard the snap of the lube bottle, then felt the slick pressure of his cock as it nudged against my entrance.

"Breathe," he murmured. "Let me in."

The stretch burned as he pushed forward. I was full of him and inside Phee at the same time. Connected to both of them in the most intimate way possible.

Then Kiernan began to thrust.

His rhythm drove me into Ophelia. Every stroke he gave me, I gave her. We moved as one. The pleasure built in waves—his cock hitting that spot inside me, Phee's walls clenching around me in response.

"You feel that?" Kiernan growled. "You feel how perfectly you fit between us?"

I could only moan as he drove deeper, making Phee cry out with every thrust. Her walls tightened as her orgasm built, and her breath came in sharp gasps.

"Help me make her come." His hand reached around to find her clit.

When I found the spot that made her scream, Phee arched off the bed, her inner walls clamping down as the orgasm ripped through her.

"Good girl." Kiernan's voice. "Now, you." His lips brushed my ear. "Come for me, Oliver."

He thrust hard, and I was gone. My own release tore through me, and I pulsed inside Ophelia while Kiernan pounded into me.

"Mine," he growled.

I woke gasping. Sweat soaked my shirt, and my cock ached against the sheets. Phee still lay beside me, but the one person we both needed—desperately—wasn't.

I pressed my face into the pillow, willing the ache away that being without him had left behind.

I stood by the window with a cup of coffee, missing Millie's morning tea, while the sun slowly cast light on the street below.

Two men in a black sedan had been there since dawn. Probably others had taken the night shift.

I checked the security panel by the door, then the lobby camera feed. Two more kept watch on the lift.

"We're boxed in," I said when Phee emerged from the bedroom.

She joined me at the panel and studied the feeds. "Four that we can see. Probably more we can't."

"If we're going to find answers, we need to find a bloody way out of here." It was more than that, though. I couldn't spend another night in his space. My erotic dreams hadn't ended with the first. They'd plagued me throughout the night. Each one made the hurt worse.

"You have someone in mind."

"Iris Beacham," I said. "She owes me one."

Phee's expression flickered. "I know of her, but we've never met."

"She's good at getting in and out of places she shouldn't be."

"So I've heard." Phee's voice was flat as she left my side and went to the kitchen.

"Ophelia?"

"I'm not jealous." She said it too quickly.

I set down my coffee, crossed to her, and took her face in my hands.

"You and Kiernan are all I want."

She held my gaze, then nodded.

I reached for my mobile and made the call.

Iris answered on the fourth ring.

"Vanguard. It's been a while."

"I need a favor."

"Of course you do." I could hear her smile. "What kind of favor?"

"I need to get out of a building in Southwark without being seen. Private residence. Detail of four minimum. Can you help?"

A pause. "What building?"

I gave her the address.

"I know of it. There's a couple of *interesting* tenants."

"Do you know it well enough to get us out?"

"Us?"

"Prima is with me."

"Fascinating," she muttered under her breath with a total lack of enthusiasm. "Give me an hour."

Forty minutes later, Iris rang.

"There's a service corridor on the thirty-second floor. Maintenance access leads to a freight elevator that opens in the sub-basement, where there's a loading dock on the east side—no camera coverage for about fifteen seconds between sweeps. I'll have a car waiting."

"How did you get building schematics in forty minutes?"

"I know a guy who knows a guy." She paused. "You'll owe me double for this."

"Roger that."

"Twenty minutes. East loading dock. Don't be late."

"Understood."

"Wait."

My stomach dropped. "What?"

"Which unit are you in?"

"Penthouse."

I heard her snicker. "Now that *is* fascinating. Archon's?" She drew out the name. "You know he's into some twisted shit, right? Alternative lifestyle. BDSM clubs. I heard he was in some kind of relationship—God, must be seven or eight years ago now. A woman died."

My grip tightened on the phone. "Do you know what happened?"

"Not the details, but it allegedly happened at a club called the Crucible." She paused. *"You aren't involved—?"*

"Iris. Can you help us get out or not?"

She sighed. "Yes, fine. Twenty minutes."

The line went dead.

Phee was still standing close enough to have heard both sides of the conversation and already had something on the screen of her mobile. "The Crucible is in Shoreditch, which isn't far from here."

"Right," I muttered, thinking through our next steps. First, we needed to escape the gilded cage Kiernan kept us in. Then we could make the next plan.

"She said seven or eight years."

"That lines up exactly with the leave," I agreed.

"The death of someone he was close to would explain taking six weeks off."

"Definitely."

The escape was clean. Mostly.

We waited until the security feed showed the guys monitoring the lobby check their phones—a synchronized moment that meant replacements were on their way. That gave us our window.

We took the internal stairs to thirty-two, our footsteps echoing off concrete walls as we made our way down. Phee went first, checking corners, signaling all clear. We worked together the way we always had in the field—silent, efficient, trusting each other without question.

The service corridor was exactly where Iris said it would be. A heavy door marked MAINTENANCE ONLY, propped open with a wedge that looked freshly placed. Perhaps Iris' work.

Beyond it, there was a narrow passage lined with pipes and electrical conduits. We went fast, staying low out of habit even though there were no cameras here.

The freight elevator was industrial—steel walls, exposed mechanics, loud enough to wake the dead. I hit the button for sub-basement, and the whole cage shuddered as it descended.

"If this thing breaks down—" Phee started.

"It won't." And thankfully, it didn't.

The sub-basement was a maze of storage units and mechanical rooms. We navigated to the loading dock, where a generator hummed in the dimly lit area.

Another door was propped open with a brick, and beyond it, there was gray daylight and the sound of traffic.

I checked my watch, counting the seconds.

"Fifteen-second gap between camera sweeps," I said. "We go on my mark."

"Roger that."

We pressed against the wall on either side of the exit, watching the camera mounted above the dock rotate away from us.

"Now."

We raced through the door, across the loading bay, and past a delivery truck that provided cover for half the distance.

"Faster," said Phee, motioning to the camera that was already swinging around.

We sprinted the last ten meters and rounded a corner into an alley just as the CCTV completed its arc. A black Audi idled at the curb with the passenger window rolled down.

Iris Beacham, with her bottle-blonde hair and red lipstick, smiled at me, then glared at Phee. "Get in," she said. "Before someone notices you're gone."

Like the SUV that delivered us to Kiernan's place, Iris hit the accelerator as soon as we were inside.

"So," she said. "Kiernan Lockhart. I have to say, Oliver, I didn't see that coming. You're usually so…conventional."

"What else do you know about the Crucible?" I asked, ignoring the jab.

"Impatient as ever." She changed lanes without signaling, cutting off a delivery van. "Not much. Underground club. Very exclusive. Very intense, from what I've heard. The kind of place where they check references before they let you in the door."

"What kind of references?"

"The kind that prove you're not going to call the police afterward. Or expose the other members." She shrugged. "I'm not into that scene myself. All that leather and submission seems exhausting. Though I suppose some people need it."

Beside me, Phee's tension was palpable.

"Is that where you're headed?" she asked.

"Not yet. We'll need somewhere to land for a few hours at least."

"I may know of a place." Her eyes flicked to Phee in the rearview mirror. The appraisal was obvious. "So, are the two of you a package deal?"

"Drop it," I seethed.

She smirked.

We drove in silence for a few minutes. The city scrolled past—office blocks giving way to residential streets, then to industrial areas at the edge of London.

"You know," Iris said, her tone casual. "Oliver and I have history."

"Iris." My voice carried a warning.

"What? I'm just making conversation." She caught my eye in the mirror again. "One night. Years ago. He was quite…memorable."

"It was a long time ago," I muttered. "And it was a mistake."

Iris laughed. "So cold. And here I thought we had something special."

"We didn't."

"No." A flash of emotion appeared on her face, but was gone as quickly as it had come. "I suppose we didn't."

She drove into the car park of a motel off the A2 that looked like it hadn't been renovated since the eighties. Maybe longer.

"It's clean—mostly—and the owner doesn't ask questions," Iris said, stopping in the parking area. "Cash only. No ID required."

We got out. Phee was already walking toward the office, her stride stiff with barely contained emotion.

"Oliver."

I turned. Iris had rolled down her window.

"Watch yourself with Lockhart." Her voice had lost its flirty edge. She sounded almost sincere. "Whatever happened at that club—people don't like to talk about it. That usually means it was bad. Really bad."

I nodded. "Thanks, Iris."

"You owe me." The smile was back. "Don't think I'll forget."

Her tires crunched on the gravel as she drove away.

Phee waited for me outside the motel office, her arms crossed and her expression unreadable.

"One night," she said. "Years ago."

"Phee…" I stepped closer and took her hands in mine. "There's no one but you. You and Kiernan. That's the only thing I want. The only thing I'll ever want."

She studied me, and whatever she found must have satisfied her, because the tension in her shoulders eased.

The room smelled like industrial cleaner and stale cigarettes. There were two double beds with floral bedspreads that had seen better decades, a television from another era bolted to the dresser, and a window with blinds that were bent and broken in several places. I swept the space out of habit—checking the bathroom, the closet, behind the furniture. Phee did the same with her phone, scanning for listening devices. We found nothing but dust.

"Clear," she said, dropping into a chair that looked less disgusting than the beds.

I sat in the other one. "We should talk about tonight."

"I've found a few mentions of the Crucible, mainly in online forums." She handed me her mobile. "It's hardly the Thorned Thistle," she added under her breath.

"I doubt many places would compare. If any."

"What's our plan?" she asked when I handed the device.

"We can't exactly walk in there, asking questions about Kiernan Lockhart."

"Right."

"So we go in as a couple," I said. "Curious. New to the scene. Looking for a club where we can explore what we want. The kind of dynamic we had at Greymarch. A triad. A dom who can handle both of us."

"And ask about safety precautions, given a rumor that's circulating about the place."

"About a woman who died." As I said the words, dread settled in the pit of my stomach.

We had six hours to prepare. Six hours to figure out how to walk into a world we'd only glimpsed at Greymarch—a world where Kiernan had been someone else before he ever found us.

My eyes met Phee's. The same trepidation stared back at me.

19

Ophelia

The Crucible occupied a narrow brick building wedged between a tattoo parlor and an abandoned print shop. No sign marked its entrance. Just a matte black door with a small camera mounted above it.

Oliver pressed the buzzer, and a voice crackled through the speaker. He gave the cover names we'd agreed on in the cab, and the door clicked open.

The interior surprised me. I'd expected the kind of place where secrets festered in dark corners. Instead, we stepped into a reception area that wouldn't have looked out of place in a high-end spa. Soft lighting, exposed brick walls hung with abstract art, and a woman behind a sleek desk smiled as we approached.

"Welcome to the Crucible. First time?"

"Yes." Oliver's charm was effortless, even now. "We've heard wonderful things."

"We require a brief orientation for new guests. Safety guidelines, consent expectations, house rules." She slid two tablets across the desk. "Please read these over. A staff member will give you a tour once you've finished reading and have added your signatures."

The guidelines were comprehensive. Safewords. Consent verification at every stage. No photography. No touching without explicit permission. Privacy expectations for members.

Where the Thorned Thistle had felt like a refuge, this place felt like a stage set. The art was too meticulously chosen. The lighting was too deliberately moody. Every element seemed designed to convey an image rather than create genuine safety.

Or maybe I was projecting my own unease onto the decor.

We signed the forms and were handed off to a young man in black who led us through a heavy door and into the club proper.

The main floor opened up before us—high ceilings with steel beams, a bar along one wall, and scattered seating areas where people gathered in small clusters. Music pulsed at a volume that allowed conversation but discouraged shouting. The crowd ranged from curious newcomers in black cocktail attire to regulars who'd shed pretense along with most of their clothing. Leather and latex caught the light. Collars gleamed at throats. A woman in nothing but a thong and nipple clamps knelt at her dom's feet while he conversed with friends. A man in a full-body harness leaned on the edge of the bar. His sub's leash was wrapped loosely around his wrist.

"The main floor is open to all members," our guide explained. "Private rooms are available by reservation on the second floor. The third floor is for members only."

"How long has the club been open?" Oliver asked.

"Ten years in this location. The original Crucible operated in Hackney for about a decade before that."

"Long history, then."

"We're proud of it." The guide gestured toward the bar. "Feel free to explore. Staff members are available if you have questions. Enjoy your evening."

He disappeared into the crowd, leaving us alone.

We made our way to the bar. Oliver ordered wine, and I asked for a vodka tonic. While we waited, I surveyed the room. Two exits were visible from here—the main entrance we'd come through and a fire door in the rear that was partially obscured by a curtain. There were probably more on the upper floors.

"First impressions?" Oliver murmured.

"Polished. Almost too much so." I accepted my drink from the bartender and took a sip. "Like they're trying very hard to look legitimate."

"Overcompensating?"

"Maybe."

We found a spot near one of the support columns where we could observe without being obvious about it. The crowd continued to thicken as the hour grew later. I counted heads, noted the ratio of staff to guests, and looked for anyone who might be watching us. Nothing stood out yet. But the night was young.

"Let's get to work," I said.

Oliver nodded and offered his arm.

We approached a group near the bar first—two women and a man whose body language read as open and relaxed. Oliver introduced us as newcomers curious about the community, and they welcomed us with enthusiasm. The taller woman said she'd been coming here for two years. The man was newer, brought in by his girlfriend. They talked about the events and the sense of belonging they'd found.

"That's wonderful," I said when she paused for a breath. "We've been looking for a place like this. Somewhere safe and established."

"Oh, it's very safe." She nodded vigorously. "Management takes it seriously."

"That's good to hear." Oliver leaned in and spoke in a lower tone. "We actually heard there might have been some kind of incident here a few years ago. We wanted to check the place out before committing."

Her companion's hand tightened on his glass, and the warmth drained from her face.

"I've not heard of anything like that," she muttered.

"No? Someone mentioned—"

"I've never had a problem." She turned to her companions with a smile that didn't reach her eyes. "We should go check on our friend."

They were gone before Oliver could respond.

We exchanged a glance at what seemed like an overreaction.

We tried again with a man standing alone near one of the observation areas. His hair was gray, his watch expensive, and he had an authoritative bearing. He was friendly at first, happy to explain the different spaces and equipment available for use.

"The private rooms are excellent," he said. "Soundproofed, well-equipped. You can book them for the evening or just a few hours."

"That's good to know." Oliver steered the conversation with the ease of long practice. "We want to find the right fit. A place with a solid reputation. No scandals, no drama."

"Every club has history," he said before excusing himself and disappearing into the crowd.

We retreated to the bar for fresh drinks. This time, I skipped the vodka and opted for lemon and tonic.

"Interesting pattern of deflection," I commented. "As the man said, every club has history."

Oliver's eyes scrunched. "Which means there's a story here."

I scanned the room a second time, and the hair on the back of my neck bristled. The energy had changed in the last hour. Everything seemed darker, more charged. The music seemed louder and the shadows deeper. The faces around us had become less distinct, as though everyone had donned masks since we arrived.

Beneath that general unease, a different sensation prickled through me. The weight of someone's eyes on us.

I'd been trained to recognize surveillance. Years of fieldwork had honed the instinct until it was as reliable as any of my other senses. Most people couldn't identify the feeling consciously—they grew uneasy without understanding why. But what I felt at the base of my skull was unmistakable.

The attention wasn't casual, and it wasn't the idle curiosity of strangers noticing newcomers in their space. This focus was intentional. Someone was tracking us.

Rather than trying to spot whoever it was, I shifted closer to Oliver, letting my lips brush his ear as though I were sharing an intimacy.

"We're being watched."

His body didn't tense, and his expression didn't change. "Where?"

"Elevated position, maybe. Above and to the left."

"The observation level?"

"Possibly."

"Coincidence? New faces attract attention."

"No." The sensation was too intense. "This feels targeted. Like whoever's watching doesn't want us here, and not because we've been asking questions."

Oliver's hand found mine on the bar. To anyone observing, we were a couple sharing a moment. Only the tension in his grip gave him away.

"Do we leave?"

I considered it. We'd gathered almost nothing useful—just the confirmation that something had happened here and no one was willing to talk about it. Leaving now meant returning empty-handed, but staying meant operating blind against an unknown threat.

"Not yet," I decided. "But stay close. Watch my back."

"Always."

We stepped away from the bar, threading through the crowd with the aimless drift of newcomers taking in the sights. I kept my posture relaxed and let my face assume an expression of mild curiosity. Inside, every nerve ending was firing.

The sensation didn't fade. If anything, it intensified. We were being tracked, and the person doing it was adjusting their position to keep us in view. I caught myself trying to spot a face that appeared too often in my peripheral vision, but I saw nothing definitive.

We paused near a scene in progress and watched a woman bound to a spanking bench while her partner worked her over with a flogger. The crowd around them was attentive. I wasn't.

If someone here knew who we were—knew we were connected to Kiernan—they could be anyone. The possibilities multiplied faster than I could sort them.

"Second level," Oliver murmured. "Two o'clock. Man in the gray shirt. He's had an eye on us for the past five minutes."

I didn't look directly. I let my gaze drift in that direction as though I were taking in the architecture. The observation level wrapped around three sides of the main floor, separated by a waist-high railing of wrought iron. I spotted the man Oliver had identified—middle-aged, forgettable face, standing with a drink in his hand.

"He's a spotter," I said.

"Working for someone else."

"Yes."

The question was who. And why.

We completed another circuit of the main floor, but with renewed purpose. I wanted to flush them out, force whoever was watching to reveal themselves, but they were too good.

Which meant we were being hunted, and I couldn't figure out by whom.

"We should go." Oliver's voice was steady, but an edge ran beneath it. "We're not going to get answers tonight, and we're exposed."

He was right. It was time to extract.

"Fire exit," I said.

My hand found Oliver's, and we quickened our pace as we walked through the crowd. The curtain in front of us was heavy velvet, and beyond it, I could see the green glow of an exit sign. We were ten meters at most.

Oliver pushed through the curtain first. I followed half a step behind into an empty corridor, already reaching for the push bar on the fire door. We made it three more steps.

The taser hit Oliver first. His body seized, and a strangled sound escaped his throat as he went down hard. I spun toward the threat, but a second set of prongs caught me in the shoulder before I could engage.

Electricity ripped through my body. Every muscle locked, and my legs buckled. The concrete floor rushed up to meet me, and I couldn't even get my hands out to break the fall.

Footsteps approached. Three sets, maybe four. Voices I couldn't process through the roar in my skull. Someone grabbed my wrists and wrenched them behind my back. Zip ties bit into my skin.

I tried to speak. Tried to fight. My body refused every command.

The last thing I saw before the hood came down was Oliver's face, blood already welling from where his head had struck the floor.

Then darkness.

I woke to cold and the taste of copper.

The hood was gone. I blinked against dim, flickering light, trying to think through the fog. My arms and legs were strapped to a chair, and when I tested the restraints, the zip ties cut deeper into my skin. A groan to my left made me turn my head. The motion sent pain lancing through my skull. Oliver was beside me, also bound the way I was. Dark and dried blood matted the hair at his temple. He was conscious, his jaw tight, and his eyes were scanning the space around us.

He tested his restraints, but they didn't give. "Phee," he whispered. "Are you hurt?"

"I don't think so, but you're bleeding."

"I know." He tried to look around. "Where in the bloody hell are we?"

I glanced around at the dim space. Low ceilings were lined with sweating pipes, and walls of old brick were stained with age. The floor was cracked concrete, sloping toward a drain in the center. There was a single heavy door at the far end but no windows.

Candles—dozens of them, maybe hundreds—covered every surface. They sat on shelves, ledges, and were clustered on the floor. A St. Andrew's cross with cracked leather straps and a padded bench, worn and abandoned, sat against the wall, and chains were coiled on the floor.

"That door is the only exit I can see."

"Same," Oliver said. "The spotter on the observation deck must've realized we planned to leave, then followed as we made our way to the exit."

We'd been outhunted. Outmaneuvered. And now, we were trapped.

Fabric shifted from the far corner of the room, then a man rose and crossed into the candlelight.

He was tall and lean, with dark hair and a face that might have been handsome years ago. He carried the stillness of someone who never wasted motion, and his eyes burned with an intensity that made my skin crawl.

The gun in his right hand was aimed at Oliver's chest.

"Good," he said. "You're awake."

"Who the fuck are you?" Oliver asked.

The man smiled, but it didn't reach his eyes.

"I've been watching you for weeks." He crossed to stand before us, just out of reach. "You're my master's newest acquisitions."

My stomach roiled, and I thought I might be sick.

"Wondering why he sent you away so abruptly?" The smile widened. "That was my doing." His tone was almost tender. "I documented everything, then warned him to get rid of you, or I'd destroy you and him."

It was as we'd both guessed somewhere deep beneath our insecurities. He'd sent us away to protect us.

"I've been waiting all this time for him to care about someone again," the man continued. "Then you two walked into his life, and I knew my patience had finally paid off."

"What do you want?" Oliver asked.

"I want him to suffer." The tenderness curdled. "I want him to know what it feels like to lose everything. And I want you to understand exactly what kind of man you gave yourselves to."

He took a mobile from his pocket, punched something on the screen, then set it aside.

"Now that he knows I have you, he'll come. He won't be able to help himself."

"If you're trying to hurt him through us—" I started.

"I'm *trying* to destroy him." He dropped into a chair with the gun resting on his knee. "And when he arrives, I'm going to tell you both who he really is and what he did."

His gaze drank in our fear.

"Like you. I was Kiernan's once," he sneered. "Before he decided I wasn't worth keeping.

20

Kiernan

The library had become a command center. Laptops were open on every surface, secure lines were established, and the fire burned low because none of us had thought to tend it. We'd been at this for hours but were no closer to figuring out who'd sent the photos.

I hadn't slept. Every time I closed my eyes, I saw Oliver's face and Ophelia's quiet devastation when I'd told them to leave. They'd looked at me like I'd betrayed them.

I had. To protect them.

The irony wasn't lost on me. Seven years ago, I'd severed ties with Elise and James to protect myself—from their growing demands, from the weight of responsibility I wasn't ready to carry. Now, I'd done it again, but for the opposite reason. This time, I'd cut them loose to keep them safe. That made the wound deeper. Because this time, I knew exactly what I was losing.

Rafe, who'd left hours ago to look into the breach at the Thorned Thistle, walked in. He looked as haggard as I felt.

"I found it. Six weeks ago, someone accessed the booking system remotely. They deleted records and created blind spots in our camera coverage."

"How did they get in?" Gus asked.

"Maintenance credential. Someone who worked for us during the east wing renovation two and a half years ago." He looked up. "The credential was never fully deactivated. Whoever did this learned our systems from the inside—every gap, every weakness."

Someone had walked our halls and exploited our vulnerabilities. I dragged my hands over my face as the possibility of who might have done this settled in. But why now?

"Kiernan." Callen's voice cut through my racing thoughts. "Snow's team just checked in."

"And?"

"Oliver and Ophelia aren't in the penthouse."

The words didn't register at first. "What do you mean?"

"His people went to do a status check, and the flat's empty."

I jumped to my feet. "*When?* How long have they been gone?"

"Working on it. I'm trying to reach Snow directly." Callen's phone was pressed to his ear.

The next few minutes were chaos. His calls went to voicemail. Finally, one of Snow's men—an operative named Harris—answered.

"Where's Snow?" Callen demanded.

I couldn't hear the response, but his face went blank. Never a good sign.

"When?" A pause. "And no one thought to inform us?" Another pause. "Right. Keep me posted."

He lowered his device. "Snow went dark in the middle of the night. His team says he got a priority call and left. No explanation, no timeline for return."

Doren Snow disappearing wasn't a surprise. He was Unit 23's ghost—the operative they sent when everyone else had failed. He answered to almost no one, disappeared for weeks at a time, and had a body count that existed only in classified files buried so deep they might as well not exist. God knew where he was now or who he'd been sent to kill.

"So what you're saying then is Oliver and Ophelia are missing and we have no idea where they are?" I said through gritted teeth.

Gus and Rafe both raised their heads.

"Harris is pulling footage now. Give him ten minutes," said Callen.

"Like hell," I muttered, opening my laptop and pulling up the penthouse building's security feeds. My building. My bloody security system. At least that gave me direct access without having to explain myself to anyone.

"Gus, take transport networks. Tube stations, bus routes, anything with cameras within a mile of the penthouse." I didn't look up from my screen.

"On it."

Callen was on his mobile again, working his own contacts. "I need eyes on every private airfield within fifty miles of London. Any flight plans filed in the last twelve hours…" He positioned himself by the window, and his voice dropped.

The lobby cameras showed nothing useful. Neither did the underground car park or the main entrance. I scrubbed backward from the current timestamp, watching Snow's team patrol the corridors, check the lift, and otherwise maintain their positions. They were professional, attentive, and completely fucking oblivious.

"Wait." I switched to the thirty-second floor. There—a service corridor marked MAINTENANCE ONLY. At eleven hundred hours, the door opened and two figures slipped through. Oliver first, then Ophelia. They were going fast and staying low like they knew exactly where they were going.

"Got 'em." I tracked them through the maintenance passage to the freight elevator. From there, to the sub-basement, then to the loading dock on the east side of the building. A fifteen-second gap existed between camera sweeps. I'd never thought to close it because who would know about it? Someone obviously had.

They'd timed it perfectly, sprinting across the loading bay and around the corner in exactly fourteen seconds.

They'd left willingly. They'd planned this. And someone had given them the blueprint to escape my own flat.

I switched to the Met's real-time CCTV feed—Unit 23 credentials opened doors that didn't exist for anyone else—and found a camera in the alley behind the building. A black Audi had been waiting. Oliver and Ophelia climbed in, and it sped off. No hesitation.

"Pulling the registration database now." Gus had already pivoted. "Cross-referencing black Audis in Greater London with—"

"Don't bother. The plates will likely be stolen or cloned." I grabbed the car's image and fed it into the CCTV network's vehicle recognition system. "I'm tracking it through the city. Gus, flag any camera gaps—if they go dark, I need to know which routes they could have taken from there."

The Audi wound through London's streets like the driver had memorized every camera placement. They avoided major intersections, stuck to secondary roads, and disappeared into known blind spots. It was methodical and deliberate.

Just not deliberate enough.

"There you are," I muttered. A camera near the A2 caught the vehicle heading southeast. I was building a pattern, predicting the gaps, jumping ahead to catch them on the other side.

"They're heading southeast," Gus confirmed, tracking parallel to my search. "Toward Kent. There's a cluster of camera dead zones around—"

"Bloody fucking hell." I froze on a grainy shot of the Audi pulling into the car park of a budget motel off the A2 at twelve hundred thirty.

I enhanced the image as far as the resolution would allow. The driver's door opened, and a woman with bottle-blonde hair and red lipstick stepped out.

"Son of a bitch," Callen said quietly from behind me. "It's Iris fucking Beacham."

"Why would she get involved?" Gus asked.

"One of them asked," I said, brushing my lower lip with my index finger. "Most likely Oliver."

"They ran missions together a few years ago," Rafe confirmed, reading something on his screen. "Knowing Iris, they have personal history along with professional."

I'd made the same assumption; however, that wasn't important now. Oliver and Ophelia had wanted out of the penthouse, and given Iris' tainted reputation within SIS, she was the most logical choice to ask for help. The woman began her career with MI5, which meant she knew every back corridor and service entrance in London—she'd know exactly how to slip surveillance.

I pulled footage from traffic cameras around the motel, tracking the Audi's exit. Iris left moments after dropping them off, and so far, there was no new movement.

Callen's hand landed on my shoulder. I looked up, knowing as soon as our eyes met that he was about to say something I didn't want to hear.

"Kier, we need to talk about who might be behind this."

"We've been over the list. Former club members with grudges. Business rivals. Foreign agents who might want leverage—"

"I'm not talking about the list." Callen's gaze held mine steadily. "The breach at the Thistle? A maintenance credential from the east wing renovation? Someone who knew exactly where our cameras had blind spots?"

He was right, and I knew it. Still, I asked, "When was that renovation?"

"Two and a half years ago." Callen's voice was quiet. "Long enough to plan something like this."

I glanced over at Gus and Rafe, who'd stopped what they were doing to listen.

While all four of my partners were aware of the trag-edy that took place, only Callen knew the full story.

"Kier?" he prompted.

I nodded. "Let's say he had opportunity. What would his motive be?"

Gus stood. "Enough with the subterfuge, Kiernan. Obviously, you and Callen know who sent the photos, or at least have a strong suspicion. Enlighten Rafe and me."

I looked at Callen, and he nodded.

I walked to the window to gather my thoughts. I'd never intended to speak of this again. Never thought there'd be reason to. "As you know, a woman I was involved with died seven years ago." I rubbed my eyes. "What you don't know is there was a third person involved. His name is James Mercer."

Gus' expression shifted from frustration to sharp attention. "Meaning he was involved with you and the woman?"

"That's right. They were my submissives for almost two years. I met them at a club in Inverness. Elise approached me first, and James came into the dynamic through her." I stared at the fire and made myself dredge up memories I'd spent years trying to bury. "James worked in IT, network security specifically. He was good at it."

The fire crackled. No one spoke.

"At first, everything was contained. We scened at the club and occasionally at Greymarch. But over time, they wanted more. They saw this place, this life, and they wanted to be part of it permanently. They wanted me to marry Elise and for the three of us to live here together, with the dynamic becoming a fully merged life.”

As hard as it was, I made myself keep going. “Things changed then. James’ submission became unhealthy. His entire identity had wrapped itself around me, around pleasing me, around earning his place here. Elise started pushing for legitimacy—the title, the security, the life of a viscountess. What we had stopped nourishing them and consumed them instead.”

“You ended it.” Rafe’s tone made it clear it wasn’t a question.

“I ended it wrong.” The admission scraped me raw. “I severed the relationship the same way I handle every threat—completely and abruptly, with no transition and no aftercare for the ending itself. I just cut them off.”

Callen’s jaw tightened. He’d heard this before, but hearing it again clearly didn’t make it easier.

“Elise spiraled. It took months, but she found another dom. She started going to the Crucible—a club in London without the kind of safety measures we now maintain at the Thistle. A breath-play scene went wrong.” I met Gus’ eyes, then Rafe’s. “She died.”

“Christ,” Gus muttered.

"James blamed me. He came to Greymarch after the funeral, screaming accusations. I had him removed from the property." I returned to my desk and took a seat. "I didn't hear from him again and assumed he'd eventually built a new life."

"But he didn't," Rafe said quietly.

"No. He didn't." I stared at the fire. "He was right to blame me. If I'd handled the ending differently…if I'd made sure they had support, that they weren't isolated…"

"You can't know that," Rafe said.

"I know I threw two vulnerable people out of my life without a safety net, and one of them is dead." My voice caught. "That's what I know."

Silence stretched between us.

"That's why you and Callen started the Thorned Thistle." Gus spoke slowly as the realization dawned on his face. "The rules. The safety measures. The obsessive attention to aftercare. We opened two years after she died."

"That's right." I met his eyes. "Every rule we enforce exists because she walked into a place that didn't have them."

Rafe opened another window on the screen and typed rapidly. "I went through our archived security footage again and looked more closely at the maintenance visits during the renovation." He paused. "There."

I stood and looked over his shoulder. So did Callen. The image was grainy, but clear enough. A man in coveralls, carrying a toolbox, walking through our service corridor. Dark hair. Average height. Face partially obscured by the angle of the camera.

"Can you enhance it?" Callen asked.

Rafe zoomed in. The man had turned slightly, offering a three-quarter profile as he punched in an access code.

My heart stopped.

"I think that could be him," I said slowly, studying the familiar angle of the jaw and the way he held himself. But it had been so long. The man I'd known had been softer, younger, still finding himself.

Callen put his hand on my shoulder. "Kiernan, that's James."

The certainty in his voice cut through my doubt. Callen had met him a handful of times, years ago. But he'd always had an eye for faces—a skill that made him invaluable in the field.

I looked again. The slope of his shoulders. The way he tilted his head. Older, harder, but unmistakably him.

James had walked into my club, worked alongside my staff, learned every vulnerability in our systems—and I'd never known. He'd been patient. Methodical. Plotting this for years.

"Son of a bitch," I seethed.

"He created a false identity," said Callen. "And he has motive."

Rafe's brow furrowed. "If he posed as staff, he had access to learn our systems from the inside. With his IT background, he could've done significant damage to our systems."

"More importantly, Oliver and Ophelia are missing," Callen finished.

"If James is behind the surveillance, he's been watching, waiting, and now—"

Rafe's laptop chimed. He glanced at the screen, then his whole body went rigid. "Oliver and Ophelia just left the motel."

I was at his shoulder in two strides, watching them climb into a cab.

"Track them," I said.

Rafe jumped between CCTV feeds as the cab wound through South London. Gus had his own laptop open, mapping the route in real time.

"They're heading north," he said. "Toward the river."

"*No.*" My blood ran cold as the pattern emerged. "They're heading northeast. Toward Shoreditch."

Rafe looked up. "What's in Shoreditch?"

"The Crucible." The words nauseated me. "That's where Elise died. If they know what happened—"

"They're walking straight into a trap," Callen finished.

"We have to get there. *Now.*"

Callen was already reaching for his mobile. "I can have the helicopter ready in fifteen minutes. We'll be in London before twenty-one hundred."

I grabbed my jacket. "Do it."

The helicopter lifted off from Greymarch at nineteen hundred hours, banking south over the dark hills. Callen was at the controls, with Gus beside him. Rafe and I sat in the back, laptops balanced on our knees, headsets crackling with the roar of the rotors.

"Two hours if conditions hold," Callen said through the comms. "Maybe a bit longer."

According to our surveillance, Oliver and Ophelia had entered the Crucible ten minutes ago. Anything could happen in two hours.

I'd called both of them several times since I realized who'd sent the photos, and each one went straight to voicemail. "They're not answering," I muttered unnecessarily.

"They're undercover at a kink club," Rafe said through the headset. "Most places like that require phones checked at the door or stored in lockers. Privacy rules."

I knew that. I'd helped write the Thistle's policies myself. But knowing didn't make the silence any easier to bear.

"What about Harris?" Gus asked. "He's still in London."

"On the wrong side of it." I was already pulling up his number. "But it's worth a try."

Harris answered on the second ring. "Sir?"

"Oliver and Ophelia. They're at a club called the Crucible in Shoreditch. 47 Grimsby Street. I need you there now."

A pause. "I'm thirty minutes out, sir, maybe more. And I don't have membership to—"

"That's ninety minutes sooner than we can get there. I don't care about membership. Head there now and take whatever backup you can put together. Watch every way in or out. Do not let them leave without contacting me."

"Understood, sir."

"Call the club directly," Callen suggested.

I found the number through a quick search and dialed. It rang eight times, then went to voicemail. "You've reached the Crucible. Leave a message, and we'll return your call during normal business hours."

No help there. At this hour, the staff would be on the floor, not answering phones.

"Police?" Gus asked, though his tone suggested he already knew the answer.

"And tell them what? Two MI6 officers are voluntarily at a legal establishment, and I'm worried they might run into my ex?" I shook my head even though no one could see it. "No crime's been committed. They won't act. And if they did, they'd blow any cover they've established and create a different disaster."

"What do we know about the club's layout?" Callen asked. "Entry points, exits, security?"

Rafe pulled up schematics on his screen. "It's a converted warehouse. Main entrance on Grimsby, service entrance in the alley behind. Three floors—ground level bar and social space, first floor private rooms, basement for"—he paused—"more intensive scenes."

The basement. Where Elise had died.

"Security?"

"Two at the front door. No weapons—this is a kink club, not a fortress. But they take member privacy seriously. We won't be able to just walk in."

"We won't have a problem. James wants me there."

"That's what worries me," Callen said quietly.

My device buzzed with a message from Harris.

Arrived at Grimsby Street. No visual on targets. Club entrance has two security. No way inside without membership. Holding position.

"How much longer?" I asked.

"Seventy minutes," Callen said. "I'm pushing it as fast as I can."

"Just get us there," I said. "Whatever it takes."

The helicopter touched down at London City Airport at twenty-one thirty. Callen had called in favors to secure emergency landing clearance, which meant we'd be on our way in minutes rather than the hour it would take to navigate Heathrow or any of the larger airports.

I was unbuckling my harness when my mobile buzzed.

Unknown number.

I opened the message, and the image that filled the screen stopped my heart.

Candles flickered around the chairs where Oliver and Ophelia sat gagged and bound. Ophelia's face was pale, but the blood matted at Oliver's temple sent chills up my spine. His recovery from the previous head injury was still tentative.

A second message followed. *You know where I am. Come alone. You have until midnight.*

"Kiernan." Callen's voice came from far away. "What is it?"

I couldn't speak. I turned the phone so they could see. Gus swore, and Rafe's face went white.

"Kiernan." Callen's voice was steady. "We go together."

"He said alone. If he sees anyone else, he'll kill them. Follow at a distance and monitor the exits. But I walk in alone."

Twenty minutes later, I stood in the alley behind the Crucible. Callen, Gus, and Rafe were nearby. If things went wrong, they'd be ready.

As expected, the service entrance was unlocked.

I checked the firearm at my hip—loaded, safety off—and started down the stairs.

James was waiting at the bottom with a gun in his hand.

"Kiernan." He looked older, harder than I remembered. "You came."

"Let them go. This is between you and me."

"I've just been telling them about Elise." His voice was eerily calm as he stepped closer, removed the two weapons I carried, and tossed them into a dark area beside us. "About what you did to us. About how she died in this very room because of what you did to her. To us."

I held his gaze. "I was not responsible for Elise's death."

"Weren't you?" He circled me. "You have no idea what it felt like to be discarded by you. To watch Elise spiral because she couldn't survive without the structure you'd given her, then ripped away."

"James—"

"No. I've waited seven years to say this to you." The calm cracked. "You moved on. You built your precious club with all your safety rules, and you told yourself that made up for it. That you'd learned your lesson." He gestured toward Oliver and Ophelia. "Now, you've found new toys to play with."

"They're not—"

"I've been watching. I've seen the way you look at them. The way you touch them. You never looked at us that way. Never touched us that way." His hand tightened on the gun. "You're capable of it. You just couldn't feel it for me. For her."

"You're right," I said quietly.

James blinked. Whatever he'd expected, it wasn't agreement.

"I couldn't give you what you needed. Either of you." I took a step closer. "You deserved a dom who could be fully present. Someone who wasn't disappearing for weeks, holding back pieces of himself. I knew I couldn't be that person, and I took you on anyway because I was selfish. Because I wanted what you offered without paying the price for it."

"Pretty words." His voice wavered.

"It's the truth." I met his eyes. "Elise went looking and found the wrong dom because I failed her. You've spent all these years in hell because I failed you. Nothing I say changes that." I spread my hands. "But Oliver and Ophelia haven't failed you. They've never even met you. Whatever justice you think you're owed, they're not part of it."

"They're part of you now."

"Then, take me." I stepped forward. "I'm right here. Willing. Let them go, and take whatever revenge you need."

Rage and grief warred across his face.

Then he looked past me. To Oliver. To Ophelia.

The moment he made his decision was written in every line of his body.

"You really do love them." He said it like a revelation. Like a knife sliding between ribs.

"James—"

The gun swung toward Oliver, and time slowed down. James' finger tightened on the trigger. Oliver's eyes went wide, and I didn't hesitate. I threw myself in the line of fire.

I felt the impact before I heard it—a punch to the chest that spun me sideways and dropped me to the stone floor. At first, there was no pain, just pressure.

Then my nerves caught fire.

I couldn't breathe. My chest was a solid wall of agony. I tried to move, to see if Oliver was okay, if the bullet had passed through me and hit him anyway, but my body wouldn't cooperate. All I could do was lie on the cold stone and feel the warmth spreading beneath me, soaking into my shirt, and pooling on the floor.

Somewhere far away, there was shouting. Footsteps on the stairs—too many of them, too fast. Callen's voice, and Gus', and Rafe's. The words blurred into a roar.

A second shot rang out. Not as loud.

Then Ophelia was there, on the floor beside me. She was crying, saying my name and other things I couldn't hear over the ringing in my ears.

Hands landed on my chest. Pressure that should have hurt, but didn't. Oliver's face swam into view above me—pale, terrified, blood still crusted at his temple. He was saying something over and over, the same words, but I couldn't make them out.

I wanted to tell him I was sorry. For sending them away. For keeping secrets. For making them think, even briefly, that I didn't want them with every fiber of my being.

I wanted to tell Ophelia that she was the bravest person I'd ever known. That her submission was a gift I didn't deserve. That the sound of her saying "yes, sir" had rewired something fundamental in me.

I wanted to tell them both that these past two weeks had been the happiest of my life. That they'd shown me what I was capable of feeling. That even if this was the end, I wouldn't trade a moment of it.

Except my mouth wouldn't form the words. Everything grew dim and cold and far away. My vision narrowed to their faces—Oliver and Ophelia, together, their hands on my chest like they could hold my life inside me through sheer force of will.

"Stay with us," Oliver was saying. I could hear him now. "Kiernan, goddamn it, stay with us. Help is coming. You have to hold on."

I tried to. I tried so hard, but the darkness was warm, and soft, and it didn't hurt anymore.

The last thing I saw was them. The last thing I felt was their hands on my skin.

If I had to die, I thought, at least I got to die for something that mattered.

Then there was nothing at all.

21

Oliver

The second shot cracked through the basement right after Kiernan hit the ground. The dark bloom was already spreading beneath James' temple. He'd turned the gun on himself.

Footsteps thundered down the stairs. Voices shouted commands I couldn't process. None of it mattered. Kiernan lay motionless on the cold stone, with blood pooling beneath him, and I couldn't reach him.

"Oliver." Rafe appeared in front of me, removed the gag, and cut my restraints. "Hold still."

"Kiernan—"

"Callen's with him."

The plastic gave way, and I was up before Rafe could say another word. My legs buckled—too long in the chair, blood flow compromised—and I caught myself on the wall, then pushed off toward Kiernan.

Callen knelt beside him and pressed a wadded jacket on Kiernan's upper left chest. In the candlelight, Kiernan's face was white and still.

I dropped to my knees on his other side. "Is he—"

"Breathing. Pulse is weak." Callen's voice was clipped, controlled, but I'd worked with him long enough to hear the fear underneath. "Ambulance is three minutes out. I need more pressure here. Can you—"

My hands covered his, then slid beneath as he repositioned. The jacket was already drenched beneath my palms. His life, draining away beneath my hands.

I pressed harder. The wound pulsed against my palms—his heartbeat, faint but present. I matched my breathing to it without meaning to. As long as I could feel that rhythm, he was still here. As long as the blood kept flowing, his heart was still pumping.

The logic was backwards. I knew that. The blood needed to stay inside him, not seep into the fabric and pool on the floor. But my brain had stopped working in straight lines.

The jacket grew heavier in my grip, but I couldn't let go. Letting go meant giving up, and giving up meant admitting that this might be the end—that Kiernan might bleed out on this basement floor while I knelt beside him and did nothing.

I'd held dying men before. In the field, in back alleys, in bombed-out buildings where the dust was still settling. This was different. This was Kiernan.

Behind me, Rafe cut Ophelia free. Her sharp intake of breath carried across the basement, followed by her footsteps. She appeared on Kiernan's other side, found his hand with one of hers, and pressed her other one to mine to add more pressure.

"Don't you dare leave us," she whispered.

Gus went to check James' body. A moment later, he crouched near us again. "He's gone."

I didn't react. Nothing existed except Kiernan's face. I willed his eyes to open, willed his chest to keep rising and falling beneath my palms. The candles flickered at the edges of my vision. Sirens wailed somewhere above us, distant and too slow.

The bullet had been meant for me.

The thought spiraled. James had shifted his aim. The movement had been unmistakable. And Kiernan had reacted faster than thought, faster than instinct, putting himself between the gun and me like his life was worth less.

I wanted to scream at him. I wanted to shake him until his eyes opened so I could tell him he was wrong.

His life wasn't a bargaining chip. His death wouldn't protect us—it would destroy us.

But he lay motionless beneath my hands, and all I could do was press harder and pray.

"Keep talking to him." Gus had a mobile pressed to his ear as he relayed information to the emergency services. "Keep him grounded."

"Kiernan." I leaned closer until my lips were near his ear. "Stay with us. Help is almost here. Just hold on."

No response. His eyelids didn't even flutter.

Ophelia stripped off her cardigan and passed it to me to replace the jacket that was now useless. I pressed it down. My hands had gone slick, and the fabric kept slipping. I adjusted my grip and pressed harder.

"Two minutes," Gus said. "They're coming in the service entrance."

I'd trained for scenarios like this. Field medicine. Emergency triage. How to keep someone alive long enough for help to arrive. But training didn't prepare you for the sound of your own voice breaking as you begged someone to hold on. Training didn't account for love.

"You don't get to do this." The words came out raw. "You don't get to throw yourself in front of bullets and leave us behind. That's not how this works."

Ophelia gripped his hand harder. "We didn't come all this way to lose you."

The absurdity of it struck me—both of us bargaining with an unconscious man, as if words could stitch wounds closed. But I couldn't stop. The silence felt too much like giving up.

"Remember what you told me? In the playroom, after you punished me." I leaned closer and pressed harder. "You said I belonged to you. Both of us did." The words caught. "Well, you belong to us too. And we're not letting you go."

His chest rose. Fell. Rose again. Each breath a victory I couldn't take for granted. Each pause between them a small death.

Footsteps echoed on the stairs. Voices called out, and torchlight swept across the space. Green uniforms descended—paramedics with equipment that looked clinical and hopeful.

"Gunshot wound to the upper left chest," Gus reported. "He's been down approximately four minutes. Breathing shallow, pulse thready."

The lead paramedic knelt beside me. "Sir, I need you to move so I can assess the wound."

I didn't want to. Every instinct screamed at me to stay where I was, to hold his life inside him with sheer will. As long as I kept pressure on the wound, he couldn't die. As long as I stayed here, I wasn't useless.

But I knew when to step aside.

I leaned away and looked down at my hands. They were covered in blood. Dark and drying at the edges, wet and red closer to my palms. It had seeped into the creases of my skin, pooled beneath my fingernails, and stained the cuffs of my shirt. All of it Kiernan's.

I'd held his life in my hands. I might not have held it well enough.

I'd done everything I could—stayed steady, talked to him, begged him to hold on. But what if everything I did wasn't enough? What if he needed more, and I'd failed him?

Ophelia gripped my wrist. Her touch anchored me.

The paramedics worked fast. They cut away his shirt, exposed the wound—a ragged hole just below his left collarbone—and applied pressure dressings. They checked his vitals, started an IV, and spoke to each other in clipped shorthand. Numbers and abbreviations. A language of crisis I couldn't follow.

Their hands swept over his body. They knew what they were doing. They had training and equipment and experience. All I'd had was a wadded jacket and the desperate will to keep him alive.

It hadn't been enough. I could see that now, watching them work. My improvised first aid had been clumsy, inadequate, the efforts of a man grasping at straws.

But it had bought time. Maybe that was all that mattered.

I should look away. I couldn't.

This was the man who'd commanded me to my knees. Who'd taken me apart with nothing but his voice and his hands. Who'd looked at me like I was worth claiming.

"BP's dropping," one of them said. "We need to move."

Rafe appeared at my shoulder as they loaded Kiernan onto the stretcher. His hand gripped my arm, and I realized only then that I was swaying.

"We'll handle the scene. Go with him."

"He's strong," Callen added. "Stubborn bastard won't go easy."

I nodded because I didn't trust my voice.

They were lifting the stretcher when Kiernan's eyes opened. Only a sliver—unfocused and glassy—but open.

His lips parted. No sound came out at first. Just the shape of a word his body was too weak to form.

I pushed forward and stood beside the stretcher. "Kiernan. I'm here. We're both here."

His eyes tracked toward my voice. Recognition flickered, dim but present. His mouth opened again.

"You're both safe?" The words were barely a whisper.

My knees nearly buckled, and I grabbed the stretcher rail to stay upright.

His pulse was dropping by the second, and his first conscious thought was to ask if we were safe.

Not "what happened." Not "am I dying." Not "where am I" or "help me" or any of the things a man with a bullet wound should be saying.

You're both safe?

That was Kiernan. That was who he was at his core—a man who would bleed out on a basement floor and use his last conscious breath to make sure we were unharmed.

The fury hit me so hard I couldn't breathe. It tangled with love and terror until I couldn't tell where one ended and the others began.

"You bastard." The words scraped out of me. "You took a bullet for us, and you're asking if we're safe?"

Ophelia appeared at my shoulder. Tears streaked her face, but her voice was steady. "We're fine. You're the one who's hurt."

"Had to." His eyes drifted closed. "Protect…"

"No." I stayed by the stretcher as the paramedics headed toward the stairs. "You don't get to sacrifice yourself and leave us. That's not protecting us. That's destroying us."

His face had gone slack. I wasn't certain he'd heard me.

Then his fingers twitched. The smallest movement, barely visible—him trying to reach for us even now.

Ophelia and I held hands as we followed the stretcher up the stairs, out of the basement, and into the cold night air, where the ambulance waited.

"We're coming with him," Ophelia said, her tone leaving no room for argument.

The paramedic glanced at us—at the blood on our clothes, the desperation in our faces—and nodded. "Family?"

"Yes." The word was instant. "We're his family."

The ambulance interior was bright and sterile. Kiernan lay on the gurney between us with an oxygen mask over his face.

The paramedic adjusted the IV drip, checked the pressure dressing, and called out numbers to her partner in the driver's seat. Systolic. Diastolic. Words that meant everything and nothing.

Ophelia held his hand. Her grip was fierce enough to anchor him to life by determination alone.

I'd been shot at. Beaten. Almost died in an op in Brodick Castle. Would have if Kiernan and Ophelia hadn't found me. Saved me.

None of it compared to this—the dread of watching Kiernan breathe and wondering if each exhale would be his last.

In the field, there was always an enemy. A target. A mission objective. My training gave me tools to survive. But there was no enemy here. No target except death itself, and I couldn't fight that. I couldn't shoot it or outrun it or negotiate with it. I could only sit here and hope.

"Is he going to make it?" The question scraped past my lips before I could stop it.

The paramedic glanced at me. Her expression gave nothing away. "He's stable for now. The doctors will know more once we get him to hospital."

Stable. Not dead. Not dying this second. It didn't mean safe. It didn't mean saved.

The ambulance swayed as it took a corner. Sirens wailed above us, and every bump in the road made me flinch. Each jolt might undo the fragile work keeping him alive.

I pressed my hand to the gurney rail as if my touch could anchor him.

"Don't leave us." Ophelia brought his hand to her lips and pressed a kiss to his knuckles.

Our gazes locked over Kiernan's still form. The same terror, grief, and fierce love that had no outlet except this vigil.

"He knew." My voice was low. "When James raised the gun. He saw where it was aimed, and he just reacted."

"That's who he is." Ophelia's voice was thick. "He'll always put himself between us and danger."

"Then, we have to be the ones who protect him from himself."

She nodded, a tear slipping down her cheek. She didn't wipe it away.

I reached out and laid my hand over Ophelia's. Kiernan's felt cold beneath ours, but his pulse was there—faint and stubborn and still fighting.

The ambulance slowed. Beyond the small window, the emergency entrance came into view. Lights blazed, and figures in scrubs rushed toward us.

"We're here." The paramedic positioned herself to help with the transfer. "They'll take good care of him."

The doors swung open. Cold air rushed in, and Kiernan was lifted out of the ambulance, away from us, to where his life would be fought for by strangers.

Ophelia climbed out first. I followed.

We walked beside the gurney, Ophelia's hand in mine, watching the paramedics call out vitals to the team that met us at the doors.

He was still breathing. Still here. The worst was over.

One of the nurses glanced at the monitor. "Pressure's dropping."

The team worked faster. The steady beep of the monitor stuttered. Skipped.

Kiernan's face had gone gray.

"He's crashing!"

The gurney disappeared through double doors. I tried to follow, but a hand grabbed my arm, holding me on the wrong side.

22

Ophelia

The doors swung shut in our faces.

Oliver stood frozen beside me.

"Sir. Ma'am." A nurse appeared at my elbow. She glanced at our hands, our clothes. "There's a washroom just there. I'll bring you some scrub tops."

I pulled Oliver into the small room. He stood at the sink like he'd forgotten how it worked, so I turned on the tap and guided his hands under the water. Red swirled down the drain. Then pink. Then clear. I washed my own hands next, scrubbing until my skin felt raw, then changed into the clean shirt the nurse had given me. It smelled like hospital laundry. It didn't help.

"The waiting area is just through there. Someone will update you as soon as we know more," another nurse who was waiting in the corridor said when we came out.

I wanted to scream at her. I wanted to put my fist through the door. Instead, I took Oliver's arm and pulled him toward the plastic chairs, because standing here, staring at nothing, wasn't going to save Kiernan's life.

Callen found us twenty minutes later.

He took one look at our faces and went straight for the doors.

A nurse stepped in front of him, but he didn't slow down. It took two orderlies to hold him back, and even then, he nearly got through.

When they finally stopped him, he didn't fight. Didn't speak. He stood there, chest heaving, staring at the doors like he could will them open.

Oliver touched his arm, and Callen flinched like he'd forgotten we existed.

We led him to the chairs, but he wouldn't sit. He stood at the window with his back to us, shoulders rigid, hands clenched at his sides.

At some point, Oliver's fingers laced through mine.

Eventually, Callen sat down.

And we waited.

The clock on the wall read zero three hundred hours. I'd been watching it, counting the seconds between each tick as if the rhythm might anchor me to the present. Oliver sat on my left, close enough that our shoulders touched. Callen was on my right, elbows braced on his knees, head bowed, utterly still.

He hadn't spoken since we'd arrived. The man who always had a dry comment, a sardonic observation, a deflection wrapped in wit, sat in silence, staring at the floor between his feet. His hands were clasped so tightly his knuckles had gone white.

Callen and Kiernan had grown up on neighboring estates. They'd served in MI6 together, joined Unit 23 together, founded the Thorned Thistle together. Kiernan was the closest thing Callen had to a brother. And now, that brother was behind those double doors, either dying or fighting to live, and none of us could do a single thing about it.

I wanted to speak, to offer comfort. But what words existed for this? I'm sure he'll be fine? I didn't believe it. He's strong? Strength didn't stop bullets.

So I sat in silence too, and we waited.

For eight years, I'd trained for every conceivable threat. I could disarm an attacker, pick a lock, and disappear into a crowd of thousands. I could assess a room in three seconds flat and identify every exit, every weapon, every person who might be a danger. I was good at my job. I was very, very good at it.

None of that mattered here. The threat wasn't a person I could fight. It was the damage already done, the minutes that might have stolen too much from him.

The helplessness was worse than fear. Fear I could work with. Helplessness sat in my chest like a stone.

As the minutes dragged past, my training took over without permission—six chairs along the left wall, four along the right, a window that faced the car park, two doors, a water dispenser in the corner. Threat assessment happened whether I wanted it to or not. The habit was so ingrained that my brain kept running calculations even when the only threat was time itself.

Oliver's knee pressed harder against mine. His breathing had gone shallow, and when I glanced at him, his face was chalk-white beneath the fluorescent lights.

"He can't die," he whispered. "Phee, he can't—"

"He won't." I didn't know if it was a promise or a plea or the only words I could think to say.

Callen didn't react. Didn't move. Didn't look up. The stillness was worse than anything he could have said.

I thought about the basement. The zip ties cutting into my wrists. The gag stuffed in my mouth. The absolute uselessness of all my training when I couldn't move or speak or do anything but watch.

I'd sat there while James ranted and Kiernan negotiated and Oliver bled from where James had struck him. I'd sat there while Kiernan stepped in front of that gun.

He'd made a choice. In that split second, he'd decided his life was worth less than Oliver's. He'd decided we would be fine without him. He hadn't asked. He hadn't hesitated. He'd acted.

The anger had been building since then, sharp and hot beneath my ribs. I loved him for it. I hated him for it. If he died tonight, he would die believing he'd done the right thing—and Oliver and I would spend the rest of our lives knowing that his protection had destroyed us.

I wanted to grab him by the shoulders and shake him. I wanted to press my mouth to his and feel him breathe. I wanted to rage at him until he understood that we didn't need a shield. We needed him alive and whole and here.

Six months ago, I hadn't known this man existed. Oliver and I had spent that time circling each other with unspoken attraction, too bound by regulations to act on what we felt. Then Kiernan had opened the doors of Greymarch, and everything had changed.

He'd seen us. Really seen us. He'd recognized desires we hadn't known how to name and given us permission to explore them. He'd commanded and directed and pushed us past every boundary we thought we had, and somewhere in the middle of all that intensity, I'd fallen for him. For both of them. For this impossible thing the three of us were building together.

And now, he might die before we'd had a chance to figure out what it meant.

My head jerked when the double doors swung open.

Callen jumped to his feet as the surgeon strode toward us. Her expression was guarded, unreadable.

"Mr. Cavendish?"

"Yes," Callen answered, standing to approach her.

"You hold Lasting Power of Attorney for Mr. Lockhart's health decisions."

"I do."

Oliver and I had risen too, flanking Callen on either side. The surgeon's gaze swept over us, assessing.

"They're family," Callen stated more than said.

The surgeon nodded once, then turned her attention to him. "Mr. Lockhart made it through surgery. The bullet entered the upper left chest and exited through the posterior deltoid. We've repaired the damage to the surrounding tissue and controlled the internal bleeding."

Callen's shoulders dropped a fraction. Beside me, Oliver made a sound—half gasp, half sob.

But the surgeon wasn't finished.

"However." She paused, and my stomach clenched. "He lost a significant amount of blood before arriving at hospital, and his body went into shock during the procedure. The next twenty-four to forty-eight hours will be critical. We're monitoring him closely for signs of infection and secondary complications."

"What are his chances?" Callen asked. His voice was steady, but the tension in his jaw and the way his hands had curled into fists at his sides communicated far more than his words alone.

"I can't make promises. He's strong—his heart never stopped during surgery, which is a good sign. But the next two days will tell us more than I can right now." She studied Callen's face. "He fought hard. That matters."

"When can we see him?"

"He's being transferred to intensive care now. You can see him once he's settled, but only briefly. He needs rest." She gave us a room number, then walked away. Her attention had already shifted to the next crisis.

He fought hard. The words echoed in my head. Of course he had. Kiernan Lockhart had never surrendered to anything in his life. He'd fought his way through operations that should have killed him, fought past the guilt that had nearly broken him after the death of a woman who'd mattered to him, fought to keep everyone at arm's length because he believed his love was dangerous.

Now, he was fighting to stay alive. And all we could do was wait to find out if fighting would be enough.

Callen stood motionless, staring at the doors she'd disappeared through. His expression hadn't changed, but his posture had shifted. The rigid control was cracking at the edges.

"Callen." I touched his arm.

He flinched like I'd burned him. Then he drew a breath, and the mask slid back into place.

"ICU," he said. "Let's go."

I caught Oliver's arm before he followed. Under the harsh fluorescent lights, the gash on his temple looked worse than it had in the basement—swollen and crusted with dried blood where James had struck him. He'd only been cleared from the doctor's restrictions a week before all this.

"You need to get that looked at."

"I'm fine."

"You were hit in the head. You're not fine until a doctor says you are."

Callen glanced back, took one look at Oliver's head, and nodded. "She's right. Get cleared. We'll be in the ICU."

Oliver opened his mouth to argue, but I was flagging down a passing nurse. Ten minutes later, he rejoined us in the corridor outside Kiernan's room, a small plaster on his temple and irritation in his expression.

"No signs of concussion," he said before I could ask. "Happy?"

I would be happy when Kiernan woke up. Until then, this would have to do.

We walked through corridors that blurred together. Oliver reached for my hand somewhere between the waiting room and the lifts, and I held on without looking at him. The fluorescent lights buzzed overhead. In the distance, a phone rang. The world continued as if nothing had changed, but everything had.

Kiernan might die. The surgeon hadn't said he would live. She'd said the next forty-eight hours would tell them more. She'd said his heart never stopped, like that was supposed to be comfort. As if the bar for hope had dropped so low that a beating heart was victory enough.

I forced myself to breathe. In through the nose, out through the mouth. The way they'd taught me during training, when they were teaching me to stay calm under fire. This was worse than fire. Fire, I could run from.

The intensive care unit was quieter than the emergency department. Softer lighting, slower rhythms, machines that beeped in steady intervals rather than urgent alarms. A nurse led us down a corridor lined with glass-walled rooms, each one containing a patient surrounded by monitors, tubes, and the apparatus of medical intervention.

Kiernan was in a room at the end of the hall.

The nurse pushed the door open and stepped aside. "Ten minutes. No more than that," she said.

Callen walked in first.

It was dim, lit only by the glow of equipment and the faint light filtering through the blinds. Kiernan lay in the center of the bed, motionless against white sheets. A thick bandage covered his left shoulder and wrapped across his chest. IV lines snaked from his arm to bags of clear fluid hanging above him. A monitor tracked his heartbeat—proof that he was alive, that his heart was still pumping, that the bullet hadn't won.

He looked wrong.

This was the man who commanded every room he entered. Who controlled scenes with nothing but his voice and his presence. Who had taken charge of Oliver and me from the moment we'd arrived at Greymarch, directing and demanding and dominating until we couldn't imagine being anywhere else. Seeing him like this—pale and still, reduced to a body in a bed—made my chest ache.

Callen crossed to the left side of the mattress and gripped the rail. He didn't speak. He stood motionless, staring down at his oldest friend, and the grief on his face was naked in a way I'd never seen from him.

I crossed to the chair on Kiernan's right side and lowered myself into it. My hand found his, the one without the IV, and I wrapped my fingers around his palm. His skin was cool. Not cold, but not warm either. The pulse at his wrist beat against my fingertips, steady enough for me to count the rhythm.

Oliver took the chair beside me. He reached out and laid his hand over mine, over Kiernan's, connecting all three of us. The warmth of his palm seeped through my skin, and I realized how numb I'd gone. Running on nothing but fear and fury and the desperate need for Kiernan to open his eyes.

"You bloody fool," Callen said quietly. The words came out ragged.

Kiernan didn't respond. His chest rose and fell in the shallow rhythm of sedated sleep.

"Thirty years." Callen's grip on the rail tightened. "Thirty years, I've known you. And you still think throwing yourself in front of bullets is an acceptable solution."

The anger in his voice matched what I'd been carrying since the basement. He understood. He'd probably watched Kiernan do this before—sacrifice himself, put his body between danger and the people he loved, refusing to let anyone else carry the weight.

"He saved Oliver," I said, hating how much it sounded like an accusation.

"That's who he is," he said. "He puts himself between the people he cares about and whatever's coming. He's been doing it since we were children."

"It nearly killed him."

"It has before." His jaw worked. "When we were twenty-three, an op went wrong. He took two rounds in his vest pulling me out of hostile territory. Refused medical attention until the field medic had finished with me." He paused. "He's never mentioned it since. Not once."

I stared at Kiernan's face, stripped of the control and command I'd come to associate with him. This was the man who would bleed out on foreign soil before letting a friend go untreated. Who would put his body between danger and the people he loved because the alternative was unthinkable.

He would destroy himself to protect us. He would burn down to ash if he thought it would keep us warm.

And we were supposed to accept that?

"No. I'm not accepting it." My voice was steady now, the anger crystallizing into resolve. "He doesn't get to make those decisions for us. He doesn't get to throw his life away and call it protection."

"You think you can change him?" Callen asked.

"I think he's going to learn that we're not standing behind him anymore." I held his gaze without flinching. "We're standing beside him. And if that means tackling him to the ground before he can throw himself in front of another bullet, then that's what we'll do."

Callen's expression shifted, and the corner of his mouth twitched—not quite a smile, but close.

"Good," he said. "He's going to need people who won't let him push them away."

I turned to Kiernan. His face was still, peaceful in a way he never was when awake. Even in sleep at Greymarch, there had been tension in the set of his jaw, the furrow between his brows. Now, there was nothing.

"You don't get to decide you're expendable," I said quietly. "Not anymore."

The monitor beeped. The IV dripped. Kiernan lay motionless.

"We didn't come here to watch you die." The words scraped past the tightness in my throat, and I squeezed his hand until my knuckles ached. "We're not leaving. No matter how many times you try to push us away."

He couldn't hear me. The sedation had pulled him somewhere far away, beyond the reach of words or anger or desperate pleas. But I said it anyway, because I needed him to know. Because if he died without hearing it, I would never forgive myself.

"You belong to us too," I said. "You claimed us. You made us yours. But you're ours now, whether you like it or not."

Oliver's fingers laced through mine. When I looked at him, tears were tracking down his cheeks in silent streams. He didn't wipe them away.

"He has to wake up," he said.

"He will."

I didn't know if I believed it. But I said it anyway, because the alternative was unthinkable.

The hours blurred together. The nurse came to tell us our ten minutes were up, took one look at Callen's face, and left without another word. Gus and Rafe arrived around zero five hundred. They stayed for an hour, speaking in low voices with Callen, then left with promises to return.

The nurses checked his vitals every thirty minutes. They adjusted his IV, noted readings on their tablets, and asked questions that Callen answered instantly. Was he allergic to anything? Did he have a history of blood clots? He rattled off information like he'd memorized Kiernan's medical file years ago. He probably had.

Somewhere around twelve hundred hours, exhaustion caught up with me. My eyes burned, my muscles ached, and the adrenaline that had kept me upright since we left the basement had finally drained away. Oliver looked even worse—gray-faced, hollow-eyed, and swaying in his chair.

"Sleep," Callen said, his voice cutting through the fog. "Both of you. There's a sofa."

"I'm not leaving him." The words came out automatic.

"I'm not asking you to leave." He nodded toward the vinyl bench beneath the window. "It's not comfortable, but it's better than collapsing. I'll wake you if anything changes."

Oliver stood, his body stiff. "He's right, Phee. We need to rest while we can."

I didn't want to let go of Kiernan's hand. For two weeks, he'd been the one in control. He'd directed and demanded and set the terms of everything between us. I'd submitted to that control willingly—more than willingly. I'd craved it. The relief of surrendering to someone stronger, someone who knew what he wanted and wasn't afraid to take it.

Now, he lay here, helpless, and I was the one keeping watch, all because he wouldn't tell us what he was up against. Why he forced us to leave. His pride and his belief that he had to protect us got in the way of us being the team he wanted us to be *personally*.

That ended now.

A soft knock came at the door. A nurse stepped inside, her gaze sweeping the room before landing on Callen.

"Mr. Cavendish? There's someone in the family waiting area asking for you."

Callen's brow furrowed. "Who?"

"She said her name is Isla MacLeod."

The change in Callen was immediate. His spine went rigid, and for a fraction of a second, raw emotion flashed across his face—longing and fear and fierce denial—before his expression locked down.

"Tell her I'll be there in a moment."

The nurse nodded and withdrew.

Callen stood motionless for a few seconds, then walked out behind her.

I released Kiernan's hand and crossed to the sofa. Oliver sat first, and I settled beside him. When his arm came around my shoulders, I leaned into him and closed my eyes.

Sleep didn't come easily. My mind kept circling back to the sound of the gunshot, to Kiernan falling. But eventually, exhaustion won, and I slipped into a thin, dreamless darkness.

I woke to a change in the room's rhythm.

The monitors beeped differently—faster, more urgent. Oliver jerked awake beside me. He was on his feet before his eyes were fully open.

I crossed the room in three strides.

Kiernan's fingers curled into the sheets. It seemed involuntary at first, then his face changed. A crease appeared between his brows, a muscle jumped in his cheek.

"Kiernan?" I grabbed his hand and held on. "Can you hear me?"

His eyelids fluttered. Once. Twice.

"We're here," Oliver said. "You're in hospital. You're safe. Take it slow."

His gaze locked on me.

I waited for the walls to go back up. For him to push us away.

He didn't.

His fingers threaded through mine. His eyes filled, one tear slid down his temple, and he let it fall.

No mask. No command. Just Kiernan. Broken open.

23

Kiernan

The first sensation I felt was pain.

My shoulder ached. The rest of my body felt disconnected, heavy, wrong.

Machines registered before I opened my eyes—the rhythmic hiss of air through tubes, an electronic tone marking time in steady intervals. The smell came next—antiseptic layered over old sweat and the sharp tang of old blood.

I was in hospital. The realization came slowly through the fog.

My eyelids refused to open. I tried again, and the muscles still wouldn't obey. My throat was dry, my tongue thick and useless against cracked lips.

Memory returned in pieces, out of order. James' face appeared, twisted with grief. A gun was in his hand, the barrel swinging away from me, toward Oliver. I acted on instinct, putting myself between the gun and him.

My whole body tried to jerk upright. Pain shot through my shoulder, and I gasped.

Had I been too slow? Were they alive? The questions slammed into me with more force than the bullet had. I needed to know if Oliver was breathing, if Ophelia's heart was still beating, if James had fired again after I went down. I needed to know, and I couldn't open my fucking eyes.

I fought my body. Screamed at it inside my own head. *Open. Move. Do something.* My eyelids twitched but wouldn't lift. My fingers clawed at the sheets but wouldn't close. I was trapped inside my own skull, and somewhere out there, Oliver might be bleeding out on a concrete floor and Ophelia might be—

There had been a second shot. I remembered that now, a crack of sound muffled by the ringing in my ears. But I had no idea what had happened after. I had no idea if I'd saved them or failed them. Not knowing was worse than the bullet. The not knowing was its own kind of death.

Something warm pressed against my right hand. Someone was touching me.

"Kiernan?" A voice. Her voice. Ophelia. "Can you hear me?"

She was alive.

My eyelids fluttered once, then twice.

"We're here," Oliver said from somewhere to my left.

Both of them were alive.

My eyes opened. The light was too bright, and shapes swam in my vision, but I turned my head toward his voice. Recognition came slowly—his face, exhausted and drawn, watching me fiercely.

"You're in hospital," Oliver said. "You're safe. Take it slow."

Ophelia sat beside my bed with her hand wrapped around mine. Dark circles shadowed her eyes, and her hair hung lank in a messy knot. She looked like she hadn't slept in days, but she was still the most beautiful thing I'd ever seen.

Relief from knowing they were both okay hit so hard my vision blurred. My chest seized, and for a moment, I couldn't tell if I was breathing or sobbing. I thanked a god I wasn't sure I believed in that James hadn't fired again. They were here and whole.

I couldn't speak. So I threaded my fingers through hers instead. Her face changed when she realized what I was doing—when she realized I wasn't pulling away.

For years, I'd kept everyone out, maintaining a controlled distance, never letting anyone close enough to see the ugly parts. I'd built walls so high I'd forgotten there was anything behind them. And now, a woman I hadn't known six months ago was holding my hand, and I was choosing to let her. I was choosing to hold on.

My eyes burned. I blinked and felt wetness slide down my temple toward the pillow.

I could have turned my head. Could have closed my eyes and pretended it wasn't happening. That's what I would have done a month ago. That's what I'd always done—hidden the weakness, masked the vulnerability, maintained the illusion of control even when everything was falling apart.

I let it fall. I let them see.

Something unknotted in my chest. Something I'd been holding so tight for so long I'd forgotten it was there.

"Kiernan." Ophelia's voice cracked on my name, and she stroked my face. "Don't try to talk yet." She reached for a cup on the bedside table and brought a straw to my lips. "Small sips."

The water tasted lukewarm and metallic. I managed two swallows before my throat closed up. She set the cup down with unsteady hands.

Oliver hadn't stirred from his chair, but his face had changed. He looked away, then back, and the warmth was gone. Now, he looked furious.

"Kiernan." His voice came out rough. He tried again. "Do you have any idea—" He couldn't finish. He stood and crossed to the bed, his hands gripping the rail until his knuckles went white. "You stepped in front of a fucking bullet."

I opened my mouth to respond and then closed it because there was no argument to make. I had done exactly that.

"You're not expendable." His tone grew louder. "You can't decide you matter less and leave us to—"

His voice broke, and he looked away, fighting for control.

"We're not going anywhere." Ophelia gripped my hand. "So don't bother trying to make us."

I wanted to argue. The words lined up in my head—*you should go, you should run*—but my body wouldn't cooperate. My throat was raw and useless. My shoulder throbbed with every heartbeat. And my fingers curled tighter around Ophelia's instead of letting go.

I closed my eyes. I was too weak to fight them right now.

I drifted after that. Sometimes, Ophelia was there; sometimes, Oliver; sometimes, they were speaking to each other in low voices I couldn't follow.

The next time I woke fully, the light had changed to flat gray evening. Oliver sat beside my bed, and Ophelia was curled up in the chair he'd vacated, asleep.

"You're more alert," Oliver said.

I swallowed. My throat still ached, but the words came easier now. "How long was I out of it?"

"Your surgery was yesterday. You've been in and out since."

An entire day lost to the fog. But the memories were clearer now—the basement, James' gun, Oliver and Ophelia bound and gagged. The way James had looked at me with grief and betrayal instead of hate after seven years of believing I'd destroyed the woman he loved. And I had. Maybe not the way he thought, but the result was the same.

"James." My voice came out hoarse. "What happened to him?"

Oliver's brow furrowed. "He's dead."

"The second shot," I said.

"After you went down. He turned the gun on himself."

The words should have meant something. They didn't. They were abstract, like a headline about a stranger.

I closed my eyes and saw him—not the man in the basement with the gun, but the one I'd known before. The first night Elise brought him to the club in Inverness. He'd worn a cable-knit jumper with a hole near the cuff that he kept touching, his nervous fingers worrying the loose threads. When I'd told him to kneel, his whole body had shuddered—in relief, I realized later. Relief at finally being told what to do.

"I don't know what's wrong with me," he'd said, barely above a whisper. "I can't stop wanting this. Wanting someone to—" He'd broken off, ashamed.

"There's nothing wrong with you," I'd told him. And I'd meant it.

He'd looked up at me then with so much hope it had made my chest hurt. Twenty-six years old. Hungry for structure. Desperate to be good for someone.

I'd made him good. For almost two years, I'd given him rules to follow and praise when he followed them. I'd watched him settle into himself, watched the anxiety bleed out of his shoulders, watched him learn to sleep through the night because he finally had someone hold-ing the shape of his world in place.

And then I'd watched it turn.

It happened slowly. So slowly, I didn't see it until the rot had already set in. James stopped having a life outside our dynamic. He quit seeing friends. Stopped talking about work except to say it didn't matter. The only thing that mattered was me—earning my approval, anticipat-ing my needs, being whatever I wanted before I knew I wanted it. His submission had been a gift. It became a void, bottomless and desperate, demanding to be filled.

Elise had changed too. She'd started wanting more than scenes—she wanted permanence. The title. The castle. She wanted me to marry her, to make her Lady Greymarch, to fold the three of us into a life that looked legitimate from the outside. "We could be so happy here," she'd say, running her hand along the stone walls like she already owned them. "Don't you want that? Don't you want us to stay?"

I didn't know how to tell her that what I'd offered was never meant to be a life. It was a container. A structure to hold them steady, not a promise of forever.

They kept asking for things I couldn't give. James wanted to be the center of my world. Elise wanted a future I'd never offered. And I—I was disappearing for weeks at a time on missions I couldn't explain, coming back hollowed out and silent, unable to be what they needed even when I was standing in front of them.

I should have ended it gently. Should have given them time, transition, and the aftercare that an ending deserves as much as any scene. Instead, I severed it. Completely. No warning. No explanation. Just get out and a closed door.

I remembered the way he'd looked at me after Elise's funeral. I'd trained myself to feel nothing by then. And now, he was gone. His grief had hardened into obsession, and he'd chosen a bullet over living another day with what I'd done to him.

Soon, the pain would hit. The hot crush of it, the way grief had swallowed me whole when my mother died, then my father. I waited for guilt to settle onto my chest like a stone.

Neither did.

There was only a strange stillness behind my ribs. A quiet where grief should have been screaming. I pressed my palm flat against my sternum, half expecting to find the wound had migrated—that the bullet had found my heart after all, and I hadn't noticed.

But it was still beating. Steady and indifferent. As if James had never mattered at all.

Maybe that was the worst part. Maybe the emptiness was the grief—proof that I'd already buried him years ago, when I'd cut him out of my life and refused to look back.

I remembered the way he used to look at Elise. Like she was the sun and he was grateful to be warm. He'd loved her more than he'd ever loved me, and I'd known it from the start. I'd been the structure. She'd been his heart.

I'd broken them both.

The thought landed with a dull thud, and in its wake, a pattern emerged that I couldn't unsee.

Elise and James were dead. My friendships survived—with Callen, Gus, Rafe, and even Snow—but the moment someone knelt for me and offered that particular kind of trust, it ended badly.

Oliver and Ophelia had both knelt. Both surrendered. Both trusted me.

"Kiernan?" Oliver's voice sharpened. "What's wrong? Should I call someone?"

When I shook my head, pains shot down my arm, and I let it ground me, let it push the panic down where it couldn't show. "I'm fine."

I wasn't. I closed my eyes because I needed to hide. I couldn't let them see what I knew with absolute certainty: I would destroy them too. It was only a matter of time.

Two more cycles of waking and sleeping passed—enough for the fog to clear, for my mind to sharpen, for my voice to return to close to normal. The pain was still there and would be for weeks, but I could think through it now and force myself to do what needed to be done.

"Ophelia stepped out to find tea," Oliver said from the chair where he sat by the window. He was scrolling through his phone, pretending not to watch me. We both knew the pretense for what it was.

This was my chance. I'd done this before—pushed people away when they got too close. One word was all it took. *Go.*

I opened my mouth to say it, and my throat locked. I tried again, forced breath through my vocal cords, and nothing came out. Not a sound.

Ophelia's cardigan lay beside me on the blanket. She'd left it when she walked out. I should have shoved it off the bed and proven I could sever connections, be the cold bastard I'd been for years. Instead, I reached for it. My fingers curled into the wool and held on.

Thirteen days. That's all it had taken for them to become part of me. And now, I couldn't say one thing to save them from me.

Oliver looked up from his phone. "Don't." The word was quiet, not a plea but a warning. "Whatever you're about to say, don't."

My mouth opened and closed and opened again. Still nothing.

"You think I don't know what's happening in your head right now?" Oliver set his phone aside and leaned forward with his elbows on his knees. "I can see you trying to find the words that will make us leave. You're building a case for why we should walk away, why it's better for everyone, why you're too dangerous to be around."

My teeth clenched. He was too bloody perceptive.

"Here's the problem with that." Oliver stood and stepped closer. "That choice isn't yours alone anymore. You gave it up in that basement."

"Oliver—"

"No. You claimed us. Both of us. You can't unclaim us because you're scared."

He called me scared. I wanted to deny it, to tell him he didn't understand, that this wasn't about fear but about fact.

He opened his mouth to say more, but the door swung open without a knock.

Callen stepped inside and closed it behind him. His eyes shifted from Oliver standing at my bedside to me with my hand wrapped in wool that wasn't mine.

"Leave us," he said to Oliver, not unkindly, but leaving no room for argument.

A muscle jumped in Oliver's cheek, and I thought he might refuse. Then he looked at me and nodded once—an acknowledgment that this was a conversation I needed to have.

"I'll be in the corridor." He touched my shoulder as he passed.

The door closed behind him.

Callen took the chair Oliver had vacated and sat. He didn't say anything for a while. He looked at me—the same way he'd looked at me after Elise's funeral, after I'd put my fist through a wall and then stood there, bleeding, while he wrapped my hand in his shirt.

"You're going to push them away," he finally said.

"Already tried."

"And?"

"Couldn't."

He nodded slowly. "Good."

"It's not good. It's—" I stopped. I didn't have words for what it was.

"It's terrifying," Callen said. "I know."

"You don't know. You weren't there when—"

"I was there for everything after." His voice was steady. "I was there when you stopped sleeping. I was there when you started drinking. I was there when you decided the only way to survive was to never let anyone that close again."

"It worked."

"Did it?" He raised an eyebrow. "You've spent seven years going through the motions. Scenes at the club. Submissives you barely remembered the names of a week later. You call that living?"

"I call it safe."

"You called it a cage and pretended it was a castle." He leaned forward, elbows on his knees. "Elise was sick, Kiernan. So was James. You know that."

"That doesn't change the outcome."

"You're a factor. You're not the cause. Elise had been struggling since before you met her. James made his own choices—years of them. You didn't find her another dom. You didn't put the gun in his hand."

"I might as well have."

"Bullshit." The word was flat, hard. "You want to spend more time in that cage? Fine. But call it what it is."

"And that is?"

"Cowardice."

"You don't understand—"

"I understand perfectly. You're scared. You found two people who actually matter to you, and now, you're terrified because caring about someone means you might lose them. So you're trying to lose them first, on your own terms, so it hurts less."

"That's not—"

"That's exactly what it is. I've watched you. Preemptive strikes against anyone who got too close." He held my gaze. "It doesn't work, Kiernan. It only means you end up alone and miserable."

I didn't have an answer for that. At least not one he wouldn't interrupt again.

"Kiernan, you have to—"

"And if Oliver and Ophelia break?" My voice came out rough.

"Then, you grieve." His voice softened. "Like the rest of us. You grieve, and you survive it, and you keep going. That's what living costs."

"I don't know if I can do it again."

"Stop making their choices for them." He stood but paused at the door. "They're not leaving. Figure out how to live with that."

He left, and the room felt empty.

Machines beeped their steady rhythm. The window showed gray sky fading to darker gray. The chair Oliver had occupied was empty. So was the one where Ophelia had slept. The corridor outside was silent—no footsteps, no voices, no indication that anyone was coming back.

This was what I wanted. Space. Distance. Room to think without Oliver's sharp gaze dissecting my every expression, without Ophelia's hand in mine, making it impossible to remember why I needed to let go.

So why did I feel more alone than I ever had in my life? Why couldn't I get past it like I always did? Why couldn't I see being on my own as a good thing anymore?

I stared at the ceiling. Counted the tiles. Lost count. Started over.

The cardigan was still in my hand. I could set it on the chair, or the windowsill, or the floor. I could prove to myself that I was still capable of releasing something.

My fingers curled deeper into the wool instead.

The silence pressed in. Not a peaceful silence. Not the comfortable quiet of being alone by choice. This was absence. This was the negative space where two people used to be.

I'd spent years cultivating solitude. I'd gotten good at it—at eating alone, sleeping alone, existing in the spaces between human contact without feeling the gaps. I'd convinced myself the emptiness was peace.

It wasn't. It was numbness. And now, Oliver and Ophelia had woken up nerves I'd thought were dead.

Now, the silence hurt.

Ophelia returned with tea she didn't drink. Oliver came back and reclaimed his post by the window. The evening deepened into night, and eventually, they both dozed—Ophelia in the chair, Oliver on the narrow bench beneath the window. Neither of them willing to go farther than a few feet from my bed.

They slept.

Oliver's face had softened, the fury and fear smoothed away. Ophelia's hand had slipped off the armrest, hanging loose. They looked exhausted, like they'd been through hell. They also looked like they weren't going anywhere.

My God, *I needed them.*

Not loved—it was too soon for that. But need. Raw, terrifying need. The kind that made my chest ache when I looked at them.

I didn't know how to be this vulnerable and survive it.

But every part of me had already decided.

I couldn't make myself let go.

The fear didn't fade, and that terrified me more than the bullet ever had.

24

Oliver

Three days in a hospital chair had done something to my spine that might be permanent.

I shifted, trying to find a position that didn't make my lower back scream, and gave up. The vinyl squeaked under me. Across the room, Ophelia was curled in the window seat, her phone abandoned beside her, asleep at last. She'd been running on caffeine and stubbornness since the night at the Crucible, and her body had finally overruled her will.

Callen sat in the corner, laptop open, doing whatever it was he did when he wasn't hovering over Kiernan's bed. Orchestrating. Arranging. Managing. Which meant he hadn't slept either. But he kept going, because that's what you did when the person closest to you was lying in a hospital bed with a hole in his shoulder.

Something else was going on with him too. That first night, a nurse had come to tell him someone was asking for him in the family waiting area. Isla MacLeod. Callen had gone rigid at her name, and when he came back twenty minutes later, he'd been different. Quieter. Whatever had passed between them, it wasn't my business.

Kiernan was asleep. Or pretending to be. His breathing had a too-even quality that meant he was aware of everything happening around him, noting it, then deciding what to do with it. Even flat on his back with a drain snaking out from under his bandages, he couldn't stop strategizing.

He lay still in the gray afternoon light, his hand curled around the edge of the blanket like he needed to hold onto something. The pallor of his skin looked wrong against the white sheets.

He hated this. Every second of it. The weakness, the dependency, the indignity of needing help for basic functions. Yesterday, I'd helped him in the loo, and the look on his face had been worse than anything James had done to us in that basement. Not pain. Shame.

I understood it. In his position, I'd feel the same. But understanding didn't make it easier to watch.

Callen's mobile chimed. He glanced at the screen, typed something, then looked up and caught me watching.

"Snow." Callen tilted the screen so I could see.

Three words. *Cleanup handled. Recovering?*

Callen typed back, *Stable. Out of ICU.*

The response came in seconds. *Good. Tell him to stop getting shot.*

Despite everything, I almost laughed. I'd never met Snow—none of us had, not really. He existed as a voice on comms, a presence in briefings, a ghost who passed through the world without leaving traces. But even ghosts, apparently, had opinions about Kiernan's self-sacrificing tendencies.

Callen pocketed his device. "He made sure there was nothing left at the scene that could cause problems."

"Problems" meaning evidence of people being present who shouldn't have been. Damage control.

"I didn't realize he was involved."

"Snow's always involved." Callen smirked. "He just doesn't advertise."

The door opened, and a nurse came in, checked the monitors, and adjusted the IV drip rate. She smiled at me with the sympathy of someone who'd seen too many worried visitors, made notes on her tablet, then left.

When she was gone, Kiernan's eyes opened.

"You're talking like I'm not here," he said. His voice was rough, scraped raw.

"You were asleep," Callen said.

"I was resting my eyes."

"You were snoring."

"I don't snore."

"You absolutely snore." Callen closed his laptop and stood, crossing to the bed. "What's your pain rating?"

"Manageable."

"That's not what I asked."

Kiernan's teeth clenched. "Six. Maybe seven."

"I'll get the nurse."

"Don't—"

But Callen was already gone, slipping out the door like a man who'd learned that arguing with Kiernan was often pointless. Even when he wasn't in hospital.

I crossed to the chair beside the bed. Kiernan tracked me.

"You look terrible," he said.

"Charming as always."

"I mean it. When did you last sleep? Actually sleep, not whatever you've been doing in that chair."

"I'll sleep when you're home."

He grimaced. "Oliver—"

"Don't tell me to leave." I reached for his hand, the one without the IV. His fingers were cool against mine. "Don't tell me to take care of myself. Don't give me the speech about how you're fine and I should go get some rest. I've heard it. I'm not interested."

His fingers curled tighter around mine.

"Stubborn bastard," he murmured.

"You like that about me."

"I tolerate it."

"Same thing."

Ophelia stirred in the window seat, stretching as she surfaced from sleep. She blinked at us, then focused on our joined hands and relaxed.

"Still here," she said. Not a question.

"Still here," I confirmed.

She unfolded herself from her perch and crossed to us, resting her arse on the edge of the bed, near Kiernan's hip.

"How do you feel?" she asked.

"Like I've been shot."

"Funny."

"I thought so."

The door opened again. I expected Callen with the nurse, but Typhon walked in.

He looked the same as he had during the Labyrinth briefings—silver threading through dark hair, a suit that cost more than my monthly salary, with a bearing that made the room feel smaller. His eyes swept the space, took in each of us, and dismissed any potential threat in under a second.

Kiernan's body language changed. The exhaustion was still there, but underneath it, he seemed more alert.

"Typhon," he said.

"Archon." The Unit 23 commander crossed to the bed and looked down with an expression that was impossible to read. "You look like shit."

"I'm aware."

"Good. Means you're not delusional on top of every-thing else." He pulled the chair I'd vacated closer to the bed and sat, crossing one leg over the other like he was settling in for a casual conversation. "The doctors tell me you'll live."

"Apparently."

"Try not to sound so disappointed about it."

Kiernan's mouth twitched. "I'll work on that."

Typhon's gaze shifted to me, then to Ophelia. The weight of his attention settled over us—not threatening, exactly, but assessing.

"Prima. Vanguard." He nodded to us in turn. "I understand you were with him when it happened."

"Yes, sir," Ophelia responded.

"And that he did what he always does."

My spine stiffened. "Yes."

"That sounds about right." Typhon shook his head. "He still thinks dying for people is easier than living for them."

"I'm right here," Kiernan griped.

"I'm aware." Typhon turned to him. "We'll debrief properly when you're recovered. For now, I wanted to see for myself that you weren't dead."

"Disappointed?"

"Relieved." The word was simple, but the weight behind it wasn't. "You're difficult to replace, Archon. Try to remember that."

He stood and buttoned his jacket. Then he paused, looking at Ophelia and me again.

"When everyone's cleared for duty, I'd like to discuss your futures with Unit 23."

I blinked. "Sir?"

"Viper's already briefed Prima on my interest. I'm extending the same consideration to you, Vanguard." He looked between us. "Think about it. We'll talk when Archon's not bleeding all over the furniture."

He left without waiting for a response. The door clicked shut behind him, and silence stretched.

"Did that just happen?" I asked.

"Typhon does what he wants," Kiernan said. His eyes had drifted closed again, but his hand was still wrapped around mine. "You get used to it."

"Unit 23." Ophelia spoke softly. "Quite an honor."

"The two of you would be brilliant." Kiernan's voice was fading, the exhaustion pulling him back under.

Callen returned with the nurse before I responded. She administered something through the IV, and within minutes, Kiernan's grip on my hand loosened as the medication pulled him into genuine sleep.

"What did Typhon want?" Callen asked, settling into his corner.

"To make sure Kiernan wasn't dead," I said. "And to recruit us for Unit 23."

Callen's eyebrow rose. "Both of you?"

"Apparently."

"Interesting." He opened his laptop again. "He doesn't do that often. He must actually like the bastard."

"Don't they work together?"

"Kiernan works for him. That's different." Callen's fingers moved over the keyboard. "Typhon doesn't make hospital visits for employees. He makes them for family."

Family. I thought about the way Typhon had looked at Kiernan with a combination of exasperation, relief, and affection. And how Callen had sat in this room for three days, like us, refusing to leave. The way Gus and Rafe had shown up at zero five hundred, speaking in low voices, their faces tight with worry.

Kiernan had spent years convincing himself he was alone. That his intensity made him dangerous, that caring about him was a death sentence, that everyone who got close would end up destroyed.

He was wrong.

The afternoon stretched into evening. Ophelia dozed in the window seat again. Callen left to make phone calls—something about the Thorned Thistle and security protocols that needed to be updated. I sat beside Kiernan's bed and watched him sleep.

Real sleep this time. Not the guarded rest of a man who couldn't stop monitoring his surroundings, but the deep unconsciousness of a body demanding recovery.

I thought about the zip ties cutting into my wrists. James' voice, going on about betrayal and justice and the woman he and Kiernan had loved. The gun, heavy and certain in his hand.

I'd been trained to resist interrogation and compartmentalize fear, to stay calm under pressure and wait for an opening. None of that had prepared me for the horror of watching someone I cared deeply for step in front of a bullet.

Kiernan's name was muffled as I screamed it through the gag. Ophelia had been sobbing beside me, both of us fighting against restraints we couldn't break. And Kiernan had lain there, motionless, while his blood spread across the concrete.

I blinked hard and forced myself back to the present. To Kiernan's chest, rising and falling.

He was still here. That was what mattered.

"You're thinking too loud."

I startled. His eyes were open, watching me.

"Sorry," I said. "Didn't mean to wake you."

"You didn't." He shifted against the pillows and winced. "What time is it?"

"Just after twenty-one hundred. Callen's making calls. Phee's asleep."

He turned his head to look at Ophelia, and his expression softened.

"The doctor came by while you were out," I said. "She said you can be discharged tomorrow if someone can manage your care."

"Good."

"We're coming with you."

His expression hardened. "Oliver—"

"This isn't a negotiation. You need care. We're providing it."

"Millie can—"

"No." I leaned forward. "We almost lost you. We sat in that waiting room for six hours, not knowing if you were going to live or die. We're not leaving you with your housekeeper and going back to London like none of this happened."

The argument built behind his eyes—the reasons we shouldn't, the risks, the thousand ways he could push us away.

"You have careers," he finally said. "Obligations. You can't—"

"Typhon offered us both positions in Unit 23. In the meantime, I'm still on leave, as is Phee." I held his gaze. "There's nothing in London that matters more than this."

"You don't know what you're signing up for."

"Then, tell me."

He looked away. Outside, the sky had gone dark.

"I'm not easy." His voice was barely above a whisper. "I'm not...I don't know how to do this. I've spent years avoiding it."

"I know."

"I'll try to protect you even when you don't need it. I'll make decisions that should be yours, because I can't stop trying to control everything."

"I know."

"Then, why—" His voice cracked. "Why are you still here?"

I stood and leaned over him, bracing my hands on either side of his head. His eyes were dark and vulnerable.

"Because we're not done with you," I said. "Because whatever you think you are—whatever you're afraid of being—we've seen it. And we still want you."

"Oliver." His hand came up, trembling, and cupped the back of my neck. "I don't know how to be what you need."

"Good thing I'm not asking you to."

I kissed him. Softly, because he was still healing. Gently, because he was still afraid. But certain, because I was done accepting his distance.

When I leaned away, his eyes were wet.

"Okay," he whispered.

Callen returned an hour later with takeaway containers and news that Rafe had completed an initial security review of the Thorned Thistle.

"Three vulnerabilities," he said, setting food on the rolling table. "All addressed. Rafe's bringing the full report to Greymarch once Kiernan's settled."

"How bad?" Kiernan asked. He was sitting up, looking more like himself despite the IV and the bandages.

"Bad enough that Rafe's taking it personally." Callen handed him a container. "Eat. You look like a corpse."

"Flattering."

"I'm not here to flatter you. I'm here to make sure you don't die of stubbornness before we get you home."

Ophelia had woken when the food arrived. She sat cross-legged on the end of the bed, picking at noodles, watching Kiernan and Callen with an expression I couldn't read.

"Gus called," she said. "He's planning to come by Greymarch in a few days. Something about a new rope technique he wants to show you."

Kiernan's mouth twitched. "He knows I can't do anything for weeks."

"I think that's the point. He wants to demonstrate on someone else while you watch and suffer."

He chuckled. "That sounds like Gus."

We ate. Nobody talked for a while. The monitors beeped. The fluorescent lights hummed. Outside, the hospital continued its endless cycle of crises and recoveries, but in this room, a change had occurred.

When the food was gone, the door opened again. The doctor—the same one who'd been checking on Kiernan since surgery and was here earlier—stepped inside with a tablet in hand.

"Good news," she said. "I'm comfortable discharging you tomorrow morning, provided you have round-the-clock care for the first week. Someone to monitor for infection and make sure you're not overdoing it."

"He does," I said before Kiernan could speak.

A dry laugh escaped him. "Apparently, I don't get a vote."

"You voted," Ophelia said. "You lost."

The doctor smiled. "I'll have the paperwork ready by ten. Get some rest tonight. All of you."

She left, and his throat worked. A war played out across his face—the part of him that wanted to shield us fighting the part that wanted to keep us.

"Fine." The word was rough. Reluctant.

But it was a door left open.

"Fine," I echoed. "We leave tomorrow."

Kiernan closed his eyes. "That wasn't surrender. That was exhaustion."

"I'll take it."

He didn't squeeze my hand. But he didn't pull away either.

I leaned in and pressed my forehead to his. He was trembling—or maybe that was me.

"We're going to figure this out," I murmured against his skin. "Whatever you need. Whatever you're afraid to ask for."

His eyes opened, and they held fear he was still trying to hide.

"Oliver." His voice was barely a whisper.

"Yeah?"

He looked at me, then at Ophelia, watching us from the end of the bed with wet eyes. Then back to me.

"Don't let me destroy you."

It wasn't a request. It was a warning.

And I had no answer for it—except a kiss.

25

Ophelia

The drive to Greymarch took five hours.

Kiernan slept for most of it, stretched across the back-seat of Callen's Range Rover, with his head in my lap and his injured shoulder braced against pillows they'd given us when he was discharged. The doctors had offered an ambulance, but Kiernan had refused with a look that ended the discussion. He'd endured enough indignity. He wasn't arriving at his own home on a stretcher.

Callen drove, Oliver sat in the front passenger seat, and I sat in the back with Kiernan's weight warm against my thighs and my fingers in his hair.

The tight control he wore like armor had loosened in slumber, showing the vulnerability underneath. He winced each time the vehicle hit a bump despite Callen navigating the roads as smoothly as he could.

Every few minutes, Oliver's eyes would glance at us, and I'd nod. We'd developed a shorthand over the past few days, a way of communicating without words. It felt natural. As though we'd been doing it for years.

We'd made this drive once before, three weeks ago, when Oliver was the one who needed care and Kiernan was the one in control, and while the landscape hadn't changed, it seemed everything else had.

"How's he doing?" Callen asked, voice low.

"Sleeping. I think."

"Good. He needs it." Callen caught my eye in the mirror. "I'll warn you; he's a terrible patient."

"I've noticed."

"No, you've seen hints." He grinned. "Wait until he's well enough to be genuinely difficult. That's when the fun starts."

Oliver snorted. "Looking forward to it."

"You say that now." But there was warmth underneath his dry tone. The warmth of someone who'd known Kiernan for thirty years and loved him despite—or because of—every infuriating quality.

We turned off the main road onto the private drive. The trees closed around us, ancient oaks forming a canopy that blocked the gray sky. When they fell away and Greymarch appeared, my shoulders dropped. It felt more like home than anywhere else I'd lived.

Kiernan stirred against my thigh. His eyes opened, and he blinked up at me.

"We're here," I said.

He struggled to sit up. I helped him, one hand braced against his good shoulder, and watched his face as he looked at the castle. "Home," he said.

The front door opened before we'd stopped, and Millie emerged, already halfway down the steps by the time Callen cut the engine.

"Hello, Millie," Kiernan said when I rolled the window down.

"Don't you Millie me." She looked him over with sharp eyes. "You went and got yourself shot. I've half a mind to finish the job myself."

"I missed you too."

"Let me see you."

Getting Kiernan out of the car was a process. He couldn't put weight on his left side without going pale, and his legs were unsteady after hours of lying down. Oliver took one side, Callen took the other, and together they maneuvered him upright while Millie watched with her hands on her hips.

"You'll be in the rooms near the library," she said once he was standing. "I've made them up fresh. You'll remain there until you can walk without looking like you're about to faint."

"Those are for guests."

"And right now, you need looking after like one." She glanced at Oliver and me. "You'll be with him."

Heat flooded my face.

"I've been keeping this house for thirty years," she said as if that explained everything. "I'll be serving dinner at seven. If you're hungry before then, you know where the kitchen is."

Once she disappeared inside, Callen laughed. "She likes you," he said.

"How can you tell?" I asked.

"She doesn't let just anyone in her domain."

It made me think of the night when the three of us had prepared dinner there together. It felt like a lifetime ago.

The rooms Millie put us in were beautiful, with high ceilings and tall windows overlooking the loch. In the largest bedroom of the three, Millie had set a table up near the four-poster bed, with medical supplies, a bell for summoning help, and a stack of books that suggested she expected Kiernan to be bedridden for a while.

He grimaced when we led him in.

"It's temporary," I said.

"I know."

"A few weeks. Maybe less."

"I know," he repeated, sinking onto the edge of the bed. The trip had taken more out of him than he wanted to admit. His face was gray, and a fine sheen of sweat had broken out across his forehead.

Oliver was already there, repositioning the pillows and helping Kiernan lie back. The ease of it struck me—the way Oliver knew exactly what to do without being told.

"Where is his pain medication?" he asked me.

"My bag. I'll get it."

Oliver handed the dose to him, while I poured a glass of water, then helped Kiernan swallow them, with one hand cupped behind his head.

"Sleep," I murmured.

Kiernan met my eyes, and in his was the helpless anger of a man who was used to being in control and now wasn't. "I've been sleeping for days."

"Would you like us to lie with you?" Oliver asked.

Kiernan's jaw worked, then loosened, and he closed his eyes. I crawled on one side, but Oliver hesitated.

He looked as exhausted as I was.

"We should rest too," I said.

"Yeah." He stayed where he was. "I keep thinking he's going to stop breathing," he admitted once Kiernan drifted off. "Every time he falls asleep, I think—"

"I know." I reached up for his hand and scooted closer to Kiernan's good side, and Oliver lay beside me.

The first few days were hard.

Kiernan was a terrible patient, as Callen had predicted. He hated being dependent, hated being weak, hated the constant reminders that his body had failed him. He pushed too hard, too fast, and twice, Oliver had to physically block him from doing things he wasn't ready for.

"I'm going for a walk," Kiernan said on day five, already reaching for his coat.

"No, you're not."

"I need air. I need to walk. I've been staring at these walls—"

"You can barely make it to the bathroom without going pale." Oliver stepped between him and the door. "You'll collapse halfway to the loch, and I'll have to carry you back."

"I'm not an invalid."

"You have a hole in your shoulder."

"Had. It's healing."

They stared at each other, two stubborn men who were used to getting their way. From the bed, I was half-amused and half-certain that Kiernan would try to push past and hurt himself.

He didn't. He turned and walked over to the window. His shoulders were rigid and his eyes furious. Worse, he didn't speak to either of us for the rest of the day.

But there were good moments too.

We eventually had dinner at the long table in the kitchen, because Kiernan refused to continue eating in bed or the suite. Millie's cooking, simple and hearty, was exactly what we all needed.

Color slowly returned to his face, and on day seven, he managed to walk to the garden without needing to rest.

The first time he laughed—really laughed—was drawn out by a terrible joke Oliver told over breakfast.

I marked each moment like a victory.

Gus arrived on day eight, although he, Rafe, Callen, and even Snow checked in regularly.

His massive frame blocked the light when he filled the doorway of the suite. A grin spread across his face when he saw Kiernan propped up against the pillows on the sofa.

"You look like shit," he announced.

"As everyone keeps telling me."

He crossed the room and rested his hand on Kiernan's shoulder. "Scared us, you bastard."

"Wasn't my intention."

"Never is." Gus' eyes shifted to Oliver and me. "You two. Keeping him in line?"

"Trying," I responded.

"Try harder. He's slippery." But there was approval in his voice. "I brought rope."

Kiernan's eyebrow rose. "I can't—"

"Not for you. For them." Gus nodded at us. "Callen mentioned they're interested in learning. I figured I'd give them a proper lesson while you watch."

"That's cruel."

"That's the point." Gus' grin widened. "Nothing motivates recovery like watching other people have fun without you."

He stayed for three hours. True to his word, he demonstrated techniques on Oliver first, then on me—nothing sexual, just the basics, like how tension and pressure could ground someone, hold them, make them feel safe.

Kiernan's fists remained clenched until Gus left. By then, he was practically vibrating with frustration.

"That was torture," he said.

"That was the point." I sat beside him and touched his face. "One more week. Then the doctor clears you."

"It feels like a year."

"I know." I kissed him. "We'll wait."

Rafe came the next day. His coiled energy and watchful silence were jarring after Gus' warmth. He arrived with a folder under his arm.

"The Thorned Thistle," he said, dropping into a chair in the sitting area. "We need to talk."

When Kiernan nodded, Oliver and I turned to leave, to give them privacy, but Rafe held up a hand.

"Don't go. You're part of this now."

We stayed.

"I found three vulnerabilities," he said, opening the folder. "James exploited all of them."

"It wasn't your fault," Kiernan muttered.

"It was. I'm head of security. The failure is mine. You know the first two, but the third was worse." Rafe was quiet for a moment, and when he spoke, pain was evident in his voice. "He accessed our database of member records. We don't know how much he copied before—" He stopped. "Before the end. I've brought in specialists to assess the damage and rebuild our security systems. But some members may have been compromised."

"Have the other partners been briefed?" Kiernan asked.

"They have. Snow is handling certain aspects. We wanted to wait until you were briefed before deciding how to proceed."

"The members need to know."

"I agree. How is the question."

"Controlled disclosure," he said after several seconds of contemplation. "Individual conversations with anyone whose records were accessed. We don't blast it out to everyone. We identify the affected members, and we talk to them personally. Let them decide how they want to respond."

Rafe nodded slowly. "That could work."

"The club remains closed until we're certain it's secure."

"Agreed." Rafe closed the folder and stood. "I'll work with Callen. We'll start reaching out." He paused at the door. "Get better, Kiernan. We need you back."

"Working on it."

Ten days after Kiernan's discharge, Callen worked some kind of magic and arranged for the doctor to pay a house call to remove the stitches.

He sat on the edge of the bed, shirtless, while she worked. I stood by the window, trying not to stare at the expanse of his back, the muscles that shifted under his skin, and the way his shoulders hunched.

"Healing well," she commented. "Better than expected. You must have a good care team."

"The best." Kiernan's gaze locked on mine.

"Light activity only for now," she continued. "No heavy lifting or strenuous exercise." She paused. "No strenuous anything."

"Define strenuous," Oliver said from the doorway.

The doctor's mouth twitched. "Use your judgment. If it hurts, you're out of breath, or if there's any pulling at the wound site, stop."

"How much longer?" Kiernan asked.

"Another few days, then we'll reassess." She packed her bag. "You're lucky, Lord Greymarch. A few inches to the left, and we wouldn't be having this conversation."

The room was quiet after she left. Kiernan sat on the edge of the bed, still shirtless, the fresh pink scar visible on his shoulder. He looked at Oliver, then at me.

"A few days," he said.

"A week at the most," Oliver added.

"I've been thinking," he said slowly. "About what you said. About needing something I've never asked for."

Oliver froze. "And?"

"I still don't know how to say it." Kiernan's hands trembled. "But I'm getting closer. And when I figure it out—when I find the words—" He looked at us with an intensity that pinned me in place. "I need to know you'll hear me. Even if what I ask for surprises you."

Oliver crossed to the bed, sat beside him, and took his hand.

"There's nothing you could ask for that would make me leave," he said. "Nothing."

"You don't know that."

"I do." Oliver's voice was fierce.

Kiernan reached up and pulled me down beside them, but his eyes stayed on Oliver. The way he looked at him—it wasn't how Kiernan usually looked at anyone. There was no command in it. No control.

Just need. Unguarded and barely contained.

26

Kiernan

The nightmare woke me at three in the morning.

I was standing in an empty room, and Oliver and Ophelia were walking away from me. I called their names, but no sound came out. I tried to follow, but my feet wouldn't move. They kept going, getting smaller, disappearing into a darkness I couldn't reach.

I woke gasping. My shoulder screamed where I'd rolled onto it, and my heart slammed into my ribs.

The bed was warm on either side of me. Oliver's front pressed into my back, and Ophelia's fingers were curled loosely over my heart. They were here. They hadn't left.

But the dream clung to me.

I lay in the dark and listened to them breathe. Oliver's slow, deep rhythm. Ophelia's softer cadence. They'd fallen asleep with me every night since my discharge, as if they could protect me from myself by sheer proximity.

They'd given me everything, and what had I given them in return? Warnings. Walls. The constant, exhausting vigilance of a man waiting for the other shoe to drop.

Don't let me destroy you, I'd said to Oliver before leaving the hospital. I'd meant it honestly. Now, I recognized it for what it was—another form of control. A way to keep them at arm's length while still keeping them close. A way to make sure that, when this ended, I could tell myself I'd warned them.

Coward. The word surfaced unbidden, and I couldn't argue with it.

I'd taken a bullet for Oliver. I'd have died for either of them without hesitation. But this—lying here with them, letting them care for me—love me—accepting what they offered without trying to manage or control or protect them from myself—this was harder than any physical sacrifice.

This required something I'd never given anyone.

Trust.

Real trust. Not the calculated risk assessment I'd always substituted for it. Not the measured parceling out of information and access, always holding something back. Real trust meant the terrifying, absolute surrender of letting someone else in—completely, without reservation, without a safety net.

I'd been dominant my entire adult life. Control was my armor. My weapon. My identity.

But lately, the ground had shifted beneath me—a change I couldn't—wouldn't—let myself examine too closely.

Not yet.

By the time gray light seeped through the curtains, I'd made a decision. Or rather, the decision had made itself.

Oliver stirred beside me, and his hand slid to my hip in a sleepy, possessive touch.

"You're awake," he murmured.

"Yes."

"Nightmare?"

"Yes."

He rolled toward me, mindful of my shoulder, and propped himself on one elbow. In the dim light, his face was soft with sleep, his hair disheveled, and his eyes still heavily lidded. But underneath that softness was the sharpness I'd come to know—the operative's alertness that never fully switched off.

"Want to talk about it?"

"No."

He studied me. I watched him assess my expression, my tension, the way I was holding myself. Reading me.

"Something's different," he said.

"Yes."

"Kiernan. What's going on?"

Ophelia shifted on my other side, making a soft sound as she surfaced from sleep. Her hand slid up my chest, and she pressed her face into my good shoulder.

"It's too early," she mumbled. "Go back to sleep."

"I can't," I said.

She lifted her head. Her eyes were bleary, but sharpened as she took in my expression. "What's wrong?"

I sat up. The motion pulled at my healing shoulder, but I ignored it. I looked at them—these two people who'd weathered every wall I'd thrown up, every attempt to drive them off—and made myself speak.

"Meet me in the playroom," I said. "Give me thirty minutes."

They exchanged a glance. Worry passed between them—the questions, the uncertainty. Oliver's expression hardened, and Ophelia reached for his hand.

"Kiernan," she started, "are you sure you're—"

"Thirty minutes."

I left before they could argue.

The playroom was cold when I arrived. I built a fire first, stacking logs and kindling. The flames caught and spread, and I fed them until the heat offset the Highland chill.

I lit candles on the mantel and on the side tables, letting their glow soften the room's edges. Then I turned down the massive bed on the far wall—custom-made for three, wide enough to sprawl without the edges getting in the way—and smoothed the silky black sheets.

This room held only one set of memories for me. Oliver and Ophelia on the night I'd prepared and claimed them. When I'd worked Oliver open with patient fingers, teaching his body to accept what I wanted to give. Making him ready. Making him mine.

I stood by the fire and waited, pulse racing.

Twenty-three minutes later, the door opened.

They came in together, wearing the silk robes I'd left outside the door. The same one I wore. Nothing beneath, if they'd followed my instructions.

"Kiernan?" Ophelia's voice was guarded. "What is this?"

I opened my mouth to explain, to deliver the speech I'd been composing in my head, the words that would make this make sense.

Nothing came out. My throat closed around everything I wanted to say. I stood there, mute and trembling.

Oliver went first.

He crossed the room with slow, measured steps, his gaze locked on mine. I tracked his approach the way I would any threat—frozen, alert, unable to look away.

He stopped an arm's length from me. Close enough to see the flecks of gold in his eyes, the faint scar above his eyebrow, the pulse beating steadily in his throat.

"You're shaking," he said.

I looked down at my trembling hands.

"I need—" The word caught. I tried again. "I want—"

"I know what you want."

My head snapped up.

Oliver's expression had shifted. The sleepy softness was gone, replaced by an edge—the dominant streak I'd helped him discover in this very room.

"You told me there was something you needed. Something you weren't ready to ask for. Every time you look at me, it's there—this thing you want but won't say." He took a step closer. "You brought us here because you're finally ready."

"Oliver—"

"Tell me I'm wrong."

I couldn't. Because he wasn't.

His eyes went dark, and he grabbed me.

One hand fisted in the front of my robe, the other clamped around the back of my neck, and he hauled me flush to him with a force that stole my breath. Our mouths crushed into each other's—not asking, not gentle, not anything close to the tender kisses we'd shared before.

This was claiming. Conquering. His teeth caught my bottom lip and bit down hard enough to sting, and when I gasped, his tongue swept in to take what it wanted.

I grabbed his shoulders for balance. My knees had gone weak, my whole body trembling with the shock of being handled like this—manhandled, controlled, overwhelmed.

He walked me backward without breaking the kiss, driving me across the room until I hit the wall. The impact jarred my healing shoulder, but I didn't care. I couldn't care about anything except his mouth on mine, his body pinning me in place, his hand pressing on my neck until I could feel my pulse thrumming beneath his palm.

"Oliver—" I managed when he finally let me breathe.

"Shut up." He bit my jaw, my throat, the tendon straining in my neck. "You don't get to talk. You don't get to strategize. You don't get to manage this." His hand yanked at my robe, pulling the tie loose. "You want this. And you're going to take it."

The robe fell open.

Oliver pulled back just far enough to look at my naked body. His gaze felt like a physical touch—my chest, my stomach, my cock already hard and straining toward him.

"Ophelia." His voice was rough. *Commanding.* "Come here."

She crossed to us with wide eyes. Not frightened. Aroused. It was apparent in the flush climbing her cheeks and the rapid rise and fall of her chest.

"He needs us," Oliver said to her. "Both of us. Do you understand what he's asking?"

"Yes." I saw the moment she knew the depth of what this meant. "I understand."

"Good." Oliver released me and stepped away. The loss of his body heat was almost painful. "On the bed. Now. Face up."

I obeyed before my mind could catch up. I crossed the room, dropped the robe, and lay on the bed.

"You prepared me in this room," Oliver said as he positioned himself over me and bracketed my body with his arms. "Remember?"

"Yes."

"You took your time. Made sure I was ready. Made sure I could take everything you wanted to give me." He lowered his head and dragged his tongue up the column of my throat. "Now, I'm going to return the favor."

His kiss was brutal and consuming as his naked body pressed into mine, his cock hard at my hip, and I arched into him.

"Eager," he murmured. "Good."

Ophelia joined us on the bed, and her hand slid down my chest, my stomach, and wrapped around my cock.

I jerked into her grip with a groan.

"Sensitive," she observed.

"He's been waiting for this." Oliver bit down on my collarbone, and I groaned. "Haven't you, Kiernan? Waiting and wanting and too stubborn to ask."

"Yes—"

"I know." He kissed down my chest, following the path Ophelia's hand had traced. "I've watched you fight it. Too proud to beg. Too scared to let go."

"I'm not—I wasn't—"

"You were." He reached my hip and bit down hard enough to leave a mark. "But you're done fighting now. Aren't you?"

"Yes."

"Good." He looked up at me, his chin resting on my hip bone, his eyes blazing with a hunger that matched my own. "Because tonight, you're mine. You're ours. And we're going to take everything you've been too afraid to give."

He shoved my thighs apart, and I let him—let him position me however he wanted, let him expose me completely. The vulnerability of it was almost unbearable. I'd never been spread open like this, never been looked at with such naked intent.

"Ophelia," Oliver said. "Keep him busy."

She traveled down my body, trailing kisses as she went. When her mouth closed over my cock, hot and wet and perfect, my hips bucked off the bed.

"Don't come," Oliver warned. "Not until I've given you permission."

I bit back a desperate sound.

He reached for the supplies on the bedside table—the same ones I'd used on him weeks ago. He slicked his fingers, settled between my spread thighs, and looked at me with a question in his eyes.

"Safeword?" he asked.

"Red."

"Use it for any reason. *Any.* I need to hear you say you understand."

"I understand."

"Good." He pressed one slicked finger against me—not pushing in, just applying pressure. "Tell me you want this."

"I want this."

"Say please."

The word stuck in my throat. I'd never—in all my years of dominance, I'd never begged for anything. I'd commanded. Demanded. Taken what I wanted because I was the one with the power.

"Kiernan." Oliver's voice cut through my hesitation. "Say it."

"Please." It came out rough, scraped raw. "Please, Oliver. I need—I need you to—"

He pushed his finger inside me.

My body tensed with the intrusion. Ophelia's mouth worked harder, drawing my attention between the stretch of Oliver's finger and the wet heat surrounding my cock. The dual sensations tangled together, pain and pleasure blurring at the edges.

"Breathe," Oliver said. "Don't fight it. Let me in."

I forced myself to exhale. To unclench. To surrender the last defense I had.

He worked me with patient ruthlessness, his finger sliding deeper, searching for the spot that would drive me mad.

"There." I arched off the bed as lightning shot up my spine. "God—there—"

"That's what I was looking for." He smiled with satisfaction.

He pressed against it again, and my vision whited out. Ophelia swallowed around me, taking me deep, and I was drowning in sensation—overwhelming and still desperate for more.

"More. Please—more—"

A second finger joined the first. The stretch burned, then eased, then transformed into pure pleasure as he found that spot again and again. I was making sounds I'd never made before—whimpers, moans, desperate pleas that I couldn't have stopped if I'd tried.

"Look at you." Oliver's voice was reverent and wrecked all at once. "Falling apart for me. For us. Do you have any idea what it means to see you like this?"

"Oliver—"

"No more walls. No more control. Just you." He added a third finger, and I cried out. "Just us."

"I love you." The words spilled out without permission. "God, Oliver—I love you—I love you both—"

He went still.

Ophelia lifted her head from my cock, her eyes meeting mine. Her lips were swollen and her cheeks flushed.

"Say it again," Oliver demanded.

"I love you." I reached for him, grabbed his arm, and pulled him up my body. "I've never—I didn't think I could—but I do."

He kissed me—fierce and tender and tasting of salt. His tears or mine, I couldn't tell.

He gasped. "God, Kiernan. I love you too."

I reached for Ophelia and cupped her cheek. "I love you, Phee." I used Oliver's pet name for her, hoping she knew the significance of my doing so.

She made her way up my body, and we kissed just as passionately as Oliver and I had, but gentler. Sweeter.

"I've never loved anyone the way I love you," she said, pulling away to look between us. "More than I dreamed possible."

As tender as this moment was, I couldn't let it end here. We needed to keep going. To close the circle. To make us complete.

I pulled Oliver closer. "I need you to——"

"Fuck you?" He laughed—a ragged, disbelieving sound. "Is that what you want?"

"Yes. Please. God. I need you inside me."

He positioned himself between my thighs while Ophelia's lips returned to mine. She swallowed my gasp as he pushed inside, then gripped my cock and stroked it in time with his thrusts.

"Look at me," Oliver commanded.

His face was tight with restraint, and his body trembled with restraint.

"Last chance," he said. "Tell me to stop, and I will. No questions."

"If you stop, I'll kill you."

He smiled—that brilliant, devastating smile I'd do anything to see.

The stretch was—I couldn't think. Couldn't breathe. Couldn't do anything except feel him filling me, inch by inch, impossibly big, impossibly deep. Ophelia's hand on my cock was the only thing keeping me from flying apart.

"Okay?" His voice was strained. Wrecked.

"Yes." I struggled to pull him deeper. "Move. Please, Oliver. Move."

He thrust. Slowly at first. Long, deep strokes that dragged against the spot inside me and made me see stars. Ophelia matched his rhythm, her hands working in tandem with his thrusts, and I was surrounded by them—filled and held and claimed in every possible way.

"Faster," I gasped. "Harder. I won't break."

"I know you won't." His hips snapped forward, driving deep, and I shouted. "You're the strongest person I've ever known. That's why you can do this. That's why you can let go."

He fucked me harder. The sound of skin on skin filled the room, punctuated by my moans and his grunts and the wet sounds of Ophelia's mouth when she leaned in to lick my shaft. It was obscene. It was perfect. It was everything.

"This is what you needed," Oliver growled.

"Yes—"

"You're not weak for wanting this." He grabbed my jaw and forced me to meet his eyes even as his hips kept driving into me. "You're brave. You're so fucking brave, Kiernan. Letting us see you like this. Letting us in."

"I love you," I said again—couldn't stop saying it, couldn't hold it back anymore. "God." The word came out reverent, wrecked. I couldn't find any others.

"We feel the same." Ophelia lifted her head, but continued stroking me.

"Even when you tried to push us away," Oliver added.

"Especially then," she murmured.

The orgasm was building at the base of my spine, inevitable and overwhelming. I fought it—one last desperate grab at control—but Oliver felt my resistance and drove into me harder.

"Let go," he commanded. "Let go, Kiernan. Come for us."

"I can't—"

"You can." Ophelia's grip tightened, twisting on the upstroke. "You can. We've got you. We'll catch you."

"Come," Oliver growled. "Now."

I shattered.

The orgasm ripped through me like nothing I'd ever experienced—not just a physical release, though that crashed over me in waves, spilling over Ophelia's hand and my stomach. But more than that. Every defense

I'd built, every barrier I'd maintained, the lies I'd told myself—all of it crumbling, dissolving, washing away.

I was dimly aware of Oliver following me over, his hips jerking, his release pulsing inside me. Of Ophelia gasping, her own hand between her legs, her whole body shuddering with her own climax.

We lay tangled together in the aftermath, but I wasn't done.

The surrender had cracked something open in me—not broken it, opened it. And what poured through wasn't weakness. It was power. Different from before. Cleaner. Not armor anymore, but choice.

I could give control. Which meant I could also take it back.

"Oliver." My voice came out rough, but underneath it was control. Command.

He lifted his head, his eyes hazy with satisfaction. "Yeah?"

"Come with me." I led him into the bathroom, where we both cleaned ourselves before turning to where Ophelia waited.

"On your knees," I ordered.

He appeared confused, then blinked when it turned into recognition, then heat.

"Kiernan—"

"Did I stutter?" I sat up, ignoring the ache in my body, the soreness that would remind me of this night for days. "On your knees. Ophelia—under him."

They shifted. Oliver rolled off me and positioned himself on all fours, still half-hard, his body flushed and slick with sweat. Ophelia slid beneath him, her thighs falling open, her eyes locked on mine.

"You're sure?" Oliver asked over his shoulder. "You just—"

"I just let you fuck me." I positioned myself behind him, my hand sliding down his spine. "And it was everything I needed. Now, you need this."

I reached for the lube and slicked myself—already hardening again, my body responding to the sight of them arranged for me, waiting for me, trusting me.

"This is who I am," I said as I positioned myself at Oliver's entrance. "All of it. The surrender and the control. The man who kneels and the man who commands."

I pushed inside him fast and hard, and he groaned, dropping his head.

"Kiernan—" Oliver's arms trembled.

"Fuck her," I commanded. "Now."

He obeyed, sinking into Ophelia's perfect pink pussy. Her back arched, and she moaned. And then I started to thrust.

The three of us were connected. Oliver between us—inside her, around me. Every thrust I gave him, he gave her. We found a rhythm together, bodies rocking in sync, pleasure building and cresting and building again.

"This," I growled into Oliver's shoulder. "This is what I want. All of us. Everything. No barriers. No holding back."

"Yes—" Ophelia's voice was broken, desperate. "God, yes—"

"Yours." I drove deeper into Oliver and felt him shudder. "Both of you. I'm yours, and you're mine, and this—this is how it's supposed to be."

Oliver came first this time—spilling into Ophelia with a hoarse shout, his whole body clenching around me. She followed seconds later when I reached around and stroked her clit.

Then, I let myself go, pouring into him, claiming him the way he'd claimed me.

We rested, caught our breath, and cleaned each other with warm cloths and gentle hands. The kind of aftercare that required no words.

But we weren't finished.

I looked at Ophelia—flushed and satisfied, sprawled across the sheets like an offering—and felt hunger stir again. Not the desperate, clawing need from before. Something deeper. The need to complete this. To close the circle.

"Ophelia." I traced my fingers down her stomach, watched her muscles flutter beneath my touch. "We haven't taken proper care of you yet."

Her breath caught. "I'm—I already—"

"Not enough." I slid two fingers inside her, and she arched off the bed. "Oliver."

He was already shifting, reading my intent. "Both of us?"

"At the same time."

Ophelia made a sound—half moan, half whimper. "I don't know if I can—"

"You can." I kissed her hard, swallowing her protest. "And you're going to because I want to feel his cock rub mine while we're both buried inside you."

When she moaned into my mouth, I pulled her on top of me, guiding her down onto my cock in one slow slide. She was drenched, open, her body welcoming me like coming home. I held her hips still, keeping her filled, waiting.

Oliver knelt behind her. I heard the slick sound of lube, felt her tense in anticipation, then shudder as his fingers worked her open.

"Ready?" he asked.

"Do it," I said.

He pressed inside her, and I nearly lost my mind.

Feeling him through that thin wall, the impossible tightness of her stretched around both of us—I had to clench my jaw to keep from coming on the spot.

"Fuck—" Ophelia's nails dug into my chest. "Oh fuck, oh God—"

"That's it." I gripped her hips, holding her steady while Oliver bottomed out. "Take all of us."

For a moment, none of us stirred. Just breathed. Adjusted. Felt.

Then Oliver started to thrust.

We found a rhythm—him driving forward while I pulled back, trading places inside her, our cocks rubbing with every stroke. Ophelia was incoherent between us, her body clenching and releasing, taking everything we gave her.

"Look at you," I breathed. "Taking both of us. So perfect. So beautiful."

"Ours," Oliver added. "You're ours."

"More," she gasped. "Please—harder—"

We gave it to her. Oliver's hands were on her hips, mine on her breasts, both of us pounding into her until the bed shook and her screams echoed off the stone walls.

"Come, Ophelia," I commanded. *Now.*

She broke apart. The double clench of her orgasm squeezed us both, milked us, dragged us over the edge with her. Oliver buried himself deep with a groan and came just as I spilled inside her.

The three of us became one. One heartbeat, one breath.

The circle, finally, completely closed. We were complete.

The fire had burned down to glowing embers. The candles guttered in their holders. Outside, morning light came in the windows, but none of us acknowledged it.

My body ached in ways I'd never experienced. The stretch and soreness of being opened, claimed, taken. The pleasant throb of well-used flesh. The lingering tremors that ran through me every time one of them shifted.

Oliver had his head on my chest, his arm thrown across my stomach. Ophelia was tucked on my other side, her leg draped over both of ours, her fingers tracing idly on my hip.

And my mind was quiet.

For the first time in seven years, the noise had stopped. The endless loop of strategy and vigilance, the constant calculation of risk, the voice that told me I was too dangerous to love—all of it had gone silent.

Not lurking at the edges. Not waiting to reassert itself. Gone.

In its place was a feeling I barely recognized—warm and settled and terrifyingly close to peace.

"How do you feel?" Oliver asked.

I considered the question. Considered him—this man who'd taken me apart with such fierce tenderness, who'd held the power I'd surrendered and used it to set me free.

"Complete," I said. "Yours."

He lifted his head. His eyes were soft, wondering. "What?"

"I feel yours." I touched his face and traced the line of his jaw. "For the first time in my life, I feel like I belong to someone. To two people. And it doesn't terrify me."

Ophelia propped herself up. "It doesn't?"

"No." I pulled her down and kissed her. "It feels like coming home."

"Kiernan…" Oliver's voice cracked.

"I love you." I looked between them, letting them see everything—no walls, no masks, no distance. "Not despite what just happened. Because of it." I pulled them both closer, one in each arm, their bodies warm next to mine. "I've never trusted anyone like this. Never let anyone see me like this. But you—" My voice broke, and I let it. "You're different. You're mine."

"Yours," Oliver agreed.

"And you're ours," Ophelia added. "That's how this works."

"I know." I pressed my lips to the top of Oliver's head, then turned to kiss Ophelia's temple. "I know that now."

The silence that followed wasn't empty. It was full—of breath and heartbeat and the weight of words finally spoken.

"Stay," I said. "Not just today. Not just until you get restless or I push you away or the world intrudes. Stay. Make this your home. Build a life with me."

"We already have," Oliver said.

"I'm asking you to make it permanent." I tightened my arms around them. "I'm asking you to let me love you for the rest of my life. To let me be yours, the way you're mine. To—" I stopped. Started again. "I've never asked anyone for forever. I'm asking you now."

Ophelia's breath caught.

Oliver lifted his head and looked at me with eyes that shone.

"Yes," he said simply.

"Yes," Ophelia echoed. "God, yes."

"Okay, then." My voice came out rough.

"Okay," Oliver repeated, and he was smiling now, that brilliant smile I'd do anything to see. "That's settled."

"Forever," Ophelia said, testing the word. "I like the sound of that."

"So do I." I kissed her, then Oliver. Then both of them together, a messy tangle of mouths and breath and laughter that shouldn't have been possible, given what we'd just done.

When we finally broke apart, the morning light had grown stronger.

"Sleep," I murmured. "We have time."

"All the time in the world," Ophelia agreed.

I pressed my lips to the top of Oliver's head and drew Ophelia closer.

For the first time in seven years, my mind was quiet.

I closed my eyes and let myself rest.

27

Ophelia

Three weeks after Kiernan's stitches came out, I woke to the sound of rain against the windows.

The bed was empty. I'd learned Kiernan liked to rise early and enjoy the quiet hours before dawn when the house was still and his mind was calm. What was new was that Oliver had gone with him. Their sides of the bed were cool, which meant they'd been up for a while.

I stretched, feeling the pleasant ache in my muscles from last night. Kiernan had topped us both—Oliver first, then me—with an intensity that left us wrung out and gasping. But afterward, when we'd collapsed into a tangle of limbs, Oliver had pressed his mouth to Kiernan's ear and murmured something I couldn't hear. Kiernan had shivered, then nodded as I'd watched Oliver's hand slide down Kiernan's spine with a possessiveness that made my breath catch.

They'd disappeared into the bathroom together. I'd fallen asleep before they came back.

I pulled on a pair of joggers and one of Kiernan's soft cotton shirts, then padded barefoot through the corridor and down the west tower stairs, toward the kitchen. Greymarch was waking up around me. Millie's voice drifted from somewhere below, giving instructions to the morning staff.

I found my two men in the kitchen. Oliver sat at the long wooden table, laptop open, a cup of tea at his elbow, and Kiernan stood at the stove, doing something with eggs and butter that filled the room with the scent of browned butter and herbs. They talked in low voices, not noticing me in the doorway.

This was what I'd been afraid to want. Not the sex, though that was extraordinary. Not even the love, though I felt it every time they looked at me. *This.* Ordinary mornings. Breakfast and the rain and the quiet domesticity of two men who'd rearranged their entire lives to be together. Here. With me and with each other.

Kiernan glanced up and smiled when he caught me watching.

"There she is." He gestured with the spatula. "Eggs?"

"Please."

Oliver looked up from his laptop, and his eyes traveled down the length of Kiernan's shirt on my body.

"That's a good look," he said. "Although it would be better with nothing underneath."

"It's comfortable."

"It's distracting." He grinned. "Come here."

I crossed to the table, and he pulled me into his lap with one arm wrapped around my waist. I settled against his chest and reached for his tea, stealing a sip.

"That's mine," he said.

"What's yours is mine."

"Is that how it works?"

"That's exactly how it works."

Kiernan set a plate in front of us—eggs, toast, and jam. He poured me my own tea, then sat across from us with his own plate.

"Viper called," I said after we'd finished, the plates were cleared, and we'd gone to the library.

Oliver was stretched on the sofa, with his head in my lap. Kiernan sat in the wingback chair by the fire, reading something on his tablet.

"And?" Oliver asked.

"She's been trying to reach you. Your medical clearance came through."

"About bloody time," he muttered. He'd been restless these past weeks, his body healed but his mind still adjusting to the stillness. Oliver wasn't built for inactivity. None of us were.

"Anything else?" Kiernan asked.

"Typhon wants an answer." I ran my fingers through Oliver's hair. "He's giving us until the end of the week."

"What do you want to do?" Kiernan asked, his eyes on me, but the question was for both of us.

"I want to say yes," Oliver said. "The work matters. And I'd rather answer to Typhon than to the bureaucratic nightmare that is MI6 middle management."

"You'd be working with me," Kiernan said. "All of us on the same team. That could be…complicated."

"It could." Oliver sat up, turning to face him. "Does that bother you?"

"No." Kiernan's answer came at once. "I'm asking if it bothers you."

"Being on a team with the two people I—" Oliver stopped, then started again. "No. It doesn't bother me."

"Say it," Kiernan said quietly.

Oliver's jaw worked. Admitting our feelings wasn't easy for any of us.

"The two people I love," he finished. "No. It doesn't bother me."

"Ophelia?" Kiernan asked.

"I want it," I said.

Kiernan's mouth curved—not a full smile, but close. "Then, that's settled."

"What about Viper?" I asked. "She's going to be annoyed about losing us to Unit 23."

"Only a little," Kiernan said. "But not as much as she's pretending. She'll survive."

"And the logistics?" Oliver asked. "Unit 23 isn't exactly a nine-to-five office job. Not that MI6 is, unless you're a bureaucrat."

"We work remotely. Missions happen when they happen, but between them—" Kiernan gestured at the room around us. "This is home base for our team."

"Speaking of the team," Oliver said. "Have you talked to Callen lately? He's seemed…off."

"He's dealing with something. Family matter at Dunravin."

"The MacLeods?"

"He hasn't said. And I haven't pushed." Kiernan's tone made it clear the subject was closed.

That evening, when we retired to the west tower, something was different. Instead of two chairs near the sitting room fireplace, there were three.

"I had the third one brought up earlier today," Kiernan said, watching my face. "It seemed…appropriate."

Oliver stood by the window, but turned to face us. "What else?"

Kiernan raised a brow. "He asks as if he doesn't already know."

Oliver smirked. "Tell us anyway."

"Tomorrow, we'll be working in the library. Setting it up as a work area for all of us."

I was stunned. Since our first day here, it had been a place we were invited into. Kiernan's place. "Are you sure you want to do that?"

"You're both welcome to set up private offices any-where you'd like. This is, after all, your home."

I blinked away tears and pinched myself. I'd never imagined such happiness was possible, whether it was with one man or two.

"There's, um, something else," Kiernan said with a hesitancy that was unlike him.

I raised my head, and so did Oliver.

"What?" he asked.

"This isn't as easy as rearranging furniture." He motioned for us to join him near the fireplace. "We have a decision to make. Decisions, actually."

"Out with it," said Oliver.

Kiernan raised a brow in his direction, then took each of our hands. "I want to make this official."

"This?" I asked, reaching for Oliver's free hand.

"Part of it can be done legally. Greymarch, as well as my other holdings, are in a trust that gets passed on to my heirs. However, in the event I predecease, either of you—"

Oliver groaned. "Kiernan."

He leveled a glare at him. "This needs to be said."

"Go on," he muttered under his breath.

"There are stipulations that would allow you to live out your lives here or anywhere else you choose to. Funds would also be provided for anything you might need."

"This is too much—"

He squeezed my hand. "I'm not finished."

I nodded once, then lowered my gaze.

"Look at me, Phee."

My eyes met his.

"There's the matter of marriage. I can marry either of you, or you can marry each other. That's all the law provides for currently."

"If this is a proposal, it's sorely lacking, Kier," Oliver teased.

His cheeks flushed in a way that he likely would've been uncomfortable with a few weeks ago. "Yes, I suppose it is."

When he lowered himself to his knees, I gasped.

He released our hands and reached into his pocket, withdrawing two rings. Simple gold bands, worn smooth with age.

"My mother's," he said, holding up one. "And my father's." He looked at Oliver, then at me. "I'm not good at asking. I'm better at commanding." A ghost of a smile crossed his face. "But I'm asking now. Be mine. Let me be yours. Wear these, and let me spend the rest of my life loving you."

Oliver went first. He dropped to his knees beside Kiernan, cupping his face with both hands.

"Yes." He kissed him—hard, fierce, certain. "You impossible, stubborn, beautiful man. Yes."

Kiernan's breath shuddered out of him. He took Oliver's hand and slid his father's ring onto his finger.

Then they both looked at me.

I was still standing. Still crying. Still trying to comprehend that this was real—that this was my life now.

"Phee?" Kiernan's voice was soft, uncertain in a way I'd never heard from him. "I need an answer."

I sank to my knees in front of him, joining them on the floor.

"Yes." I kissed him through my tears. "Yes, yes, yes."

He slid his mother's ring onto my finger. It fit perfectly, as if it had been waiting for me.

The three of us knelt there together, foreheads touching, hands intertwined, the firelight flickering across our faces.

"Forever," Kiernan said quietly.

"Forever," Oliver echoed.

"Forever," I whispered.

"There's one more thing," Kiernan said, his voice dropping low. "Tomorrow night. The Thistle." His eyes shifted between us, hungry and possessive. "I want to show you off. Both of you. Let everyone see what's mine."

"Yours?" Oliver's eyes scrunched.

"Ours," Kiernan amended, but his smile said he wasn't sorry. "Let them see what's ours."

Epilogue

I woke before dawn on my wedding day and lay still in the gray half-light, listening as the ancient castle settled.

Greymarch had stood for three hundred years. Generations of Lockharts had loved and lost within these walls. My parents had married in this castle, as had my grandparents before them. They'd followed tradition, done what was expected, and lived lives that fit neatly into the world's understanding of how things should be.

Today, something new would happen here. Ophelia, Oliver, and I would defy convention and marry. Our union would exist outside the law but would be real, nonetheless.

The kilt I wore had been my father's. It was a dark tartan in the Lockhart hunting pattern, and the wool remained supple despite the decades. I dressed slowly and deliberately. Putting on the crisp white shirt, then the waistcoat, then the jacket with its silver buttons bearing the family crest. The *sgian-dubh* slid into my sock, its handle worn smooth by the hands that had carried it before mine.

In the mirror, I saw my father's jaw and my mother's eyes. They would not have understood what I was about to do—a ceremony binding me to two people instead of one. I didn't care. I'd never been more confident of any decision I'd made in my life.

Oliver's parents and sister had flown in from Australia. Ophelia's family had come from Nigeria. We'd braced ourselves for the worst when we told them, and rehearsed explanations and justifications that none of them had needed.

Ophelia's father had simply said, "My daughter has never stayed in one place long enough to call it home. If you and Oliver are the reason she's finally found one, then I have nothing but gratitude."

Oliver's mother had looked at the three of us across the dinner table and said, "Well, you'll need a bigger Christmas tree." His father had laughed and poured another round of wine.

We'd spent weeks dreading rejection that never came.

A knock came as I finished adjusting my cuffs. Millie stood in the doorway, already fighting her tears. "Let me look at you."

I turned so she could inspect me. She crossed the room and straightened my collar, though it needed no straightening.

"Your father wore this kilt the day he married your mother." Her fingers lingered on the wool. "I pressed it myself that morning."

Her hands trembled as she smoothed the front of my jacket. "I wondered if I'd ever see you wear it." She cleared her throat and brushed away a single tear. "They're beautiful, your two. They shine when they look at you. Did you know that?"

I hadn't noticed. But Millie had, and if she said they shone, I believed her.

"Go on, then." She waved me toward the door. "Oliver's been pacing in the library for twenty minutes."

I found him in a room I used to consider my private sanctuary, but which now belonged to the three of us equally. He turned from the window when he heard me, and for a moment, neither of us spoke. His charcoal suit was impeccable, and his hair looked soft enough that I wanted to run my fingers through it. His gaze moved over the kilt, the jacket, the full Highland regalia, and his composure fell apart.

"Sir. You look—"

"Come here."

He crossed to me. His hands reached for my lapels, but stopped short, waiting for permission.

I took his face in my hands and kissed him hard. I kissed him like he was mine, because he was.

When I released him, his chest heaved.

"I'm going to marry you today," I said. "Both of you. And tonight, after the reception, I'm taking you both to the Thistle."

He swallowed hard. "The collaring."

"Yes." I traced my thumb along his jaw. "You'll kneel for me in front of witnesses. You'll wear my collar for the rest of your life. If that's what you want."

"It's what I want." He said it without hesitating.

I kissed him again, softer this time. "Go on now. I'll see you at the altar."

The great hall had been transformed. Winter roses and heather lined the aisle, candles burned in silver holders along the walls, and the massive fireplace had been lit before dawn and fed through the morning until the whole room glowed. I stood at the front with the officiant—a friend from Edinburgh, a judge who'd agreed to preside over the ceremony.

The first part, between Ophelia and me, would be legally binding. She would become my viscountess, and our children would be heirs not only to Greymarch, but to the entirety of the family's holdings. That didn't mean Oliver would be left out. My attorney had drafted a document, giving him equal ownership of unentailed assets, and the rights to reside on any of the estate's properties for the rest of his life.

Oliver sat in the front row, beside Callen, Gus, and Rafe. His hands were folded, and his eyes were on me.

When the harpist and violinist began to play Pachelbel's "Canon in D," I motioned for him to stand beside me.

Then the doors opened, and Ophelia appeared on the threshold on her father's arm.

Her gown was made of ivory silk, and her dark hair was swept up while loose curls framed her face. Her father's eyes were bright, and his smile broad. When they reached me, he placed her hand in mine, then held my gaze long enough to make his meaning clear before stepping away.

After she handed her bouquet of white roses and thistles to her mother, I took her hands. They were cold from nerves, and I rubbed my thumbs across her knuckles until the tension eased.

"Kiernan," she said, low enough that only I could hear. "I love you."

"I love you," I said. "Both of you. More than I knew I was capable of."

The officiant led the ceremony in a way that weaved legalities with the parts we'd added.

We exchanged vows we'd written—about protection and partnership, trust freely given, and dominance earned, a life that belonged to no template but our own.

When it came time for the rings, I produced two bands of platinum, each engraved on the inside—Ours to keep.

I slid the first onto Ophelia's finger. I wasn't surprised when she didn't cry. She was too stubborn to break in front of witnesses.

When I slid the second onto Oliver's, tears slid down his cheeks as he stared at the band on his hand.

Then Oliver reached into this pocket, and together, he and Ophelia placed the band on my ring finger.

"You may kiss your—" The officiant paused.

"Partners," I said. "I may kiss my partners."

I cradled the back of Ophelia's neck, and brought my lips to hers. Then I turned to Oliver and kissed him the same way, with the same intention. Then they kissed each other.

When I lifted my head, the room burst into applause. Callen was grinning. Ophelia's mother and Oliver's mother and sister were crying.

The reception was brief by design. We drank champagne, listened to toasts, and posed for photographs by the fireplace. After dinner, when the guests drifted to their rooms, I caught Ophelia's eye and inclined my head toward the door. When she touched Oliver's arm, he looked at me and nodded.

We slipped away without fanfare, changed out of our wedding attire and into what I'd chosen for us to wear tonight.

Ophelia's was a deep-emerald corset with black boning that cinched her waist and lifted her breasts, paired with a black silk skirt that skimmed the tops of her thighs and nothing beneath it. Black stilettos added four inches to her height. Oliver and I wore black trousers, black shirts open at the collar, and matching leather cuffs at our wrists. We looked like what we were—two men who owned the woman between us.

Callen drove us to the Thorned Thistle. Gus and Rafe, who'd used the tunnels, said they'd be waiting inside when we arrived.

I helped Ophelia out of the SUV, then waited for Oliver to come around from the other side of the vehicle. Then we joined hands.

"From this point forward, you are mine." Both of them responded the way they always did—spines straightened, breath quickened. "You will not speak unless I give permission. You will keep your eyes on me. You will trust that everything I do tonight is because I love you."

"Yes, sir," they said in unison.

I pushed the door open and led them to the room where the next ceremony would take place. The walls of the small and intimate space had been draped in burgundy velvet. Candles burned in iron sconces, and in the center sat a polished obsidian altar bearing two black boxes.

At the entryway, I helped Ophelia remove her shoes like Oliver and I had.

The only witnesses invited were the three men who were my partners and closest friends. Snow wasn't in attendance, but he'd arranged to watch remotely. These were the people who'd built this place with me and who would hold us accountable to the promises made tonight. While Ophelia and Oliver could've had guests of their own, both chose not to.

I guided them to the center and positioned them side by side, facing the altar, then moved to stand before them.

"Kneel."

They sank together, heads bowed, hands resting on their thighs. I let the silence hold.

"What I'm about to give you is not jewelry. It is not a symbol or a gesture. When I place a collar around your throat, I am claiming responsibility for your well-being—your safety, your pleasure, your growth. I am promising to lead with intention, to correct with care, and to push you toward becoming the people you are capable of being. This belonging is the most sacred thing I know how to offer."

I reached for the first box. Inside, against black velvet, lay a collar of burnished leather with a single titanium ring at the front.

"Oliver."

His head came up, his eyes wet and his jaw tight.

"The submission you offer me is the bravest thing I have ever been given. Do you accept this collar, knowing that it binds you to my authority? Knowing that I will make demands of you and hold you to standards and expect your obedience even when it's difficult?"

"Yes, sir."

"Freely? Because it's what you want?"

"More than anything."

I settled the collar around his throat and fastened it. The leather sat snug—not tight enough to restrict, but he would always know it was there. I cupped his jaw and tilted his face up.

"Mine."

"Yours."

We kissed more deeply than we had at the marriage ceremony. When I released him, tears streamed down his face, and he made no effort to hide them.

"Stay."

Ophelia's collar was different—thinner, more delicate, the leather dyed a deep wine red, but the titanium ring matched Oliver's. She looked up at me the way she always did when she was about to give me something that cost her—chin lifted, eyes fierce, daring me to be worthy of it.

"Ophelia. Do you accept this collar, knowing that it requires your vulnerability? Knowing that I will ask things of you that terrify you, and hold you through the fear, and refuse to let you retreat?"

"Yes, sir."

"Freely?"

"I want to be yours." Her hands trembled in her lap. "I never wanted anything as much as I want to be yours."

I settled the collar around her throat and traced my thumb along the edge of the leather. She shuddered.

"Good girl."

One tear slipped down her cheek, and I caught it with my thumb.

I stepped back and looked at them both—kneeling, collared, mine. I had given them rings and spoken vows earlier. This was the final commitment. What bound us together forever.

"You may rise."

They stood together, and we embraced as one.

—Oliver—

When he released us, Ophelia and I knelt without being commanded to do so. Kiernan's eyes scrunched, and his brow furrowed. He believed the ceremony was complete, that the claiming only flowed in one direction. He was wrong.

I caught Ophelia's eye, and she nodded once.

"Sir." I kept my voice steady. "The ceremony isn't finished."

"What do you mean?"

"Permission to rise?"

"Of course."

We stood together and flanked him.

"You collared us," I said. "You claimed responsibility. You gave us visible proof that we belong to you."

"That's what a collaring is."

"That's what a collaring used to be. Before us."

Callen moved forward from his place along the wall. In his hands, he carried an aged wood box with the Lockhart crest carved into the lid.

Kiernan's brow furrowed as he studied it.

"We talked about this," I said. "Ophelia and I. What it would mean to belong to you. What we would gain." I took a breath. "We also talked about what you would be giving up."

"I'm not giving anything up."

"You're giving up control." Ophelia stepped closer. "Not all of it. Not even most of it. But some. You're trusting us to see the parts of yourself you've hidden from everyone else."

"That's not—"

"It is." I cut him off, and the shock on his face was almost worth the terror of interrupting him. "You kneel for us too, Kiernan. Maybe not physically. But you kneel."

Callen opened the box.

Inside lay a torque of hammered silver, thick and heavy, designed to sit at the base of the throat. It was open at the front with two terminals that would rest against his collarbones.

I pointed to one terminal. "The Thornwood crest."

Ophelia touched the other. "A rose. My middle name."

"Do you accept this?" I forced the words out. "Do you accept that you belong to us as we belong to you? That our claim on you is as real and as permanent as your claim on us?"

He looked at the torque, then at me, then Ophelia.

"Yes."

I lifted the torque from the box. The silver was warm and heavier than I expected. Ophelia placed her hands on his shoulders from behind.

"Kneel," she said.

His knees bent, then he sank to the floor in front of us and looked up with an expression I'd never seen on his face before.

I settled the torque around his throat, and Ophelia's hands joined mine on the metal.

"Ours," she said.

"Yours," he answered.

From behind us, Callen added, "Witnessed and sealed."

After several seconds, Kiernan stood. "I believe," he said, "we have a marriage to consummate."

Our three guests departed with handshakes and murmured congratulations.

Once they were gone, Kiernan reached for Ophelia first, pulled her against his chest, and kissed her hard. She pressed into him, fingers clutching his shirt. I watched, and what I felt wasn't jealousy. It was want.

"Come here."

He gripped the back of my neck and pulled me in. His mouth was on mine, hot and demanding. Ophelia kissed my jaw, then my throat, then the edge of my collar.

"The bed," Kiernan said against my mouth. "Now."

Our clothes came off as we moved toward it. Ophelia's silk skirt slid down her hips, and I unlaced her corset.

"Remove my shirt," he said once she was naked. "Oliver, you're overdressed."

Kiernan moved behind me after I took off my shirt. His bare chest pressed against my back as he unfastened my belt. "I've been thinking about what I wanted to do to both of you once you were collared," he said against my ear.

"What did you come up with?" I gasped when he reached into my trousers and gripped my cock.

"Everything. I want to watch Ophelia ride your face while I fuck you. I want to bury myself inside her while you take me from behind. Then spend hours making you scream and beg and come so hard you forget your own name."

I pulsed in his hands.

"To start," Kiernan continued, "I want you inside me while I'm inside her."

I pressed my mouth to his shoulder. "Then, that's what you'll get."

We removed the rest of our clothes, then stood at the end of the bed, where Ophelia lay waiting.

Kiernan positioned himself between her thighs, and I knelt behind him and ran my hands down the line of his back.

I slicked my fingers and worked him open. His head dropped forward, and Ophelia stroked his face while I stretched him. He pushed back against my hand, impatient, demanding more without words. I gave it to him.

When he was ready, I slicked my cock and pushed forward. He groaned as I seated myself fully. Beneath us, Ophelia gasped as he pushed inside her.

"Move," he said.

I didn't need to be told twice. I gripped his hips and thrust deep, angling to hit the spot that made him curse. Kiernan was between us, taking and giving at once. I found my rhythm, and he matched it, driving into her as I drove into him.

"Harder," he demanded.

Ophelia cried out beneath him, her back arched, and her nails raked down his arms.

"I'm close," she gasped. "Kiernan—Oliver—"

"Let go," he told her. "Come for us."

Her orgasm hit hard. She screamed his name, then mine. Kiernan kept moving through it, drawing it out, and I kept building toward my own release.

He buried himself deep inside her and clenched around me as he came. The sensation pulled me over with him.

We collapsed together. He rolled to his side and pulled us both with him, refusing to break contact. I pressed against his back, and Ophelia curled into his front.

We lay there until the candles burned low. Eventually, we cleaned ourselves and the room, dressed, and returned to Greymarch through the tunnels. We climbed the stairs to Kiernan's bedroom—our bedroom—without encountering anyone.

The bed was vast, and the sheets were already turned down. We stripped again, then climbed in with Kiernan in the center, Ophelia on one side, and me on the other. Our legs tangled under the covers.

I lay awake after they drifted off. Moonlight crossed the ceiling, and Kiernan's chest rose and fell against my palm. I closed my eyes and slept.

—Ophelia—

I woke to warmth on both sides, and the unfamiliar weight of the collar at my throat.

For a moment, I didn't move. Kiernan's arm was draped across my waist, Oliver's back pressed against mine, and pale winter light filtered through the curtains. My whole life, I'd woken in temporary places—embassy residences, safe houses, hotel rooms that looked the same in every city. This was the first time I'd woken somewhere permanent.

I let myself feel it. The solidity of the bed beneath me, the sound of their breathing, the way neither of them stirred when I shifted slightly. They slept like men who trusted the world around them. I wasn't sure I'd ever slept that way.

Kiernan's eyes opened, and his gaze held mine, unhurried.

"Good morning, wife."

The word landed somewhere deep in my chest. "Good morning, husband."

Oliver stirred behind me. "Too early for talking."

"It's nearly ten, other husband," Kiernan said.

"Still too early."

Kiernan's mouth curved, and he reached across me to grip Oliver's hip. "Get up. There's another gift."

That got Oliver's attention. He propped himself on one elbow, suddenly awake. "Now?"

"Now."

After we put on robes and slippers, they refused to tell me where they were taking me.

They made me close my eyes while they led me through the castle, one hand in each of theirs. We stopped, and heavy-sounding doors creaked open.

"Open," Kiernan whispered as each man kissed my neck.

The conservatory stretched before me, and it was nothing like the ruin I remembered.

The iron framework had been restored, and each arch and strut gleamed. Hundreds of glass panels had been replaced with crystal-clear panes that caught the winter light. Heat circulated through the space where tropical palms rose toward the glass ceiling, flowering vines climbed the framework, and orchids hung in baskets among the ferns. A stone path wound through the greenery to a clearing at the center.

"We started weeks ago," Oliver said. "You said it must have been magnificent once. So we brought it back."

We'd stood in the ruin together, and I'd said something offhand while stepping around a dead palm frond. I barely remembered.

But Oliver had.

"I found specialists for the restoration," Kiernan said. "Oliver researched the plants. Millie supervised when we couldn't."

"We left space," Oliver added. "For whatever you want to grow."

The tears came before I could stop them, and I could barely speak. "It's perfect."

I pulled Oliver to me first and held him hard. Then Kiernan. I buried my face against his chest.

We walked the path to the clearing, and I sank onto a wrought-iron, cushioned love seat. They settled on either side of me.

Outside, snow streaked past the glass. Inside, the air was warm and the plants reached toward the light.

"We should get ready," Kiernan said after a while. "Our honeymoon flight leaves at four."

"Our what?" I gasped. "Where are we going?" I looked over at Oliver, who shrugged.

"It's a surprise," Kiernan said, reaching into my robe to cup my breast before lowering his head and sucking my nipple into his mouth.

"What, um, should I pack?" I asked, having trouble speaking, especially when Oliver pushed my legs open and thrust a finger into my already-drenched pussy.

Kiernan raised his head. "You won't be needing clothes. Either of you. I plan to keep your bodies naked and available to me the entire time we're gone."

Oliver sank to the floor, spread my legs wider, then licked through my folds. "Sounds like a perfect honey-moon to me," he muttered before latching his lips to my clit.

"Me too," I groaned as my body spasmed with an orgasm I hadn't gotten permission to have.

"Tsk, tsk," Kiernan scolded. "We may have to wait until we're on the plane to punish you for that."

I stuck out my lower lip in a pout, and Oliver raised his head.

"Is that look because you've earned a punishment or because you'll have to wait to get it?"

I smirked. "Both."

Keep reading for a sneak peek at
the next book in
Merrigan Calder's
Thorned Thistle series—
Possessed.

He's waited years to claim her.
She's spent years denying what she needs.
When danger strikes, his possession becomes
her surrender—and her salvation.

CALLEN

I've wanted Isla MacLeod since we were teenagers—the estate manager's proud daughter who looked at me with equal parts fascination and resentment. She was forbidden then, too young and too good for someone like me. Now her father's in prison, her life's in ruins, and the people who used her as leverage think she knows secrets worth killing for. She needs protection whether she admits it or not. She needs me. And I'm done waiting.

ISLA

Callen Cavendish was supposed to stay in my past—the wealthy boy who made my pulse race and my pride sting. But when my father's former associates come hunting for information I don't have, Callen is suddenly everywhere: protective, commanding, refusing to let me push him away. He wants me to surrender, to trust him, to stop fighting. He wants to possess me. The terrifying part? I want it too. I want to stop being strong. I want to be his.

Prologue

Callen

The invitation had been sitting on my desk for a week before I opened it.

Hand-lettered calligraphy on heavy cream stock, sealed with wax the color of old blood. The kind of thing that arrived at Dunravin regularly—charity galas, estate auctions, the tedious social obligations that came with being heir to a dukedom.

I'd planned to decline like I always did. Then I'd seen the host's name.

Lazzaro Benedetti. It meant nothing to most people, but in certain circles—my circles—it carried weight. He ran the Copper Chalice, one of Europe's most exclusive private clubs. It was headquartered in a Renaissance villa outside Florence. Not the kind of establishment with dress codes and champagne toasts. The kind where discretion was currency and desire was the only language spoken.

I'd heard whispers about the event he was hosting at the villa. A week-long gathering for select members of the international community. Invitation only. Heavily vetted.

I shouldn't have cared. I had responsibilities at home—the estate, my work with Unit 23, the Thorned Thistle. Kiernan, still recovering from the gunshot wound that had nearly killed him, was wrapped up in his new life with Oliver and Ophelia, and someone needed to keep the club running smoothly in his absence.

But something had been gnawing at me for months. A restlessness that no scene at the Thistle seemed to fill anymore.

So I'd packed a bag and flown to Florence. Told myself it was networking. International relationship-building that would benefit the club.

I was lying, of course. I'd known I was lying even as I boarded the plane.

The villa rose from the Tuscan hills like something lifted from a Renaissance painting—honey-colored stone and terra-cotta tiles, cypress trees standing sentinel along the winding drive. The setting sun painted everything in shades of amber and rose, and the warm air carried the scent of lavender and ripening grapes.

I moved through the club's public rooms with a glass of wine I barely tasted, exchanging nods with faces I recognized from clubs across the continent. The ground floor was civilized enough—a cocktail party like any other, beautiful people making small talk. But I could feel the undercurrent beneath the surface. The anticipation. Everyone here knew what would happen when the sun finished setting and the real activities began.

I climbed the curved staircase to the observation gallery that overlooked the main salon. Benedetti had designed the space for voyeurs—comfortable seating arranged behind one-way glass, allowing guests to watch the scenes below without interruption. A handful of people were already there, drinks in hand, their attention fixed on the room beneath us.

I found a spot in the shadows, and when I looked down, the glass in my hand shattered.

I didn't feel the wine soaking my fingers or the bite of broken crystal. I only saw her.

Isla MacLeod's auburn hair, longer than I remembered, spilled down her bare back in waves that caught the candlelight like fire. Her pale skin was scattered with the freckles I'd traced with my fingertips years ago. Her wrists were bound behind her back—red rope expertly tied, the kind of *kinbaku* that required training and trust.

She knelt on a platform in the center of the room with her head bowed while some Italian bastard trailed a flogger across her shoulder.

When she arched into his touch, I clenched my fists.

I'd spent years convincing myself she was too innocent for my world. Too bright. Too good. I'd watched her grow from a shy teenager into a stunning woman, and I'd kept my distance, protecting her from my darkness. I'd told myself that wanting her was a sin I'd carry silently to my grave.

Yet, here she was.

She'd crossed a fucking continent to keep this secret, come all the way to Tuscany so no one from home would ever know. And I'd found her anyway.

I was moving before I made the conscious decision. Four strides carried me down the stairs and across the salon floor.

The dom looked up as I approached, startled, but whatever he saw in my face made him take an instinctive step back.

"This scene is over," I said with a level of control I didn't feel.

Isla's head snapped up, and her blue-green eyes—the color of the sea off the Scottish coast, the color I saw every time I closed mine—went wide with shock.

"Callen?"

"Get up. We're leaving."

"You can't just—" She was trembling. "You have no right—"

"I have every right." The words ripped out of me, raw and honest in a way I'd never allowed myself to be with her. I let her see it all—every year of wanting, every lie I'd told myself. "Get. Up."

She raised her chin. "I don't belong to you."

"Not yet." I stepped closer, close enough to see her pulse hammering in her throat. "But you will."

She stared at my hand. Then took it.

About Merrigan Calder

Merrigan Calder is the author of wickedly sexy, dangerously addictive, deliciously dark romance.

She's the darker-romance pen name of USA Today best-selling author Heather Slade. Merrigan's heroes—while morally gray—are sublimely sexy, seductive alphas, and her heroines are confident, strong, resilient, and determined. Both are always shamelessly sexy.

The road to HEA in Merrigan's books may be a little longer, tougher to navigate, and filled with a higher level of angst, but no less satisfying at the journey's end.

Learn more and follow here:

Website: https://oashort.com/s/bob_mc_w

Newsletter signup: https://oashort.com/s/bob_mc_nl

Facebook: https://oashort.com/s/bob_mc_fb

Instagram: https://oashort.com/s/bob_mc_ig

Tiktok: https://oashort.com/s/bob_mc_tt

YouTube: https://oashort.com/s/bob_mc_yt

Amazon: https://oashort.com/s/bob_mc_a

Goodreads: https://oashort.com/s/bob_mc_gr

Bookbub: https://oashort.com/s/bob_mc_bb

–More coming soon–
from author Merrigan Calder

Thorned Thistle

Commanded

Possessed

Obsessed

Surrendered

Captured

Copper Chalice

Auctioned

Claimed

Owned

Ruined

Kept

Velvet Viper

Roped

Branded

Broken

Spurred

Mastered